The Comic Romance

Paul Scarron

Translated by Jacques Houis

ALMA CLASSICS LTD
London House
243-253 Lower Mortlake Road
Richmond
Surrey TW9 2LL
United Kingdom
www.almaclassics.com

The Comic Romance first published in French in 1651–57
This edition first published by Alma Classics Ltd in 2012

Cover image © Getty Images

Translation and Extra Material © Jacques Houis, 2012

Printed and bound by CPI Group (UK) Ltd, Croydon, CRO 4YY

Typeset by Tetragon

ISBN: 978-1-84749-220-3

Contents

The Comic Romance

TO THE COADJUTOR[*]

That Is Saying It All

Y ES, MONSIGNOR,
Your name alone carries with it all the titles and all the praise
that can be given to the most illustrious persons of the century. It
will make my book seem good, however bad it may be; and even
those who find that I could have done a better job of writing it
will have to admit that I could not do a better job of dedicating
it. Were the honour you do me by the affection you have shown
me through so much kindness and so many visits not to incline
me to seek out carefully the means to please you, I would be so
inclined anyway. Thus my novel was destined for you from the
time I had the honour of reading you the beginning, which you
found to your liking. This, more than anything else, gave me the
courage to finish it, and prevents me from blushing while giving
you such a bad gift. Should you value it for more than it is worth,
or should the least part of it please you, I would not trade places
with the healthiest man in France. But, Monsignor, I do not dare
hope that you will read it; it would be too much time wasted for
someone who uses his time as effectively as you, and who has
more important things to do. I will be sufficiently rewarded for
my book should you merely deign to receive it and should you
take my word – as it is the only faculty I have left – that I am,
with my entire being,

Monsignor,

Your most humble, most obedient and most obliged servant,

Scarron

TO THE READER WHO IS SCANDALIZED

By the Typographical Errors Contained in My Book

I AM NOT GOING TO GIVE YOU any errata from my book other than the book itself, which is full of errors. The printer is less to blame than I, whose bad habit it is often to write what I give the printer on the eve of the day it is printed. So much so that, my head still full of what I just finished writing, I reread the pages I am given to correct in roughly the same way I recited in school the lesson I had not had time to learn – I mean by glancing at a few lines and skipping over what I had not yet forgotten. Those who know how to discern the good from the bad in what they read will soon recognize the errors I was able to make, and those who do not understand what they read will not notice my failures. That, benevolent or malevolent reader, is all I have to say; if you like my book enough to want it to be more correct, buy enough copies to warrant a second printing, and I promise it will be reviewed, augmented and corrected.

Scarron

FIRST PART

———

CHAPTER I

A Theatre Troupe Arrives in the Town of Le Mans

THE SUN HAD COMPLETED more than half of his journey, and his chariot, having reached the downward slope of the world, moved faster than he wanted. Had his steeds wished to take advantage of their downhill course, they could have completed what was left of the day in less than ten minutes; but instead of pulling with all their might, they frolicked and curvetted about, breathing the sea air which made them whinny as it alerted them to the proximity of the sea, where, it is said, their master sleeps every night. To put it in simpler, more human terms, it was between five and six o'clock in the afternoon when a cart pulled into the marketplace of Le Mans. Hitched to four rather emaciated oxen led by a brood mare whose colt sauntered all around it like the little devil he was, the cart was piled high with trunks, chests and big bolts of painted canvas, forming a pyramid on top of which sat a lady wearing a patchwork of town clothes and country clothes. A young man, whose clothing was as shabby as his bearing was noble, walked beside the cart. A large bandage on his face covered one eye and half of his cheek. He shouldered a long rifle he had used to murder several magpies, blue jays and crows. These he wore strung together like a bandolier at the bottom of which hung, by their feet, a hen and a gosling, in all likelihood pilfered. Instead of a hat, he wore a nightcap bound by garters of several colours, and this headgear looked like a kind of rough, unfinished turban. His doublet was a grisette coat with a strap for a belt, which also served to hold up a sword of such great length it was impossible to wield effectively without a stand. He wore tucked breeches like those worn by actors when they portray heroes of antiquity, and instead of shoes he had a tragedian's buskins covered with mud up to the ankles. An old man, less irregularly though very poorly dressed, walked beside him. He carried a bass viol on his shoulders and, because he stooped a bit as he walked, from a distance he could have been mistaken for a big tortoise walking on its hind legs. Now some critic will probably grumble about this comparison because of the disproportion between a tortoise and a man, but I am referring to the giant tortoises found in the Indies and, moreover, I have it on my own authority.

Let us return to our caravan. It passed in front of a tennis* court called The Doe, at the door of which many of the town's most prominent citizens were gathered. The novelty of the rig and the noise made by the rabble crowded around the cart caused all of these honourable bourgeois to look over at our strangers. A sheriff's lieutenant named La Rappinière, among others, accosted them with a magistrate's air of authority, demanding to know what kind of people they were. The young man I described earlier spoke up and, without removing his turban, because he held his rifle with one hand and the hilt of his sword with the other, to keep it from hitting his legs, told him that they were French by birth, actors by profession, that his own stage name was Destiny, his old companion's Grudge, and the lady's, who was perched on top of their luggage like a hen, Cave. This bizarre name made several in the group laugh, whereupon the young actor added that the name Cave should seem no more far-fetched to thinking men than those of Mountain, Valley, Rose or Thorn.

6

The conversation was interrupted by the sound of punches and cursing coming from the front of the cart. It was the tennis court's servant who had attacked the driver, because his oxen and mare were helping themselves to a pile of hay in front of the door. The combatants were separated, and the tennis-court keeper, who loved the theatre more than she did sermons or vespers, with a generosity unheard of in a tennis-court keeper, allowed the driver to let his animals eat their fill. He accepted her offer, and while the animals ate, the author rested awhile and began to think about what he would say in the second chapter.

CHAPTER II

The Sort of Man the Sieur de La Rappinière Was

IN THOSE DAYS THE SIEUR DE LA RAPPINIÈRE was the town joker of Le Mans. Every small town has its joker, and the city of Paris has its fair share of them. There is a joker in every neighbourhood, and I myself would have been my neighbourhood's joker if I had wanted to, but as everyone knows, I forsook the vanities of this world a long time ago. But to return to the Sieur de La Rappinière, he soon resumed the conversation which had been interrupted by the fist fight and asked the young actor if their troupe consisted only of Mademoiselle Cave, Monsieur Grudge and himself.

"Our troupe is as complete as the Prince of Orange's or His Grace the Duke of Épernon's," he replied, "but because of a mishap we suffered in Tours, where our scatterbrained doorkeeper killed one of the royal intendant's riflemen, we were forced to escape with one shoe off and one shoe on, in the sorry state you see us in now."

"Those riflemen did the same thing at La Flèche," said La Rappinière.

7

"May St Anthony's fire burn them up!" said the tennis-court keeper. "Thanks to them we won't be having a play."

"Not if it were up to us," replied the old actor. "If we had the keys to our trunks and we could get to our clothes, we would entertain you townsmen for four or five days before heading to Alençon, where we are supposed to meet up with the rest of the troupe."

Everyone's ears pricked up at the actor's words. La Rappinière offered Cave one of his wife's old dresses and the tennis-court keeper offered Destiny and Grudge two or three outfits she was keeping on deposit. "But," added someone in the group, "there are only three of you."

"I've acted an entire play all by myself," said Grudge. "I was the king, the queen and the ambassador, all at the same time. I played the queen in falsetto, and the ambassador in a nasal voice, turning towards my crown, which I had placed on a chair. As the king I returned to my seat, my crown and my dignity, and I spoke in a deeper voice. We'll be glad to show you how it's done. If you compensate our driver, pay our hotel expenses and furnish our costumes, we'll play before dark. If not, please allow us to have a drink and get some rest, because we've had a long trip."

Everyone liked the proposal, and La Rappinière, who always had a trick up his sleeve, said that no clothes were needed other than those belonging to two young townsmen who were playing some tennis, and that Lady Cave, in her street clothes, would be up to any role called for in a play. No sooner said than done: in less than ten minutes the actors had a few drinks, got into costume, and the crowd, which had grown, settled into an upper room. When a dirty sheet was raised, the audience saw the actor Destiny lying on a mattress, wearing a small basket on his head in lieu of a crown. He was rubbing his eyes like someone just waking up, and reciting, in the style of Mondory, the part of Herod that starts with:

"Dangerous ghost who troubles my sleep."*

The bandage that covered half his face did not prevent him from showing that he was an excellent actor. Mademoiselle Cave performed wonders in the roles of Marianne and Salomé. In the other roles, Grudge pleased everyone, and the play was about to be successfully wrapped up, when the Devil, who never sleeps, got involved and caused the tragedy to end, not with Marianne's death and Herod's despair, but with a thousand punches, as many slaps, a frightful number of kicks, too many curses to be counted, and then, with a beauty of a last word, crafted by the Sieur de La Rappinière, the greatest of experts in matters of this kind.

CHAPTER III

The Play's Deplorable Outcome

IN ALL THE TOWNS OF THE KINGDOM, there is usually a tennis court where the local loafers gather every day, some to play, others to watch. There, blasphemy acquires a rhetorical flourish, little consideration is shown for the feelings of others, and those who are not there are stabbed in the back by wagging tongues. No one is spared. Each behaves like a sworn enemy of the other, and all are invited to jeer and mock to the best of their God-given ability. Now, if memory serves me, it was in one of those tennis courts that I left three thespians performing *Marianne* to an honourable company presided over by the Sieur de La Rappinière. Just as Herod and Marianne began to quarrel, the two young men whose clothes had been so freely borrowed entered the room wearing breeches, each holding his racket. They had come straight to see the play without waiting to be towelled off. When they noticed that Herod and Pherore were wearing their clothes, the more hot-tempered of the two called out to the tennis-court valet. "You son of a bitch," he said, "why did you give my clothes to that clown?" The valet, who knew he was dealing with a real brute, answered meekly that he wasn't to blame.

"Who is, then? You cuckold's beard."

The poor servant didn't dare point a finger at La Rappinière in his presence; but, being the most insolent of men, La Rappinière himself stood up from his chair and said: "I am. What do you have to say to that?"

"That you are a cuckold," retorted the other, bringing his racket down hard on La Rappinière's head. La Rappinière, who was used to being the first to take such actions, was so stunned that he didn't move, either out of surprise or because he wasn't angry enough yet, since it took a lot to draw him into a fight, even if only a fist fight. Things might have gone no further had his valet, who was angrier than he was, not thrown himself on the attacker, landing a punch (with all of its consequences) right in the middle of his face. To this he added many other punches wherever he could land them. La Rappinière then attacked his adversary from behind, and started to pummel him as if he, La Rappinière, were the injured party. Whereupon one of the man's relatives began to administer the same treatment to La Rappinière. Wanting to create a diversion, a friend of La Rappinière fell upon the relative. He was attacked by another, who was himself attacked. Finally, everyone in the room joined in. Some swore. Others cursed. They all fought. As she watched her furniture being destroyed, the tennis-court keeper filled the air with pathetic cries. It looked like they would all perish in a hail of kicks, punches and footstools, had not several of the town's magistrates been alerted to the commotion, while happening to be walking through the market with the Seneschal of Maine, des Essarts. The magistrates considered throwing buckets of water on the combatants, a remedy that might have proven effective, when fatigue separated the warring parties. Moreover, two Franciscan Brothers, who had charitably waded into the battle, got the combatants to agree, if not to a firm peace treaty, at least to a truce, during which negotiations continued, without prejudice to the taunts and rejoinders that shot back and forth. Such was the actor Destiny's punching prowess that it is still celebrated in the town of Le Mans, in stories told by the two youths who started the fight, with whom he tangled directly, raining upon them with his fists, and by the many other adversaries he knocked out with a single punch. He lost his bandage during the mêlée, and one could see that he was as good-looking as he was well built. Bloody faces were washed off with cool water, torn collars replaced, poultices applied as needed, some wounds stitched and the furniture put back where it belonged, though not in the condition it had been before being disturbed. After a few minutes no sign was left of the brawl save the animosity that showed on the faces of those who had squared off.

The poor actors left with La Rappinière, who got in the last word. As they entered the marketplace, on their way out of the tennis court, they were set upon by seven or eight ruffians armed with swords. La Rappinière was very frightened, as was his custom, and thought he might experience something even worse than fear, had Destiny not generously thrown himself in front of a blade that would have run La Rappinière through. Destiny warded off the stroke, though not without sustaining a slight wound to his arm. But he quickly drew his own sword and in no time disarmed two adversaries, split open two or three skulls, battered several faces, and so thoroughly routed the gentlemen of the ambush that all who witnessed it swore they had never before seen a more valiant man. The trap thus foiled had been set for La Rappinière by two squires, one of whom had married the sister of the youth who had started the tennis-court brawl with a hard smash of his racket. In all likelihood La Rappinière would have been harmed, had it not been for the defender God sent him in the form of our valiant actor. This good deed found a place in his heart of stone and, without allowing the poor remnants of this dilapidated troupe to spend the night in an inn, he brought them to his home, where the driver of the cart unloaded their baggage and returned to his village.

CHAPTER IV

Which Continues to Be about the Squire
de La Rappinière and What Happened
in His House during the Night

M ADAME DE LA RAPPINIÈRE greeted her company with
compliments galore, being, in all the world, the woman
who most enjoyed giving them. She wasn't bad-looking, though
so thin and dry that she couldn't snuff a candle with her fingers
without setting them on fire. I could tell you a hundred strange
things about her but I won't, for fear of being long-winded. In
no time the two ladies became such close friends that they called
each other dear and dearest. As he came in, La Rappinière, who
was as boastful as a town barber, gave orders to the kitchen and
pantry to hurry supper. It was pure braggadocio; aside from his
old valet, who doubled as a groom, the staff included only a young
maid and a lame old woman who had a very hard time of it. La
Rappinière was punished for his vanity. He usually ate at the tavern,
on some dupe's tab, while his wife and servants made do with
the region's traditional cabbage soup. Hoping to shine in front
of his guests by giving them a treat, he attempted a secret hand-
off, behind his back, of some money for the valet to buy dinner.
Through the fault of either valet or master, the money fell on the
chair where he sat, and from there to the floor. La Rappinière
turned crimson, his wife blushed, the valet swore, Cave smiled,
while Grudge may not have noticed anything. As for Destiny, I
never did find out what effect this incident had on him. The money
was picked up, and the group chatted while waiting for supper.
La Rappinière asked Destiny why he hid his face behind a patch.
He told him that he had a good reason, and that being disguised
by accident, he had also wanted to deprive some enemies he had
of the opportunity to see his face.

Good or bad, supper finally arrived. La Rappinière drank so
much he got drunk, and Grudge also had his fill. Destiny dined

like a sober gentleman, Cave like a famished actress and Madame de La Rappinière like a woman who wanted to take advantage of the opportunity, so much so that she ended up with the runs. While the servants ate and the beds were made, La Rappinière bombarded them with a hundred tales filled with vanity. Destiny slept alone in a small room. Cave shared a closet with the chambermaid. Grudge slept with the valet I don't know where. They were all sleepy. Some from fatigue, others from having eaten too much, and yet they hardly slept, so true is it that nothing is certain in this world. Shortly after falling asleep, Madame de La Rappinière woke up needing to go where even kings have to report in person. Her husband woke up soon afterwards. He could tell he was alone, even though he was quite drunk. He called for his wife but she didn't answer. Suspecting something, getting mad, getting out of bed in a rage, everything happened at once. On the way out of his room, he heard steps in front of him. He followed the sounds and, in the middle of the hall that led to Destiny's room, got so close to what he was following that he thought he was stepping on its heels. He threw himself on what he thought was his wife, grabbed her and yelled, "You whore!" But his hands met no resistance, while his feet struck something, so he pitched forward and felt something sharp stick into his stomach. He let out horrifying cries of "Murder!" and "I've been stabbed!" without letting go of his wife, whom he thought he had by the hair as she struggled under him. His cries, insults and curses alerted the whole house, and everyone came to his aid at the same time – the chambermaid with a candle; Grudge and the valet in dirty nightshirts; Cave in a cheap skirt; and Destiny, sword in hand. The last to arrive, Madame de La Rappinière, was amazed, as were the others, to see her husband furiously wrestling a nanny goat, there to nurse a litter of puppies who had lost their mother. Never was anyone more taken aback than La Rappinière. His wife, who suspected what he was up to, asked him if he were crazy. Not knowing what to say, he answered that he had mistaken the goat for a thief. Destiny guessed what had happened. Everyone went back to bed with their own version of the incident, and the goat was locked in with her puppies.

CHAPTER V

Which Does Not Contain Much

T HE ACTOR GRUDGE, one of the major heroes of our novel (who are not lacking in this book; and since there is nothing more perfect than the hero of a book, a half-dozen heroes or so-called heroes will do more honour to mine than a single hero, who might turn out to be the one people talk about least, since everything is a matter of luck in this world) – Grudge, then, was one of those misanthropes who hate everyone and who don't love themselves, and I've heard from many people that he was never known to laugh. He had some wit, and he could compose passable doggerel; hardly a man of his word in any case, as mischievous as an old monkey and as envious as a dog. He found fault with everyone in his profession. Bellerose was too affected; Mondory too crude; Floridor too stiff,* and so on. I think he might easily have welcomed the conclusion that he was the only actor without faults; and yet the troupe tolerated him only because he had grown old in the profession. In the days when the theatre was limited to the plays of Hardy,* he played nursemaid roles, wearing a mask and speaking in falsetto. When the theatre began to improve, he supervised the box office, played confidants, ambassadors and bodyguards, whenever a king needed to be accompanied or someone needed to be arrested or attacked, or a battle waged. His nasty tenor could be heard when trios were in fashion and he put flour on his face to play the farce. These talents formed the basis of his insufferable vanity, to which were added constant mockery, endless slander and a fiery temper that was, nevertheless, not entirely without valour. All this made his companions fear him; only with Destiny was he meek as a lamb, showing himself to be as reasonable as his nature would allow. Rumour had it that Destiny had beaten him, but this didn't last long; neither did the rumour that he loved other people's possessions to the point of appropriating them; all that aside, you couldn't find a better man. It seems to me that I told you he shared a bed with La Rappinière's valet, whose name was Doguin. Either the bed he slept in was no good or Doguin wasn't much of a room-mate, for he didn't sleep at all that night. He got up at dawn, along with Doguin, who was called by his master, and, passing by La Rappinière's room, stopped in to say good morning. La Rappinière received his compliments with the all the pomp of a provincial magistrate, and reciprocated with fewer than one tenth of the civilities he received, but, since actors play all sorts of characters, Grudge did not take it personally. La Rappinière bombarded him with questions about the theatre, and, one thing leading to another, asked him how long Destiny had been in their troupe, adding that he was an excellent actor. "All that glitters isn't gold," replied Grudge. "In the days when I played leading men, he would only have played a page: he shouldn't be expected to know what he never learnt. He hasn't been in the theatre very long. Actors don't come about as easily as mushrooms. People appreciate him because of his youth. You wouldn't be half as impressed if you knew him like I do. He acts the man about town, as if he were some great lord, but he won't reveal who he is, or where he's from; neither will the beautiful Cloris, who is with him, whom he calls his sister, and God only knows if she is! I may not look like it, but I saved his life in Paris, not without suffering two bad sword wounds. He was so ungrateful that, instead of following me when I was carried to the surgeon's, he spent the night looking through the mud for some piece of diamond jewellery or other – which was probably just Alençon quartz – that he said those who attacked us had taken from him." La Rappinière asked Grudge how this misfortune had happened to him. "It was Twelfth Day, and we were on the Pont-Neuf," answered Grudge. These words were extremely troubling to La Rappinière and his valet Doguin.

Both of them blanched and blushed; and La Rappinière changed the topic so quickly and with so much confusion that Grudge was amazed. The town's executioner and several archers entered the room, interrupting the conversation, to the great relief of Grudge, who could tell that something he had said had struck a nerve in La Rappinière. What it was, he could not guess.

Meanwhile, poor Destiny, the topic of so much conversation, was having a hard time; Grudge discovered him with Mademoiselle Cave, not having much success making an old tailor admit that his hearing was of poor quality, and that his workmanship was even worse. Their disagreement stemmed from Destiny's having found, as he unloaded the troupe's costumes, two doublets and a pair of very worn breeches. He had given them to this old tailor to turn into some form of garment more fashionable than the page's breeches he had on; and the tailor, instead of using one of the doublets to mend the other and the breeches too, by an error of judgement unworthy of someone who had spent his whole life mending old garments, had patched the two doublets with the best parts of the breeches, to such an extent that poor Destiny, with so much in the way of doublets and so little in the way of breeches, was left to choose between keeping to his room and causing children to run after him, as they did when he was in costume. La Rappinière's generosity repaired the mistake of the tailor – who inherited the patched doublets – and Destiny was given a suit of clothes that had belonged to a robber whom La Rappinière had recently had broken on the wheel. The executioner, who was in attendance, and who had left the suit for safekeeping with La Rappinière's maid, quite impudently said that the suit was his, but La Rappinière threatened to have him removed from his duties. The clothes fit Destiny, who went out with La Rappinière and Grudge. They dined at a tavern, at the expense of a burgher who had business with La Rappinière. Mademoiselle Cave passed the time washing her dirty lace collar and keeping her hostess company. That same day, Doguin encountered one of the young men he had beaten the day before at the tennis court, and returned with two sword wounds and many bruises; and because these wounds were bad, Grudge, after dinner, went to a nearby inn to spend the night, exhausted from having combed the city, along with Destiny, in the company of La Rappinière, who wanted to obtain satisfaction for his wounded valet.

CHAPTER VI

The Chamber Pot Adventure; the Bad Night Grudge
Gave the Inn; the Arrival of a Part of the Troupe;
Death of Doguin and Other Memorable Things

GRUDGE ENTERED THE INN a little more than half drunk. La Rappinière's maid, who was helping him, told the hostess to prepare a bed for him. "That's all we need!" she said. "If our other guests were like him, we couldn't afford to pay the rent!"

"Don't be silly," said her husband, "Monsieur de La Rappinière does us too great an honour; prepare a bed for this gentleman."

"As if I had one," said the hostess. "I just gave the last one to a merchant from the Bas Maine."

The merchant happened to come in then, and, upon hearing the subject of the dispute, offered half of his bed to Grudge, either because he had business with La Rappinière or because he was obliging by nature. Grudge thanked him as much as the curtness of his manners would allow. The merchant dined, the host kept him company and Grudge didn't have to be asked twice to join them and start drinking afresh. They talked taxes, cursed the tax collectors, put the state's affairs in order, but neglected to keep order themselves, starting with the host, who took out his purse and asked to settle the bill, forgetting he was at home. His wife and his maid dragged him into his room by the shoulders and put him on a bed, fully clothed. Grudge informed the merchant that he suffered from bladder problems, and that he was sorry

17

to have to inconvenience him; to which the merchant replied that a night was soon over. The bed was against the wall. Grudge jumped in first, and the merchant having got in afterwards in the good part of the bed, Grudge asked him for the chamber pot. "What do you want to do with it?" asked the merchant. "Keep it near me, so I don't have to inconvenience you," said Grudge. The merchant answered that he would give it to him when he needed it; to which Grudge only reluctantly agreed, protesting that he was truly desperate not to inconvenience him. The merchant fell asleep without answering him; and scarcely had he started to sleep soundly than the mischievous actor, who would willingly lose an eye if it caused the other fellow to suffer the same fate, tugged at the poor merchant's arm, and cried out: "Monsieur, oh! Monsieur!" With a yawn, the sleepy merchant asked him: "What would you like?"

"Give me the chamber pot," said Grudge. The poor merchant leant out of bed and, grasping the chamber pot, put it in Grudge's hands, who endeavoured to piss, and, after having tried a hundred times, or pretended to, after having sworn a hundred times through clenched teeth and bitterly complained about his condition, gave the pot back to the merchant without having pissed a single drop. The merchant put it back on the floor and said, with a yawn as wide as an open oven door: "Really, Monsieur, I feel sorry for you," and promptly went back to sleep. Grudge allowed him to sail forth into sleep, then, when he saw him snore like he hadn't ever done anything else his whole life, the traitor woke him up again and asked him for the chamber pot as maliciously as he had the first time. The merchant put it in his hands as nicely as he had before, and Grudge placed it where the piss comes out, with as little desire to piss as he had to let the merchant sleep. He yelled even more loudly than before and took twice as long not pissing, while he begged the merchant not to go to the effort of handing him the chamber pot again, that it wasn't reasonable, and that he could get it himself. The poor merchant, who would have given all his earthly possessions for a good night's sleep, answered him with a yawn that he could do as he pleased, and put the chamber pot back in its place. They said goodnight to one another quite politely, and the poor merchant would have bet anything that he was about to enjoy the best sleep of his life. Grudge, who knew otherwise, let him sink into a deep sleep again and, without letting it trouble his conscience to awaken a man who was sleeping so well, pressed his elbow into the merchant's stomach, leaning over him with the weight of his entire body, as he stretched his other arm out of the bed, the way you do when you want to pick something up off the floor. The poor merchant, unable to breathe and feeling his chest being crushed, awoke with a start and yelled horribly: "*Morbleu*! Monsieur, you're killing me!"

Grudge, in a voice as sweet and composed as the merchant's was vehement, replied: "I'm so sorry, I was trying to get the chamber pot."

"*Vertubleu*!" cried out the merchant. "I'd much rather hand it to you and not sleep a wink; you've given me a bruise I'll feel for the rest of my life."

Grudge did not reply and started to piss so abundantly and so hard that the noise of the chamber pot alone would have been enough to wake the merchant. He filled the pot, praising the Lord with loutish hypocrisy. The poor merchant congratulated him as best he could for this copious flow of urine that held out the hope of an uninterrupted night's sleep, when the dastardly Grudge, pretending to put it back on the floor, dropped the chamber pot and all of its contents on the merchant's face, his beard and his stomach, while crying out hypocritically: "Oh! Monsieur, I'm so sorry!" The merchant did not reply, because as soon as he felt himself drowning in piss, he stood up and screamed, like a madman, that he needed a candle. Grudge, coolly enough to make a priest swear, said: "What a shame!" The merchant continued to scream. The host, the hostess, the maids and valets came. The merchant told them that he had been made to sleep with a devil and asked that a fire be built for him in another room. They asked him what was wrong. He was so angry he didn't answer, took his clothes, and went to the kitchen to dry off, where he spent the night on a bench, next to the fire. The host asked Grudge what he had done. Feigning complete innocence, he told him, "I don't know what he's complaining about. He woke up and woke me up, screaming bloody murder. He must have had a bad dream, or else he's crazy. He wet the bed too." The hostess felt the bed and said it was true that the mattress was soaking wet, and swore to God that the merchant would pay. They said goodnight to Grudge, who slept all night as peacefully as the just, making up for the bad night he had spent at La Rappinière's. He woke up earlier than expected, though, because La Rappinière's maid hurriedly summoned him to come see Doguin, who was dying and who asked to see him before he died. He hurried over, anxious to know what a dying man who had only known him for a day could possibly want from him. But the maid was wrong: having heard the dying man ask to see the actor, she had mistaken Grudge for Destiny, who had just gone into Doguin's room when Grudge arrived, and locked himself in, having heard from the priest who confessed Doguin, that the wounded man had something to tell him that was important for him to know. He had been there for less than ten minutes when La Rappinière returned from town, where he had gone at first light to take care of some business. On arrival, he learnt that his valet was dying, that the bleeding could not be stopped because a large blood vessel has been cut, and that Doguin had asked to see the actor Destiny before dying. "And did he see him?" asked La Rappinière, visibly concerned. He was told that they were locked in together. These words struck him like a thunderbolt, and he ran, as if possessed, to knock on the door of the room where Doguin was dying, just as Destiny was opening it to call for help because Doguin was losing consciousness. Shaken, La Rappinière asked him what his crazy valet wanted. "I think he's dreaming," replied Destiny, coldly, "because he told me he was sorry over and over, and I don't think he has ever given me offence; but he should be attended to, for he is dying." They gathered around Doguin's bed just as he let out his last breath, which seemed to make La Rappinière more cheerful than sad. Those who knew him thought it was because he owed his valet back wages. Only Destiny knew the real story.

Just then two men entered the house, whom our actor recognized as his associates and about whom we shall speak in greater detail in the next chapter.

CHAPTER VII

The Adventure of the Litters*

THE YOUNGEST OF THE ACTORS who entered La Rappinière's house was Destiny's valet. He told Destiny that the rest of the troupe had arrived, except for Mademoiselle Star, who twisted her ankle several miles from Le Mans. "What made you come here? And who told you where we were?" asked Destiny.

"The plague prevented us from going to Alençon, and we stopped at Bonnétable," answered the other actor, called Olive, "and some people we met there told us you had performed here, that you had a fight and were wounded. Mademoiselle Star is worried about you, and wants you to send her a litter."

The owner of the inn next door, who came running when he heard about Doguin's death, said that he had a litter, and that, for a fair price, it would be ready to leave at noon, carried by two good horses. The actors settled on one écu for the litter, and took rooms at the inn for the troupe. La Rappinière volunteered to get the Lieutenant General's permission to put on a play, and at noon Destiny and his friends started out for Bonnétable. It was a very hot day. Grudge slept in the litter. Olive rode the rear horse, and one of the host's valets led the front one. Destiny was on foot, shouldering his rifle while his valet related what had happened between Château-du-Loir and the little village near Bonnétable where Mademoiselle Star twisted her ankle getting off a horse.

Just then, two men, riding fine horses and hiding their faces from Destiny behind upturned collars, approached the litter from the open side, and, finding nothing but an old man asleep, the one on the best horse said: "I think all the demons are in league against me today, disguised as litters to drive me crazy." Having said that, he rode off through the fields, followed by his companion. Olive called over Destiny, who was too far away to have heard anything, and told him what had happened. It meant nothing to Destiny and did not trouble him.

A mile farther down the road, the litter driver, made drowsy by the heat, drove the litter into a mud hole, scaring Grudge, who thought he would fall in too. The horses broke their harness, and had to be unhitched and pulled out by the neck and tail. They picked up the wreckage, and made it to the next village as best they could. The equipment needed major repairs. While these were being made, Grudge, Olive and Destiny's valet had a drink at the door of the village inn. Now another litter accompanied by two footmen also stopped in front of the inn. No sooner had it arrived than another one appeared, a hundred paces behind it, coming from the same direction. "There must be a very important meeting of all the litters in the province," said La Rappinière. "Let them get on with their convention, because it doesn't look like any more litters are going to show up!"

"Here comes another one anyway, who doesn't want to miss the party," said the hostess. And, indeed, they saw a fourth litter coming from the direction of Le Mans, which made them laugh heartily, all except Grudge, who never laughed, as I have already told you. The last litter joined the others. Never before had so many litters been seen in one place. "If the litter-seekers we met a little while ago were here, they'd be pretty happy," said the driver of the first litter. "I came across them too," said the second driver. The troupe's driver said the same thing, and the last one to pull up confessed he had feared they would beat him. "Why is that?" Destiny asked him. "Because," he replied, "they were looking for a lady who twisted her ankle that we took to Le Mans. I never saw such angry men. They were taking it out on me that they hadn't found what they were looking for." Hearing this, the actors were all ears, and questioned the driver, who told them that the wife of the lord of the village where Mademoiselle Star hurt herself visited her and had her transported to Le Mans with great care.

The conversation among the litter drivers lasted a while, as they discussed their encounters with the litter-seekers. The first litter carried the parson of Domfront, who was stopping by Le Mans for a medical consultation on his way back from the Bellême hot springs. The second litter carried a wounded gentleman returning from the army. The litters split up. The actors' and the parson's returned to Le Mans, and the others went where they were supposed to go. The sick priest stayed at the same inn as the actors. We'll let him rest in his room and take a look, in the next chapter, at what was going on in the actors' room.

CHAPTER VIII

In Which Several Things Are Revealed That Need
to Be Known in Order to Understand this Book

THE TROUPE WAS MADE UP OF DESTINY, Olive and Grudge, each of whom had a servant who aspired to become a lead actor some day. Among these servants, a few could already recite without blushing and getting flustered. Destiny's servant was one of those who managed quite well, understood what he was saying, and was quite witty. Mademoiselle Star and Mademoiselle Cave's daughter played leads while Cave played queens and mothers, and performed farce. The troupe also had a poet or, if you will, an author, since all the grocery stores in the kingdom were full of his works, in verse as well as prose. This wit had joined the troupe almost in spite of itself. Since he did not share in the profits, and spent some of his own money feeding the actors, he was given the smallest parts, which he nevertheless tended to butcher. He was obviously in love with one of the two actresses, but he was so discreet, although a little crazy, that no one had been able to discover which of the two he meant to seduce with the promise of immortality. He threatened to write many plays for the troupe, but he had spared them so far. It was known only through conjecture that he was writing one, entitled *Martin Luther*, found in a notebook he denied owning, even though it was written in his own hand.

When our actors arrived, the actresses' room was already filled with the town's most impertinent fops, some of whom were partially deflated by the cool reception they had encountered. They were all talking at the same time about theatre, good poetry, authors and romances. Never before had so much noise been made in a room where no fighting was going on. Surrounded by two or three others who must have been the local wits, the troupe's poet was telling, until he was blue in the face, of how he had seen Corneille, caroused with Saint-Amant and Beys, and lost a good friend when Rotrou died.* Mademoiselle Cave and Mademoiselle Angélique, her daughter, unpacked as calmly as if they were all alone in the room. Angélique's hands were squeezed or kissed from time to time by the notoriously lecherous country gentlemen; but a swift kick in the shins, a slap across the face or a bite, as the situation warranted, soon rid her of these unwanted suitors. She was not rude or shameless, but her playful, uninhibited temperament left little room for formality. Otherwise she possessed wit and was a very decent girl. Mademoiselle Star had the opposite temperament. You could not find a more modest, sweet-tempered girl. She was so kind on this occasion that she didn't have the heart to kick all these ogling fops out of her room, even though her twisted ankle was giving her a lot of pain and she badly needed to rest. She was fully dressed on a bed, surrounded by four or five of the most persistent coxcombs, her head spinning from many of those double entendres that pass for wit in the provinces, and often forcing a smile in response to things that hardly pleased her. This is one of the great drawbacks of an acting career, which, combined with having to laugh or cry when they feel like doing something altogether different, greatly diminishes the pleasure actors derive from sometimes being emperors or empresses, or being called a Greek god when they aren't even close, or a young beauty when they've grown old on the stage and their teeth and hair are now part of their wardrobe. There are many things to be said on this subject but, for variety's sake, they must only be brought up sparingly at different points in my book.

Let us return to poor Mademoiselle Star, besieged by country squires, the most annoying of men, all of them big talkers, some of them very impertinent, and among whom were a few fresh out of college. In the crowd was a short widower, a lawyer and court officer in a small jurisdiction nearby. Since the death of his little wife, he had threatened the women of the town to remarry, and the clergy of the province to become a priest, if not a preaching prelate. He was the biggest little nut to have run amok since Roland.* He had studied his whole life, and although study weds knowledge to truth, he lied like a page. He was presumptuous and opinionated like a pedant, and a bad enough poet to be hanged, if only there were law and order in the kingdom. When Destiny and his companions entered the room, without giving them the time to get their bearings, he offered to read them a play he had written entitled *The Life and Times of Charlemagne in Forty-Eight Acts*. This scared the assembly so that everyone's hair stood on end. Destiny, who managed to preserve some judgement amid the general terror, said that there wouldn't be enough time to hear him out before supper. "Well," he said, "in that case I'm going to tell you a story taken from a Spanish book* sent to me from Paris that I want to adapt to the stage." They tried to change the subject three or four times to avoid having to listen to what they assumed would be an imitation of, say, *Donkey Skin*,* but the little man did not get discouraged and, by dint of starting his story over from the beginning each time he was interrupted, he at last forced them to listen. As it turned out, no one minded, for the tale was a good one and belied people's low opinion of anything that came from Ragotin, as this finger puppet was called. You will hear this story in the next chapter, not as Ragotin told it, but as it was told to me by one of those who heard it. So Ragotin isn't the one who is speaking; I am.

CHAPTER IX

The Tale of the Invisible Mistress

D ON CARLOS OF ARAGON was a young gentleman who bore the name of an illustrious family. He performed wonders at the games the Viceroy of Naples held for the public to celebrate the wedding of Philip the second, third or fourth, I don't remember which. The day after a running at the ring won by Don Carlos, the Viceroy allowed the ladies to visit the city in disguise and wear masks, in the French style, for the convenience of the foreign ladies who had come to the city for the festivities. That day Don Carlos put on his best clothes and appeared, with a number of other tyrants of the heart, in the church of gallantry. Churches are profaned as often in that country as in our own, to the eternal shame of those who seek to woo customers from other churches by drawing them, in this way, to their own. Thus does the house of God become a meeting point for coquettes and fops. These abuses ought to be curbed. People should be assigned to chase fops and coquettes away from churches the way they keep out dogs and bitches. Those who say this is none of my business haven't seen anything yet! Let the fool who takes offence know that all men are fools here below, as well as liars, some more so than others; and I, who am talking to you, am perhaps more foolish than the rest, although I am honest enough to admit it. Since my book is no more than a load of foolishness, I hope that every fool who isn't too blinded by his own ego will see some aspect of himself reflected in it. To get back to my story then, Don Carlos was in a church with a number of other Italian and Spanish gentlemen showing off their feathers like peacocks, when three masked ladies accosted him in the midst of these proud Cupids. One of the ladies said this to him, or something to the effect of, "Lord Don Carlos, there is a lady in town to whom you are much obliged. In all the ring races and jousts she rooted for you to win, which you did."

"The best thing about what you are telling me," replied Don Carlos, "is that I am learning it from someone who seems to be a person of merit. I must admit that, had I dared to hope a lady would take my side, I would have taken greater care to be worthy of her approval." The unknown lady told him he had neglected nothing in proving himself one of the most dextrous men in existence, and that his black-and-white livery indicated he was not in love with anyone. "I've never really known the meaning of colours," answered Don Carlos, "but I do know that my failure to love is due less to indifference than to the knowledge I have that I am unworthy of being loved." They said many more such fine things to each other that I won't repeat, because I don't know what they were and I wouldn't dare make them up, lest I wrong Don Carlos and the unknown lady, both of whom were much wittier than I am, as I recently learnt from an honest Neapolitan who knew them both. In short, the lady in the mask told Don Carlos she was the one who had a penchant for him. When he asked to see her face, she told him he wasn't ready yet, that she would find a better opportunity, and that, in order to prove she wasn't afraid to meet with him alone, she would give him a token. As she said this, she took off her glove and, showing the Spaniard the loveliest hand he had ever seen, presented him with a ring that he received in such a state of surprise at the whole adventure that he almost forgot to bow as she left. The other gentlemen, who had discreetly kept their distance, now returned to his side. He told them what had happened to him and showed them the ring, which was quite valuable. Everyone gave his opinion, and Don Carlos proved to be as smitten by the unknown lady as if he had seen her face, such is the power of wit over those who share it.

A week went by without news of the lady, and I never found out whether he worried about it much. Every day he would go to an infantry captain's house where several gentlemen met to gamble. One evening that he hadn't played, and was on his way home earlier than usual, he heard someone calling him by name from the parlour of a large house. He approached the window, which had a grate, and recognized his invisible mistress by the sound of her voice. She said, "Come closer, Don Carlos. I've been waiting for you here in order to settle our quarrel."

"You're nothing but a braggart," Don Carlos told her. "At first you are insolent and defiant. Then you go into hiding for a week, only to reappear at a barred window." "We'll see each other when the time comes," she told him. "I wasn't afraid to see you. I simply wanted to know you before letting you see me. You are aware that duelling adversaries must fight with equal weapons. Should your heart not be as free as mine, you would have an advantage over me. That is why I wanted to learn about you."

"And what did you learn about me?" asked Don Carlos.

"That we are on equal footing," the invisible lady replied. Don Carlos told her they were not equal, "because you see me and know who I am, but I don't see you or know who you are. What conclusions do you think I have to draw from the care you take to conceal your identity? People don't hide when their intentions are good, and it's easy to fool an unsuspecting person. But you don't fool that person twice. If you're using me to make someone else jealous, I should tell you I'm not suited for that. I'm only suited for loving you."

"Are you done with your rash suspicions?" said the lady.

"They aren't exactly unfounded," replied Don Carlos.

"Please understand," she said, "that I am very truthful, as you will see in all our dealings, and that I want you to be too."

"Fair enough," said Don Carlos, "but it's also fair that I know who you are."

"You soon will," said the invisible lady. "Don't become impatient. That is how you will be worthy of what you expect from me. And I assure you (so that your gallantry is not unfounded and without hope of being rewarded) that my birth is not inferior to yours, that I have sufficient wealth for you to live as magnificently as any prince of the realm, and that I am closer to pretty than ugly; as for wit, you have too much of it yourself not to have discovered whether or not I possess it." With that, she withdrew, leaving Don Carlos with his mouth hanging open, ready to answer, so surprised by what she had said, so in love with someone he couldn't see, and so puzzled by her strange behaviour which might turn out to involve some deception, that he spent the better part of a half-hour pondering his extraordinary adventure. He knew there were several princesses and ladies of quality in Naples. But he also knew there were many greedy courtesans there who target foreigners, and who are all the more dangerous because they are beautiful. I won't tell you whether or not he had supper or went to bed on an empty stomach, as do the writers of certain novels who set an exact schedule for their heroes: have them get up early, tell their story until lunch, eat a light lunch, and continue with their story afterwards or wander into the woods to speak to themselves – or is it that they have something to share with the rocks and the trees? At dinner time they happen to be in an eatery, where they sigh and daydream instead of eating, and then go off and build castles in Spain on some terrace overlooking the sea, while a squire reveals that his master is so-and-so, the son of such-and-such a king, that there isn't a better prince anywhere, and that even though he's the most handsome mortal in existence, you should have seen him before he was disfigured by love.

Getting back to our story, Don Carlos returned to his spot the next day. The invisible lady was already waiting for him. She asked him if he had been confounded by their earlier conversation, and whether he doubted everything she said. Without answering her, Don Carlos asked her to tell him what risk she ran by showing herself, since they were equals and the result of their courtship would meet with everyone's approval. "The risk is great, as you will discover in time," the lady said. "Rest assured that I'm for real, and that I've been very modest in what I've told you about myself." Don Carlos did not press her further. They shared their love even more than they had before, and parted with the promise to keep their rendezvous every day.

The next day there was a great ball at the Viceroy's. Don Carlos hoped to recognize his invisible lady there, yet tried, nevertheless, to find out who owned the house where he was so favourably received. He learnt from the neighbours that it belonged to a very retiring old lady, the widow of a Spanish captain, who had neither daughters nor nieces. He asked to meet her. She let it be known to him that she had stopped seeing anyone since her husband's death. This further puzzled him. That evening Don Carlos attended a gathering of the most brilliant society at the Viceroy's. There he carefully observed all the ladies who might be his unknown mistress. Finally, he settled on the daughter of a marquis from Lord knows what marquisate; for it is the last thing I will swear to in this day and age, when everyone has become a marquis on their own say-so. She was young and beautiful, and something in the sound of her voice reminded him of the one he was looking for. But after a while he found so little in common between her wit and the invisible lady's that he began to regret having made so much progress so quickly with this attractive lady that, without flattering himself, he had reason to believe she did not despise him. They danced together all evening. When the ball ended, a dissatisfied Don Carlos left his captive to bask in the glory of having had, all to herself, in such a glittering assembly, a dancing partner envied by all the men and admired by all the women. As soon as he left the ball, he went home to pick up his weapons, and from there to the fatal grate, which was nearby. His lady, who was waiting, asked him for news of the ball, even though she had attended it. He frankly admitted he had danced several times with a beautiful lady and that they had spent the rest of the time talking. She asked him several questions that betrayed jealousy. Don Carlos, for his part, let her know he worried that her absence at the ball cast doubt on her quality. Realizing this, to put his mind at ease, she was more charming than ever and favoured him as much as one can in a conversation through a grate, to the point of promising him she would soon reveal herself. Then they parted; he doubting whether to believe her, she jealous of the beautiful lady with whom he had spent the ball.

The next day, Don Carlos, having gone to mass, offered holy water to two masked ladies who wanted some at the same time as he. The better-dressed of the two told him she could not accept compliments from someone with whom she had reason to quarrel. "If you aren't in too much of a hurry," Don Carlos told her, "I will try to satisfy your objections."

"Follow me into the chapel," replied the unknown lady. She went in first, followed by Don Carlos, who thought she wasn't his lady, although they were about the same size, because her diction seemed somewhat affected. This is what she told him after they had locked themselves in the chapel: "Lord Don Carlos, the entire city of Naples is talking about the lofty reputation you have acquired in the short time you have been here. You are considered the noblest gentleman there is. The only thing that seems strange to us is that you have failed to notice the ladies of quality and merit in this city who have such a high opinion of you. They have expressed their feelings as much as decency allows, and although they ardently wish to make you aware of them, they would prefer it if your neglect were caused by obliviousness rather than a feigned lack of awareness motivated by indifference. I know of one lady who values you enough to warn you, at the risk of compromising her own reputation, that your nocturnal adventures have been discovered, that you are recklessly involved in loving the unknown; and since your mistress does not show herself, she must be ashamed of loving you, or of being unworthy of your love. I don't doubt that the object of your contemplative love is a lady of great quality and wit, and that you have imagined an adorable mistress. But, Lord Don Carlos, don't trust your imagination more than your judgement; beware of a person who hides, and don't persist in these nocturnal conversations. But why should I wear this disguise? I am the one who is jealous of your ghost, who does not want you to speak to her, and since I have revealed myself, let me tell you that I will foil her plans and emerge victorious from a battle I have every right to wage since I am her equal in beauty, wealth and quality, and all the other things that make someone desirable. Heed my advice, if you are wise." She left as she said these words, without giving Don Carlos the time to reply. He wanted to follow her, but was prevented by a gentleman at the door of the church who engaged him in a conversation he could not avoid, which lasted quite a while. He spent the rest of the day dreaming about this adventure, and at first suspected that the lady from the ball and this latest masked woman were one and the same person, but he soon realized that this lady had shown herself to be very witty, whereas he remembered that the lady from the ball was anything but. He did not know what to believe, and even wished he were not committed to his mysterious mistress, so he could devote himself completely to the one he had just met. He told himself that, after all, she was no more of a known quantity than his invisible mistress, whose wit had charmed him so in the conversations they had had, and hesitated no further. Since he was not easily intimidated, he did not worry much about the threats that had been made against him.

That very evening, he was at his grate at the usual time, when he was seized by four masked men, strong enough to disarm him and carry him by force to a waiting coach. I leave it to the reader to imagine the names he called them, and how he reproached them for unfairly outnumbering him. He even tried to win them over with promises, but instead of persuading them, he only succeeded in making them more careful, depriving him of any hope he might have had of freeing himself through courage or strength. Meanwhile, the coach and the four horses drove away at a full trot. It left the city, and after an hour entered a magnificent house whose gate was held open to receive it. The four masked men got off the coach, holding Don Carlos under the arms like an ambassador being introduced to the emperor of the Turks. In this manner he was carried up a flight of stairs, where two masked ladies holding torches met him at the door of a vast room. The masked men let him go and took their leave with a deep bow. In all likelihood they did not return his pistol or his sword, nor did he thank them for the pains they had taken to guard him. I won't go on about the ladies' torches being silver, for they were of chiselled gold leaf. And the room was the most magnificent in the entire world, as beautifully furnished, if you will, as some of the apartments in our romances, like Zealander's ship in *Polexandre*, Ibrahim's palace in *Illustre Bassa*, or the room where the King of Assyria received Mandane in *Cyrus*,* which is, along with those I have already mentioned, the world's most well-furnished book. Imagine how our Spaniard felt at finding himself in this superb apartment, with two masked ladies who led him into an adjacent room that was even more sumptuously furnished than the previous one. There they left him alone. Had he been of Don Quixote's ilk, he would have milked the situation for everything it was worth, imagining himself to be no less than Esplandián or Amadís.* But our Spaniard was no more concerned than if he had been in his own inn. He did sorely miss his invisible mistress, and constantly thought about her, so that he found this beautiful room sadder than a prison, which only ever looks good from the outside. He did find it easy to believe that he was not in danger from whoever had provided him with such comfortable lodgings. He surmised that the lady who had spoken to him the day before in church was the magician behind all these enchantments. He thought to himself how much he admired women's fancies, and the way they act so quickly on their resolutions. For his part, he resolved to wait patiently for the end of the adventure and stay faithful to the mistress at the grate, no matter what promises or threats he encountered. A little while later, well-dressed masked servants set the table and served supper. Everything about it was magnificent. Music and perfumes were not forgotten, and our

Don Carlos, along with the senses of smell and hearing, found his sense of taste more satisfied than I would have thought possible under the circumstances. I mean he ate his fill. Call it intestinal fortitude. I forgot to tell you that I think he washed his mouth, for I am told he took great care of his teeth. The music lasted for some time after supper and, everyone having withdrawn, Don Carlos wandered around for a long time reflecting on all these enchantments or something else. Two masked ladies and a masked dwarf spread out a magnificent toilette and began to undress him without asking him whether he felt like going to bed. He was very submissive. The ladies made the bed and withdrew. The dwarf removed his shoes or boots and then the rest of his clothes. Don Carlos went to bed without so much as a word being exchanged. He slept quite well for someone who was in love. The birds from an aviary woke him at dawn, and the masked dwarf came in to serve him, bringing the whitest, most perfumed, most beautiful towels. If you don't mind, we shall skip what he did before lunch, which was the equal of dinner, and move right to the point where one of the masked ladies broke the silence by asking Don Carlos if he would like to see the mistress of this enchanted palace. He said he would welcome the opportunity. She came in soon thereafter, followed by four very richly dressed ladies in waiting:

> More than Cythera be warned
> When lit up by a new flame
> She'll rise perfumed and adorned
> The better to capture her game.

Never had our Spaniard seen a more comely person than this unknown Urganda.* He was so carried away and surprised at the same time that he stumbled at every bow and step he made, as she took him by the hand and ushered him into the next room. All the beautiful things he had seen in the rooms I have already spoken of were nothing compared to what he found in this one, and it was embellished further by the masked lady's presence.

They walked on the finest carpet ever seen. The Spaniard was steered to an armchair, and the lady, having seated herself on a mountain of plush cushions facing him, in a voice as melodious as a harpsichord, spoke words to this effect: "I do not doubt, Lord Don Carlos, that you are very surprised by all the things that have happened in my house since yesterday. And if it hasn't made much of an impression on you, it has at least shown you that I know how to keep my word; and by what I have already done, you should be able to judge what I am capable of doing. Perhaps my rival, through her tricks and the blind luck of having struck first, has already become the absolute ruler of the heart to which I nevertheless dispute her claim. A woman is not discouraged by the first setback, and if my fortune, which is nothing to laugh at, and everything else that may be had with me cannot persuade you to love me, I will at least have the satisfaction of not having to conceal myself out of shame or deceit, and to have preferred being despised for my actual faults to being loved for my imagined virtues." As she uttered these words she took off her mask, revealing heaven in all its glory or, if you prefer, heaven in miniature: the world's most beautiful head, held up by the finest figure he had ever admired; all of which put together added up to a perfectly divine person. Judging by the freshness of her complexion, she appeared to be no more than sixteen, but a certain attitude, at once regal and relaxed, that youngsters do not yet possess, hinted that she was closer to twenty. Don Carlos did not answer her right away. He was almost angry at his invisible lady, who kept him from giving himself over entirely to the most beautiful woman he had ever seen. He hesitated about what to say and what to do. Finally, after an internal conflict that lasted long enough to worry the lady of the enchanted palace, he firmly resolved not to hide his innermost feelings from her; it was without doubt his finest hour. This was his answer, which some have found too blunt: "I cannot deny, my lady, that I would be the most fortunate man indeed to appeal to you, had I been fortunate enough to be able to love you. I am well aware that I am leaving the most beautiful person in the whole world for another whose beauty may only exist in my imagination. But, my lady, would you have found me worthy of your affection had you believed me capable of infidelity? And could I be faithful if I could love you? Pity me instead of blaming me; or rather let us pity ourselves together, you for being unable to obtain what you desire, and me for being unable to see the one I love." This he said so sadly that the lady could tell he was speaking from the heart. She neglected none of the things that could persuade him. He turned a deaf ear to her pleas and failed to be moved by her tears. She went on the attack several times. He countered every charge. Finally she resorted to blame and insults and told him

> Everything rage makes us say
> When it commands the senses,

leaving him there, not to pick straws but to curse his misfortune, which was caused by an excess of good fortune.

A little while later, a damsel came to tell him he was free to take a walk in the garden. He walked through all the beautiful apartments without encountering anyone until he reached the stairway, at the bottom of which he saw ten masked men guarding the door, armed with lances and carbines. As he crossed the courtyard to enter the garden, which was as beautiful as the rest of the house, one of these archers of the guard walked by, and without looking at him, told him, as though afraid of being overheard, that an old gentleman had entrusted him with a letter for Don Carlos and that he had promised to deliver it by hand, although he risked his life should he be discovered, but that a gift of twenty pistoles and the promise of as much again made him risk everything. Don Carlos promised to keep his secret and quickly entered the garden to read the letter.

> *You can imagine my distress since I lost you, by your own distress, if you love me as much as I love you. I do feel some consolation at having discovered where you are. Princess Porcia is the one who had you abducted. She does not let much stand*

*in the way of her desires, and you are not the first Rinaldo of
this dangerous Armida.* But I will break all her spells and soon
pull you away from her arms, so that I may give you, in mine,
all that you deserve, if you are as faithful as I wish.*

The Invisible Lady

Don Carlos was so delighted to hear from his lady, with whom
he was truly in love, that he kissed the letter again and again, and
sought out, at the garden gate, the one who had given him the
letter, to reward him with a diamond he wore on his finger. He
lingered for some time in the garden, unable to contain his amazement at this Princess Porcia, whom he had often heard spoken of
as a very wealthy young lady from one of the noblest houses of
the kingdom, and as he was quite virtuous, he felt such an aversion
to her that he resolved, at the risk of his life, to do all he could
to escape her prison. As he left the garden, he encountered an
unmasked damsel (masks were no longer being worn in the palace)
who had come to ask him if he would mind if her mistress ate with
him that day. I leave it to you to imagine whether or not he said she
would be welcome. Soon thereafter lunch or dinner was served, for
I no longer remember which it should be. Porcia appeared more
beautiful, as I said earlier, than Cythera, but there should be no
problem to say here, for diversity's sake: more beautiful than day
or dawn. At the table, she was as charming as can be, and showed
so much wit to the Spaniard that he was secretly displeased to
see, in a lady of such high birth, so many excellent qualities put
to such bad use. He forced himself as best he could to appear to
be in a good mood, although he continually thought about his
unknown lady, and burned with a violent desire to return to her
grate. As soon as the table was cleared, they were left alone, and as
Don Carlos was silent, either out of respect or to force the lady to
speak first, she broke the silence with these words: "I don't know if
I can expect anything from the cheerful expression I seem to have
noticed on your face or whether mine, which I have shown you,
has not seemed attractive enough to make you wonder whether

the one that is being hidden from you is more capable of inspiring love. I haven't hidden what I wanted to give you because I didn't want you to be able to repent for having taken it, and although someone who is accustomed to receiving pleas and entreaties can easily be offended by a refusal, I won't hold against you the one I have already received, so long as you repair it by giving me what I think I deserve more than your invisible someone. Let me know your final decision so that, if it is not to my advantage, I may seek, in mine, reasons that are strong enough to fight those I think I have had to love you." Don Carlos waited for some time for her to resume speaking and, seeing that she had fallen silent, staring at the ground, waiting for him to decide her fate, he acted on the resolution he had already made to speak to her frankly and dash any hope that he might ever belong to her. This is how he went about it: "My lady, before giving you an answer concerning what you want from me, you must, with the same honesty you desire from me, sincerely reveal your feelings about what I am going to say to you. If you had caused someone to love you," he added, "and, through all the favours a lady may bestow without harming her virtue, obliged him to swear an inviolable oath of fidelity, wouldn't you consider him the most cowardly and treacherous of men if he failed to live up to his promise? And wouldn't I be that coward and that traitor, if for you I left someone who has reason to believe in my love?" He was going to formulate any number of other convincing arguments, but she did not give him the time. She abruptly stood up, saying that she could see where he was headed, that she could not help admiring his commitment, even though it was so contrary to what would have brought her peace of mind, that she was giving him back his freedom, and that he would oblige her by waiting for nightfall before returning the same way he had come. She held her handkerchief in front of her eyes while she spoke, as if to hide her tears, leaving the Spaniard somewhat taken aback and yet so filled with joy to be free that he could not hide it, had he been the world's biggest hypocrite; and I believe that, had the lady noticed it, she would not have been able to refrain from scolding him. I don't know if night was long in coming, because, as I have already told you, I no longer bother to keep track of time or hours. You will only know that it came and that he got into a closed coach, which dropped him off at home after a rather long drive. As he was a wonderful master, his servants thought they would die of happiness when they saw him, and risk smothering him with their hugs; but they did not enjoy his company for long. He picked up some weapons and, accompanied by two of his servants who were not the kind to let themselves be beaten, he hastened to his grate so quickly that those who were with him had a hard time keeping up. No sooner had he made the customary sign than his invisible deity answered. They exchanged such tender words that it brings tears to my eyes whenever I think of them. Finally, the invisible lady told him she had just had a vexing experience in the house where she was staying, and that she had sent for a coach in order to leave it, but that this would take a long time, while his own coach could be ready much sooner. So she asked him to send for it and to take her to a place where she would no longer hide her face from him. The Spaniard didn't have to be asked twice. He made a mad dash to his servants, whom he had left at the end of the street, and sent them to fetch his coach. When the coach arrived, the invisible lady was true to her word and got in with him. She told the coachman which way to go, making him stop next to a great house, into the courtyard of which they entered by the light of several torches, which had already been lit when they arrived. A grand staircase led the Spaniard and his lady to an upper hall where he was not without worry, since she had yet to remove her mask. Finally, several richly adorned damsels bearing torches having come to greet them, the lady was no longer invisible. Removing her mask, she showed Don Carlos that the lady at the grate and Princess Porcia were one and the same. I won't try to describe Don Carlos's pleasant surprise. The beautiful Neapolitan told him she had abducted him a second time in order to know his final decision, and that the lady at the grate had ceded to her any claim she had to him. To this she added many other things as witty as they were flirtatious. Don

Carlos threw himself at her feet, embraced her knees and thought he would eat her hands he kissed them so much, thereby saving himself from saying the nonsense one says when one is too happy. When these first transports had passed, he used all his wit and all his charm to praise his mistress's amusing conceit. He acquitted himself so well, in terms so flattering to her, that she was more certain than ever not to have been mistaken in her choice. She told him she did not want to trust anyone but herself when it came to something without which she would have been unable to love him and that she would never have given herself to a man less true than he. Whereupon Princess Porcia's parents, who had been informed of her plan, arrived. Since she was one of the most important persons in the kingdom and Don Carlos a man of high birth, they easily obtained a dispensation from the archbishop for their marriage. They were married that very night by the parson of the parish, who was a good priest and a great preacher, so don't ask me if he made a fine exhortation. It is said that they got up quite late the following morning, which I do not find hard to believe. The news was soon divulged, which so pleased the Viceroy, who was a friend of Don Carlos, that public celebrations began anew in Naples, where they still remember Don Carlos of Aragon and his invisible lover.

CHAPTER X

How Ragotin Had His Fingers Smacked with a Corset Stay

R AGOTIN'S STORY WAS GREETED by applause from everyone. He was as proud of it as if he had written it himself. With this added on to his natural vanity, he began to treat the actors with disdain and, going over to the actresses, he grabbed their hands without their consent and tried to fondle them, a form of provincial gallantry more in keeping with a satyr than a gentleman.

Mademoiselle Star was content to remove her white hands from his grimy and hairy ones, while her companion, Mademoiselle Angélique, gave him a big smack on the fingers with a corset stay. He left them without uttering a word, blushing with shame and vexation, and returned to the group, where everyone was speaking as loudly as possible without listening to what the others were saying. Ragotin silenced most of them by shouting to ask them what they thought of his story. A young man whose name I forget replied that the story didn't belong to Ragotin any more than to anyone else, since he had found it in a book, and as he said this he pointed out a book that was sticking out of Ragotin's pocket and snatched it from him. Ragotin scratched the young man's hands trying to get it back, but only managed to get it into someone else's hands, from whom Ragotin tried to wrest it just as unsuccessfully as before. The book, having already gone to a third party, was passed in this way to five or six different pairs of hands which Ragotin could not reach because he was the shortest person in the room. Finally, having stretched five or six times unsuccessfully, having torn as many sleeves and scratched as many hands, while the book was still making the rounds of the room, poor Ragotin, who saw that everyone was laughing at his expense, threw himself furiously upon the author of his misfortune and punched him in the stomach and thighs, not being able to reach any higher. The other's hands, having a strategic height advantage, fell squarely on the top of his head five or six times, with such force his hat was pushed right down to his chin, which so rattled the seat of his reason that the little man no longer knew where he was. As a final insult, as he was leaving, his adversary kicked him on the top of the head, making him land on his arse at the feet of the actresses, after a very sudden fall. I ask you to imagine the fury of a little man more vainglorious than all the barbers of the realm, at the moment of his greatest triumph, the triumph of his story, in front of actresses whose lover he wanted to be, for, as you shall see later on, he did not yet know which one of them would most touch his heart. Truth be told, his little body fallen on its arse,

41

through the various movements of his arms and legs, even though his face was not visible, because his head was encased in his hat, so excellently expressed the fury of his soul that the assembled company thought it wise to close ranks and form a barrier between Ragotin and the one who had offended him, who was whisked away, while the charitable actresses put the little man back on his feet. He bellowed all the while in his hat like a bull, because it blocked his eyes and mouth and interfered with his breathing. Removing it was difficult. It was shaped like a butter pot, with a rim narrower than its body, and Lord knows whether a head which had been forced into it, with a very big nose, could exit as it had entered. This misfortune was the cause of a greater good, because Ragotin had likely reached the peak of his anger, which would probably have had consequences of great magnitude if his hat, which was suffocating him, had not made him think about his own salvation rather than another's destruction. He did not ask for help, because he could not speak; but, when he was seen raising his trembling hands to his head in a vain effort to free it, and stamping his feet with rage at breaking his nails to no avail, it became uppermost in everyone's mind to come to his aid. The first efforts to remove his hat were so violent that Ragotin thought they were trying to tear off his head. Finally, at the end of his rope, he made a sign with his fingers for his headdress to be cut off with scissors. Mademoiselle Cave removed those she wore on her belt, and Grudge, who performed this successful operation, after pretending to make his incision across the face (throwing quite a scare into Ragotin), split the felt on the back of his head from top to bottom. As soon as some air had returned to his face, everyone burst out laughing to see him puffed up to the point of popping from the quantity of humours that had risen to his face and, what's more, because he had skinned his nose. Things would have ended there, though, had not a smart alec told him his hat needed to be mended. This untimely piece of advice so revived his lingering anger that he grabbed one of the andirons by the fireplace and, threatening to throw it at the whole troupe, caused such a fright among the boldest of them that everyone tried to flee through the door in order to avoid being struck. They pushed so hard only one person was able to get out, by falling forward at that, his spurs having got caught on someone else's. Ragotin himself started to laugh, which reassured everyone. His book was returned to him, and the actors gave him an old hat. He vented his anger at the one who had so mistreated him but, as he was more vain than vindictive, he told the actors, as if he were promising them something rare, that he wanted to turn his story into a play and that, given the manner in which he would go about it, he was sure to reach in a single bound heights that other authors had only achieved gradually. Destiny told him his story was entertaining, but that it wasn't any good for the theatre. "Who are you to tell me so?" said Ragotin. "My mother was the author Garnier's* godchild and I who am speaking to you still have his writing case in my possession." Destiny told him that Garnier himself would not have helped his reputation with this adaptation. "And what do you find so difficult about it?" asked Ragotin. "That it cannot be made into a play without breaking the rules of propriety and sound judgement," replied Destiny. "A man of my calibre can make up the rules as he wishes," said Ragotin. "Wouldn't you consider it," he added, "both a new and magnificent thing to see a great church portal in the centre of a theatre, in front of which twenty gentlemen, at least, with an equal number of damsels, made gallant conversation: it would delight everyone."

"I agree with you," he continued, "that nothing must be done against decorum or propriety, which is why I wouldn't want to make my actors speak inside a church." Destiny interrupted to ask him where he planned to find so many gentlemen and so many ladies. "And how do they do it in the schools, where they stage mock battles?" said Ragotin. "At La Flèche School I acted in the rout of Ponts-de-Cé,"* he added, "more than a hundred soldiers from the Queen Mother's side appeared on stage, not counting those from the King's army, who were even more numerous. I remember that, because of a downpour which interrupted the show; it was said that all the feathers of the local gentry, which had been borrowed for the occasion, would never recover." Destiny, who enjoyed making Ragotin say such judicious things, retorted that schools had plenty of students, whereas they were only seven or eight in their troupe when it was at full strength. Grudge, a worthless soul, as you already know, took Ragotin's side, the better to egg him on, and said he disagreed with his colleague, that he had acted longer than Destiny, that a church portal was the most beautiful stage set anyone had ever seen and, as far as the number of gentlemen and ladies was concerned, some could be rented and the rest made of cardboard. Grudge's cardboard solution made everyone laugh, including Ragotin, who swore he had thought of it too, but hadn't wanted to say so. "And how about the coach," he added. "What a novelty that would be in a play! I once played Toby's dog, and I played it so well the audience was delighted. As far as I'm concerned," he continued, "if things are judged by their effect on the mind, every time I've seen *Pyramus and Thisbe*, I wasn't as touched by Pyramus's death as I was frightened of the lion."* Grudge backed Ragotin's ideas with others that were just as ridiculous, thereby ingratiating himself to such an extent that Ragotin took him out to dinner. All the other intruders also dispersed, leaving the actors, who were more in the mood to dine together than to socialize with the town's loafers, at liberty.

CHAPTER XI

*Which Contains What You Shall See
if You Bother to Read It*

R AGOTIN LED GRUDGE TO A TAVERN where he ordered their best offerings. It's been said that he didn't invite him to his home because what was served there wasn't very good. I won't comment on this for fear of passing judgement too lightly, and I haven't wanted to delve too deeply into this question because it isn't worth the trouble and I have far more important things to write about. A very discerning man who could quickly size people up, Grudge no sooner saw two partridges and a capon being served to the two of them than he suspected that Ragotin wasn't treating him so well simply for his merit or to repay him for how he had obliged him by agreeing that his story would make a good play, but that he had something else in mind. So he got ready to hear some new extravagance from Ragotin, who didn't reveal right away what he was up to and continued to talk about his story. He recited a number of satirical verses he had made up about most of his neighbours, about unnamed cuckolds and about some women. He sang drinking songs and showed Grudge many anagrams, because this is how would-be poets, through such products of their misshapen minds, start out bothering honest folk. Grudge resumed his fawning. He exaggerated everything he heard by raising his eyes to the sky. He swore, like a losing gambler, that he had never heard anything as beautiful and even pretended to tear out his hair, so moved was he. From time to time he would tell Ragotin, "How sad it is for you, and for us too, that you don't devote yourself entirely to the theatre. In two years' time Corneille would be as forgotten as Hardy is today. I'm a stranger to flattery, but to encourage you, I have to tell you that when I met you I knew right away you were a great poet, and you can ask the others in my troupe what I told them. I'm rarely mistaken. I can spot a poet a mile away. When I first saw you, I felt I knew you as well as if I'd raised you myself." Ragotin swallowed this whole, along with several glasses of wine, which intoxicated him even more than Grudge's praise, who was holding his own, eating and drinking with great gusto, from time to time crying out: "For God's sake, Monsieur Ragotin, put your talent to use. You're a mean man not to enrich yourself and us too. I can scribble as well as the rest of them, but if I could write verses half as good as those you just read me, I wouldn't be reduced to scraping by. I'd live off my income like

Mondory. Work, Monsieur Ragotin, work. And if by winter we don't wow those gentlemen from the Hôtel de Bourgogne and the Hôtel du Marais, let me never set foot on stage again without breaking an arm or a leg. I have nothing more to say. Let's drink." He kept his word and having filled his glass to the brim, he raised it to the health of Monsieur Ragotin with Monsieur Ragotin himself, who raised another one to the health of the actresses, which he drank with his head bare and with so much emotion that, without noticing it, he broke the stem when he put his glass back down on the table. He tried several times to make it stand again, thinking he had tipped it over. Finally he threw it over his head and pulled on Grudge's arm to call his attention to it, not wanting to waste the reputation of having broken a glass. He was a little saddened that Grudge didn't laugh. But, as I've already told you, Grudge was more of an envious animal than one endowed with the capacity for laughter. Grudge asked him what he thought of the actresses. The little fellow blushed without answering and, what with Grudge repeating the question, stammering, blushing and expressing himself very badly, he finally made it understood that one of the actresses greatly appealed to him. "Which one?" asked Grudge. The little man was so embarrassed to have said so much that he answered, "I don't know." "Neither do I," said Grudge. This embarrassed him even more and, taken aback, made him add, "It's... it's..." He repeated the same word four or five times, to which the actor, losing patience, said, "You're right. She's a very good-looking girl." This completed Ragotin's discomfiture. He was never able to say who it was he had in mind, and maybe he didn't even know as yet, having less love in his heart than vice. Finally, when Grudge named Mademoiselle Star, he admitted that she was the one he was in love with. As for me, I think that had Grudge named Angélique or her mother, Cave, Ragotin would have forgotten the one's smack and the other's age and surrendered himself body and soul to whichever one was named, such was the old goat's confused state of mind. The actor made him drink a big glass of wine, which cleared up part of his confusion, and drank one himself, after which he told him, speaking in a low voice and looking around the room even though they were the only ones there: "Your wound isn't fatal and you have found a man who can cure you, so long as you are willing to believe him and keep your secret. It's true that yours is a very difficult undertaking: Mademoiselle Star is a tigress and her brother Destiny a lion, but she isn't used to seeing men like you, and I know just what to do. Let's finish our wine and tomorrow it will be day." The conversation was interrupted while each drank a glass of wine. Ragotin was the first to speak again. Listing his achievements and riches, he told Grudge that he had a nephew who was the clerk of a financier; that this nephew had become a close friend of the tax collector La Rallière when he had been in Le Mans to settle an excise there, and that Grudge had reason to hope for a stipend equal to that of the King's actors, thanks to the influence of this nephew. He also told him that if anyone in his family had children, he could get them sinecures, because his niece had married the brother of a woman who was kept by the steward of an abbot of the province who was entitled to make lucrative ecclesiastical appointments. While Ragotin recounted his exploits, Grudge, who was visibly affected by drink, did nothing but refill both glasses, which were emptied at once, Ragotin not daring to turn down anything from someone who would do so much for him. Finally, by dint of swallowing, they filled up. As was his custom, Grudge grew more serious, while Ragotin became so leaden and stupefied that he leant over the table and fell asleep. Grudge called over a maid to make a bed, because no one was awake at his inn. The maid told him that she might as well make two beds and that in his present state Monsieur Ragotin didn't need to be awakened. He certainly didn't wake up, and never has anyone slept or snored better. Sheets were put on two of the three beds in the room without waking him. He rained insults on the maid and threatened to beat her when she informed him that his bed was ready. Finally,

Grudge having turned him in his chair towards the fire that had been lit to warm the sheets, he opened his eyes and allowed himself to be undressed without saying anything. He was helped into bed with some effort and Grudge got into his bed after having shut the door. An hour later Ragotin got out of bed. I've never been able to know just why. He got so lost in the room that after having knocked over all the furniture and himself, several times, without finding his bed, he finally found Grudge's and woke him up by uncovering him. Grudge asked him what he was looking for. "I'm looking for my bed," said Ragotin. "It's to the left of mine," said Grudge. The little drunkard turned right and climbed between the cover and the straw foundation of the third bed, which had neither a mattress nor a featherbed, where he slept the night quite peacefully. Grudge got dressed before Ragotin woke up. He asked the little drunkard if it was to mortify his flesh that he had left his bed to sleep on straw. Ragotin insisted that he hadn't got up and that the room must be haunted. He quarrelled with the innkeeper, who defended the reputation of his establishment and threatened to sue him for defamation. But I've been boring you for too long with this account of Ragotin's revels. Let's return to the actors' inn.

CHAPTER XII

A Fight in the Night

I AM TOO MUCH A MAN OF HONOUR not to warn the benevolent reader that, if he is scandalized by all the foolishness he has seen up to now in the present book, he would do well to stop reading; for in good conscience he won't see anything else, were the book as long as *Cyrus the Great*. If, by what he has already seen, he finds it difficult to imagine what he will see next, it may be that I share his vantage point, that one chapter brings forth the next and that in my book I do as those who place the bridle on their horse's neck and let it wander wherever it will. It may also be that I have a plan and that, without filling my book with examples to imitate, with actions and things condemnable or ridiculous, I seek to instruct by entertaining, the way a drunk gives aversion for his vice and can sometimes give pleasure through the extravagant behaviour caused by his drunkenness.

But let me stop moralizing and return to our actors, whom we had left at the inn. As soon as their room emptied out and Grudge left with Ragotin, the troupe's doorkeeper, whom they had left in Tours, entered the inn leading a horse loaded with baggage. He sat down to dine with them. Through what he related and what they learnt from one another, it became known how the royal overseer of the province had not been able to harm them, having himself had a very hard time escaping the people's wrath, along with his infantrymen. Destiny told his comrades how he had fled in his Turkish costume, in which he intended to play Mairet's *Soliman*,* and that upon learning that the plague was in Alençon, he had come to Le Mans with Cave and Grudge, in the manner described at the beginning of these very realistic and hardly heroic adventures. Mademoiselle Star also told them about the help she had received from a lady from Tours, whose name I never learnt, and how thanks to this lady she was escorted to a village near Bonnétable, where she sprained her ankle falling off a horse. She added that, having learnt the troupe was in Le Mans, she had herself carried there in a litter which the lady of the village generously lent her.

After dinner, Destiny alone remained in the ladies' room. Cave loved him like her own son. Mademoiselle Star was no less dear to her. Angélique, her daughter and sole heir, loved Destiny and Star like her own brother and sister. She didn't really know who they were or why they joined the theatre, but she realized that, although they called each other brother and sister, they were more close friends than close relatives; that Destiny lived with Star most respectfully; that she was very virtuous and that, while Destiny

49

was witty and showed he had been well brought up, Mademoiselle Star seemed more like a young lady than a touring actress. While Destiny and Star were loved by Cave and her daughter, they showed themselves worthy of it by reciprocating, which wasn't difficult, as the two actresses deserved to be loved as much as any actresses in France, although through misfortune rather than lack of merit they had never had the honour of climbing onto the stage of the Hôtel de Bourgogne or du Marais, both of which are the *ne plus ultra* for actors. Those who don't understand these three little Latin words (that I couldn't help using here, so apropos were they) should have someone explain them, if they wish. To end the digression, after such a long absence, Destiny and Star did not hide their displays of affection from the two actresses. They expressed as best they could the worries they had about each other. Destiny informed Mademoiselle Star that he thought he had seen their old nemesis during the last performance in Tours, that he had spotted him in the crowd, despite his attempts to hide his face in his coat, and that this was why Destiny had worn a bandage on his face on the way out of Tours: in order to make himself unrecognizable to his enemy, being unable at the time to defend himself should he be attacked by a force of men. He then told her about the great many litters they had encountered on their way to meet her, and that, unless he was sadly mistaken, their common enemy was the unknown man who had carefully examined the litters, as was recounted in Chapter 7. While Destiny spoke, Star could not help shedding a few tears. This greatly moved Destiny, and after having consoled her as best he could, he added that if she would only allow him to devote as much care to seeking out their common enemy as he had devoted until now to avoiding him, she would soon find herself free of his persecutions, or he would lose his own life in the process. These words only increased her distress. Destiny was not stoic enough not to be distressed too; and Cave and her daughter, who were of a very compassionate nature, became distressed out of sympathy or by contagion, and I even think they cried. I don't know whether

Destiny cried, but I do know that he and the actresses did not speak for quite a while, during which time anyone who wished to cry did so. Finally, Cave put an end to the pause occasioned by the tears, and reproached Destiny and Star for having so little trust in her and her daughter – despite the time they had spent together, which had allowed them to appreciate just how much of a friend to them she was – that she and Angélique still didn't know their birth and quality. And she added that she had been persecuted enough in her own lifetime to be able to counsel unfortunates such as they appeared to be. Destiny answered that it wasn't out of distrust that they hadn't revealed themselves to her, but that he thought the story of their misfortunes would be quite boring. He then offered to tell it whenever she wished, whenever she had some time to kill. Cave wanted to waste no time in satisfying her curiosity, as well as her daughter, who fervently wanted the same thing, having sat down next to her, on Star's bed. Destiny was about to begin telling his story when they heard a commotion in the next room. Destiny listened for a while, but instead of stopping, the noise increased and someone even cried out: "Help! Murderer!" Destiny bounded out of the room, sacrificing his doublet in the process, which was torn by Cave and her daughter when they tried to restrain him. He entered the room the noise was coming from, where he couldn't see a thing, and where punches, slaps and the mixed-up voices of several men and women beating up one another, blending with the muffled sounds of bare feet stamping around the room, made an unbearable racket. He imprudently went to mingle with the combatants and immediately caught a punch on one side and a slap on the other. This changed the good intention he had of separating those hobgoblins into a violent desire for vengeance. He began to move his hands and windmill with his arms, mistreating more than one jaw, as the evidence of his bloody hands would later reveal. The brawl lasted long enough for him to receive about twenty blows and dishing out twice as many. At the height of the fighting, he felt a bite on his thigh, and when, reaching for it, his hand encountered something furry, he thought he'd been bitten by a dog. But Cave and her daughter, appearing at the door with a light – like St Elmo's fire after a storm – saw Destiny and revealed to him that he was in the midst of seven people in their nightshirts who were fighting most ferociously, but stopped of their own accord as soon as the light came on. It didn't stay calm for long, though. The innkeeper, who was one those seven white penitents, fell upon the poet once more. Olive, who was there too, was attacked by the innkeeper's footman. Destiny wanted to pull them apart, but the innkeeper's wife – who turned out to be the beast who had bitten him, and whom he had mistaken for a dog because her head was bare and she had short hair – leapt at him, with the help of two maids as dishevelled and undressed as she was. The shouting resumed. The slaps and punches rang out with renewed intensity and the brawl heated up even more than before. Finally, several people who had been awakened by the noise entered the battlefield and separated the combatants, resulting in a second ceasefire. The cause of the quarrel was sought. What disagreement had brought together seven undressed people in the same room? Olive, who seemed to be the calmest, said that the poet had left their room, only to return faster than his footsteps, followed by the innkeeper who wanted to beat him; that the innkeeper's wife had followed her husband and pounced on the poet; that, as he tried to separate them, a valet and two maids had attacked him, and that the light, which had gone out just then, was the reason why the fight had lasted so long. It was the poet's turn to plead his case. He said he had just composed the two most beautiful stanzas anyone had ever made and, for fear of forgetting them, he had asked the inn's maids for a candle; that they had made fun of him; that the innkeeper had called him food for the gallows; and that, not wanting to be without a retort, he had called the innkeeper a cuckold. No sooner did he utter this word than the innkeeper, who was within striking distance, slapped him. As soon as the slap was delivered, and as if by plan, the innkeeper's wife, his valet and maids pounced on the actors, who met them with well-thrown punches. This final encounter was rougher and lasted longer than the previous ones. Taking hold of the fat maid, Destiny hitched up her skirts and gave her a vigorous spanking. Olive, seeing how this made people laugh, did the same thing to the other maid. The innkeeper was dealing with the poet. And the innkeeper's wife, who was the most enraged, had been restrained by several of the spectators, which made her so angry she yelled that she was being robbed. Her yells woke La Rappinière, who lived next door to the inn. He had the doors opened. Thinking he would find no fewer than eight bodies, given the noise he had heard, he made the fighting stop in the name of the King and, having learnt the cause of all this disorder, he exhorted the poet not to compose verses at night and considered beating the innkeeper and his wife, because they had heaped abuse upon the poor actors, calling them buffoons and idlers and swearing to kick them out the next day. But La Rappinière, to whom the innkeeper owed money, made him shut up by threatening to call in his loans. La Rappinière went home, the others returned to their rooms and Destiny went back to the actresses' room, where Cave asked him not to postpone any longer telling her his adventures and those of his sister. He told them he'd be glad to, and began his story in the manner you shall see in the following chapter.

CHAPTER XIII

Longer than the Preceding One.
Destiny and Mademoiselle Star's Story

" I WAS BORN IN A VILLAGE near Paris. If I wanted to, I could make you believe that I am from a very illustrious family, as unknown people find it easy to do. But I am too sincere to deny my low birth. My father was among the most prominent and prosperous men of his village. I have heard him say he was the son of a poor gentleman, that he had gone off to war in his youth, which, having earned him nothing but injuries, led him to becoming the gentleman usher of a wealthy Parisian lady, and that, having accumulated some savings, because he was also her steward and bookkeeper – which means that he may have lined his own pockets – he had married an old lady-in-waiting of the house, who made him her heir and died soon thereafter. He quickly tired of being a widower and, being just as tired of service, took as his second wife a peasant woman who supplied bread to his mistress's house. I was the product of this second marriage. My father's name was Garigues. I never learnt where he was from. As for my mother's, it adds nothing to the story. Suffice it to say that she was stingier than my father and he was stingier than her. They both had a flexible conscience. My father had the honour of being the first person to have held his breath while being measured for a suit, so that less cloth would be used to make it. I could tell you a hundred such tales of avarice, which earned him a well-deserved reputation as an inventive and witty man; but, for fear of boring you, I'll settle for telling you two that are hard to believe, but quite true nevertheless. He had amassed a large quantity of wheat to resell at a great profit during a lean year. Then there were such good harvests that the price of wheat dropped. He was in such despair and felt so neglected by God that he went to hang himself. One of his neighbours, who happened to be in his room when he came in to carry out his noble plan, and who hid for fear of being seen – I don't really know why – was quite surprised when she saw him hanging from a chevron on his doorway. She ran to him, calling for help, cut the rope and, helped by my mother who arrived just then, removed it from his neck. They may have repented this good deed because he beat them both silly and made the poor woman pay for the rope she cut by withholding some of the money he owed her. The other feat is just as strange. In the year that scarcity made food so expensive that the old people of the village couldn't recall a worse one, he regretted everything he ate, and, his wife having given birth to a boy, he got it into his head that she had enough milk to feed both his son and himself, hoping that, by suckling his wife, he could save on bread and consume a food that is easy to digest. My mother's wit was not as great as his, but her avarice was, and while she did not come up with ideas like my father did, once she understood them she applied them more thoroughly than he. So she tried to breastfeed her son and her husband at the same time, as well as herself, so stubbornly that the poor innocent creature starved to death, and my mother and father were so weak and famished that they overate and were both sick for a long time. My mother became pregnant with me some time later and, after the happy delivery of a most unhappy creature, my father went to Paris to ask his mistress to be my godmother, along with a good churchman who resided in his village, where he had a sinecure. As he was returning home at night in order to avoid the daytime heat and was passing through a main street of the *faubourg*, where most of the houses were still under construction, he glimpsed at a distance, by the light of the moon, something shiny crossing the street. He didn't pay much attention to it, but hearing what sounded like the moans of a suffering person coming from the area where what he had seen had disappeared, he boldly entered a large unfinished building, where he found a woman sitting on the ground. The building let in enough moonlight so that my father could see that she was very young and very well dressed; her dress made of silver brocade was what had caught his eye from afar. You mustn't doubt that my father, who was quite bold by nature, was less surprised than this young lady; but she was in a state where nothing worse could happen to her than what already had. This emboldened her to speak first and tell my father that, if he were Christian, he should take pity on her; that she was ready to give birth; that having gone into labour and failing to see a servant return who had left to fetch a trustworthy midwife, she had slipped out of her house without waking anyone, her servant having left the door open in order to get back in without making any noise. She had scarcely related her story than she successfully delivered a child that my father received in his overcoat. He did the best he could at being a mid-wife, and the young lady beseeched him quickly to take away the little creature, to take care of it, and to be sure in two days' time to contact an old churchman, whose name she provided and who would give him money and all the necessary instructions on how to feed the child. Hearing the word "money", my father, who had a miserly soul, wanted to show off his eloquence as a gentleman usher; but she didn't give him time. She handed him a ring as a token for the priest whom he was supposed to find for her, had him bundle her child in her shawl, and made him leave quickly, despite his protestations about abandoning her in the state she was in. I do believe she must have had a hard time getting home. As for my father, he went back to his village, put the child in his wife's care and, two days later, made sure he found the old priest and showed him the ring. From him he learnt that the child's mother was the daughter of a very old and wealthy family; that the father was a Scottish lord who had gone to Ireland to recruit soldiers for the King's army and that this foreign lord had promised to marry her. The priest told him that because of her hurried delivery she was sick to the point of risking her life, and that in this extreme situation she had told her parents everything. They had consoled her instead of getting angry at her, because she was their only daughter. He added that the event was not known to the rest of the household. Finally, he assured my father that he had only to care for the child and keep the secret for his fortune to be made. Thereupon he gave my father fifty écus and a small bundle containing all the clothing the child would need. My father returned to his village after having had a good lunch with the priest. I was sent to a wet nurse, while the stranger took my place. A month later, the Scottish lord came back and, finding his mistress in such bad shape that she had only a short time to live, he married her the day before she died, and thus became a widower as soon as he married. He came to our village two or three days later with his wife's parents. Tears flowed and the child was kissed so much he risked being smothered. My father had reason to be pleased with the lord's generosity, and the grandparents didn't neglect him either. They returned to Paris delighted with the care my mother and father were giving their grandson, whom they didn't want to bring back to Paris yet, because the marriage was being kept secret for reasons I never learnt.

As soon as I could walk, my father brought me to his house so I could keep the little Count of Glaris (so named after his father) company. The antipathy said to have existed between Jacob and Esau,* even in their mother's womb, cannot have been greater than that between the young count and me. My father and mother loved him tenderly while having an aversion for me, even though I gave as many signs of one day becoming a gentleman as Glaris gave few. There was little about him that wasn't common. As for me, I appeared to be what I wasn't; much less Garigues's son than the son of a count. And if I have ended up as an unfortunate actor, it is probably because Fortune wanted to take revenge upon Nature, which tried to make something of me without its consent, or, if you will, because Nature sometimes enjoys favouring those for whom Fortune has an aversion.

I'll skip relating the childhood of the two little peasants, for Glaris was one by nature more than I, and our most exciting adventures were merely a succession of punches thrown. In all of our quarrels, I always had the upper hand, unless my mother and father stepped in, which they did so often and so passionately that it shocked my godfather, Monsieur de Saint-Sauveur, who asked my father to put me in his care. My father happily gave me up, and my mother regretted my departure even less than he. So here I was, at my godfather's, well-fed, well-dressed, shown much affection and never beaten. He spared nothing to teach me to read and write and, as soon as I was old enough, to learn Latin. He arranged with the lord of the village, who was a true gentleman and very wealthy, that I would study along with his two sons under the tutelage of a scholar whom he had brought from Paris and was paying handsomely. This nobleman, the Baron d'Arques, was having his children brought up with great care. The elder,

Saint-Far, was quite good-looking, but an incurable beast, even if there had been a cure for it. The younger, as if to compensate, besides being better-looking than his brother, had a mind as lively and a soul as generous as his body was beautiful. Indeed, I don't think it is possible for a boy to inspire greater hopes of his becoming a true gentleman than this young nobleman, named Verville, did in those days. He honoured me with his friendship, and I loved him like a brother, while still respecting him as a master. As for Saint-Far, he was only capable of base passions, and I cannot better express the feelings he harboured towards his brother and me than by telling you that he did not love his brother more than me, about whom he felt indifferent, and he did not despise me more than his brother, whom he hardly liked. His entertainments were different from ours. He only enjoyed hunting and hated his studies. Verville rarely went hunting and derived great pleasure from studying, in which there existed between us a marvellous conformity, which seemed to extend to all things. I can honestly say that I didn't need to make much of an effort to accommodate myself to his temperament, and had only to follow my own inclinations.

The Baron d'Arques had a very large collection of novels in his library. Our tutor, who in Latin Land* had never read any, who at first forbade reading them and who repeatedly condemned them in front of the Baron d'Arques, in order to render them as odious to him as the Baron had found them entertaining, became so taken with them himself that, after devouring the old ones and the modern ones, he admitted that reading good novels educated while entertaining, and that he thought they were no less able to instil noble sentiments in young people than Plutarch.* Thus he encouraged us to read them as much as he had previously steered us away from them. He advised us to start with the moderns, but they were not yet to our taste and, until the age of fifteen, we enjoyed reading the likes of *Amadís of Gaul* far more than the likes of *L'Astrée** and the other beautiful novels written since, through which the French have shown, in this as well as a thousand other things, that while they do not invent as much as other nations, they perfect more. So we spent most of our free time reading novels. Saint-Far, who called us the readers, spent his hunting or beating peasants, the latter with considerable success. The inclination I had to do good endeared me to the Baron d'Arques, who loved me as if I were a close relative. He did not want me to leave his children when he sent them to the Academy, and so I accompanied them more as a classmate than as a servant. We spent two years learning our lessons there and, upon leaving the Academy, since a nobleman related to the Baron d'Arques was raising an army for the Venetians, Saint-Far and Verville persuaded their father to let them go with this relative to Venice. The good gentleman wanted me to accompany them once again, and Monsieur de Saint-Sauveur, my godfather, who loved me dearly, generously gave me a letter of credit of considerable value, for me to use as needed, so that I would not be a burden to those I had the honour of accompanying. We took the long way in order to see Rome and the other beautiful cities of Italy – in each of which we stayed – with the exception of those ruled by the Spanish. In Rome I fell ill, and the two brothers pursued their journey; their relative didn't want to miss the opportunity of travelling on the Pope's galley, which was going to join the Venetian army at the Dardanelles Strait, where it was waiting for the Turks. Verville greatly regretted leaving me, and the idea of being separated from him at a point when I could have shown myself worthy of his friendship caused me to despair. As for Saint-Far, I think he left me as though he had never known me, and I only gave him a thought because he was the brother of Verville, who gave me, as he left, as much money as he could. I don't know whether it was with his brother's consent.

So there I was, sick in Rome, without any acquaintances besides my host, a Flemish pharmacist who gave me extraordinary care during my illness. He was not ignorant of medicine and, as far as I could tell, I found him more knowledgeable than the Italian doctor who regularly visited me. Finally I recovered, and was soon strong enough to visit Rome's remarkable sites, where foreigners easily find enough to satisfy their curiosity. I loved visiting the vineyards (which is what they call several parks that are more beautiful than the Luxembourg or the Tuileries; the Cardinals and other persons of quality make sure they are manicured, more out of vanity than for pleasure, as they never or very rarely go there). One day, as I was strolling in the most beautiful of these parks, I saw two well-dressed women whom two young Frenchmen wouldn't let pass unless the youngest of the women lifted a veil that covered her face. One of these Frenchmen, who seemed to be the other's master, was even insolent enough to uncover her face by force, while his servant held the one who wasn't veiled. I wasted no time wondering what to do. I told these rude men that I would not tolerate their violent treatment of the ladies. Seeing me speak to them with such resolve, they were both surprised enough to be taken aback, as they would have been even if, like me, they had had their swords. The two women stood next to me, and the young Frenchman, preferring to suffer an affront rather than a beating, said to me as he left: "Mr Soldier, we'll meet again, when the swords won't all be on one side." I replied that I would not hide. His man followed him, and I stayed with the two women. The one who was not wearing a veil appeared to be around thirty-five. She thanked me, in French that owed nothing to Italian, and told me, among other things, that if all my countrymen resembled me, Italian women would have no trouble living in the French style. After that, as if to reward me for my help, she added that, having stopped her daughter from being seen without her consent, it was only fair that I should see her of her own free will. "Raise your veil, Leonora, so that Monsieur may see that we are not com- pletely unworthy of the honour he has done us in protecting us." No sooner had she finished speaking than her daughter removed her veil, or rather dazzled me. I have never seen anything more beautiful. She raised her eyes two or three times to steal looks at me, and as our eyes met each time, she blushed, which made her more beautiful than an angel. I could see that her mother was extremely fond of her, because she seemed to share the pleasure I took in looking at her daughter. Since I wasn't used to encounters of this sort and since young people are easily disconcerted in the company of strangers, the compliments I gave them when they left were clumsy and may have given them a low opinion of my wit. I was angry at myself for not having asked where they lived, and for not having offered to escort them there. It was too late to run after them. I tried to ask the gatekeeper if he knew them. We spent a long time failing to understand one another, as his French was no better than my Italian. Finally, more through sign language than anything else, he made me understand that he did not know them, or that he didn't want to admit knowing them. I returned to my Flemish pharmacist a changed man, that is to say in love and anxious to know whether this beautiful Leonora was a courtesan or an honest woman, and whether she had as much wit as her mother had shown. I started daydreaming and flattered myself with a thousand answered prayers, which entertained me for a while but worried me greatly once I began to realize how impossible they were. After having made countless useless plans, I settled on systematically looking for them, as I couldn't imagine that they would be able to remain invisible much longer in a city as sparsely populated as Rome, to a man as in love as I was. That very day I searched everywhere I thought I could find them, and I came home more tired and sadder than I had been when I left. The next day, I searched even more carefully and ended up being only more tired and more worried. From the way I scrutinized the blinds and the windows, as well as the impetuousness with which I chased after every woman who reminded me of my Leonora, I was often taken for the craziest of all the Frenchmen, who have contributed most to discrediting their nation in Rome. I don't know how I was able to recover my health during this time when I was such a lost soul. I became perfectly healthy in body, though my mind remained sick and so split between the honour which called me to Candia and the love which kept me in Rome that I wondered sometimes whether I would obey the letters I often received from Verville, who urged me in the name of our friendship to join him, without taking advantage of his right to order me.

On the eve of my departure, Signor Stephano Vanbergue (this was my host's name) told me he wanted to invite me to lunch at the home of one of his friends, and see if I would agree that his taste wasn't bad for a Flemish man. He added that he had waited for the eve of my departure because he was somewhat jealous. I accepted his invitation more out of a sense of obligation than anything else, and we went there at lunchtime. The lodgings we entered had neither the appearance nor the furniture one would expect from those of a pharmacist's mistress. We walked across a well-appointed parlour into a magnificent room where I was greeted by Leonora and her mother. You can imagine how I was pleased by this surprise. This beautiful girl's mother expected to be greeted in the French manner, and I must admit that she kissed me more than I kissed her. I was so inhibited I couldn't see a thing, and I didn't understand her compliments. Finally, I recovered my wits and my eyesight, and saw that Leonora was even more beautiful and charming than I had remembered, but I wasn't sure enough of myself even to say hello. I immediately recognized my mistake, and without having the presence of mind to correct it, shame made me blush as much as modesty had Leonora. Her mother told me that, before I left, she wanted to be sure to thank me for the efforts I made to find out where she lived. Her telling me this only added to my embarrassment. She dragged me into a sitting area, decorated in the French style, to which her daughter did not accompany us, probably finding me too dull to be worth the effort. She stayed with Signor Stephano, while I got to show her mother who I really was – a country bumpkin that is. She was kind enough to hold up both ends of the conversation with excellent wit, although nothing is quite as difficult as exhibiting it with someone who has none. As for me, I never had less than during this encounter, and if she wasn't bored then, she has never been bored by anyone. Afterwards she told me several things which I barely answered with yes or no, that she was French by birth and that Signor Stephano would tell me what kept her in Rome. It was time for lunch, and I had to be dragged into the dining room as I had been before to the bedroom sitting area, because I was so perturbed I could barely walk. I was just as dumb before and after lunch, during which I did nothing with self-confidence except incessantly look at Leonora. I think this bothered her and, to punish me, she kept her eyes lowered. If her mother hadn't kept talking, the lunch would have been as silent as in a monastery, but she discussed the affairs of Rome with Signor Stephano, at least that's what I imagine, because I didn't pay enough attention to what she was saying to be able to talk about it with any authority. Finally, we left the table, to everyone's relief but my own, for I was visibly deteriorating. When it was time to leave, they said many obliging things to me, which I only answered with the kind of things one puts at the end of a letter. What I did on the way out that I hadn't on the way in is that I kissed Leonora goodbye and completely lost my mind. Stephano couldn't get a word out of me during the entire trip home. I shut myself in my room and threw myself on the bed without taking off my coat or my sword. There I thought about everything that had happened to me. Leonora appeared to my imagination even more beautiful than she had to my eyes. I remembered the lack of wit I had shown to the mother and daughter, and each time this came to mind, the shame of it would set my face on fire. I wanted to be rich; I was pained by my low birth; I imagined countless adventures favourable to my fortune and my love. Finally, thinking of nothing but an honest pretext for staying, and not finding one, I was desperate enough to wish getting sick again, something to which I was only too predisposed. I tried to write to her. But nothing I wrote satisfied me, and I pocketed the beginning of a letter I might not have dared send once I had finished it. After having tormented myself, and able to think of nothing besides Leonora, I wanted to visit the park where I had seen her for the first time in order to abandon myself completely to my passion, and I also planned to pass by her home. This park was one of the city's most out-of-the-way places, surrounded by several old, uninhabitable buildings. As I walked, daydreaming under the ruins of a portico, I heard footsteps behind me, and at the same time felt a sword strike my lower back. I spun around drawing my own sword and, finding myself face to face with the servant of the young Frenchman I told you about before, I intended at least to return the blow he had treacherously dealt me. But while I was moving forward without being able to reach him, because he was backing up as he parried, his master came out of the ruins and, attacking me from behind, struck me on the head and again in the thigh, which made me fall. It didn't look like I'd be able to escape, being caught by surprise the way I was; but because committing a bad deed can cloud your judgement, the servant wounded the master's right hand and, at the same time, two Franciscan friars from the Trinity of the Mount, who were walking nearby and who saw that I was being attacked, rushed to my aid, and my aggressors fled, leaving me with three wounds. I was very fortunate that these good friars were French, because in such an out-of-the-way place an Italian seeing me in such bad shape would have left me rather than help me, for fear that, being discovered helping me, he would himself be suspected of having attacked me. While one of these charitable friars took my confession, the other ran to my lodgings to tell my host about my misfortune. He rushed to my side and had me carried, half-dead, to my bed. With so many wounds and so much in love, it wasn't long before I had a violent fever. Everyone feared for my life, and I saw no reason to be more hopeful than they were.

Yet my love for Leonora did not fade. On the contrary, it grew as my strength decreased. Being unable to bear any longer such a heavy burden, and not wanting to die without being able to tell Leonora that I would only have wanted to live for her, I asked for a quill and ink. I was thought to be dreaming, but I asked so insistently and protested so well that I would be brought to despair if I were not granted what I asked for that Signor Stephano, who had recognized my passion and who was perceptive enough more or less to guess my intention, gave me everything I needed to write with, and stayed alone with me in my room. I reread the few sheets I'd written not long before, in order to use the thoughts I'd had on the same subject. This is what I wrote to Leonora:

As soon as I saw you, I could not help loving you. My reason did not argue against it; it told me, as much as my eyes, that you were the most worthy of being loved in the whole world, instead of telling me that I wasn't worthy of loving you. But reason would only have aggravated my condition with useless remedies and, after offering some resistance, would have yielded to the need to love you that you impose upon all who see you. I have therefore loved you, beautiful Leonora, with so respectful a love that you must not hate me for it, even though I am bold enough to reveal it to you. But how to die for you and not glory in it! And how hard can it be for you to forgive me for a crime you will have so little time to reproach me for? It is true that to have you as the cause of my death is a reward that can only be earned by service, and you may regret to have so favoured me without intending to. Don't hold it against me, loveable Leonora, since you can no longer make me lose it, and since it is the only favour I have ever been granted by Fortune, who will only be able to pay the debt she owes to your merit by giving you worshippers as superior to me as all the beauties of the world are inferior to you. I am not vain enough to hope that the least feeling of pity...

I was unable to finish my letter; suddenly I was too weak to continue and the quill dropped from my hand, my body being unable to keep up with my racing mind. Otherwise, this long introduction to a letter that I just recited for you would have been only a small part of what I would have written, so much did love and fever overheat my imagination. I was unconscious for a long time, without giving any sign of life. Signor Stephano, who noticed this, opened the door and sent for a priest. At the same time, Leonora and her mother came to see me. They heard I'd been wounded, and because they thought it had only happened to me because I'd come to their rescue, and that they were therefore the innocent cause of my death, they didn't hesitate to come see me despite the state I was in. I was unconscious for such a long time that they left before I came to, quite upset it seemed, and believing that I wouldn't recover. They read what I'd written, and the mother, who was more curious than the daughter, also read the papers I left on the bed, among which was a letter from my father, Garigues. I was between life and death for a long time, but finally youth prevailed. I was out of danger after two weeks, and after five or six weeks I began to walk around my room. My host often gave me news of Leonora. He told me about her and her mother's charitable visit, which caused me extreme joy, and while I was a little unhappy that my father's letter had been read, I was very glad that mine had been read too. Every time I found myself alone with Stephano, I couldn't talk about anything besides Leonora. One day, remembering that Leonora's mother had said that he could tell me who she was and what kept her in Rome, I asked him to share what he knew. He told me her name was Mademoiselle de La Boissière, that she had come to Rome with the wife of the French ambassador, that a man of quality, a close relative of the ambassador, had fallen in love with her, that she hadn't hated him, and that as a result of a clandestine marriage they had had the beautiful Leonora. What's more, he told me that, because of it, this lord had a falling-out with the ambassador's entire family, and had to leave Rome and live for some time in Venice with Mademoiselle de La Boissière, to let time heal the rift with the embassy, and that, having brought her back to Rome, he had furnished a house and given all the necessary instructions for her to live like a person of her rank, while he was in France, where his father had summoned him, and where he hadn't dared bring his mistress, or his wife if you will, knowing full well no one would approve of his marriage. I must admit I couldn't help wish sometimes that my Leonora weren't the legitimate daughter of a nobleman, so that the flaw in her birth would bring it closer to the lowliness of my own. But I would soon repent such a criminal thought and wish her a fortune as advantageous to her as she deserved; although this idea made me feel strangely desperate, because, loving her more than my own life, I could well foresee that I could never be happy without possessing her, nor possess her without making her unhappy.

While I finished my convalescence and the only thing left of such a serious condition was my extreme pallor, due to the quantity of blood I had lost, my young masters returned from the Venetian army. The plague that infected the entire Levant no longer allowed them to prove their courage there. Verville still loved me as he always had and Saint-Far didn't yet show his hatred of me, as he has since. I recounted everything that happened to me, leaving out my love for Leonora. They expressed an acute desire to meet her, which I increased by exaggerating the merits of both mother and daughter. You should never praise the one you love in front of others who might love her too, since love enters the soul through the ears as well as the eyes. It is a folly that has often hurt those who have indulged in it, as I can tell you from experience. Saint-Far asked me every day when I would take him to Mademoiselle de La Boissière's. One day, when he was pressuring me more than he ever had before, I told him I didn't know if she would agree to it, because she was quite withdrawn. "I see you are in love with her daughter," he replied and, adding that he could perfectly well see her without me, he offended me so much, and I seemed so taken aback, that he no longer had any doubts about what he might not have suspected before. He then mocked me mercilessly, and left me so helpless and confused that Verville took pity on me. He led me away from this brute to visit the Corso, where I was very sad, despite Verville's efforts to entertain me, thanks to goodness truly extraordinary in someone of his age and of a birth far loftier than my own. Meanwhile his coarse brother was working at satisfying himself, or rather ruining me. He went to Mademoiselle de La Boissière's, where he was at first mistaken for me, because he had my host's footman with him, who had accompanied me there several times; I don't think he would have been received otherwise. Mademoiselle de La Boissière was quite surprised to see a strange man. She told Saint-Far that, since she didn't know him, she didn't know to what she owed the honour of his visit. Saint-Far bluntly told her he was the master of a boy who had been lucky enough to be wounded while doing her a small favour. Having started off with an account that pleased neither mother nor daughter, as I would find out later, and these two witty persons not caring to risk the reputation of their wit with a man who had shown them right away that he scarcely had any, the brute did not find them entertaining, and they were quite bored with him. What drove him crazy was that he didn't even have the satisfaction of seeing Leonora's face, no matter how much he implored her to lift the veil she usually wore, as do girls of noble birth in Rome who are not yet married. Finally, this gallant man got bored of boring them. He freed them from his painful visit and returned to Signor Stephano's, with very little advantage gained from the disservice he had done me. Since that time, as brutes have a strong tendency to wish harm to those they have harmed themselves, his expressions of contempt towards me became so unbearable and he offended me so often that I would have lost a hundred times over the respect I owed his station, had not Verville's unstinting kindness helped me endure his brother's rudeness. I didn't yet know the harm he had done me, although I often felt its effects. I found Mademoiselle de La Boissière more reserved than she had been when I first knew her, but, being polite, she didn't make me feel like a bother. As for Leonora, she seemed very dreamy in front of her mother and, when she wasn't being observed by her, it seemed to me that her face appeared less sad and that I received more favourable looks."

Destiny was telling his story and the actresses were listening to him attentively without showing any signs of tiredness, when the clock struck two in the morning. Mademoiselle Cave reminded Destiny that he was supposed to accompany La Rappinière the next day to a house he owned two or three leagues from the city, where he had promised to treat them to the pleasures of hunting.

Destiny took leave of the actresses and went to his room, where it appears he slept. The actresses did the same and what was left of the night went by very peacefully, the poet thankfully not having given birth to any new rhymes.

CHAPTER XIV

Abduction of the Parson of Domfront

T HOSE WHO HAD ENOUGH TIME to waste to spend it reading the preceding chapters surely know, if they haven't forgotten, that the parson of Domfront was in one of the litters that turned up in a party of four in a little village, by way of an encounter that may never have happened; but, as everyone knows, it is more likely for four litters to meet up than four mountains. This parson then, who was staying in the same inn as our actors, had his gravel examined by the doctors of Le Mans, who told him in quite elegant Latin that he had the gravel (something the poor man already knew only too well) and, after having concluded other business, the nature of which I never discovered, he left the inn at nine in the morning in order to go home and tend to his flock. A young niece of his, dressed like a lady, whether she was one or not, sat in the front of the litter, at the feet of her uncle, who was short and fat. A peasant named Guillaume led the front horse by the bridle, according to the parson's instructions, to prevent him from stumbling; and Julian, the parson's servant, took care of prodding the rear horse, who was so reticent that Julian was often forced to push him by the hindquarters. The parson's chamber pot, made of copper that shone like gold because it had been scoured at the inn, hung from the right side of the litter, making it far more respectable than the left side, which was only adorned by a hat in a cardboard box that the parson had retrieved from the Paris mail coach for a gentleman, a friend of his, who had a house near Domfront.

About a league and a half from town, as the litter was slowly making its way down a sunken path, bordered by hedgerows as strong as walls, three horsemen, backed up by two men on foot, stopped the venerable litter. One of them, who seemed to be the leader of these highwaymen, exclaimed in a terrifying voice: "I'll kill the first one who utters a sound!" and waved the barrel of his pistol just inches away from the eyes of the peasant Guillaume, who was leading the litter. Another did the same thing to Julian, and one of the men on foot took aim at the niece of the parson, while he slept quietly in his litter and so was spared the horrible fear that gripped his peaceful little caravan. These villains made the litter go faster than the nags who carried it wanted to go. The parson's niece was more dead than alive. Guillaume and Julian were crying without daring to open their mouths, because of the terrifying sight of the firearms, and the parson was still asleep, as I told you before. One of the horsemen broke away from the pack at a gallop and rode ahead. Meanwhile, the litter neared a wood, at the entrance of which the lead horse who, maybe because he was dying of fear like the man leading him, or maybe out of pure mischief or because he was being made to go faster than his heavy and lethargic nature would allow – this poor horse caught his hoof in a rut and stumbled with such force that Monsieur the parson woke up and his niece fell from the litter onto the nag's narrow hindquarters. The parson called to Julian, who didn't dare answer; he also called to his niece, who took care not to open her mouth; the peasant was as unresponsive as the rest, and the parson got downright angry. It has been said that he swore to God, but I can't believe such a thing from a parson of Bas-Maine. The parson's niece had got up off the horse's croup and gone back to her seat without daring to look at her uncle, and now the horse, having vigorously stood up, was moving faster than he ever had, notwithstanding the noise made by the parson, who was shouting as if from his pulpit: "Stop! Stop!" His reiterated cries excited the horse and made him go even faster. He repeatedly called Julian first, then Guillaume and, more often than them, his niece, to whose name he often attached the epithet "double rascal". She could well have spoken, if she had wanted to, because the guard who was making them keep so silent had gone over to the horsemen who were ahead of the litter at a distance of forty or fifty yards, but her fear of the carbine made her oblivious to the insults of her uncle, who ended up screaming and yelling "Help!" and "Murder!" when he saw he was being so stubbornly disobeyed. At that point, the guard fetched the two horsemen who had ridden ahead and they returned to the litter, making it stop. One of them said to Guillaume in a frightening voice: "Who is that madman yelling in there?"

"Alas, you know better than me," replied poor Guillaume. The horseman struck him in the teeth with the barrel of his pistol and, showing it to the niece, ordered her to take off her mask and tell him who she was. The parson, who could see everything that was going on from his litter, and who was in the midst of a lawsuit against a local gentleman by the name of de Laune, thought that this de Laune was the one who wanted to kill him. He started to shout: "Monsieur de Laune, if you kill me, you'll have God to answer to. I'm a consecrated priest, and you'll be excommunicated like a werewolf." Meanwhile his poor niece was taking off her mask, showing the horseman a frightened, unfamiliar face. This produced an unexpected effect. The angry man shot the lead horse in the stomach and, with another pistol he kept in his saddle, shot one of his footmen right in the head, saying "Let this be a lesson to those who provide false intelligence!" This sent the parson's and his entire caravan's fear through the roof. The parson asked to be confessed; Julian and Guillaume got down on their knees and the parson's niece went to her uncle's side. But those who had frightened them so much had already left, and had gone as far away as their horses could carry them, leaving behind the one who had been shot dead. Julian and Guillaume stood up trembling, and told the parson and his niece that the armed men had left. They had to unharness the rear horse, so that the litter wouldn't tilt forward so much, and Guillaume was sent to a nearby village to find another horse. The parson didn't know what to think of what had happened to him. He couldn't imagine why he had been abducted, why they had left without robbing him or why the horseman had killed one of his own, which the parson didn't find as upsetting as the killing of his horse, who, in all likelihood, had no quarrel with that strange man. He continued to think that de Laune wanted to have him killed, and that he would find out why. His niece claimed it wasn't de Laune, that she knew him well; but the parson wanted it to be him so he could have a big criminal trial, perhaps trusting in the paid witnesses he hoped to find in Gorron, where he had relatives.

As they argued about this, Julian, who saw some riders appear in the distance, ran away as fast as he could. The parson's niece, who saw Julian flee, figured he must have had a good reason and ran away too; this made the parson think he was losing his mind, since he didn't know what to make of so many extraordinary events. Finally, he also saw the riders Julian had seen and, worse, he saw they were coming straight at him. This troupe was made up of nine or ten horses, in the middle of which there was a man on a nag, who was tied up, gagged and haggard, like those who are being taken to be hanged. The parson began to pray to God, and wholeheartedly put himself in God's hands – without forgetting his remaining horse – but he was amazed and reassured all at once when he recognized La Rappinière and some of his archers. La Rappinière asked him what he was doing there and whether he was the one who killed the man lying dead next to the horse's body. The parson told him what had happened and again opined that the one who tried to have him killed was de Laune, to which La Rappinière replied with a lengthy speech. One of the archers ran to the nearest village to have the body removed, and returned with the parson's niece and Julian, who were reassured and had met Guillaume returning with a horse for the litter. The parson went home, without any more nasty encounters, to Domfront where, for the rest of his life, he will tell the story of his abduction. The dead horse was eaten by wolves or wild dogs; the body of the man who was killed was buried I know not where; and La Rappinière, Destiny, Grudge and Olive, the archers and the prisoner returned to Le Mans. And such was the outcome of La Rappinière's and the actors' hunt, which bagged a man instead of bagging a hare.

CHAPTER XV

Arrival of a Surgeon at the Inn.
Continuation of Destiny and Star's Story

Serenade

Y OU'LL REMEMBER, IF YOU PLEASE, that in the preceding chapter, one of those who abducted the parson of Domfront had left his companions and gone at a gallop to who knows where. As he was prodding his horse on a very narrow and sunken path, he saw in the distance several horsemen coming towards him; he wanted to retrace his steps to avoid them and turned his horse so sharply and quickly that it reared up and fell on him. La Rappinière and his troupe (for they were the ones he saw) thought it quite strange that a man who was coming towards them so quickly should want to go back the same way. This gave La Rappinière cause for suspicion. He was already naturally suspicious, on top of which his post called for him to expect the bad rather than the good. His suspicion grew a lot more when, being next to this man whose leg was under his horse, he noticed that the man didn't seem to be as frightened of his fall as he was of there being witnesses to it. Since he didn't risk anything by increasing the man's fear and knew his job better than a royal magistrate, he said as he approached him, "Looks like you've been caught, honest fellow! I'll put you in a place from where you won't fall so heavily!" These words seemed to stun the wretch more than his fall, and La Rappinière and his men noticed such clear signs of a guilty conscience on his face that anyone, even someone less enterprising than La Rappinière, wouldn't have hesitated to arrest him. So he ordered his archers to help him get back up, and had him tied and gagged on his horse. La Rappinière's subsequent encounter with the parson of Domfront, amidst the chaos you witnessed, with a dead man and a horse shot to death, made him feel he hadn't been mistaken; a feeling that was much reinforced by the prisoner's fear, which visibly increased with the encounter. Destiny observed him more attentively than the others, thinking he recognized him, but not being able to recall where he had seen him. He searched his memory in vain while they were en route. He just wasn't able to remember. Finally, they arrived in Le Mans, where La Rappinière had the presumed criminal put in jail, and the actors, who were due to go on stage the next day, retired to their inn to put their affairs in order. They were reconciled with the innkeeper; and the poet, who had the generosity of a poet, wanted to pay for supper. Ragotin, who was in the inn, and couldn't stay away since he had fallen in love with Star, was invited by the poet, who was crazy enough also to invite all the spectators of the battle that had taken place the previous night, in nightclothes, between the actors and the innkeeper's family.

Just before supper, the good company at the inn was increased by the arrival of a surgeon and his entourage, which was made up of his wife, an old Moorish servant woman, a monkey and two footmen. Grudge had known him long ago; they greeted each other warmly, and the poet, who found it easy to make new acquaintances, only left the surgeon and his wife after having made them promise to do him the honour of being his guests at supper, by dint of pompous compliments that didn't actually say much. Nothing unusual happened during supper; there was a lot of drinking, and eating to match. Ragotin feasted his eyes on Star's face, which intoxicated him as much as the wine he drank, and he didn't say much during the supper, even though the poet provided him with ample reason for argument by directly criticizing the verses of Théophile,* whom Ragotin greatly admired. The actresses conversed for a while with the surgeon's wife, who was

Spanish and not disagreeable. They then retired to their room, where Destiny accompanied them to finish his story, which Cave and her daughter were dying of impatience to hear. Star meanwhile began to study her part; and Destiny, having taken a chair next to the bed where Cave and her daughter were sitting, picked up his story where he had left off:

"You've seen me up to now very much in love, and in a difficult situation owing to the effect my letter may have had on Leonora and her mother; you're going to see me even more in love and the most despairing man alive. I called on Mademoiselle de La Boissière and her daughter every day, so blinded by my passion that I didn't notice the reserve with which I was greeted, even less did it occur to me that they might find my too frequent visits annoying. Mademoiselle de La Boissière was quite bothered by them, ever since Saint-Far told her who I was, but it wouldn't have been civil of her to bar me from her home after what I had been through for her. As for her daughter, judging by what she's done since, she felt sorry for me, and did not share the feelings of her mother, who never lost sight of her so that we would never find ourselves alone together. To tell the truth, if this beautiful girl had wanted to treat me with less reserve than her mother, she never would have dared to in front of her. So I suffered the torments of hell, and my frequent visits were only good for making me seem more repellent to those I wanted to appeal to. One day, Mademoiselle de La Boissière received letters from France, and needed to go out. As soon as she had read them she sent for a rented carriage and for Signor Stephano, so that he could accompany her, since she didn't dare go out alone ever since the frightening encounter during which I had been of service. I was readier and more appropriate to serve as an escort than the one she sent for, but she didn't want to receive the slightest favour from someone she wanted to get rid of. As luck would have it, Stephano couldn't be found, and she was forced to express in front of me her unhappiness at not having anyone to escort her, so that I would offer my services, which I did with as much joy as she had resentment at being reduced to taking me along. We visited a cardinal, who represented the interests of France at the time, and who fortunately granted her an audience as soon as she requested one. Her business must have been important and not without difficulty, because she spent a long time talking to him in private in a kind of grotto, or rather a covered fountain, that was in the middle of a beautiful park. Meanwhile, all those who were with the cardinal wandered around their favourite parts of the park. So here I was, on a wide walkway between rows of orange trees, alone with the beautiful Leonora, as I had wished so many times, yet even less bold than I had ever been. I don't know whether she noticed and so was the first to speak out of kindness. 'My mother,' she said, 'has good reason to be mad at Signor Stephano for being absent today and causing us to make you go to so much trouble.'

"'And I,' I replied, 'am much obliged to him for having unknowingly procured for me the greatest happiness I shall ever experience.'

"'I am sufficiently obligated to you,' she retorted, 'to take part in anything that is favourable to you; so tell me, please, what happiness he procured for you, if it is something a girl can know, so that I may be delighted by it.'

"'I would be afraid,' I said, 'that you would make it stop.'

"'I!' she continued. 'I have never been envious and even if I were of everyone else, I would never envy someone who risked his life for me.'

"'You wouldn't do it out of envy,' I said.

"'And what other motive would make me opposed to your happiness?' she replied.

"'Out of contempt,' I said.

"'You'll make me very sad,' she added, 'if you don't tell me what I hold in contempt and how my contempt for something makes it less appealing to you.'

"'It's easy for me to explain,' I answered, 'but I don't know that it is something you will want to hear.'

"'Don't tell me then,' she said, 'for when we aren't sure how something will be received, it is a sign that it is either unintelligible or offensive.' I must admit that I've always been amazed how I answered her, thinking far less about what she was telling me than about her mother, who could return and make me lose my opportunity to talk to her about my love. I finally became emboldened and, without wasting more time on a conversation that wasn't getting me quickly enough where I wanted to go, I told her, without replying to her, that I had been waiting a long time for the opportunity to speak to her in order to confirm what I had been bold enough to write to her, and that I would never have taken this risk if I hadn't learnt that she had read my letter. I then repeated most of what I had written to her and added that, being ready to leave for the war the Pope was waging against some Italian princes, and having resolved to die there since I wasn't worthy of living for her, I wanted to know what feelings she would have had for me if my fortune were more in keeping with the boldness I had had to love her. She admitted, blushing, that my death would not leave her indifferent. 'And if you are the kind of man who thinks of his friends,' she added, 'preserve one who has been so helpful to us, or at least, if you are in such a hurry to die, for a reason that is greater than the one you've just told me, defer your death until such time as we've been able to see each other in France, where I have to return soon with my mother.' I pressed her to tell me more clearly what feelings she had for me, but by then her mother was so close to us that she wouldn't have been able to answer me if she had wanted to. Mademoiselle de La Boissière gave me a cold look, maybe because I had time to speak to Leonora in private, and this beautiful girl herself seemed to be somewhat pained by it. It was why I dared only spend a short time at their house. I left them as happy as I could be, drawing conclusions from Leonora's answer that were very advantageous to my love.

"The following day I went to see them, as was my custom; I was told they had gone out and I was told the same thing for the three days running that I went back without getting discouraged.

Finally, Signor Stephano advised me not to go there any more, because Mademoiselle de La Boissière would no longer allow me to see her daughter, adding that he thought me too reasonable to seek an entry that would be refused. He revealed the cause of my disfavour: Leonora's mother had found her writing me a letter and, after reprimanding her harshly, she had ordered her people to tell me she and Leonora were out every time I came to visit them. It was then that I learnt of Saint-Far's disservice and that since then my visits had upset the mother. As for the daughter, Stephano assured me on her behalf that my merit would have made her forget my fortune if her mother had been as disinterested as she.

"I won't attempt to describe the despair I felt as a result of this bad news. I was as distressed as if Leonora were being unfairly taken away from me, even though I had never hoped to possess her. I was furious at Saint-Far, and even considered fighting him. But when I thought about what I owed his father and brother, tears were my only recourse. I cried like a baby and I was uncomfortable being alone. I had to leave without seeing Leonora. We were in the Pope's army for an entire campaign, where I did everything I could to get myself killed. Fate was against me the way it has been in all things. I couldn't find the death I was looking for and I acquired a certain reputation I wasn't seeking, which would have pleased me at another time, but just then nothing could satisfy me besides the memory of Leonora. Verville and Saint-Far had to go back to France, where the Baron d'Arques greeted them as a father who idolizes his children. My mother greeted me coldly. My father was staying in Paris, where he had been chosen to be the governor of the Count of Glaris's son. The Baron d'Arques, who had learnt what I'd done during the war of Italy, where I'd even saved Verville's life, wanted me to live in his household as a gentleman and companion. He allowed me to visit my father, whose welcome was even worse than his wife's. Any other man of his station, with a son as accomplished as I was, would have presented him to the Scottish count, but my father hurriedly removed me from the house, as if he were afraid I would dishonour him.

During the time we spent together, he did nothing but reproach me for being too elegant and too vain, and he told me I would have been better off learning a trade than dragging a sword around. You can well imagine that such words were hardly music to the ears of a young man who had been well brought up, who had earned something of a reputation in war, who had dared to love a beautiful girl, and even show her his passion. I'll admit to you that the feelings of respect and friendship due to a father didn't stop me from considering him a very unpleasant old man. He walked up and down a few streets with me, flattering me in the manner I just described and suddenly left me, expressly forbidding me to come see him again. I didn't have a hard time resolving to obey him. I left him and went to see Monsieur de Saint-Sauveur, who welcomed me like a father. He was very indignant about my own father's brutish behaviour and promised not to abandon me. The Baron d'Arques had business that required him to move to Paris. He made his residence at the end of the Faubourg Saint-Germain, in a beautiful house that was recently built, along with many others that have made this suburb as beautiful as the city. Saint-Far and Verville made their appearance at court, strolled on the Cours-la-Reine and went visiting. They did everything young people of their rank do in this big city, which makes the inhabitants of the other cities of the kingdom seem like country folk. As for me, when I wasn't accompanying them, I trained in all the fencing schools, or I went to the theatre, which may be why I've become a decent actor.

"One day, Verville took me aside and told me he had fallen madly in love with a young lady who lived on our street. He informed me that she had a brother named Saldagne, who was as jealous of her and another sister as if he were their husband. He told me he had made enough progress with her that he had persuaded her to let him in the garden the following night through a back door which opened onto the countryside, like the one at the Baron d'Arques's. After confiding in me, he asked me to accompany him and do all I could to charm the girl who would be attending her. Because of the friendship Verville had always shown me, I couldn't refuse to do anything he wanted. We went out by the back door of our garden at ten o'clock at night, and were met in the one where the mistress and her maid were waiting for us. Poor Mademoiselle de Saldagne trembled like a leaf and didn't dare speak. Verville wasn't much more confident. There wasn't a peep out of the maid, and I, who was only there to accompany Verville, didn't speak and didn't feel like speaking. Finally Verville summoned his courage and took his mistress to a sheltered path, after having urged the maid and me to be sure to stand watch; this is what we did, so vigilantly that we walked around for quite a while without exchanging a single word. At the end of a path we came across the young lovers. Verville asked me quite loudly if I had conversed with Miss Madelon. I answered by saying that I didn't think I had given her reason to complain. 'Certainly not,' said the chambermaid, 'because he hasn't said a thing yet.' Verville laughed and assured this Madelon that I was worth having a conversation with, even though I was given to melancholy. Mademoiselle de Saldagne spoke up to say that her chambermaid wasn't a girl to be dismissed either. At this point the happy lovers left us, reminding us to make sure no one could catch them by surprise. I prepared myself to be very bored by a servant girl who would probably ask me what my wages were, what maids I knew in the neighbourhood, if I knew any new songs and whether I had many benefits from my master. After that, I expected to hear all the secrets of the Saldagne family and all his faults, and those of his sisters too, because few personal servants meet without telling everything they know about their masters and without criticizing the little care these take to increase their own fortune and that of their servants; but I was surprised to find myself conversing with a chambermaid who started right away with: 'I conjure you, mute spirit, to confess whether you are a valet, and if you are, by what admirable virtue you have managed until now to keep yourself from saying anything bad about your master.' These words, which were so extraordinary coming from a chambermaid, amazed me.

I asked her in the name of what authority was it her business to exorcize me. 'I can see,' she said, 'that you are a stubborn spirit, and that I will have to redouble my efforts to conjure you. Tell me, O rebellious spirit, by the power that God has granted me over smug and proud valets, tell me who you are.'

"'I'm a poor boy,' I told her, 'who would like to be asleep in his bed right now.'

"'I see,' she replied, 'that I'll have a hard time getting to know you; at least I've already discovered that you are hardly gallant, because,' she added, 'weren't you supposed to speak to me first, to sweet-talk me, to want to take my hand, to be slapped two or three times, kicked just as often, and scratched too, and end up going home what they call a lucky man?'

"'There are girls in Paris,' I interrupted, 'whose marks I would be delighted to bear; but there are others that I wouldn't even want to look in the face for fear of having nightmares.'

"'You mean,' she said, 'that maybe I'm ugly. Hey, Mr hard-to-please, don't you know that all cats are grey at night?"

"'I don't want to do anything at night,' I replied, 'that I'll regret in the morning.'

"'And what if I'm beautiful?' she said.

"'Then I wouldn't have shown you enough respect,' I told her. 'Moreover, with the wit you've exhibited, you deserve to be properly served and wooed.'

"'And would you properly serve a smart girl?' she asked me.

"'Better than any other man in the whole world,' I said, 'provided I loved her.'

"'Why would you care,' she added, 'so long as she loved you?'

"'Both would have to be combined in any gallant adventure I'd undertake,' I replied. 'Really,' she said, 'if I were to judge the master according to the servant, I would say my mistress chose well with Monsieur de Verville, and the servant girl who wins your heart will have good reason to boast.'

"'It isn't enough to hear me speak,' I said, 'you also need to see me.'

"'I don't think,' she replied, 'I need to do either.'

"Our conversation could not last any longer, because Monsieur de Saldagne was loudly knocking on the front door, which no one was rushing to open, by order of the sister, who wanted to have the time to go back to her room. The lady and her chambermaid left in such a state of agitation and in such a rush that they didn't even say goodbye as they ushered us out of the garden. Verville wanted me to follow him to his room as soon as we got home. I have never seen a man more in love and more satisfied. He exaggerated his mistress's wit and told me he wouldn't be content until I saw her. He kept me up all night repeating himself, and I was only able to go to bed when the first light of dawn began to appear. As for me, I was amazed to have found a serving girl who was such a good conversationalist, and I must admit I wanted to know if she was pretty, although the memory of my Leonora made me quite indifferent to all the beautiful girls I saw every day in Paris. Verville and I both slept until noon. As soon as he woke up, he wrote to Mademoiselle de Saldagne, and sent his letter with his valet, who had already delivered others there and knew her chambermaid. This servant was from Lower Brittany, with an unfortunate face and a wit that was even worse. It occurred to me, when I saw him leave, that if the girl I'd conversed with saw how ugly he was and talked to him for a second, she wouldn't suspect him of being the one who had accompanied Verville. The big oaf acquitted himself quite well for an oaf. He found Mademoiselle de Saldagne with her older sister, who was called Mademoiselle de Léry, to whom she had confided Verville's love for her. As he was waiting for her reply, Monsieur de Saldagne was heard singing as he climbed the stairs. He was on his way to see his sisters, who hustled our Breton into an armoire. The brother wasn't very long with his sisters and the Breton was pulled from his hiding place. Mademoiselle de Saldagne went into a little office to answer Verville, and Mademoiselle de Léry conversed with the Breton, who most likely did not entertain her much. Her sister, having finished the letter, delivered her from our lummox by sending him back to his master with a note promising to wait for him at the same time in the same garden.

"As soon as night fell, you can be sure Verville was ready for the rendezvous he'd been given. We were let into the garden and once again I was with the girl I'd found so witty the night before. She seemed even more so now, and I have to admit that the sound of her voice and the way she expressed herself made me hope she was pretty. Meanwhile, she couldn't believe I was the Lower Breton she'd seen, nor understand why I had more wit at night than in the daytime because, while the Breton had told us that the arrival of Saldagne in his sisters' room had frightened him, I made it a point of pride to protest to this witty servant girl that I hadn't feared so much for myself as for Mademoiselle de Saldagne. This removed all doubts she may have had that I wasn't Verville's valet, and I noticed that, after this, she started to speak like a real servant. I learnt that Monsieur de Saldagne was a horrible man, and that having found himself at a young age without a mother or father, he ruled like a tyrant over his sisters to force them to become nuns, treating them not only like an unjust father, but also like a jealous and unbearable husband. It was my turn to tell her about the Baron d'Arques and his children when the garden door, which we hadn't closed, opened, and we saw Monsieur de Saldagne enter, followed by two lackeys, one of whom carried a torch. He was returning from a house at the end of the street, where there was gambling every day, and where Saint-Far often went for entertainment. They had both gambled that day, and Saldagne, having lost his money early, had entered his house by the back door, which was not his custom, and, having found it open, surprised us in the way I just described. The four of us were on a sheltered path, which allowed us to move out of sight of Saldagne and his people. The young lady remained in the garden under the pretext that she was getting some air, and to make this seem more plausible, she started to sing, without being much in the mood to, as you can imagine. Meanwhile Verville, having climbed the wall by means of a trellis, had leapt to the other side; but another of

Saldagne's lackeys, who hadn't come in yet, saw him jump, and told his master that he had just seen a man jump from the garden wall into the street. At the same time they heard me fall into the garden with a crash, the same trellis Verville had used to escape having unfortunately given way beneath me. The sound of my fall, combined with the lackey's report, alerted everyone in the garden. Saldagne ran towards the noise, followed by three of his lackeys, and, seeing a man with sword in hand (for as soon as I stood back up I got ready to defend myself), he attacked me, with his men backing him up. I quickly showed him I wasn't going to be easy to beat. The lackey who carried the torch moved closer than the others. This allowed me to see Saldagne's face, which I recognized as belonging to the same Frenchman who had tried to kill me in Rome for having stopped him from molesting Leonora, as I told you earlier. He recognized me too and, thinking I had come that night to repay him the favour, he shouted that I wouldn't get away this time. He redoubled his efforts, and I found myself hard-pressed, with my leg, which been almost broken by the fall, making things worse. I retreated to a summer cottage that I'd seen Verville's mistress enter, weeping. She didn't leave this cottage when I arrived, either because she didn't have enough time or because she was too frightened to move. As for me, I took courage when I saw that I could only be attacked through the doorway, which was quite narrow. I wounded Saldagne on the hand and the most dogged of his lackeys on the arm, which gave me some breathing room. Still, I didn't hold out any hope of escaping, expecting that in the end I'd be shot to death by pistol after I'd made it difficult for them to do it by sword; but Verville came to my rescue. He wasn't going to go home without me, and when he heard the commotion and the sounds of a sword fight, he arrived to save me from the peril he'd exposed me to, or at least to share it with me. Saldagne, whom he had already met, thought he was coming to his aid, as a neighbour and friend. He felt much obliged, and greeted him by saying, 'Do you see, Monsieur, how I am attacked in my own home?' Verville, who could tell what he was thinking, answered without hesitation that he was his servant against anyone else, but that he was there with the intention of serving me against one and all. Saldagne, enraged by his mistake and swearing, said he could finish off two traitors all by himself, and furiously charged Verville, who met him vigorously. I came out of my cottage to join my friend, and caught the lackey who was holding the torch by surprise. I didn't want to kill him, so I swatted him on the head with the flat of my sword, which gave him such a scare he ran out of the garden deep into the countryside, yelling, 'Thief! Thief!' The other lackeys ran away too. As for Saldagne, just as we ran out of torchlight, I saw him fall into the shrubbery, either because Verville had wounded him, or by accident. We didn't think it wise to help him up, but rather to leave as quickly as possible. Saldagne's sister, who knew that her brother was capable of being very violent with her, came out of the cottage and, speaking softly and crying at the same time, asked us if we could take her with us. Verville was delighted to have his mistress in his care. We found our garden door open, as we had left it, and we didn't close it to save ourselves the trouble of opening it if we needed to go out.

"In our garden there was a low room, painted and well-decorated, where we ate in the summertime and which was separate from the rest of the house. My young masters and I sometimes used it for fencing practice and, as it was the most pleasant room in the house, the Baron d'Arques, his children and I each had a key, so that the valets couldn't have access to it and the books and furniture in there would be secure. This was where we put our young lady, who was inconsolable. I told her we were going to look after our safety and her own, and that we would return momentarily. Verville spent a good fifteen minutes waking his Breton valet, who had made merry that evening. As soon as he lit a candle, we spent some time thinking about what we would do with Saldagne's sister; finally we decided to put her in my room, which was at the top of the house and was only frequented by my valet and me. We returned to the garden room with a light. Verville let out a loud cry as he went in, which startled me. I didn't have time to ask him what was wrong, because I heard talking at the door of the room that someone opened just as I snuffed my candle. Verville asked, 'Who is it?' His brother Saint-Far answered, 'It's me. What the devil are you doing at this hour without a candle?'

"'I was talking to Garigues because I couldn't sleep,' Verville answered.

"'And I,' said Saint-Far, 'couldn't sleep either, so it's my turn to use the room; please leave me alone there.' We didn't make him ask twice. I spirited our young lady away as discreetly as I could, having stood between her and Saint-Far, who was on his way in. I led her into my room while she continued to despair and returned to Verville's room, where his valet lit the candle. Verville, who appeared crestfallen, told me he had to return to Saldagne's. 'And what do you want to do?' I asked. 'Finish him off?'

"'Ah! Poor Garigues,' he cried. 'I'll be the unhappiest man in the whole world if I don't free Mademoiselle de Saldagne from her brother's grasp!'

"'But how could she be there, since she's in my room?' I replied.

"'I wish to God she were!' he said, with a sigh.

"'I think you're dreaming,' I said.

"'I'm not dreaming,' he continued. 'We mistook Mademoiselle de Saldagne's older sister for her.'

"'What!' I said immediately. 'Weren't you together in the garden?'

"'Nothing could be more certain,' he told me.

"'Then why do you want to get yourself killed at her brother's, since the sister you want is in my room?'

"'Ah! Garigues,' he cried out again, 'I know what I saw.'

"'So do I,' I told him, 'and to show you I'm not mistaken, let's go see Mademoiselle de Saldagne.' He told me I was crazy, and so the most tormented man in the whole world followed me. But my surprise was no lesser than his torment when I saw in my room a young lady I had never seen before, who wasn't the one I had brought there. Verville was as surprised as I was, but as a reward the most satisfied man alive, because he was reunited with Mademoiselle de Saldagne. He admitted that he was the one who was wrong, but I couldn't answer him, being unable to understand by what enchantment a young lady I had not let out of my sight had turned into another one between the garden room and my room. I looked attentively at Verville's mistress, who certainly wasn't the one we brought from Saldagne's, and who didn't even look like her. Verville, seeing me so bewildered, asked me what was the matter. 'I have to confess once more that I was wrong,' he said.

"'If Mademoiselle de Saldagne came in with us earlier, I am even more mistaken than you,' I said.

"'But with whom did she come in then?' he asked.

"'I don't know,' I answered, 'nor do I know who does, besides Mademoiselle herself.'

"'I also don't know with whom I came, unless it was with Monsieur,' said Mademoiselle de Saldagne, referring to me, 'because,' she went on, 'it wasn't Monsieur de Verville who took me from my brother's. It was a man who came in right after you left. I don't know whether my brother's cries were the reason, or whether our lackeys, who came back at the same time, told him what had happened. He had them carry my brother to his room, and my chambermaid, having come to tell me everything I just told you and that she noticed that this man was an acquaintance of my brother and our neighbours, I went to wait for him in the garden, where I pleaded with him to take me home with him until the next day, when I would go to a lady friend's to await the passing of my brother's fury, which, I assured him, I had every reason to dread. This man offered, with much civility, to escort me anywhere I wanted to go. And he promised to protect me against my brother, even if he risked his life. It was with him that I came to this house, where Verville, whose voice I recognized, spoke to this same man, after which I was taken to the room where you see me now.'

"What Mademoiselle de Saldagne told us didn't enlighten me entirely, but at least she helped me guess roughly how the thing happened. As for Verville, he was so busy looking at his mistress that he didn't pay much attention to what she told us; he began to say sweet nothings to her, without worrying how she had come to be in my room. I took a light and, leaving them together, returned to the garden room to speak to Saint-Far, even though he was sure to say something disagreeable, as was his custom. But I was surprised to discover, instead of him, the same young lady I knew with certainty I had brought from Saldagne's. My surprise was compounded by seeing that she was dishevelled, like someone who had been manhandled. Her hair was a mess, and the kerchief that covered her breast was bloody in places, as was her face.

"'Verville,' she said to me as soon as she saw me. 'Don't come near me unless it's to kill me. You'd better not attack me again. If I was strong enough to fight you off the first time, God will give me enough strength to tear your eyes out if I can't kill you. So that's the violent love you claimed to have for my sister?' she added, crying. 'Oh, am I ever paying dearly for indulging my sister's whims! And when one doesn't act as one should, it serves one right to suffer the evils one fears most! But what's stopping you?' she said, seeing me standing there stunned. 'Are you feeling remorse for what you did? If that's the case, I'm willing to forget this happened. You're young, and it was foolhardy of me to trust the discretion of a man your age. Send me back to my brother, I beg you. As violent as he is, I'm less afraid of him than you. You're just a brute, or rather our family's mortal enemy. It wasn't enough for you to seduce a girl and try to kill a gentleman. You had to add an even greater crime.' As she finished speaking these words, which she uttered with great vehemence, she started to cry so bitterly that I have never seen anyone as distraught. I must admit that that was when I lost whatever presence of mind I had left in such a confusing situation, and if she herself hadn't paused, I wouldn't have dared to interrupt her, both because I was stunned and because of the authority with which she reproached me. 'Mademoiselle,' I answered. 'Not only am I not Verville, but I can also assure you that he isn't capable of an evil deed like the one you complain of.'

"'What!?' she replied. 'You're not Verville? I didn't see you fight my brother? A gentleman didn't come to your aid? And you didn't, as I requested, bring me here, where you tried to do violence unworthy of both you and me?' She was so choked with emotion she couldn't go on. As for me, I have never been more confounded, being unable to understand how she knew Verville and didn't know him. I told her that the violence done to her was unknown to me, and since she was Monsieur de Saldagne's sister, I would take her, if she wished, to see her sister. As I finished speaking, I saw Verville enter the room with Mademoiselle de Saldagne, who wanted to be taken back to her brother's. I don't know where she had got such a dangerous notion. The two sisters embraced as soon as they saw each other and started crying again. Verville urged them to quickly go back to my room, explaining how difficult it would be to get them to open up at Monsieur de Saldagne's, the house being on the warpath, not to mention the peril they faced at the hands of a brute; that they wouldn't be discovered here; that it would soon be light; and that, according to the news we would receive from Saldagne, we would decide what to do then. It wasn't very difficult for Verville to get them to agree, as the two poor young ladies felt reassured by each other's presence. We went up to my room where, after having carefully reviewed the bizarre events that gave us so much trouble, we believed as surely as if we had seen it that the violence done to Mademoiselle de Léry surely came from Saint-Far, knowing all too well, Verville and I, that he was capable of something even worse. It turned out to be as we surmised. Saint-Far had gambled in the same house where Saldagne had lost his money and, passing by the garden minutes after the altercation, he came across Saldagne's lackeys, who recounted what had happened to their master, claiming he'd been attacked by seven or eight thieves in order to excuse the cowardice they had shown when they abandoned him. As his neighbour, Saint-Far felt obliged to offer his help, and didn't leave Saldagne until he was carried to his room, after which Mademoiselle de Saldagne asked Saint-Far to shelter her from her brother's violence.

She had gone with him, as her sister had with us. He had wanted to put her in the garden room where we were, as I told you, and, because he was no less afraid that we might see his young lady than we were that he might see ours, and that by chance the two sisters were next to each other, when he went in and we went out, I found myself holding the hand of his at the same time as he made the same mistake with mine, and thus the young ladies were switched. All this was feasible because I had put out the light and they were both dressed alike, and so dazed – as were we – that they didn't know what they were doing. As soon as we had left her in the room, seeing that he was alone with a beautiful girl and being endowed with far more instinct than reason, or, to speak of him as he deserves, being baseness incarnate, he tried to take advantage of the opportunity, without thinking of what could happen or that he was perpetrating an irreparable offence to a girl of quality who had sought shelter in his arms. His brutality got the punishment it deserved. Mademoiselle de Léry defended herself like a lioness. She bit him, scratched him and bloodied him. His reaction to all this was none other than to go to bed and sleep as peacefully as if he hadn't attempted the most unreasonable act there is.

"You're probably wondering how Mademoiselle de Léry came to be in the garden when her brother surprised us there, she who hadn't come the way her sister had. This confused me too, but I learnt from both of them that Mademoiselle de Léry had accompanied her sister in the garden in order not to have to rely on a servant's discretion, and that she was the person I had conversed with, who went by the name Madelon. I was no longer surprised to have found so much wit in a chambermaid; and Mademoiselle de Léry confessed that after having conversed with me in the garden and found me wittier than valets usually are, she was astonished to meet Verville's the next day, whom she still took to be me but who proved to be witless. Since that time we have had something more than esteem for one another, and I daresay she was at least as pleased as I was that we could share each other's affection with more equality and proportion than if one of us had been a valet or a maid.

"The day broke and we were still together. We left our young ladies in my room, where they could sleep if they wished, while Verville and I pondered what we needed to do next. Not being in love like Verville, I was dying to go to sleep, but it wouldn't have been right to abandon my friend when he had a pile of urgent business to attend to. I had a lackey who was as clever as Verville's valet was dim. I filled him in as much as I could, and sent him to find out what was going on at Saldagne's. He acquitted himself well, with the discretion born of wit, and reported that Saldagne's people said that thieves had badly wounded him; and there was no more talk of his sisters than there would have been if he hadn't had any, either because he didn't care about them or because he had forbidden his people to talk about them in order to stifle rumours that would harm his reputation. 'It's obvious that this is going to lead to a duel,' Verville said. 'And maybe murder,' I replied, informing him that Saldagne was the one who tried to kill me in Rome, that we had recognized each other, and I added that, if he believed I was the one who had made an attempt on his life, it was very likely he didn't yet suspect us of having any kind of relationship with his sisters. I went to tell those poor girls what we had learnt, while Verville went to see Saint-Far to find out what his feelings were and if we had guessed right. He saw that Saint-Far's face bore many scratches but, no matter how many questions Verville asked him, all he could get from his brother was that on his way home from gambling he had found the door to Saldagne's garden open, his house abuzz and Saldagne himself badly wounded in the arms of his servants who were carrying him to his room.

"'This is a terrible thing,' said Verville, 'and his sisters must be very upset. They're good-looking girls. I think I'll pay them a visit.'

"'What do I care,' answered the brute, who then began to whistle, and did not respond to his brother, no matter what he said.

"Verville left him and returned to my room, where I was using all my eloquence to console our beautiful damsels in distress. They despaired, expecting only extreme violence from their brother's strange personality, who was without doubt more the slave of his passions than anyone else in the whole world. My lackey brought them some food from the restaurant nearby, which he continued to do for the two weeks we kept them in my room, where, luckily, no one found them, because they were at the top of the house, far from anyone else. They wouldn't have minded staying in a religious establishment but, because of their unfortunate adventure, they had reason to fear not being able to leave a convent whenever they wanted, once they had entered it.

"In the meantime, Saldagne's wounds were healing, and Saint-Far, whom we watched, visited him every day. Verville didn't budge from my room, to which the household paid no attention, since it had grown accustomed to him spending entire days reading or conversing with me. His love for Mademoiselle de Saldagne grew daily, and she loved him as much as he loved her. Her older sister didn't find me unattractive, and I wasn't indifferent to her. It wasn't that my passion for Leonora was diminished, but I had nothing to hope for in that realm. And if I could have possessed her, her unhappiness would be on my conscience.

"One day Verville received a note from Saldagne, who wanted to see him, sword in hand, and who was waiting for him with one of his friends on the Grenelle plain. In the same note, Verville was asked to bring along none other but me. I suspected he wanted to catch both of us in the same net. This suspicion was well founded, since I had experienced what he was capable of. But Verville refused to consider it, having resolved to give him all kinds of satisfactions, even offering to marry his sister. He sent for a rented coach, even though there were three at home. We went where Saldagne was waiting for us, and Verville was astonished to find his brother serving his enemy. We neglected neither expressions of respect nor entreaties in the hope of reaching a compromise. Fighting the two least rational men in the whole world proved unavoidable. I tried to tell Saint-Far I was in despair at the idea of drawing my sword against him, and I responded respectfully and submissively to all the outrageous things with which he tried my patience. Finally, he brutally told me I had always displeased him, and that if I wanted to be back in his good graces I needed to taste his sword two or three times. As he said this, he charged me furiously. I was content to parry for a while, resolved as I was to avoid grappling with him, at the risk of suffering some wounds. God smiled on my good intentions. He fell at my feet. I let him get up, which only excited his rage. Finally, having lightly wounded me on the shoulder, he yelled at me, like a boastful lackey, that I had 'got a taste' with such insolent anger that my patience wore out. I pressed him, and having broken down his defences, I moved in close enough to be able to grab his sword by the hilt. 'This man you hate so much,' I told him then, 'will nevertheless not take your life.' He made many useless efforts, without saying a word, like the brute he was, although I kept trying to tell him that we had to separate Saldagne and his brother, who were rolling around on the ground; but I realized he had to be treated differently. I didn't hold back, and I thought I would break his hand with the effort I made to tear his sword away from him and throw it out of his reach. I immediately ran over to lend a hand to Verville, who was grappling with his man. As I approached, I saw, in the distance, horsemen riding towards us. Saldagne was disarmed and, at the same time, I felt a sword strike me from behind. It was the generous Saint-Far, in such a cowardly manner, using the sword I had left him. I could no longer control my feelings. I struck back, inflicting a serious wound. The Baron d'Arques, who arrived just then, and saw me wound his son, wished me ill, all the more because he had always wished me all the best. He prodded his horse towards me and struck me on the head with his sword. Those who came with him swooped down on me. I held off my many enemies quite well, but I would have succumbed to greater numbers had not Verville, the most generous friend in the whole world, risked his life to step in between them and me. With the flat of his sword he whacked the ear of his valet, who was pressing me harder than the rest in an attempt to stand out from the crowd. Holding it by the hilt, I offered my sword to the Baron d'Arques. This didn't mollify him. He called me a rascal and an ingrate and every name he could think of, even threatening to have me hung. I proudly replied that, rascal and ingrate that I was, I had spared his son's life and that I only wounded him after he treacherously struck me. Verville told his father that what I said was true, but he still said that he never wanted to see me again. Saldagne and the Baron d'Arques got into the coach where Saint-Far was put, and Verville, who didn't want to leave me, took me with him in the other one. He dropped me off at the townhouse of one of our princes, where he had friends, and retired to his father's. Monsieur de Saint-Sauveur sent me a coach that very night and secretly put me up in his home, where he took care of me as though I were his son. Verville came to see me the next day and told me his father found out about our fight from Saldagne's sisters, whom he had found in my bedroom. With much joy, he then told me that the whole affair would be resolved by a double marriage as soon as his brother's wound, which was not in a dangerous location, was healed and that it was up to me to be on good terms with Saldagne; as for his father, he wasn't angry any more, and felt bad about mistreating me. Verville then wished that I would soon be healed, so I could take part in the festivities. But I answered that I could no longer stay in a country where my low birth could be held against me, the way his father had when he called me a scoundrel, and that I would soon leave the kingdom to be killed in war or to acquire a fortune that was proportionate to the feelings of honour his example had given me. I have reason to believe my resolution saddened him, but a man who is in love is not preoccupied for long by any feeling other than his own passion."

Destiny was going on with his story, when the sounds of a gunshot, immediately followed by organ music, came from the street. This instrument, which may never heretofore have been heard at an inn's doorstep, made everyone who had been awakened by the shot run to their window. The organ continued to be played, and those who were expert in the matter could even tell that the organist was playing a hymn. No one could make head nor tails of this devout serenade, which hadn't yet been recognized for what it was. But any lingering doubts were dispelled when two nasty voices were heard, one singing soprano while the other groaned out the bass. These two caterwauling voices accompanied the organs to create a concert that made all the dogs in the area howl. They sang:

"With our voices and ivory lutes,
Let us ravish every soul…"

and the rest of the song. After this old ditty was badly sung, the voice of someone was heard speaking very softly – as loudly as he could, scolding the singers for always singing the same thing. The poor singers replied that they didn't know what they were supposed to sing. "Sing whatever you want," the same person replied half out loud. "You have to sing, since you're being paid handsomely." After this explicit order, the tone of the organ changed, and a good *Exaudiat** was played and sung with convincing devotion. No one in the audience had dared to speak, for fear of interrupting the music, when Grudge, who would not have kept quiet on such an occasion for all the riches in the world, shouted at the top of his lungs, "Are you conducting a church service in the street?" One of the listeners spoke up to say that you could call what they were doing singing *Tenebrae*, in the true sense of the word. Another added that it was a nocturnal procession; finally all the inn's jokers enjoyed the music without any of them being able to guess who was performing it, even less for whom or why. Nevertheless the *Exaudiat* played on, when ten or twelve dogs that were following a bitch of ill repute ran along with their mistress between and around the musicians' legs. As several rivals in the same place don't tend to agree for long, after having grumbled and sworn at one another for a while, they suddenly turned on each other with so much animosity and fury that the musicians,

fearing for their legs, fled, leaving their organ for the dogs to use
at their discretion. These intemperate lovers did not make good
use of the instrument. They knocked over a trestle table that held
the harmonious machine, and I wouldn't put it past a few of
those damned dogs to lift their leg and piss on the fallen organ,
these animals being quite diuretic by nature, especially when a
bitch of their acquaintance is in the mood to proceed with the
multiplication of her species. The concert being thus disconcerted,
the innkeeper had the doors to the inn opened in order to bring
the organ, the table and the trestles indoors. As he and his valets
busied themselves with this charitable task, the organist returned
to his organ, accompanied by three people, among whom were a
woman and a man who was hiding his face behind his coat. The
man was none other than Ragotin himself, who wanted to give
Mademoiselle Star a serenade and, to do this, had hired a diminutive castrato, who played the organ in a church. It was this monster,
neither man nor woman, who sang soprano and played the organ
his servant girl had brought, while a choirboy whose voice had
already broken sang bass, and all this for the sum of two testons,
the cost of living having already increased so much in the good old
land of Maine. As soon as the innkeeper recognized the authors
of the serenade, he said, loudly enough to be heard by all those
who were at the windows of the inn, "So you're the one, Monsieur
Ragotin, who is singing vespers at my door. You'd be better off
sleeping and letting my guests sleep." Ragotin replied that he was
mistaking him for someone else, but he said it in such a way as to
reinforce the idea he pretended to deny. Meanwhile, the organist
who found his bellows ruptured and who was short-tempered, as
all beardless creatures are, swore at Ragotin, telling him he would
have to pay the damage. Ragotin told him he couldn't care less
about that. "Whether you care or not," replied the castrato, "I
want to be paid." The innkeeper and his valets sided with him,
but Ragotin informed them, as one would ignorant people, that
this simply wasn't customary when serenading. That said, he left,
taking great pride in his gallant gift. The musicians loaded the

organ onto the back of the castrato's servant. The castrato went home in a foul mood, with the table balanced on his shoulder, followed by the choirboy who carried the two trestles. The inn was locked up. Destiny said goodnight to the actresses and postponed the end of his story until the next opportunity.

CHAPTER XVI

Opening of the Theatre and Other Things
of No Less Consequence

T HE NEXT MORNING the actors gathered in one of the rooms they occupied in the inn, in order to rehearse the play they were going to perform after lunch. Grudge, to whom Ragotin had already confided his role in the serenade and who feigned disbelief, warned his companions that the little man would soon make an appearance to hear them sing his praises for his refined gallant gift, and added that any time he tried to bring it up they should cleverly change the subject. Ragotin entered the room in short order, and, after saying hello to the actors in general, he wanted to talk about his serenade to Mademoiselle Star, who proved to be a wandering planet, because she changed her seat without answering him each time he asked her at what time she had gone to bed, and how she had spent the night. He left her for Mademoiselle Angélique, who did nothing but continue to study her part instead of answering him. He accosted Cave, who didn't so much as look at him. All the actors, one after the other, followed Grudge's instructions to the letter and either didn't respond to what Ragotin said or changed the subject every time he wanted to speak about the previous night. Finally, unable to contain his vanity or let his reputation languish any longer, he said aloud, addressing everyone, "Would you like me to tell you the truth about last night?"

"Do as you please," someone answered.

"I was the one who gave you the serenade," he added.

"Is it the custom in these parts to give them with organ music?" asked Destiny. "And for whom was it intended? Wasn't it," he continued, "for the beautiful lady who caused so many gentle dogs to fight each other?"

"No doubt about it," said Olive, "because these animals of a biting nature wouldn't have disturbed such harmonious music unless they were rivals, and jealous ones at that, of Monsieur Ragotin." Someone else spoke up to say it was clear his mistress favoured him, and that his intentions were honourable, since he was so open about it. Finally, all those who were present took a shot at Ragotin and his serenade, with the exception of Grudge, who spared him, having been privileged by the honour of his confidence. It looked like this dog mockery would exhaust all those who were in the room, if the poet, who in his own way was as foolish and vain as Ragotin, and never missed an opportunity to satisfy his vanity, hadn't doggedly changed the subject by saying, in the voice of a nobleman or of someone pretending to be one, "Speaking of serenades, I remember I was given one for my wedding that lasted two weeks and involved over a hundred instruments. It made the rounds of the Marais. The loveliest ladies of the Place Royale adopted it. Several beaux claimed it as theirs, and it even inspired jealousy in a nobleman, who had his people attack those who were giving it to me. The gentleman's people were easily driven off by my friends, who were all my countrymen – men as brave as they come – most of whom had been officers in a regiment I raised to put down an uprising in our region." Grudge, who had suppressed his natural inclination for mockery for the sake of Ragotin, wasn't as kind to the poet, whom he continually persecuted. He took the floor and said to the Muses' darling, "Your serenade, as you describe it, sounds more like a charivari which disturbed the nobleman, who sent his riff-raff to make it stop or drive it away. What makes me believe this even more is that your wife died of old age six months after your nuptials, to use your expression."

"But she died of mother's womb sickness," said the poet.

"You mean grandmother's or great-grandmother's," replied Grudge. "Her womb hadn't bothered her since the reign of Henri IV," he added, "and to show you I know more about her than you do, although you talk about her so often, I want to tell you something about her you never learnt. In the court of Queen Marguerite…" This promising start to a story attracted all who were in the room to Grudge's side. They knew he had chronicles against the entire human race. The poet, who was extremely wary of him, interrupted him by saying, "I bet one hundred pistoles to the contrary." This abrupt challenge made everyone laugh, which drove the poet from the room. It was always through wagers of large sums that the poor man defended his daily hyperboles, which amounted to thousands in the course of a week, not including the outright lies. Grudge was the critic-in-chief of his actions as well as his words, and the influence he wielded over him was so great that I dare compare it to Augustus's over Antony.* I mean this only as regards influence, and no comparison is made between two provincial actors and two Romans of that calibre. Grudge having embarked on his tale, and having been interrupted by the poet, as I just told you, everyone asked him to finish it. But he excused himself, promising to tell them someday the poet's entire life story, and that the wife's would be included.

They rehearsed the play they were going to perform that afternoon at a nearby tennis court. Nothing remarkable happened during the rehearsal. They performed after lunch and they performed nicely. Mademoiselle Star was ravishing, Angélique had her fans, and each of them played their role to everyone's satisfaction.

Destiny and the other men also outdid themselves, and those in the audience who had often been to the theatre in Paris had to admit that the King's players would not have done a better job. Ragotin silently ratified the donation he had made of his body and soul to Mademoiselle Star, previously submitted to Grudge, who kept promising him to make the actress accept it. Without this promise, despair would soon have created a grand, moving subject for a tragic story out of a pathetic little lawyer. I won't tell whether the actors appealed to the ladies of Le Mans as much as the actresses did to the men – even if I knew I wouldn't tell – but, since even the wisest man isn't always the master of his tongue, I'll end this chapter now, to avoid all further temptation.

CHAPTER XVII

The Unfortunate Outcome of Ragotin's Civility

AS SOON AS DESTINY CHANGED out of his old embroidery and into his everyday clothes, La Rappinière brought him to the town's prison, because the man they'd captured the day the parson of Domfront was abducted was asking to speak to him. Meanwhile the actresses returned to their inn with a big procession of Manceaux.* Having found himself next to Mademoiselle Cave as she was leaving the tennis court where the play had been performed, Ragotin presented his hand to escort her back, although he would have preferred to serve his dear Star in this manner. He took Mademoiselle Angélique's hand as well, so that he became a squire to both the left and the right. This double civility caused a triple inconvenience, because Cave, who walked farthest from the gutter, as befitted her seniority, was pressed against the side of the buildings by Ragotin, so that Angélique wouldn't have to step into the sewage. Moreover, the little man, who only came up to their waist, pulled down so hard on their hands that it was difficult for them to keep from falling on him. What added to their discomfort was that he was constantly turning around to look at Mademoiselle Star, whom he heard behind him speaking to two fops who were escorting her, whether she wanted them to or not. The poor actresses often tried to free their hands, but Ragotin held on so tight they would rather have been in fetters. Again and again they told him he needn't go to the trouble. He simply replied, "Your servant! Your servant!" (this was his standard expression of civility), and he squeezed their hands even more tightly. They would have to grin and bear it until they reached the stairway to their room, when they could hope to be set free. But Ragotin wasn't going to be impolite. While he continued to reply, "Your servant! Your servant!" to everything they could say, he first tried to go straight up the stairs with the two actresses; this turned out to be impossible, because the stairs were too narrow. With her back to the wall Cave went up first, pulling Ragotin, who pulled Angélique, who didn't pull anything, but who laughed hysterically. A new obstacle soon arose. Only four or five steps from their room, they encountered one of the innkeeper's valets, carrying a bag of oats that was too heavy for him, who told them, with much effort because he was weighed down by his burden, that they had to go back down because he could not carry such a heavy load back up. Ragotin tried to reply; but the valet swore that he would let his bag fall on them. So they sought to unmake quickly the progress they had so deliberately made, with Ragotin still attached to the actresses' hands. The valet, burdened by the oats, leant over them strangely, causing Ragotin to stumble, although this would not have made him fall, since he gripped the actresses' hands the way he did; but Cave, who was holding him up more than her daughter was, thanks to a more secure position on the stairs, was pulled back and fell on top of Ragotin, with her feet on his chest and stomach, while striking her daughter's head so hard with her own that both of them fell down. The valet, who thought to himself it would be some time before everyone got back up, and who couldn't stand the weight of the bag of oats any longer, finally spilt it onto the steps, swearing like an innkeeper's valet. The innkeeper arrived and was mad at his valet; the valet was mad at the actresses; the actresses were mad at Ragotin who was madder than any of those who were mad, because Mademoiselle Star, who arrived at the same time, witnessed this misfortune, which was almost as embarrassing as the one with the hat they had to cut off his head with scissors a few days earlier. Cave swore that Ragotin would never escort her again, and showed Mademoiselle Star her hands, which were bruised. Star told her that God had punished her for stealing Monsieur Ragotin, for whom she had waited in front of the theatre, because he was supposed to escort her. She added that she was happy about what happened to the little man as he hadn't been true to his word. He didn't hear any of this, because the innkeeper was talking about making him pay for the loss of his oats, having already, for the same matter, tried to beat his valet, who called Ragotin a defender of lost causes. Angélique turned against him as well, complaining that she had been his second choice. In short, Fate demonstrated that she had yet to play any part in Grudge's promises to make Ragotin the most fortunate lover in the whole land of Maine, including even Le Perche and Laval. The oats were picked up and the actresses went up to their room one after the other, without incident. Ragotin did not follow them, and I don't really know where he went. Dinner time came, and the troupe dined at the inn. They went their own ways after dinner, while Destiny joined the actresses to continue his story.

CHAPTER XVIII

The Story of Destiny and Star Continued

I MADE THE PREVIOUS CHAPTER a little short. Maybe this one will be longer. But I'm not really sure. We'll see. Destiny took his usual seat and picked up the thread of his story as follows: "I'm going to try to finish as succinctly as possible the story of a life with which I've bored you for too long already. Having come to see me, as I told you, and being unable to persuade me to return to his father's, Verville left me very saddened by my resolution, or so it seemed to me, and went home, where, soon after, he married

Mademoiselle de Saldagne, and Saint-Far married Mademoiselle de Léry. She was as sharp as he was dull, and I couldn't imagine how two such unequal minds could ever agree. Meanwhile, I recovered fully and the generous Monsieur de Saint-Sauveur, having approved of my resolution to leave the kingdom, gave me money for my trip, while Verville, who didn't forget me simply because he was married, gave me a good horse and one hundred pistoles. I followed the road that goes to Lyon and then to Italy, in order to stop by Rome, where I planned to see my Leonora for the last time before seeking death in Candia, which would put me out of my misery. At Nevers, I stayed at an inn near the river. Having arrived early, and not knowing what to do for entertainment while I waited for dinner, I went for a stroll on a big stone bridge over the Loire. Two women were also walking on the bridge, one of whom, who looked sick, walked with difficulty, leaning on the other one. I tipped my hat without looking at them as I passed by and walked on the bridge for some time, thinking about my bad luck and, more often, about my love. I was quite well dressed, as must be those whose birth cannot excuse a shabby outfit. When I walked by the women again, I overheard one of them say, 'I'd really think it was him if I didn't know he was dead.' I don't know why I turned to look, as I had no reason to think those words referred to me. They hadn't been said with anyone else in mind. I saw Mademoiselle de la Boissière, her face drawn and pale, leaning on her daughter Leonora. I went straight towards them with more self-confidence than I used to have in Rome, because I had greatly developed my body and mind during the time I spent in Paris. I found them so surprised and frightened that I think they would have fled if Mademoiselle de la Boissière were able to run. This surprised me as well. I asked them what happy coincidence had brought me together with the two people in the world I held most dear. My words reassured them. Mademoiselle de la Boissière told me that I shouldn't be shocked they had reacted to me with astonishment; Signor Stephano had shown them letters he received from one of the gentlemen I had accompanied in Rome, informing him that I had been killed during the war in Parma. She said she was delighted that this piece of news which had upset her so much had turned out to be wrong. I replied that death was not the greatest misfortune that could befall me, and that I was on my way to Venice in order to spread rumours of the same nature, only more truthful ones this time. They were distraught by my resolution, and the mother began to show me great affection; I could not imagine why. Finally, I learnt from her why she was so warm. I could still be of service to her, and her circumstances didn't allow her to show contempt for me and give me the cold shoulder the way she had in Rome. They had experienced a setback serious enough to leave them in need. Having sold all their furniture, which was of very high quality and included many pieces, they left Rome with a French maid who had long been in their service, and Signor Stephano had given them his valet, who was also Flemish and who wanted to return to his country. This valet and this maid were in love and planned to get married, but no one knew about it. Upon arriving at Roanne, Mademoiselle de La Boissière took a boat downriver. At Nevers, she felt so sick she was unable to continue. During her sickness, she was hard to please, and her maid wasn't up to her usual standard. One morning, the maid and the valet disappeared, and what was worse, the poor lady's money disappeared as well. The distress this caused aggravated her condition, and she was forced to stay in Nevers, to wait for news from Paris where she hoped to find the resources she needed to continue her trip. Mademoiselle de La Boissière told me this sad adventure in a few words. I escorted them back to their inn, which was also mine, and after spending some time with them I retired to my room to let them eat dinner. As for me, I didn't eat, although I felt like I'd spent several hours at the table. I went to see them as soon as I heard from them that I'd be welcome. I found the mother in bed and the daughter appeared with a face as sad as it had been happy only moments earlier. Her mother was even sadder than her, and I became sad as well. We spent some time looking at one another without speaking. Finally, Mademoiselle de La Boissière showed me letters she had received from Paris which made her and her daughter the unhappiest women alive. She told me the reason for her distress with so many tears, and her daughter, who was crying as much as her mother, touched me so much that I doubted my ability to express the extent of my commiseration, even though I offered them whatever I had, in such a way as to remove any doubts regarding my sincerity: 'I don't know yet what you are so upset about,' I told them, 'but if my life is all that's needed to relieve your sorrow, you can put your minds at ease. Just tell me, Madame, what to do. I have money, if you need it. I have courage, if you have enemies. And for all the services I am offering I require only the satisfaction of having served you.' My face and my words showed them so clearly what was in my soul that their great sorrow was somewhat alleviated. Mademoiselle de La Boissière read me a letter in which a lady friend of hers told her that someone unnamed, whom I understood to be Leonora's father, had been ordered to leave the court and had gone to Holland. Thus the poor lady found herself far from home, without money and lacking the means of obtaining any. I once again offered what I had, which might have amounted to five hundred écus, and I told her I would take her to Holland or to the ends of the earth, if that was where she wanted to go. Finally, I assured her that she had found in me someone who would serve her like a valet but who would love and respect her like a son. I blushed when I uttered the word 'son', but I was no longer the odious man who was turned away at the door in Rome and for whom Leonora was unapproachable. And for me, Mademoiselle de La Boissière was no longer a strict mother. To all the offers I made her, she always replied that Leonora would be much obliged to me. Everything was in Leonora's name, and you would have thought that her mother was only a lady-in-waiting speaking on behalf of her mistress. So it is that most people only show consideration to those they deem useful to themselves.

"I left them very relieved and retired to my room as contented as could be. I spent a very pleasant though sleepless night, falling asleep near dawn and getting up quite late. That day Leonora was more nicely dressed than the day before, and she could not have failed to notice that I too had gone to some effort to look good. I took her to mass without her mother, who was still too weak. We had lunch together, and since that time we have been but the same family. Mademoiselle de La Boissière was very grateful for my help and often protested that she wouldn't die in my debt. I sold my horse, and as soon as she recovered enough of her strength, we took a flatboat and went down the river to Orléans. While we were on the water, I enjoyed the great felicity of Leonora's conversation without being interrupted by her mother. I found the wit of this attractive girl as dazzling as the light of her eyes. As for my own mind, which might have appeared suspect in Rome, it did not disappoint her on this occasion. What more can I say? She came to love me as much as I loved her; and you must have noticed that, ever since you have known us, this reciprocal love has not diminished."

"What!" interrupted Angélique. "Mademoiselle Star is Leonora?"

"None other," Destiny replied. Mademoiselle Star spoke up and said that her fellow actress was right to doubt that she was the Leonora whom Destiny had depicted like the beauty in a novel. "That isn't the reason," said Angélique. "It's because we always find it difficult to believe something we really wished for." Mademoiselle Cave said she never had any doubt, and didn't want the discussion to continue, so that Destiny could get on with his story, which he did as follows:

"We docked in Orléans, where our arrival was so entertaining that I want to tell you the details. A bunch of porters, who were waiting at the dock for arriving passengers with luggage, crowded onto our boat. They were more than thirty in all to lift two or three small bags that the weakest among them could have carried under his arms. If I'd been alone, I probably wouldn't have been restrained enough not to lose my temper at their insolence. Eight of them grabbed a small chest that didn't weigh twenty pounds and, after pretending to have a hard time lifting it off the ground, they finally hoisted it above their heads, balancing it on their fingertips. All the rabble of the port laughed at this, and we were forced to follow suit. Still, I was blushing with shame at having to travel across an entire town in such a procession, because the rest of our luggage, which one man could have carried, kept twenty occupied, while my pistols alone required four men. We entered the town in the following order. Eight big drunk candidates for the gallows – or who deserved to be – together carried a small chest, as I already told you. My pistols followed, one after the other, each carried by two men. Mademoiselle de La Boissière, who, like me, was fuming, came next. She was sitting on a big wicker chair supported by two long rafting poles carried by four men who relayed one another and had many insolent things to tell her along the way. The remainder of our luggage followed. It was made up of a small suitcase and a canvas-covered bundle that seven or eight of these rascals were tossing around while they walked, as though they were playing the game of broken pot. I brought up the rear of this triumphal parade, holding Leonora's hand. She was laughing so hard that I had to take pleasure in this swindle despite myself. During our march, the passers-by stopped in the street to gawk at us, and the ensuing noise brought everyone to the window.

"Finally we arrived at the faubourg on the outskirts of town, facing Paris, followed by much rabble, and we lodged at the Emperors' Inn. I ushered my ladies into a low room and then threatened those rascals so sincerely that they were glad to get the little I gave them, the innkeeper and his wife having scolded them as well. Mademoiselle de La Boissière, whom the joy of no longer being without money had cured more than anything else, felt strong enough to travel by coach. We reserved three seats on the one leaving for Paris the next day, and in two days we arrived in Paris without incident. It was when I got off at the coach house that for the first time I met Grudge, who had come from Orléans like us, on a coach that accompanied ours. He heard me asking where the inn of the Calais coaches was; he told me he happened to be on his way there and that if we hadn't already reserved our lodgings he would find us some, if we wished, at the place of a woman he knew, who rented out furnished rooms where we would be very comfortable. We believed him, and we were glad we did. This woman was the widow of a man who had spent his whole life partly as the doorkeeper and partly as the stage designer for a theatre troupe. He had even tried to act, but without success. Having accumulated some savings while serving in the theatre, he had turned to providing furnished rooms and taking boarders, thereby becoming prosperous. We rented two quite comfortable rooms. Mademoiselle de La Boissière received confirmation of the bad news she had had from Leonora's father, and she learnt more things that she kept from us and that upset her enough to make her get sick again. This made us postpone for some time our trip to Holland, where she had decided I would escort her; and Grudge, who was going there to meet up with a theatre troupe, was willing to wait for us after I promised to cover his expenses.

"Mademoiselle de La Boissière was often visited by one of her friends, who had served the wife of the French ambassador to Rome at the same time she had and been her confidant during her relationship with Leonora's father. It was from this friend that she learned about her illegitimate husband's banishment, and she helped us out several times while we were in Paris. I went out as little as possible, for fear of being seen by someone I knew. And I didn't find it difficult to stay home since I was with Leonora and the care I took of her mother only enhanced me in her eyes. The woman I mentioned before persuaded us to go on an outing to Saint-Cloud so that Mademoiselle de La Boissière could get some fresh air. Our hostess joined us, as did Grudge. We took a boat and went for a walk in the most beautiful parts of the park and, after we had a snack, Grudge led our little troupe toward our boat, while I stayed behind going over the bill in a tavern with an unreasonable hostess who delayed me longer than I expected. I escaped her grasp as cheaply as I could and left to catch up with my companions.

But I was astonished to see quite far away on the river our little boat taking my people back to Paris without me, without even leaving behind a little lackey who carried my sword and my coat. As I stood at the water's edge, at a loss to know why no one had waited for me, I heard a commotion coming from one of the flatboats and, having approached it, I saw two or three gentlemen, or so they appeared to be, who were trying to beat a boatman because he refused to follow our boat. I jumped onto this boat as it was pulling away from the shore, because the boatman was afraid of being beaten. But while I was taken aback by my companions leaving me in Saint-Cloud, I was no less confounded to see that the person responsible for the violence I had just witnessed was the same Saldagne I had so many reasons to despise. In the moment I recognized him, he moved from the end of the boat where he had been to where I was. Not quite knowing what to do with myself, I tried to hide my face as best I could, but being so close to him it would be impossible for him not to recognize me and, being without a sword, I made a desperate decision, which hatred alone would not have made me capable of had it not been augmented by jealousy. I grabbed him at the very moment he recognized me, and threw myself into the river with him. He couldn't retaliate, either because his gloves didn't allow him to or because he was too surprised. He came as close to drowning as it is possible to. Most of the boats went to his rescue; everyone thought we had fallen in by accident. Saldagne alone knew what had happened, and he was in no shape to complain or get someone to chase after me. I made it to the riverbank without much effort, as I was wearing a light outfit that didn't interfere with my swimming, and, the circumstances warranting speed, I was far from Saint-Cloud by the time Saldagne was fished out. While they had a hard time saving him, I imagine it was even harder to believe his story of the risk I took in order to rid myself of him, since I don't see why he would have kept it secret. I returned to Paris by a roundabout route,

entering the city at night. I didn't need to dry off as the sun
and all the running I had done left very little moisture in my
clothes. Finally, I was back with my dear Leonora, whom I
found to be in real distress. Grudge and our hostess were overjoyed to see me, as was Mademoiselle de La Boissière, who,
the better to make Grudge and our hostess believe I was her
son, played the distraught mother quite well. She apologized
to me in private for not waiting, and confessed that she had
been too preoccupied by her fear of Saldagne to think of me;
besides, with the exception of Grudge, the rest of our troupe
would only have got in the way if I tangled with Saldagne. I
learnt then that upon leaving the inn or the tavern where we
had eaten, this gentleman followed them to the boat; that he
very impolitely asked Leonora to unmask, and that her mother,
having recognized him as the same man who had tried the
same thing in Rome, returned to her boat very frightened, and
made it cast off without waiting for me. Saldagne meanwhile
was joined by two men of the same ilk. After consulting with
them for a few minutes on the riverbank, they had got on the
boat, where I found them threatening the boatman to make
him go after Leonora. This adventure caused me to venture
out even less often. A little while later, Mademoiselle de La
Boissière fell ill again, with melancholy playing a major role,
so we spent a part of the winter in Paris. We were informed
that an Italian prelate returning from Spain was on his way to
Flanders via Péronne. Grudge had enough influence to get us
included on his passport as actors. One day that we went to
visit this Italian prelate, who was living on the Rue de Seine,
we had dinner, on a whim, in the Faubourg Saint-Germain with
some actor acquaintances of Grudge's. As we were, he and I,
crossing the Pont-Neuf on the way home late at night, we were
attacked by five or six wool-snatchers.* I fought back as well
as I could, and I have to admit that Grudge did all that could
be asked of a courageous man and even saved my life. This
didn't prevent me from falling into the hands of these thieves,

my sword having unfortunately fallen. Grudge, who valiantly extricated himself from them, only lost a tattered coat. I lost everything except my clothes. What made me despair was that they took a portrait box that held Leonora's father's likeness on enamel, of which Mademoiselle de La Boissière had asked me to sell the diamonds. I found Grudge at a barber-surgeon's at the end of the Pont-Neuf. He had wounds on his face and arm. I had only a light head wound. Mademoiselle de La Boissière was very upset about the loss of her portrait, but the hope of soon seeing its subject consoled her. Finally, we left Paris for Péronne; from there we went to Brussels and from Brussels to The Hague.

"Leonora's father had left there two weeks earlier to go to England, where he went to serve the King against the Roundheads. Leonora's mother was so distraught by this news that she fell ill and died. As she was dying, she could see I was as unhappy as I would be had I been her son. She entrusted her daughter to me and made me promise I wouldn't abandon her, and that I would do everything in my power to find her father and put her into his hands. Not long afterwards, I was robbed by a Frenchman of all the money I had left, and the need in which I found myself with Leonora was such that we joined your troupe thanks to Grudge. You know the rest of my adventures. Since that time they've been the same as yours until Tours, where I think I saw that devil Saldagne again. I don't think I'm mistaken when I say that I won't be in this area for long without crossing paths with him, which I don't fear as much for myself as for Leonora, who would lose a faithful servant if she lost me or if some misfortune separated us."

That was how Destiny finished his story and, after consoling Mademoiselle Star, who cried as much when recalling her sorrows as she would if they were just beginning, he said goodnight to the actresses and went to bed.

CHAPTER XIX

Several Remarks Which Are Not Irrelevant. Ragotin's New Misfortune and Other Things You Will Read, if You Wish

L OVE, WHICH LEADS THE YOUNG to undertake anything and the old to forget everything, which caused the Trojan War and so many others I don't want to bother remembering, wanted to show, in the town of Le Mans, that it is no less formidable in a dubious inn than anywhere else. It wasn't content to make the lovesick Ragotin lose his appetite. It inspired thousands of unruly desires in La Rappinière, who was very susceptible to them, and made Roquebrune fall in love with the surgeon's wife, adding to his vanity, bluster and poetry a fourth folly, or rather a double infidelity, because he had long spoken of love to Star and Angélique, who both advised him not to go to the trouble of loving them. All this pales in comparison to what I am going to tell you. It also triumphed over the misanthropic and insensitive Grudge, who also fell in love with the surgeon's wife. Thus did the poet Roquebrune, to pay for his sins and expiate the miserable books he had wrought, acquire as his rival the meanest man in existence. The lady's name was Doña Inezilla del Prado, born in Malaga, and her so-called husband's, Lord Ferdinando Ferdinandi, Venetian gentleman born in Caen, Normandy. In the same inn there were yet others suffering from the same illness as those whose secrets I have just revealed; but I will let them be known at the right time and place. La Rappinière had fallen in love with Mademoiselle Star when he saw her in the role of Chimène,* and resolved at that time to divulge his secret to Grudge, whom he judged capable of doing anything for money. The divine Roquebrune had imagined that the conquest of a Spanish lady was a worthy object for his bravery. As for Grudge, I don't know what charms this foreign lady possessed that could make a man who hated everyone capable of love. The old actor, who'd tasted damnation while still alive – I mean who'd fallen in love before he died – was still in bed when

Ragotin, troubled by his passion as if it were a stomach ache, sought him out. He wondered if Grudge had any more thoughts about his chances, and wanted Grudge to take pity on him. Grudge promised him he wouldn't let the day go by without promoting Ragotin's cause to his mistress in a major way. La Rappinière entered the room at the same time, while Grudge finished getting dressed, and, having pulled him aside, confessed his infirmity and told him that if he could arrange for him to be in Mademoiselle Star's good graces, there wasn't anything he wouldn't do for him, including a position as an archer and La Rappinière's own niece in marriage, who would inherit from him since he had no children. The deceitful Grudge promised him even more than he had to Ragotin, which led this harbinger of the hangman to harbour substantial hopes. Roquebrune also came to consult the oracle. He was the most incorrigibly presumptuous person ever to come from the banks of the Garonne. He had got it into his head that everyone believed what he said about his great family, wealth, poetry and valour, so much so that he didn't take offence at Grudge's continual put-downs and persecution. He thought that Grudge only did it to round out the conversation; besides, he understood mockery better than anyone, and endured it like a Christian philosopher, even when it hit home. So he thought all the actors admired him, including Grudge, who had enough experience to admire few things and who, far from having a good opinion of this laurel-muncher,* had ample enough information about who he was to know whether the bishops and great lords of his country whom he constantly claimed as his relatives were truly the branches of a family tree that this genealogy and heraldry fanatic (among his other forms of craziness) had had drawn up on old parchment. He was disappointed not to find Grudge alone, although it should have bothered him less than someone else, since he had the bad habit of always whispering in people's ears and turning everything and often nothing into a secret. He therefore took Grudge aside, and admitted that he really needed to know whether the surgeon's wife was a woman of substantial wit, because he had loved women of every nationality except Spanish, and was she was worth it? He wouldn't be any the poorer for giving her a gift of one hundred pistoles, a sum he offered to spend on every occasion, as often as he spoke of his illustrious family. Grudge told him he didn't know Doña Inezilla well enough to speak for her wit, but that he had often come across her husband in the best cities of the kingdom, where he sold mithridate,* and that to learn what he wanted to know, he had only to converse with her, as she spoke French reasonably well. Roquebrune wanted to show her his genealogy on parchment, to impress the Spanish lady with the splendour of his race. But Grudge told him this was better suited to making him a Knight of Malta than making a lady attracted to him. Roquebrune thereupon made the gesture of a man counting money in his hand and said to Grudge, "You know very well what kind of man I am."

"Yes, yes," answered Grudge, "I know what kind of man you are and will be your whole life long." The poet left, and Grudge, at one and the same time his rival and his confidant, approached La Rappinière and Ragotin, who were rivals without being aware of it. Beside the fact that it is easy to hate those who stake a claim to what we thought destined only for us, and that he naturally hated everyone, old Grudge had always had a great aversion for the poet, who, no doubt, did nothing to lessen it by confiding in him. Grudge therefore resolved, right then and there, to play the nastiest tricks imaginable on him; a task to which his monkey brain was very well suited. So as not to waste any time, he started that very day by borrowing money from Roquebrune, which he used to outfit himself from head to foot, and bought new underwear. He'd been a slob all his life, but love, which accomplishes even greater miracles, made him care about his grooming in his later years. He took to wearing clean underwear more often than was appropriate for an old country actor and started to dye and shave his beard with so much care that his fellow actors noticed.

That day the company had been retained to perform a comedy for one of the town's wealthiest bourgeois, who was giving a great banquet and ball for the wedding of a young lady, a relative who had once been his ward. The party took place in one of the area's most beautiful houses, which he owned, located about a league outside of town – I never did learn exactly where. The company's stage designer and a carpenter had gone there in the morning to set up a theatre. The whole troupe travelled there in two coaches, leaving Le Mans at eleven in order to arrive at lunchtime, when they were supposed to perform the play. The Spanish lady Doña Inezilla came along, invited by the actresses and Grudge. Ragotin, who knew the schedule, waited for the coaches at an inn on the outskirts of town, and tied a horse he'd borrowed to the gate of a lower hall that opened onto the street. He had barely sat down to lunch when he was informed that the coaches were approaching. He flew to his horse on the wings of love, a long sword by his side and a carbine slung over his shoulder. He never said why he attended a wedding with such an arsenal, and even Grudge, his dear confidant, never found out. When he untied his horse's bridle, the coaches were so close to him that he didn't have time to find a leg up in order to cut a dashing figure astride his horse like a mini St George. Since he wasn't a very good rider and wasn't ready to display his agility in front of so many people, he accomplished the task most awkwardly. The horse was as long in the legs as Ragotin was short. He nevertheless reached the stirrup and hoisted himself up, swinging his right leg over to the other side of the saddle, but the straps, which were a bit loose, played a dirty trick on the little man, because the saddle rotated on the horse just as he tried to get on. Still, things weren't going badly up to that point, but the accursed carbine, which was supposed to be held by a strap slung over his shoulder and across his chest but instead hung from his neck like a necklace, had, unbeknownst to him, unfortunately migrated between his legs to such an extent that his rear end didn't come close to touching the saddle. The carbine rested across its length, from the pommel to the crupper. He was uncomfortable, and couldn't touch the stirrups with his toes. At that point the spurs with which his short legs were equipped made themselves known to the horse in a location no spur had ever touched before. This made it take off with more zest than was needed by a little man seated on nothing but a carbine. He squeezed his legs, the horse raised its rump, and Ragotin, following the downward slope that nature dictates to bodies endowed with weight, found himself on the horse's collar, where he smashed his nose, the horse having raised its head as a result of a furious jerk to the reins administered by its foolhardy rider. Trying to repair the damage, Ragotin let up on the bridle. This made the horse jump, which caused the patient's rear end to travel the entire length of the saddle and leave him on the rump, with the carbine still between his legs. Not used to carrying anything there, the horse bucked, putting Ragotin back on the saddle. Our inadequate equestrian squeezed his legs again and the horse bucked even harder, and then the unfortunate Ragotin ended up with his rear end stuck on the pommel, where we shall leave him as on a pivot, in order to get a little rest because, on my honour, this description has taken more out of me than the rest of the book, and I'm still not entirely satisfied with it.

CHAPTER XX

The Shortest of the Current Book. Ragotin's Fall Continued and Something Similar That Happened to Roquebrune

WE LEFT RAGOTIN SITTING on the pommel of a saddle, looking very embarrassed and worried about what would happen to him next. I don't think the late Phaeton,* sadly remembered, was more challenged by his father's four fiery steeds than was our little lawyer sitting on a horse as sweet as an ass. If he didn't lose his life like that reckless son, Fortune is to blame, whose whims would offer me much room for discussion, if I weren't obligated, in all good conscience, to rescue Ragotin quickly from the peril he faces, since we will make good use of him when our theatre troupe is in the town of Le Mans.

As soon as the unfortunate Ragotin felt only the pommel of a saddle between the two most fleshy parts of his body, ones he was accustomed to sit on, like all other animals endowed with reason – I mean, as soon as he realized he had very little to sit on, he gave up on the bridle like a man exercising good judgement, and grabbed the mane of the horse, which immediately broke into a gallop. Then the carbine went off. Ragotin thought he'd been shot through the body. The horse thought the same thing, and stumbled so violently that Ragotin lost the pommel that served as his seat, so much so that he dangled for a while from the horse's mane, one foot stuck to the saddle by a spur, while the other foot and the rest of his body waited for the spur to work itself free in order to fall to earth, together with the carbine, the sword and the bandolier. Finally the foot broke free, his hands let go of the mane and he had to fall. He did so far more gracefully than when he had climbed on. All this happened in sight of the coaches which had stopped to rescue him, or rather to have the pleasure of rescuing him. He cursed the horse, which had calmed down after his fall, and he was invited, as consolation, into one of the coaches, where he took the seat occupied by the poet, who was happy to be on horseback, so he could ride next to where Inezilla sat and flirt with her. Ragotin left him the sword and the firearm, which he wore in martial fashion. He lengthened the stirrups, adjusted the bridle and did a better job of climbing onto his horse than Ragotin had. But some spell had been cast on this unfortunate animal. The badly strapped saddle turned, as it had with Ragotin, and what held up his trousers having broken, the horse carried him for some distance one foot in the stirrup, the other serving as a fifth leg for the horse, with the hindquarters of the citizen of Parnassus exposed for all to see, his trousers having fallen down to his calves. None of the spectators had laughed when Ragotin fell, because they feared he might hurt himself. But Roquebrune's accident was accompanied by great peals of laughter from the coaches. The coachmen stopped so they could get their fill of laughter and all the spectators let out a great hoot in the direction of Roquebrune, at the sound of which he fled into a nearby house, leaving the horse to fend for itself, which it did badly, as it trotted off in the direction of town. Ragotin, who was afraid he might have to pay for it, left the coach to go after it. The poet, who had covered up his posterior, climbed into one of the coaches, at once self-conscious and intrusive, poking people with the weapons that belonged to Ragotin, who had now experienced a third misfortune in front of his mistress, upon which we shall end the twentieth chapter.

CHAPTER XXI

Which May Not Be Found Very Entertaining

THE ACTORS WERE MADE to feel welcome by their host, who was an *honnête homme,** one of the most respected in the area. They were given two rooms in which to store their clothing and prepare themselves for the play, which was postponed until evening. They were served lunch together, and afterwards those who wanted to go for a walk could choose from beautiful gardens and ample woods. A young counsellor of the Rennes parliament, a close relative of the host, accosted our actors and stopped to converse with them, having noticed that Destiny had wit and that the actresses, besides being quite beautiful, had more to say than memorized lines. The conversation concerned things which conversations with actors usually do: plays and those who write them. The young counsellor said that the known subjects about which it is possible to make plays that respect the rules had all been covered, that history had been exhausted, and that ultimately the twenty-four-hour rule would have to be ignored, that the people and most of society didn't know what the strict rules governing theatre were good for, that it was more enjoyable to see actions take place on stage than to hear descriptions of them, and that, this being the case, successful plays could be written without being extravagant like the Spanish or tortured by the rigour of Aristotle's rules.* The conversation moved from theatre to novels. The counsellor said that nothing was more entertaining than certain modern novels; that only the French knew how to write good ones and that the Spanish had the secret of writing short stories they called novellas, which are far more instructive for us and within human reach than those imaginary heroes of Antiquity, who are sometimes annoying by virtue of being too perfect; and finally, that examples which are capable of being imitated were at least as useful as those that are almost impossible to imagine. He concluded that, were novellas written in France which were as good as some of Miguel de Cervantes's, they would be as popular as heroic novels. Roquebrune didn't agree. He said with absolute conviction that there was no pleasure to be derived from reading novels if they weren't made up of the adventures of lords, and of powerful lords at that. For that reason, he had found only parts of L'Astrée appealing. "And in which histories will we find enough kings and emperors to write your new novels?" the counsellor replied. "They should be written," said Roquebrune, "like those completely imagined novels that have no basis in history."

"I can tell," answered the counsellor, "that Don Quixote isn't your cup of tea."

"It is the silliest book I've ever seen," Roquebrune continued, "although it appeals to many discerning people."

"Take care," said Destiny, "that it doesn't displease you through your fault rather than his." Roquebrune would have come up with a retort if he had heard what Destiny said, but he was busy recounting his exploits to several ladies who had approached the actresses. He promised to write no less than a novel in five parts, each one with ten volumes, which would surpass Cassandre, Cléopâtre, Polexandre and Cyrus, even though the latter's nickname is Great, just as the son of Pippin's.*

Meanwhile, the counsellor was telling Destiny and the actresses that he had tried to write novellas in the Spanish style, and that he wanted to show them a few. Inezilla spoke up and said, in French that owed more to Gascon than Spanish, that in the court of Spain her first husband had the reputation of being a good writer, that he had written many novellas which were well received and that she still had some in handwritten manuscript form that would be successful in French if they were well translated. The counsellor was very curious about this kind of book. He told the Spanish lady he would be very happy if she would allow him to read them, which she graciously agreed to. "And," she added, "I even think I'm as expert in this as anyone. Since several women of our nation do write them, as well as poems, I've tried my hand at it, and can also show you some of my own." As was his custom, Roquebrune boldly offered his services as a translator. Inezilla, who might have been the cleverest Spanish woman ever to cross the Pyrenees into France, replied that it wasn't enough to be well acquainted with French, that one also had to know Spanish, and that she would have no problem giving him her novellas to translate once she had learnt enough French to judge whether he was capable of translating them. Grudge, who hadn't yet spoken, said that it shouldn't be open to doubt, since Roquebrune had been a proofreader. No sooner had he uttered these words than he remembered that Roquebrune had lent him money. He didn't give him his customary push, seeing how the poet was already befuddled by what he had said and admitting with great confusion that, although he really had corrected proofs for printers, they had only been those of his own works. Mademoiselle Star then said to Doña Inezilla that, since she knew so many tales, she would often pester her to tell some. The Spanish lady offered to tell one right away. She was taken at her word. Everyone took a seat around her, and she began a story, not in the words used in the next chapter, but intelligibly enough to show she possessed a great deal of wit in Spanish, since she showed quite a bit in a language of which she did not know the subtleties.

CHAPTER XXII

Every Rogue Has His Match

I N THE ABSENCE OF HER BROTHER, who was a cavalry captain in the Netherlands, a young lady from Toledo, named Victoria, from the ancient house of Portocarrero, had retired to a house she owned on the banks of the Tagus, a half-league from Toledo. She had remained the widow, at seventeen, of an old gentleman who became wealthy in the Indies and who, after becoming lost at sea six months after his wedding, had left his wife a substantial inheritance. Since the death of her husband, this beautiful widow had moved in with her brother, and had led a life that earned everyone's approval, to the extent that at the age of twenty, mothers held her up as an example for their daughters, husbands for their wives and would-be lovers as a challenge for themselves, as a conquest worthy of their merit. While her retirement had cooled off several suitors, it had increased the esteem in which she was held by society. She freely enjoyed the pleasures of the countryside in her rustic home, when one morning her shepherds brought her two men they had found stripped of all their clothes and tied to trees, where they had spent the night. Each one had been given a mean shepherd's cape to wear and it was in these handsome outfits that they appeared before the beautiful Victoria. The cheapness of the costume could not hide the rich bearing of the youngest, who complimented her in gentlemanly fashion and told her he was a gentleman from Cordoba named Don López de Góngora, that he was on his way from Seville to Madrid on important business, and that having taken a break to gamble at a half-day's distance from Toledo, where he had lunched the previous day, nightfall had caught them by surprise, and both he and his valet had fallen asleep while waiting for a mule driver who had stayed behind. Thieves had then found them while they slept, and had tied them to a tree, after having stripped them down to their underwear. Victoria didn't doubt he was telling the truth; his demeanour spoke in his favour, and the generous thing to do was to help a stranger in such unfortunate circumstances. It so happened that, among the clothes her brother had left behind there were several outfits, for Spaniards never throw away their old clothes when they acquire new ones. The most handsome one that fit him best was chosen for the master, and the valet was dressed in the most suitable one for him. Lunchtime having arrived, this stranger whom Victoria invited to eat at her table seemed so attractive and conversed with so much wit that she thought her help couldn't ever be put to better use. They spent the rest of the day together and were so attracted to each other that that very night they slept less than they usually did. The stranger wanted to send his valet to Madrid to pick up some money and have some suits made, or at least he pretended to. The beautiful widow wouldn't hear of it, and promised to give him some to finish his trip. That same day she listened to his talk of love. Finally, after two weeks, the convenience of the location, the equal merit of the two young people, many oaths on one side and too much frankness and credulity on the other, a promise of marriage made and reciprocal pledges given in the presence of an old gentleman butler and a lady-in-waiting made her commit a fault of which she would never have been thought capable, and put this lucky stranger in possession of the most beautiful lady in Toledo. For eight days in a row there was nothing but fire and flames between the young lovers. When they had to separate, there were only tears. Victoria had every right to make him stay. But the stranger explained that he was neglecting very important business in favour of her love, that winning her heart was making him lose a lawsuit in Madrid and hurting his standing at the royal court. Victoria was the first to hasten his departure. She didn't love him so blindly as to prefer the pleasure of being with him to his advancement. She had suits of clothes made in Toledo for him and his valet, and gave him as much money as he wanted. He left for Madrid, seated on a good mule with his valet on another. The poor lady was truly overcome with sadness when he left, and if he wasn't deeply affected, he pretended to be with the greatest hypocrisy. The very day of his departure, a maid cleaning the room where he had slept found a portrait box wrapped in a letter. She brought the whole package to her mistress, who saw in the box a perfectly lovely young face, and read in the letter these words, or others to this effect.

Monsieur my cousin,
I enclose the portrait of the beautiful Elvira de Silva. When you see her you will find her even more beautiful than the painting. Her father, Don Pedro de Silva impatiently awaits your arrival. The terms of your marriage are as you wished and are most advantageous, or so it seems to me. All this is reason for you to hurry your voyage.
> *Don Antonio de Ribera*
>> *From Madrid, etc.*

The letter was addressed to Fernando de Ribera, Seville. I invite you to imagine Victoria's shock when she read this letter, which gave every appearance of being intended for her López de Góngora. She realized, too late, that this stranger she had so greatly and so quickly obliged had disguised his name and, by this disguise, she could be certain of his infidelity. The beauty of the lady in the portrait was no less painful, and this marriage, of which the terms were already set, really drove her to despair. Never has anyone been in such distress. She felt like her sighs would suffocate her and cried so much it gave her a headache. "What a miserable creature I am!" she would sometimes tell herself, her old usher and lady-in-waiting, who had witnessed her marriage. "Have I been good for so long only to commit an irreparable fault, and did I need to resist so many persons of quality among my acquaintances who would have been happy to possess me, only to give myself to a stranger who might be mocking me after having made me unhappy for the rest of my life? What will they say in Toledo? And what will they say in the whole of Spain? Will a cowardly and deceitful young man ever be discreet? Did I have to tell him

I loved him before I knew whether he loved me? Would he have concealed his name if he had been sincere, and should I now expect him to hide the advantage he has over me? What won't my brother do to me, after what I've done to myself, and what good to him are the honours he is acquiring in Flanders if I dishonour him in Spain? No, no, Victoria. I have to be ready for anything since I let go of everything. But before proceeding to revenge and extreme remedies, I must try to regain through skill what I lost through carelessness. I'll still be able to sacrifice myself if all hope is lost."

Victoria was very tough-minded to be able to make a good resolution quickly in such a bad situation. Her old butler and lady-in-waiting wanted to give her advice. She told them she knew very well what they could say to her, but that the time had come to take action. That very day a cart and a wagon were loaded with furniture and tapestries and, Victoria having spread the news among her servants that she had to go to court to tend to urgent business on her brother's behalf, she entered a coach with her butler and her lady-in-waiting, and took the road to Madrid, followed by her luggage. As soon as she arrived, she found out where Don Pedro de Silva lived, and rented a place in the same neighbourhood. Her old butler was named Rodrigo Santillane. As a young man he had been supported by Victoria's father and loved his mistress as if she were his own daughter. Having many friends and acquaintances in Madrid, where he had spent his youth, it didn't take him long to learn that Pedro de Silva's daughter was marrying a gentleman from Seville, named Fernando de Ribera, that one of his cousins by the same name had arranged this marriage and that Don Pedro was already thinking about the people he would provide for his daughter. The very next day, Rodrigo Santillane, elegantly clad, Victoria, dressed like a widow of modest means, and Beatrix, her lady-in-waiting, playing the part of the mother-in-law, Rodrigo's wife, went to Don Pedro's and asked to speak to him. Don Pedro received them very politely and Rodrigo told him, with great self-confidence, that he was a poor gentleman from the mountains of Toledo, that he had an only child, a daughter from his first wife,

Victoria, whose husband had recently died in Seville where he lived, and that seeing his daughter widowed with limited means, he had brought her to court to find her a position. That was where he heard that Don Pedro was ready to marry his daughter, and thought he would be pleased to be offered a young widow, very well suited to serve as the new bride's *dueña*. He added that his daughter's merit emboldened him to offer her, and that Don Pedro would be at least as satisfied with her as he may already be with her demeanour. Before going any further, I should inform those who don't already know it that Spanish ladies have *dueñas* at their side. These *dueñas* are more or less like our governesses or ladies of honour attached to women of quality. I should also tell you that these *dueñas* are strict and inflexible creatures, at least as dreaded as stepmothers. Rodrigo played his part so well, and Victoria, beautiful as she was, seemed in her simple clothes so appealing and so promising that he hired her on the spot for his daughter. He even offered Rodrigo and his wife a position in his household. Rodrigo told him he was unable to accept this honour for several reasons but, since he lived in the same neighbourhood, he would be at his service whenever he was needed.

So Victoria lived in Don Pedro's house. He and his daughter Elvira liked her very much. All the valets coveted her. Don Antonio de Ribera, who had arranged his unfaithful cousin's marriage to Pedro de Silva's daughter, often visited to tell him that his cousin was on the way, and that he had written when he left Seville. Yet this cousin kept not arriving, which upset him. Don Pedro and his daughter didn't know what to think, and Victoria was even more concerned. Don Fernando wasn't about to return quickly. The very day he left Victoria's, God punished him for his perfidy. As he arrived in Illescas, a dog suddenly ran out of a house, startling his mule, which then crushed his leg against a wall and threw him to the ground. Don Fernando dislocated his hip and was in such pain after his fall that he couldn't continue his trip. He spent seven or eight days in the hands of the local doctors and surgeons, who weren't among the best, and as his condition worsened by the day, he alerted his cousin and asked him to send a litter. Everyone was distressed by his fall, but relieved to know what had become of him. Victoria, who still loved him, was very worried. Don Antonio sent for Don Fernando. He was brought to Madrid where, while clothes were made for him and his retinue, which was imposing (for he was beloved by his family and very rich), the Madrid surgeons, who were more skilful than those of Illescas, healed him completely. Don Pedro de Silva and his daughter Elvira were informed of the day Don Antonio de Ribera would bring them his cousin Don Fernando. It is likely young Elvira did not neglect herself and that Victoria was not impassive. She watched her unfaithful lover enter, adorned like a newly-wed, and, while he had appealed to her dishevelled and badly dressed, in his wedding clothes she thought he was the best-looking man she had ever seen. Don Pedro was equally satisfied, and his daughter would have been demanding indeed, had she found anything about him to object to. All the servants looked at their mistress's fiancé with wide eyes, and everyone in attendance felt joy in their hearts, except Victoria, whose heart was in her throat. Don Fernando was charmed by Elvira's beauty and admitted to his cousin that she was even more beautiful than her portrait. His compliments were those of a sensible man, and as he spoke to her and her father, he avoided as much as possible the silly clichés a man who is asking to be married typically says to a father-in-law and a fiancée. Don Pedro de Silva shut himself in his study with the two cousins and a lawyer to add something that was missing to the terms. Meanwhile Elvira remained in the room, surrounded by all her ladies, who were thrilled by her fiancé's good looks. Only Victoria remained calm and serious amidst the others' excitement. Elvira noticed this and took her aside to tell her she was surprised she had nothing to say about the happy choice her father had made of a son-in-law who seemed to have so much merit, adding that, out of flattery or politeness she should at least say something. "Madame," said Victoria, "what can be seen of your intended is so obviously flattering to him that I do not need to praise it. The reserve you've noticed does not come from indifference, and I would be unworthy of all your kindness if I didn't care about everything that concerns you. So, I would have been as delighted about your marriage as the others if I knew less about the man who is supposed to become your husband. Mine was from Seville and his house was not far from the house of your intended's father. He is from a noble family, he is rich and handsome, and I believe him to be intelligent. In short he is worthy of you. But you deserve a man's undivided affection and he won't be able to give you what he doesn't have. I would love not having to say things that may upset you, but I wouldn't be able to pay back the debt I owe you if I didn't tell you all I know about Don Fernando, when your future happiness is at stake." Elvira was shocked by what her governess said. She asked her not to wait any longer to shed some light on the doubts she had planted in her mind. Victoria said it couldn't be explained in front of her servants, or in few words. Elvira pretended to have some business in her bedroom, where Victoria told her, as soon as they were alone, that, in Seville, Fernando de Ribera was involved with a Lucretia de Monsalve, a lovely though poor damsel; that having promised to marry her, she had given him three children; that they had kept the affair secret during his father's lifetime; and that after his death, when Lucretia asked Fernando to keep his promise, he had cooled considerably; that she had complained to two gentlemen of her family; that it had caused a scandal in Seville; and that Don Fernando had left Seville for a time, heeding the advice of his friends, to escape Lucretia's relatives, who were looking for him everywhere in order to kill him. She added that the affair had reached that point when she left Seville, and that a rumour was circulating at the same time that Don Fernando was going to get married in Madrid. Elvira couldn't help but ask if this Lucretia was very beautiful. Victoria told her that she only lacked wealth, leaving Elvira to wonder and decide to tell her father right away what she had just learnt. Elvira left. Victoria was still in the anteroom when the same valet entered who had accompanied her unfaithful lover back when she had so generously welcomed him into her house near Toledo. This valet was bringing his master a packet of letters that the Seville post had given him. He was unable to recognize Victoria, who was disguised by her widow's hairdo. He asked her if he could speak to his master, so he could give him his letters. She told him he wouldn't be able to see his master for quite a while, but that if he wanted to give her the packet, she would see that it got to Don Fernando as soon as he was available. The valet didn't make a fuss and, having handed over the packet, went about his business. Victoria, who had thought of everything, went to her bedroom, opened the packet, and in no time closed it again, adding a letter to it she quickly wrote. Meanwhile the two cousins concluded their visit. Elvira saw Don Fernando's packet in the hands of her governess and asked her what it was. Victoria told her that Don Fernando's valet had given it to her to transmit to his master and that she was going to send for him because she wasn't there when he went out. Elvira told her that they didn't run any risk by opening it, and that it might contain something related to the affair she had just heard about. Victoria, who had just that in mind, opened it again. Elvira looked at all the letters, and didn't fail to stop at the one she saw written in a woman's hand, addressed to Fernando de Ribera, in Madrid. This is what she read:

Your absence and the news I have received that you were being married at court will soon cause you to lose someone who loves you more than life itself, if you do not return soon to prove her wrong and accomplish what you can no longer defer or refuse her without manifest indifference and treachery. If what they are saying about you is true and you are no longer concerned about me and our children, you should at least be concerned about your own life, that my cousins will cause you to lose, once you have left me no choice but to ask them, for you currently owe it only to my having asked them not to take it from you.

Lucretia de Monsalve

From Seville, etc.

After reading this letter, Elvira no longer questioned anything her governess had told her. She showed it to her father, who could not get over the idea that a gentleman of quality could be spineless enough to be unfaithful to a damsel who was his equal and with whom he had children. On the spot, he went to collect more information from a gentleman friend of his from Seville, who had informed him earlier about Don Fernando's fortune and activities. He had barely left when Don Fernando came to ask for his letters, followed by his valet, who had told him that his mistress's governess was keeping them for him. He found Elvira in the room and told her that, even though two visits were allowable given the terms they were on, he hadn't come so much to see her as to ask for the letters his valet had left with her governess. Elvira answered that she had taken them and was curious enough to open the packet, figuring that a man his age might have some romantic attachment in a big city like Seville and that, while her curiosity hadn't made her very happy, it had taught her that those who married without knowing one another beforehand were taking a great risk. She added that she didn't want to delay any longer the pleasure he took in reading his letters and, curtseying, left him without waiting for a reply. Don Fernando was quite surprised by what he heard his mistress say. He read the fake letter and saw there was an attempt to undermine his marriage. He spoke to Victoria, who was in the room, without paying much attention to her face, and said that some rival or evil person had forged the letter he had just read. "Me, a wife in Seville! And children!" He cried out in amazement. "If that isn't the most impudent sham ever, let them cut off my head!" Victoria told him that he might well be innocent, but that his mistress couldn't do otherwise than to make sure, and that surely the wedding wouldn't happen until Don Pedro consulted a gentleman from Seville, a friend of his who would be able to tell him whether this intrigue was real or invented. "This is what I desire," replied Don Fernando. "If there is a single lady in Seville with the name Lucretia de Monsalve, I no longer want to pass for a man of honour, and I beg you," he continued, "if you have some influence over Elvira, and I think you do, please tell me, so that I may urge you to put a word in on my behalf."

"Without boasting," replied Victoria, "I don't think she would do for someone else what she refused me, but I also know her temperament, and she isn't easily appeased when she thinks she has been wronged. And since my fortune is entirely dependent on her good will, I am not about to be found lacking in kindness towards her for having been found too kind to you, and risk being on bad terms with her by trying to rid her of the low opinion she has of your sincerity. I am poor," she added, "and for me, not winning means losing a lot. If what she promised me in order to remarry were to be missing, I would be a widow all my life, although, young as I am, I can still attract some man of distinction; but they say that, without money…"

She was going to launch into a long governess rant, because to do a good impersonation she had to talk a lot, but Don Fernando interrupted her to say, "Do me the favour I ask, and I will make it possible for you to do without your mistress's rewards. And to show you," he added, "that I want to give you more than words, bring me ink and paper and I'll write you a promissory note for whatever amount you want."

"Jesus! Monsieur!" exclaimed the fake governess. "A gentleman's word is sufficient, but, to please you, I'll go get the items you've requested." She returned with all that was needed to make a promise of a hundred million in gold, and Don Fernando was such a gallant man, or rather he so desired to possess Elvira, that he wrote his name on a blank piece of paper to compel her by this demonstration of trust to serve him with zeal. Victoria was on top of the world; she promised to accomplish miracles for Don Fernando and told him she wanted to be the most wretched creature if she didn't work on this affair as though it were her own. And she wasn't lying. Don Fernando left her, filled with hope, and Rodrigo Santillane, her butler, who passed for her father, having stopped by to learn how far along she was with her plan, she told him and showed him the signed blank paper, for which they both thanked God. He pointed out that everything seemed to be going her way. In order not to waste any time, he returned to his dwelling, which Victoria had rented near Don Pedro's, as I told you, and there he wrote, above Don Fernando's signature, a promise of marriage, signed by witnesses and dated during the time Victoria's unfaithful lover stayed at her country house. Rodrigo was as skilled at handwriting as anyone in Spain, and he copied Don Fernando's handwriting so well, using a poem he'd written for Victoria, that Don Fernando himself would have been fooled by it.

Don Pedro de Silva didn't find the gentleman he'd sought out for information regarding Don Fernando's marriage. He left his calling card and returned home, where that very evening Elvira confided in her governess and assured her she would disobey her father rather than ever marry Don Fernando, moreover confessing that she had long been engaged by affection to a Diego de Maradas; that in deference to her father she had stifled her inclination to please him; that since God had permitted Don Fernando's bad faith to be discovered, she thought that by spurning him she was obeying the will of God, who seemed to be choosing a different husband for her. You can well imagine that Victoria endorsed Elvira's resolutions and did not speak to her on behalf of Don Fernando. "Don Diego de Maradas," Elvira then told her, "is dissatisfied with me because I left him to obey my father, but I have only to favour him with a single look, and I am sure to make him come back, were he as distant from me as Don Fernando now is from his Lucretia."

"Write to him, Mademoiselle," said Victoria, "and I will deliver the letter." Elvira was overjoyed to find her governess in favour of her plans. She had the coach readied for Victoria, who climbed in with a *billet-doux* for Don Diego and, after having herself dropped off at her father Santillane's, she sent home her mistress's coach, telling the driver she felt like walking where she needed to go. Good old Santillane showed her the promise of marriage he had made, and she sat down to write two notes, one to Diego de Maradas, the other to Pedro de Silva, her mistress's father. These notes, signed *Victoria Portocarrero*, informed them of her address and invited them to join her regarding an affair of great importance to them. While the notes were delivered to their recipients, Victoria changed out of her widow's outfit and dressed elegantly, let out her hair, which I am told was exceptionally beautiful, and wore it like a lady of the court. Don Diego de Maradas arrived right after she had finished, curious to know why a woman he had never heard of wanted to see him. She received him most politely, and scarcely had he sat down next to her than she was informed that Pedro de Silva wished to see her. She invited Don Diego to hide in her alcove, assuring him that it was extremely important to him that he hear the conversation she was about to have with Don Pedro. He didn't resist the wishes of such a beautiful and elegant woman, and Don Pedro was ushered into Victoria's room. The elegance of her clothing, and her hairdo, which was so different from the way she wore her hair at his house, had improved her appearance and changed the look of her face to such an extent that he didn't recognize her. She steered Don Pedro to a seat from where Don Diego could hear everything she said to him, and spoke to him as follows: "I think, Monsieur, that you must first learn who I am, so that you are no longer kept impatient to know. I am from Toledo, from the house of Pontecorvo. I was married at sixteen and widowed six months after my wedding. My father wore the cross of Santiago and my brother belongs to the order of Calatrava." Don Pedro interrupted her to tell her that her father had been one of his closest friends. "What you are telling me makes me very happy," replied Victoria, "because I will need many friends in the affair that I want to talk to you about." She then told Don Pedro what had happened to her with Don Fernando, and provided him with the promise forged by Santillane. As soon as he read it she continued to speak, "You know, Monsieur, what honour requires a person of my quality to do. Even if I were to be denied justice, my relatives and friends have a great deal of influence, and are sufficiently wounded by this affair to serve my interests to the fullest. I thought, Monsieur, that I should warn you about my claim, so that you don't go through with Mademoiselle your daughter's marriage. She deserves more than an unfaithful man, and I think you are too wise to give her out of stubbornness a husband who could be disputed."

"Were he a prince of Spain," answered Don Pedro, "I wouldn't want him if he were unjust. Not only won't he marry my daughter, but I'll even forbid him from entering my house. For you, Madame, I offer whatever I have in the way of influence and friends. I was already warned that he was someone who would take his pleasure wherever he found it, even seek it at the expense of his reputation. Being that way, even though he wouldn't be yours, he would never belong to my daughter, who, God-willing, will find a husband in the court of Spain."

Don Pedro didn't stay any longer with Victoria, seeing that she had nothing more to tell him. Victoria called Don Diego to come out of his alcove, where he had been able to hear her entire conversation with his mistress's father, and so she didn't tell her story a second time. She handed him Elvira's letter, which delighted him and, because she would have been hard-pressed to tell him how she obtained it, she confided in him her metamorphosis into a *dueña*, knowing that it was as much in his interest as hers to keep it a secret. Before leaving Victoria, Don Diego wrote a letter to his mistress in which the joy of seeing his hopes resurrected allowed one to gauge the extent of the sadness he felt when he thought they had died. He took leave of the beautiful widow, who put on her governess outfit and went back to Don Pedro's.

Meanwhile, Don Fernando de Ribera had gone to his mistress's with his cousin Don Antonio, in order to try and repair the damage done by Victoria's forged letter. Don Pedro found them with his daughter, who was at a loss for words when, to justify Don Fernando, they seemed eager for a search to be conducted in Seville to see if a Lucretia de Monsalve had ever existed. To Don Pedro they repeated everything that could serve to exonerate Don Fernando. To which Don Pedro answered that, if the relationship with the lady from Seville was a fraud, it would be easy to expose, but that he had just met a lady from Toledo, named Victoria Portocarrero, whom Don Fernando had promised to wed and to whom he was even more indebted because she had generously helped him without knowing him; and that Don Fernando couldn't deny it because he had given her a promise written in his own hand. He added that a gentleman of honour shouldn't think about getting married in Madrid when he already was in Toledo. As he concluded, he showed the two cousins the promise of marriage. Don Antonio recognized his cousin's handwriting and Don Fernando himself, who was also fooled by it, even though he knew very well he'd never written it, became as befuddled as could be. The father and daughter withdrew after bidding them a rather frosty farewell. Don Antonio scolded his cousin for having used him in one matter when he had his mind on another. They climbed back into their coach, where Don Antonio, having made Don Fernando admit to his bad behaviour with Victoria, reproached him repeatedly for the darkness of his deed and pointed out the serious consequences it could have. He told him he should forget about getting married, not only in Madrid but in all of Spain, and that he should consider himself lucky if he got away with just wedding Victoria, without having to pay with his blood, if not his life, since Victoria's brother wasn't the kind of man to be content with an apology when his honour was at stake. Don Fernando was quiet while his cousin berated him. His conscience sufficed to convince him that he had misled and betrayed someone who had rescued him, while the promise was making him crazy, since he couldn't understand what spell had been cast to make him write it.

Victoria, having returned to Don Pedro's dressed as a widow, gave Don Diego's letter to Elvira, who told her that the two cousins had come to clear Don Fernando, but that it turned out there was something to hold against Don Fernando that surpassed his liaison with the lady from Seville. Elvira then related what Victoria knew better than Elvira, to which she reacted with amazement, bitterly condemning Don Fernando's reprehensible behaviour. That same day, Elvira was invited to see a play that was being performed at a relative's house. Victoria, with the Don Fernando matter still in mind, expressed the hope that if Elvira were willing, this play could help to advance her plans. She told her young mistress that if she wanted to see Don Diego, nothing could be easier; that her father Santillane's house was the most convenient place for such a meeting; and that since the play didn't begin until midnight, she could leave early and see Don Diego without arriving too late at her relative's. Elvira, who really did love Don Diego, and who had only consented to marry Don Fernando out of deference for her father, did not object to Victoria's proposal. They climbed into a coach as soon as Don Pedro went to bed, and got off at the home Victoria had rented. Santillane, as master of the house, showed them around, assisted by Beatrix, who pretended to be his wife, Victoria's stepmother. Elvira wrote a note to Don Diego which was delivered right away, and Victoria privately wrote one to Don Fernando, in Elvira's name, in which she informed him that it was up to him to make their marriage happen, that she believed him to be worthy, and that she didn't want to be made unhappy by being too compliant with her father's bad moods. In the same note she gave him directions to her house that were so detailed he couldn't fail to find it. The second note left some time after Elvira had written to Don Diego. Victoria wrote a third one that Santillane delivered directly to Pedro de Silva, through which she informed him, in her role as an upstanding and honourable govern-ess, that his daughter, instead of attending the play, had wilfully had herself driven to Santillane's home, that she had sent for Don Fernando in order to marry him and that, knowing full well he would never consent to this, she, Victoria, had thought she had better warn him and show him that he hadn't been mistaken in his high opinion of her when he chose her as Elvira's governess. Santillane, moreover, advised Don Pedro not to come without an *alguacil*, or what in Paris is called a *commissaire*.* Don Pedro, who was already in bed, had himself dressed hastily, the angriest man you can imagine. While he gets dressed and sends for a constable, let's see what is going on at Victoria's.

By good fortune the notes were received by the two lovers. Don Diego, who received his first, was the first to arrive at the rendezvous. Victoria met him and put him in a room with Elvira. I won't try to relate the tender words the young lovers exchanged. Don Fernando knocking at the door doesn't give me enough time. Victoria opened the door herself, after making it clear what a great favour she was doing him, for which the amorous gentleman thanked her profusely, promising her even more than he had already given. She led him into a room, where she asked him to wait for Elvira, who was about to arrive, and shut the door without giving him any light, telling him this was the way her mistress wanted it and that after they had spent a few moments together she was sure her mistress would let herself be seen, but concessions needed to be made to the modesty of a young lady of quality who, having undertaken such a bold act, would find it difficult to see, before anything is said, the one for whose love she was doing this. That done, Victoria, as quickly as possible, dressed very elegantly and adjusted her hair and make-up as much as the short time allowed. She entered the room where Don Fernando stood, without giving him the least suspicion she wasn't Elvira, being as young as her and wearing clothes and Spanish perfumes which would make the lowest scullery maid pass for a person of quality. Just then Don Pedro, the constable and Santillane arrived. They entered the room where Elvira was with her suitor. The young lovers were very surprised. Don Pedro was so blind with rage he was about to use his sword on the one he thought was Don Fernando. The constable, who recognized Don Diego, grabbed his arm, shouting that he should be more careful, that it wasn't Fernando de Ribera who was with his daughter but Don Diego de Maradas, a man his equal in quality and wealth. Don Pedro acted wisely and helped his daughter to her feet after she had fallen on her knees before him. He realized that if he hurt her by opposing her marriage he would be hurting himself, and that he couldn't have found a better match if he had chosen it himself. Santillane asked Don Pedro, the constable and all those who were in the room to follow him, and led them into the one where Don Fernando was closeted with Victoria. It was opened in the name of the King. Having opened it and seeing Don Pedro in the company of a constable, Don Fernando told them, with a great deal of self-confidence, that he was with his wife, Elvira de Silva. Don Pedro replied that he was mistaken, that his daughter was married to someone else, "As for you, you can no longer deny that Victoria Pontecarrero is your wife." Victoria proceeded to reveal her identity to her unfaithful lover, who could not have been more confounded. She reproached him for his ingratitude, to which he had no reply. He had even less to say when the constable told him that he had no other choice than to take him to prison. Finally, his remorse, the fear of going to prison, Victoria's tears, her beauty – which was not inferior to Elvira's – and, more than anything else, a remnant of generosity which had been conserved in Don Fernando's soul despite all the debauchery and recklessness of his youth, forced him to surrender to reason and to Victoria's merit. He kissed her tenderly. She thought she would faint in his arms, and it seems that Don Fernando's kisses played no small part in preventing this. Don Pedro, Don Diego and Elvira shared in Victoria's happiness, and Santillane and Beatrix thought they would die of joy. Don Pedro lauded Don Fernando for having mended his ways. The two young ladies embraced with such fervent expressions of friendship you would have thought they were kissing their lovers. Don Diego de Maradas reiterated pro-testations of obedience to his soon-to-be father-in-law. Before going home with his daughter, Don Pedro invited everyone to lunch at his house the following day, where, for two whole weeks, he wanted the festivities to make them forget the anxieties they had suffered. The constable was invited. He promised to come. Don Pedro gave him a ride home and Don Fernando remained with Victoria, who now had as much reason to be delighted as she previously had to be distressed.

CHAPTER XXIII

*An Unexpected Misfortune Which Caused
the Performance to Be Cancelled*

INEZILLA TOLD HER STORY with marvellous elegance and charm. Roquebrune was so pleased with it he took her hand and kissed it by force. She told him in Spanish that one tolerated everything from great lords and madmen, for which Grudge was silently grateful. The face of this Spanish woman was starting to fade, but beautiful remains were still visible and, had she been less beautiful, her wit would have made her preferable to a younger woman. All those who heard her story agreed that she had made it pleasing in a language she hadn't yet mastered, and in which she was sometimes forced to mix Italian and Spanish to make herself understood. Star told her that instead of excusing herself for having made her speak at such length, she expected thanks from her for giving her the opportunity to show off her wit. The remainder of the afternoon was spent in conversation. The gardens were filled, until dinner time, with ladies and the town's most notable citizens. They dined in the manner of Le Mans, which is to say exceptionally well, and everyone took a seat to watch the play. But Mademoiselle Cave and her daughter weren't there. They were sent for. They weren't heard from for a half-hour. Finally, there was a commotion outside the hall and almost at the same time poor Cave entered, dishevelled, her face bloodied and bruised, and yelling like a madwoman that her daughter had been abducted. Because of the sobs that were choking her, she had such a hard time speaking that it took quite a while to learn that unknown men had entered the garden by a back door while she was rehearsing her part with her daughter; that one of them had grabbed her, whose eyes she tried to tear out, seeing that the two others were taking her daughter; that the man who was responsible for the shape she was in left on horseback with his companions, one of whom held her daughter. She then said she had followed them for a long time, yelling "Thieves!" but since no one heard her she had come back to look for help. As she finished speaking, she began to cry so hard that everyone took pity on her. The entire audience was moved. Destiny got on a horse which Ragotin had just ridden from Le Mans (I don't know whether it was the same one that had thrown him earlier). Several young men in attendance took the first horses they could find and ran after Destiny, who was already far away. Grudge and Olive went on foot, following those who had gone on horseback. Roquebrune stayed with Star and Inezilla, who were consoling Cave as best they could. He was criticized for not following his companions. Some thought it was out of cowardice, others who were more indulgent said it wasn't a bad idea to stay with the ladies. Meanwhile, those who remained were reduced to dancing to their own singing, since the host hadn't hired violins on account of the play. Poor Cave felt so bad she needed to lie down on one of the beds in the room in which the actors kept their costumes. Star took care of her as if she were her own mother, and Inezilla made herself most helpful. Cave asked to be left alone and Roquebrune led the two ladies into the room where the company was.

They had hardly got there when a servant came to tell Star that Cave was asking for her. She told the Spanish lady and the poet she would return, and then went to see her friend. In all likelihood, if Roquebrune were a clever man, he took advantage of the opportunity and declared his passion to the appealing Inezilla. Meanwhile, as soon as Cave saw Star, she asked her to close the door and come closer to the bed. When Star was close to her, the first thing Cave did was to cry as though she were just starting to and take her hands, which she wet with her tears while sobbing in the most pitiful way imaginable. Star wanted to console her by holding out the hope her daughter would soon be found, since so many people had gone after the abductors. "I hope she never comes back," answered Cave, as she cried even harder than before. "I hope she never comes back," she repeated, "and that I had only to regret her, but I have to condemn her. I have to hate her and rue the day I brought her into this world. Here," she said, showing Star a piece of paper, "see what an honest colleague you had, and read in this letter my death warrant and my daughter's infamy." Cave started to cry again, and Star read what you are going to read, if you bother to.

You must not doubt all I have told you about my lineage and my wealth, since it would not do for me to mislead through deception someone that I can only appeal to through my sincerity. It is in this manner, beautiful Angélique, that I may be worthy of you. Therefore do not postpone promising what I ask since you will only have to give it to me when you will no longer be able to doubt what I am.

As soon as she had finished reading this letter, Cave asked her if she recognized the handwriting. "Like my own," Star told her. "It's Léandre's, my brother's valet, who writes all our parts."

"He's the traitor who will cause my death," answered the poor actress. "See how well he goes about it," she added, giving Star another letter from the same Léandre. Here it is, word for word.

My happiness will depend on you if your resolution of two days ago still holds. My father's tenant, who lends me money, sent me one hundred pistoles and two good horses. It's more than we need to go to England, where, unless I am badly mistaken, a father who loves his only son more than life itself will agree to anything to make him return soon.

"Well, what do you have to say about your chum and your valet, about this girl I brought up so well and this young man whose wit and wisdom we all admired? What surprises me most is that we've never seen them speak to one another, and that my daughter's playful temperament would never have made anyone suspect she could fall in love like that, and yet she has, my dear Star, and so head over heels it resembles madness more than love. I caught her writing to her Léandre and using such passionate expressions I wouldn't believe it if I hadn't seen it. You've never heard her speak seriously? Oh, she sure speaks a different language in her letters and, if I hadn't torn up the one I took from her, you'd have to admit that at sixteen she is as knowledgeable as those who have grown old in *coquetterie*. I had brought her to the little wood where she was abducted in order to complain without witnesses that she wasn't repaying me well for all the pain I have endured for her. I'll tell you what I meant by that," she added, "and you'll see if there ever was a daughter more obligated to love her mother." Star didn't know what to say to these well-founded complaints, and it seemed the right thing to do to let such distress express itself. "But," Cave continued, "if he loves my daughter so much, why manhandle her mother? For his companion who grabbed me beat me cruelly and even continued long after I had stopped resisting. And if this godforsaken boy is so rich, why is he abducting my daughter like a thief?"

Cave went on for some time with her complaints and Star consoled her as best she could. The host stopped by to see how she was and to tell her that a coach was ready if she wanted to return to Le Mans. Cave asked him if he would mind her spending the night in his house, and he was glad to oblige her. Star stayed to keep her company and several ladies of Le Mans invited Inezilla into their coach, who didn't want to be separated from her husband for so long. Roquebrune, who decorously didn't dare leave the actresses, was quite upset about it, but in this life you don't get everything you want.

END OF THE FIRST PART

SECOND PART

CHAPTER I

Which Serves Only as an Introduction to the Others

THE SUN WAS PLUMB ABOVE our antipodes and only lent his sister enough light to find her way in a very dark night. Silence reigned over the earth, with the exception of those places where crickets, owls and serenade-givers are found. Yes, everything in nature was asleep or, at least, was supposed to be asleep, not counting a few poets whose brains were bedevilled by verses difficult to compose, a few unhappy lovers, those who are called *damned souls*, and all those animals, whether brute or endowed with reason, who, that night, had business to attend to. I don't need to tell you that Destiny was among those who weren't sleeping, as were Mademoiselle Angélique's abductors, whom he pursued as much as a horse could gallop when clouds often obscured the moon's feeble light. He felt a tender love for Cave, both because she was so nice and because she loved him in return, and her daughter was no less dear to him. Moreover, his Mademoiselle Star, having found it necessary to become an actress, could not have found among all the caravans of country actors two more virtuous actresses than those two. This isn't to say that there aren't any in that profession who aren't lacking in virtue. But according to society's opinion, which may be wrong, they are less encumbered by it than by make-up and old embroidery.

Our generous actor was therefore running after the abductors faster and with more animosity than the Lapiths ran after the Centaurs* with. At first he followed a long lane which led to the garden door through which Angélique had been abducted. After galloping for some time, he entered a sunken path, as most are in Maine. This path was full of ruts and stones, and even though there was a full moon, it was so dark Destiny could not make his horse go any faster than a walk. He was cursing the sorry path to himself when he felt some man or some devil jump onto his horse's croup and put his arms around his waist. Destiny was very frightened and his horse had such a scare it would have thrown him if the ghost who possessed him and was hugging him hadn't helped secure him in the saddle. His horse bolted as frightened horses do, and Destiny spurred him on, not knowing what he was doing, unhappy to feel two arms around his waist and against his cheek a cold face breathing to the cadences of the galloping horse. The ride was long because the path wasn't short. Finally, when they entered a prairie the horse moderated his impetuous pace, and Destiny his fear, because we eventually get used to the most unbearable pains. The moon was bright enough to show him he had a big naked man sitting behind him and an ugly face next to his. He didn't ask him who he was; I don't know whether out of discretion or not. He continued to make his winded horse gallop, when, against all hope, the naked stowaway let himself fall to the ground and began to laugh. Destiny urged his horse on even more and, looking back, saw his ghost running at full speed in the direction he had come from. Destiny has since confessed that you can't be more scared than he was. A hundred paces from there he found a highway that led to a hamlet where all the dogs were awake, which led him to believe that those he was pursuing might have passed through there. To shed some light on the situation, he did what he could to awaken the sleeping occupants of three or four houses that were on his path. He was unable to rouse anyone and succeeded only in infuriating their dogs. Finally, hearing children cry in the last house he found, he was able to get the door opened by means of threats and learnt from a woman in a smock, who trembled as she spoke, that troopers had passed through their village not long before, and that they were taking with them a woman who cried a lot and whom they were having a hard time keeping quiet. He told the same woman about the encounter he had with the naked man and she told him that he was a peasant from their village who had gone mad and who lived in the fields. What this woman told him about the horsemen passing through her hamlet gave him the courage to press on and to hurry his horse's pace. I won't tell you how many times it stumbled and was afraid of its own shadow. It's enough you know he got lost in the woods and that, sometimes unable to see a thing and sometimes lit by the moon, at daybreak he came upon a small farm where he thought it was time to let his horse feed, and here we shall leave him.

CHAPTER II

The Boots

WHILE DESTINY GROPED HIS WAY after Angélique's abductors, Grudge and Olive, who didn't take the abduction as much to heart, didn't chase after them as fast as he did; besides they were on foot. So they didn't get very far and, having found in the next town an inn that was still open, they asked to sleep there. They were put in a room where there was already a guest, noble or commoner, who had dined there and who, needing to tend to urgent business, the nature of which I never learnt, planned to leave at daybreak. The actors' arrival didn't fit into his plan to be on horseback at an early hour, because they woke him and maybe he cursed them silently, but the presence of two relatively respectable men might explain why he kept silent. Grudge, whose demeanour was sociable, began by apologizing for interrupting his sleep, then asked him where he was from. He told him he was from Anjou and that he was on his way to Normandy for a pressing matter. While Grudge was getting undressed and the sheets were being heated, he continued his questions, but since they were of no utility to either of them, and didn't suit the poor fellow who had been awakened, he asked to be allowed to sleep. Grudge apologized quite cordially and, at the same time, the love of self* causing him to forget to love his neighbour, he forged a plan to appropriate a new pair of boots that a servant boy had just delivered to the room after cleaning them. Olive, who felt like doing nothing other than sleep, threw himself on the bed and Grudge stayed next to the fire, not so much to watch the last of the wood that had been lit as to fulfil his noble ambition of acquiring a pair of brand-new boots at someone else's expense. When he thought the man he was going to rob was sound asleep, he took his boots, which were at the foot of his bed, and, having pulled them onto his bare feet, without forgetting to attach the spurs, he got in bed next to Olive. He must have been careful to stay on the edge of the bed, for fear that his armed legs might touch the bare legs of his comrade, who wouldn't have kept quiet about this novel way of sleeping between two sheets, and could have aborted his enterprise.

The rest of the night went by peacefully. Grudge slept or pretended to sleep. The roosters crowed, day came and the man who was sleeping in our actors' room had a fire lit and got dressed. Time came to put his boots on. A maid brought him Grudge's old boots, which he gruffly rejected; he was assured they were his; he got angry and made a diabolical fuss. The innkeeper entered the room and gave him his master cabaret-tender's word that there weren't any boots other than his, not only in the inn but in the whole village, as even the parson never went anywhere on horseback. Thereupon, he wanted to talk about his parson's good qualities and tell him how he got his parsonage and since when.

The innkeeper's chatter made him lose his patience. Grudge and Olive, who were awakened by the noise, learnt what was going on and Grudge exaggerated the importance of the case, telling the innkeeper that it was really bad. "I care about a pair of new boots about as much as I do a single clog," the poor bootless man was telling Grudge, "but what is at stake is a matter of great importance to a man of quality I care more about disappointing than my own father. And if I found the worst pair of boots for sale I would give more than the asking price." Grudge, who sat up in bed, shrugged his shoulders from time to time and didn't answer, feasting his eyes on the innkeeper and the maid, as they unsuccessfully looked for the boots, and on the wretch who lost them, who meanwhile cursed his existence and might have been planning something dire when Grudge, with unparalleled and atypical generosity, said out loud, while snuggling into bed like a man who is dying to go back to sleep, "*Morbleu*! Monsieur, don't make such a fuss about your boots and take mine, but only if you let us sleep, like you wanted me to let you yesterday." The wretched man, who no longer was one since he recovered a pair of boots, couldn't believe his ears. His awkward thanks amounted to a lot of gibberish expressed in such a passionate tone of voice Grudge feared he would end up climbing into his bed to embrace him. So he exclaimed angrily and swore learnedly, "Hey, *morbleu*! Monsieur, what a pain you are when you lose your boots and when you thank those who give them to you! For God's sake, take mine. I'm telling you again I'm not asking for anything in return except you letting us sleep, or give me back my boots and make as much of a racket as you want." He opened his mouth to reply, when Grudge cried out "Oh my God! Let me sleep or let me keep my boots!" The innkeeper, who had gained a lot of respect for Grudge because of his imperious way of speaking, pushed his guest out of the room, seeing him so grateful for a pair of boots generously given that he seemed bent on having the last word. He nevertheless had to leave the room and put on his boots in the kitchen, while Grudge drifted off to sleep more peacefully than he had at night, his ability to sleep being undermined no longer by the desire to steal the boots and the fear of being caught in the act. As for Olive, who had made better use of the night than Grudge, he rose early and ordered some wine, having nothing better to do for entertainment than to drink.

Grudge slept until eleven. As he was getting dressed, Ragotin entered the room. He had visited the actresses that morning and, having been reproached by Mademoiselle Star for not being one of her friends, since he wasn't among those who were chasing after her companion, he promised her not to return to Le Mans until he had some news of her; but he couldn't find a horse to rent or borrow, and he wouldn't have been able to keep his promise if his miller hadn't lent him a mule, which Ragotin rode without boots and arrived, as I just told you, in the town where the two actors had slept. Grudge had great presence of mind. No sooner did he see Ragotin wearing shoes than he thought luck was giving him a golden opportunity to hide his larceny; a problem he had not been able to solve. So, first he asked Ragotin to lend him his shoes and to be good enough to wear his boots, which were giving him a blister because they were new. Ragotin joyfully accepted the proposal because, while riding his mule, the tongue of the stirrup buckle had torn his stocking, making him regret he wasn't wearing boots.

The subject of lunch arose and Ragotin paid for the actors and his mule. Since his fall from the horse, when the carbine discharged between his legs, he swore never to ride again without exercising extreme caution. He used a leg up to climb onto his mount, but despite his precautions he had a very hard time getting onto the packsaddle. His impetuous nature didn't allow him to be judicious and he had mindlessly pulled up Grudge's boots, which came to his waist, making it impossible for him to bend his legs, which weren't the strongest in the province. Finally, Ragotin on his mule and the actors on foot, they followed the first path they encountered and, along the way, Ragotin revealed to the actors his plan to join them on stage, assuring them that although he was bound soon to become the greatest actor in France, he didn't intend to derive any income from his craft, that he wanted to do this only out of curiosity and to show that he was born to do anything he wanted to undertake. Grudge and Olive backed his noble wish, and by dint of praise and encouragement, put him in such a good mood that, seated on his mule, he began to recite verses from *Pyramus and Thisbe* by Théophile. Several peasants who accompanied a full cart along the same road thought he was preaching the word of God, seeing him declaim like a madman. While he recited, they bared their heads and respected him like an itinerant preacher.

CHAPTER III

Cave's Story

THE TWO ACTRESSES, whom we left in the house from which Angélique had been abducted, hadn't slept any more than Destiny. Mademoiselle Star had got into the same bed as Cave, so as not to leave her alone with her despair and try and persuade her not to be as devastated as she was. Finally, realizing that such justified affliction was not short of reasons with which to defend itself, she no longer tried to come up with her own. Instead, to create a diversion, she began to bemoan her own bad luck as strongly as her companion did hers, and thus adroitly got her to recount her adventures, all the more easily as Cave could not tolerate someone claiming to be more miserable than she was. So she wiped away her tears, which covered her face, and, starting with a deep sigh so as not to have to interrupt herself for some time, she began her story as follows:

"I was born an actress, daughter of an actor whom I never heard say he had relatives in any other profession. My mother was the daughter of a merchant from Marseilles, who gave her to my father in marriage to reward him for having risked his life to save hers, when she was attacked by an officer of the galleys who wanted her as much as she despised him. It was a stroke of luck for my father, who was given, without having asked, a beautiful young woman who was much wealthier than a country actor would expect to find. His father-in-law did what he could to make him leave the profession, pointing out that being a merchant was more honourable and profitable, but my mother, who loved the theatre, made him stay. He wouldn't have minded following his wife's father's advice, knowing better than she that life in the theatre is not as happy as it seems. My father left Marseilles shortly after his wedding, and took my mother, who was more impatient than he, on her first tour, and quickly taught her to become an excellent actress. She got pregnant during the first year of her marriage and gave birth to me behind the theatre. A year later I acquired a brother whom I loved dearly and who loved me too. Our company was made up of our family and three actors, one of whom was married to an actress who played supporting roles. One day we were passing through a town in the Périgord, during a holiday. My mother, the other actress and I were on the cart that carried our luggage, and our men escorted us on foot when our little caravan was attacked by seven or eight loutish men, so drunk that having decided to shoot a harquebus in the air to frighten us, I was covered in shot and my mother was wounded on the arm. They seized my father and two of his companions before they could defend themselves, and beat them cruelly. My brother and the youngest of the actors fled and, since that time, I haven't had any news of my brother. The townsfolk joined those who were visiting violence on us and made us turn around. They marched proudly and hurriedly, like people who have plundered a treasure and want to put it in a secure place, and they made such a racket they couldn't hear each other speak. After an hour's walk, they made us enter a castle where, as soon as we entered, we heard several people shouting with joy that the Gypsies had been captured. This made us aware that we had been mistaken for others, which gave us some consolation.

The mare that pulled our cart died of exhaustion after being driven too hard and beaten. The actress she belonged to, who rented her to the company, reacted with cries as heartrending as if she had seen her husband die. My mother fainted at the same time from the pain in her arm, and the cries I let out for her were even greater than the actress's for her mare. Our noise, and the noise of the brutes and drunkards who brought us, caused the lord of the castle to leave his quarters followed by four or five rather scary-looking musketeers or redcoats. He first wanted to know where the thieving Gypsies were, and gave us quite a fright; but seeing only blonds among us, he asked my father who he was and no sooner did he learn we were unfortunate actors than, with an impetuosity that amazed us, swearing more furiously than anyone I've ever heard and brandishing his sword, he charged the ones who had taken us. They fled at once, some wounded, the others quite frightened. He had my father and his companions untied and ordered that the women be given a room and our luggage stored in a safe place. Maids came in to serve us and made a bed for my mother, who was in pain from the wound on her arm. A man, who had the look of a butler, apologized to us on behalf of his master for what happened. He told us the rabble that had made such a grievous mistake were expelled and most of them beaten or maimed, that a surgeon in the next town was being sent for to bandage my mother's arm, and asked if anything had been taken from us. He suggested we check our luggage to see if anything was missing.

"At dinner time food was brought to our room; the surgeon who had been sent for arrived; my mother was bandaged and went to bed with a high fever. The following day the lord of the castle summoned the actors to appear before him. He asked after my mother's health and said he didn't want to let her leave until she was well. He was good enough to order a search of the area for my brother and the young actor who had run away. They were never found, and this increased my mother's fever. A doctor and a surgeon who were more experienced than the one who bandaged her the first time were brought in from a nearby town. As it turned out, we were treated so well we eventually forgot we had been treated badly.

"The gentleman at whose castle we were staying was very wealthy, more feared than loved in the area, as violent in all his actions as a governor of a frontier town and reputed to be as brave as it is possible to be. He was called the Baron de Sigognac; in those days he would have been a marquis at the very least and, at that time a petty tyrant of the Périgord. A group of Gypsies, who were living on his land, had stolen the horses from a stud farm he owned a league from his castle and his people, whom he sent after them, made an error at our expense, as I've already told you. My mother recovered fully, and my father and his companions, to show their gratitude for having been treated so well – to the extent that poor actors could – offered to put on a play in the castle if it would please the Baron de Sigognac. A big page, who was at least twenty-four years old and who was without a doubt the kingdom's senior page, along with some kind of gentleman-in-waiting, learnt the parts of my brother and the young actor who fled with him. The news spread throughout the region that a troupe of actors was going to stage a play at the Baron de Sigognac's. Many Périgordian nobles were invited, and when the page learnt his part, which was so difficult for him that it had to be cut and reduced to two verses, we performed *Roger et Bradamante* by Garnier.* The audience was resplendent, the hall well lit, the theatre very convenient and the set appropriate to the subject matter. We all tried to do our best and we succeeded. My mother looked as beautiful as an angel, armed like an Amazon and, as she was still a little pale from her sickness, her complexion was more radiant than all the lights of the hall. Although I have every reason to be very sad, I can't think about that day without laughing at the funny way the big page played his part. My bad mood shouldn't deprive you of something so amusing. Maybe you won't find it so, but I can tell you it made the audience laugh and that I've laughed about it since, either because it really is funny or because I'm one of those people who laugh easily. He played the part of the old Duke Aymond's page and only had two lines to recite in the whole play. This is when the old man gets terribly angry at his daughter Bradamante for not wanting to marry the Emperor's son, because she is in love with Roger. The page says to his master:

'Monsieur, let's go inside; in this great heat
You don't seem very steady on your feet.'

This big oaf of a page, even though his part was easy to remember, didn't fail to flub his lines and said, clumsily and trembling like a criminal:

'Monsieur, let's go inside; in this great heat
You don't seem very steady on your legs.'

The false rhyme surprised everyone. The actor in the role of Aymond burst out laughing, and could no longer play an angry old man. The entire audience laughed as well. I was sticking my head out through the opening in the backdrop in order to see and be seen, when I thought I would fall down laughing. The lord of the castle, who was one of those melancholiacs who rarely laugh and never laugh without a good reason, found so much to laugh about in his page's memory lapse and in his bad way of declaiming verses that he thought he would burst if he continued to force himself to retain a little gravity. But he eventually had to laugh as much as everyone else and his servants had to admit they had never seen him laugh as much. Since he had acquired great authority in the region there was no one in the audience who did not laugh at least as much or more than he did, either willingly or obsequiously."

"I fear," added Cave, "that I've done like those who say: I'm going to tell you a story that will have you holding your sides, and then don't keep their word, because I admit I've built up my page story too much."

"No," Star replied, "I found it to be just as you had led me to expect. It is true that it may have seemed funnier to those who witnessed it than to those who hear it narrated; the page's flub contributes a lot to making it so. Also, the time, the place and the natural inclination we have to join in with other people's laughter may have given it advantages it can no longer enjoy."

Cave made no more excuses for her tale and picked up where she had left off: "After all the actors and spectators had laughed as much as their ability to laugh would allow, the Baron de Sigognac wanted his page to return to the stage to correct his mistake, or rather to make the audience laugh some more. But the page, who was the biggest dolt I've ever seen, wanted no part of it, no matter what one of the most brutal masters imaginable ordered. He took it about as well as he was capable of taking it, which was very badly. His displeasure, which would have been very slight had he been reasonable, ended up causing the greatest misfortune that could have befallen us. Our play was applauded by the entire audience. The farce was even more entertaining than the play, as it usually is anywhere besides Paris. The Baron de Solignac and the gentlemen who were his neighbours enjoyed it so much they wanted us to perform again. Each gentleman chipped in for the actors, according to his generosity. The baron made the first contribution, to set an example for the others, and the play was scheduled for the next holiday. We performed for a month in front of this Périgordian nobility, commissioned as a gift by men and women alike. The troupe even benefited from some slightly used clothes. The Baron had us eat at his table, where we were fussed over by the servants who often told us they were indebted to us for the good mood of their master, who seemed to them a changed man since he had been humanized by the theatre. The page alone viewed us as those who had ruined his reputation and the verse he mangled, which everyone in the castle, down to the least kitchen boy, recited back to him on every occasion, was like a dagger to his heart that he swore to avenge on some member of our troupe. One day when the Baron de Sigognac had gathered together his neighbours and peasants to rid his woods of a great number of wolves who lived there and menaced the countryside, my father and his companions each carried a harquebus, as did the Baron's servants. The nasty page was armed as well and, thinking he had found the perfect opportunity to carry out his evil plan, he no sooner saw my father and his companions separated from the others, reloading their harquebuses and passing powder and lead back and forth, than he shot his from behind a tree and pierced my poor father with two bullets. His companions, who were busy holding him up, didn't think at first to go after the murderer, who got away and has since fled the country. Two days later my father died of his wounds. My mother almost died of grief, fell ill again, and I was as upset as a girl my age could be. As my mother's illness lingered, our troupe's actors and actresses took their leave of the Baron de Sigognac and went elsewhere to find another company to join. My mother was sick for more than two months until she finally got well, after receiving from the Baron de Sigognac expressions of generosity and kindness that weren't in keeping with the reputation he had in the region of being the greatest tyrant who ever inspired fear in a land where most of the gentlemen try to do so. His valets, who had always known him to be without humanity and without civility, were surprised to see him be so obliging toward us. He was thought to be in love with my mother, but he almost never spoke to her and never came into our room, where he had our meals served to us ever since my father's death. It is true that he often sent for news of us. The local gossips were kept busy, as we later learnt. But my mother, who could not decently remain in the castle of a man of such quality, had already thought about leaving, and had decided to retire to Marseilles, near her father. She informed the Baron de Solignac of this, thanked him for his kindness, and asked him to add to all the obligations she already had to him that of providing her and me with mounts until I forget which town, and a cart to carry our baggage that she wanted to sell to the first merchant she came across, no matter how little he would pay for it. The Baron seemed quite surprised by my mother's request, and she was more than a little surprised at not being able to get him to agree to it or turn it down.

"The next day, the parson of one of his parishes came to see us in our room. He was accompanied by his niece, a nice, pleasant girl who had become my friend. We left her uncle and my mother together and went for a walk on the castle grounds. The parson spent a long time in conversation with my mother and only left at dinner time. I found her quite preoccupied. I asked her two or three times what was wrong without getting an answer. I saw her cry and I started to cry too. Finally, after making me close the door to our room, she told me, crying even harder than before, that the parson informed her the Baron de Solignac was head over heels in love with her and moreover assured him he held her in such high esteem he had never dared tell her or have her be told he loved her and wanted to marry her. As she finished speaking, her sighs and sobs seemed like they would suffocate her. I asked her again what was the matter. 'My girl!' she said. 'Haven't I told you enough for you to understand that I couldn't be more miserable?' I told her it wasn't such a misfortune for an actress to become a woman of quality. 'Ah, poor little girl,' she said to me, 'how you do speak like a young inexperienced girl! If he's deceiving the good old parson in order to deceive me,' she added. 'If he doesn't plan to marry me like he wants me to believe, shouldn't I fear a man who is entirely a slave to his passions? And if he truly wants to marry me and I accept, who in the whole world will be as miserable as me once he gets over his whim? And how much will he hate me if one day he repents having loved me? No, no, my daughter, it isn't good fortune that has come knocking, like you think, but a horrible misfortune which, after having taken from me a husband I loved and who loved me, wants to force one on me who, maybe, will hate me and force me to hate him.' Her distress, which seemed unfounded to me, increased so much she thought she would suffocate while I helped her get undressed. I consoled her as best I could and, to combat her despair, I used all the arguments of which a girl my age was capable. I didn't neglect to tell her that the respectful and obliging manners this least civil of men had always shown us seemed like a good omen to me, and especially the lack of boldness he showed when declaring his passion to a woman in a profession that does not always inspire respect. My mother let me say anything I wanted, went to bed very upset and tossed and turned all night instead of sleeping. I tried to resist sleeping, but I had to give in and I slept as much as she slept little. She got up early, and when I woke up, I found her dressed and quite calm. I was anxious to know what decision she had made because, to tell the truth, I flattered my imagination with the future grandeur I hoped to see my mother achieve if the Baron de Sigognac was expressing his true feelings and if my mother could limit her own to giving him what he wanted from her. The idea of hearing my mother called Madame Baroness happily occupied my mind and ambition gradually began to take over my young brain."

Cave was telling her story and Star was listening to her attentively, when they heard the sound of footsteps in their room, which seemed all the stranger since they both remembered very well having locked the door shut. Yet they continued to hear someone walking. They asked who was there. No one answered. A moment later Cave saw, at the foot of the bed, which was open, the shape of someone she heard sigh and who, leaning against the foot of the bed, pressed against her feet. She sat up to try and see what was beginning to frighten her and, resolved to speak to him or her, she poked her head into the room, but saw nothing. The least company is sometimes reassuring, but sometimes also fear is not diminished by being shared. Cave was scared by not seeing anything and Star was scared that Cave was scared. They sank into their bed, pulled the covers over their heads and held on to each other, being very frightened and almost not daring to speak. Finally, Cave told Star that her poor little girl was dead and that it was her soul that had come to sigh beside her. Star might have been going to reply when they again heard someone walking in the room. Star sank even farther into the bed than before and Cave, emboldened by her idea that it was her daughter's soul, sat up in bed again as she had before and, once again seeing the same shape which sighed again and pressed against her feet, she extended her hand and touched an extremely hairy one that made her let out a horrifying shriek and fall backwards on the bed. At the same moment they heard barking in their room, like when a dog is scared of what it encounters in the night. Cave was bold enough to look at what it was and then she saw a big greyhound barking at her. She threatened it in a loud voice and it ran away barking towards a corner of the room where it disappeared. The brave actress got out of bed and, in the moonlight, she discovered in the corner of the room, where the phantom greyhound had disappeared, a little door to a little hidden stairway. It was then easy to understand that the family greyhound had used it to enter the room. He wanted to sleep on their bed but, not daring to do so without the consent of the occupants, he let out a dog sigh and put his front legs on the bed, which was high on its own legs, as all old-fashioned beds are, and hid underneath it when Cave stuck her head out into the room the first time. She didn't immediately disabuse Star of her belief that it was a spirit, and spent a long time making her understand that it was a greyhound. As distressed as Cave was, she made fun of her companion's cowardice and postponed the end of her story to some other time when sleep wouldn't be as necessary as it was then. Day was starting to break. They fell asleep and awoke around ten, when they were informed that the coach that was supposed to take them to Le Mans was ready to leave whenever they were.

CHAPTER IV

Destiny Finds Léandre

MEANWHILE, DESTINY WAS GOING from village to village, trying without success to gather information that would help him find what he was looking for. He covered a lot of ground, and only stopped around two or three, when his hunger and his horse's fatigue made him return to a big village he'd just left. There he found a decent inn, because it was on the highway, and didn't forget to ask if anyone had heard of a gang of riders who had abducted a woman. "There is a gentleman upstairs who has," said the village surgeon, who happened to be there. "I think," he added, "he had some quarrel with them and they roughed him up. I just applied an anodyne and resolutive cataplasm on a livid tumour he has on the neck vertebrae, and dressed a large wound he received on the occiput. I wanted to bleed him, because his body is covered with contusions, but he didn't want me to; he certainly needs it. He must have taken a nasty fall and been badly beaten." This village surgeon so enjoyed using the terminology of his art that even though Destiny had left and no one was listening to him, he went on for a long time with the speech he had started until someone fetched him to bleed a woman who was dying of a stroke.

Meanwhile, Destiny headed towards the room of the man the surgeon treated. There he found a well-dressed young man with a bandaged head, who was resting on a bed. Destiny wanted to excuse himself for having entered his room before knowing whether he was welcome, but the first words were scarcely out of his mouth when the young man got up from the bed and came over to embrace him. It was his valet Léandre, who had left him four or five days earlier without saying goodbye and whom Cave believed was her daughter's abductor. Destiny did not know how to address him, as he looked like a gentleman in both dress and mien. While Destiny examined him, Léandre regained his composure, because he was quite disconcerted at first. "I am very embarrassed," he told Destiny, "that I wasn't as honest with you as I should have been, since I hold you in such high esteem; but I hope you'll excuse an inexperienced young man who, before getting to know you well, assumed you were like others in your profession and didn't dare confide a secret on which his happiness depends." Destiny told him that he could only know from Léandre how he hadn't been as honest as he should. "I have many more things to tell you if you don't maybe already know them," Léandre answered, "but first I need to know what brings you here." Destiny related how Angélique was abducted. He told him he'd been pursuing her abductors and that when he entered the inn he learnt Léandre had found them and could give him news of them. "It's true I found them," Léandre sighed, "and I fared as well against them as an outnumbered man could; but my sword having broken off in the body of the first man I wounded, I was unable to serve Mademoiselle Angélique in any way or die serving her, committed though I was to one or the other eventuality. They put me in the state in which you see me now. I was knocked out by a back stroke to the head. They thought I was dead and left in a hurry. That's all I know about Mademoiselle Angélique. I'm waiting here for a valet who'll have more information. He followed them from a distance after helping me recover my horse, which they probably left behind because it isn't worth much." Destiny asked him why he had left so abruptly, where he was from and who he was, there being no longer any doubt in his mind that Léandre had concealed his name and his quality. He admitted that Destiny was on to something, and having lain back down because the blows he'd received had left him in considerable pain, Léandre told him, Destiny sitting at the foot of the bed, what you are going to read in the next chapter.

CHAPTER V

Léandre's Story

"I'M A GENTLEMAN FROM A FAMILY that is quite well known in the province. I hope one day to inherit at least twelve thousand pounds per annum if my father ever dies, because although he has, for eighty years, driven everyone crazy who is a dependant of his or who has done business with him, he is in such good health that

I have more reason to fear that he will never die than I do to hope that I will one day succeed him as the owner of the three beautiful estates that make up his fortune. He wants me to be a counsellor at the parliament of Brittany, even though I have no interest in this. That is why he started my education early. I was a student at La Flèche when your troupe played there. I saw Mademoiselle Angélique and fell in love with her to the point that I couldn't do anything else but love her. I did far more. I was bold enough to tell her I loved her, and she didn't take offence. I wrote to her. She received my letter, and her expression did not betray displeasure. From then on an illness that confined Mademoiselle Cave to her room, while you were at La Flèche, made the conversations her daughter and I had much easier. She would probably have prevented them, so strict is she despite belonging to a profession which is supposed to dispense those who practise it from scruples and severity. Since I fell in love with her daughter, I stopped attending school, but I didn't miss a single performance of the troupe. The Jesuit fathers wanted me to do my duty, but I no longer wanted to obey those unpleasant masters after choosing the most charming mistress imaginable. Your valet was killed at the door of the theatre by Breton students, who were very disorderly in La Flèche that year, because they were in a large group and wine was cheap. This was partly why you left La Flèche for Angers. I wasn't able to say goodbye to Mademoiselle Angélique, since her mother didn't let her out of her sight. All I could do was appear before her as she was leaving, in tears, with my face expressing despair. A sad look in my direction almost killed me. I locked myself in my room. I cried the rest of the day and all night, and that very morning, changing my clothes for those of my valet, who was my size, I left him at La Flèche to sell my school supplies, with a letter for one of my father's farmers who gives me money when I ask, and instructions to meet up with me in Angers. I went there after you and caught up with you at Duretail, where several persons of quality who were running the hounds kept you for about a week. I offered you my services and you took me as your valet, either because you were tired of not having one, or because my mien and my face, which you did not find unpleasant, compelled you to hire me. My hair, which I had cut very short, made me unrecognizable to those who had often seen me with Mademoiselle Angélique; besides, the ugly valet outfit, which I wore as a disguise, made me look very different from how I looked in my own, which was better than what students usually wear. Mademoiselle Angélique recognized me immediately, and has since admitted she didn't doubt my passion for her was very intense, because I had left everything to follow her. She was generous enough to try to dissuade me and help me recover my reason, which she could see I'd lost. For a long time she made me endure rigours that would have cooled off anyone less in love than I was. Finally, by dint of loving her, she began to love me as much as I loved her. Since you have the soul of a person of quality, and a particularly beautiful one to boot, you soon recognized that mine wasn't the soul of a valet. I was in your good graces and I earned the approval of the entire troupe; even Grudge didn't despise me, he who is reputed to like no one and hate everyone.

"I won't waste your time repeating everything two young people in love say every time they see each other. You already know it from experience. I'll just tell you that Mademoiselle Cave, suspecting our communication, or rather having no doubts about it, forbade her daughter to speak to me. She disobeyed her mother, who caught her writing to me and treated her so cruelly both in public and in private that it was easy for me to persuade her to have herself abducted. I'm not afraid to admit it to you, knowing that you are as generous as can be and at least as much in love as I am." Destiny blushed at the last words uttered by Léandre, who continued his narrative, telling Destiny that he had only left the company in order to be able to carry out his plan: one of his father's farmers had promised to give him money and he was hoping for more still in Saint-Malo from a merchant's son, a close friend, who had recently come into possession of his inheritance through his parents' deaths. He added that, with the help of his friend, he hoped to travel easily to England, and from there make peace with his father without exposing to his wrath Mademoiselle Angélique and her mother, against whom he would likely have engaged in all sorts of hostile actions with all the advantages a wealthy man of quality has over two poor actresses. Destiny made Léandre admit that, because of his youth and quality, his father would be sure to accuse Mademoiselle Cave of abduction. He didn't try to make him forget his love, knowing full well that people who are in love are incapable of listening to any advice other than the dictates of their passion and are more worthy of pity than blame. But he strongly disapproved of his plan to run away to England and tried to paint a picture of what it would be like for two youngsters together in a foreign land: the fatigue and the hazards of a sea voyage; the difficulty of obtaining money should they need to; finally the enterprises undertaken against them because of Mademoiselle Angélique's beauty and their youth. Léandre didn't try to defend an unworthy cause. He once again asked Destiny to forgive him for having hidden who he was for so long, and Destiny promised he would use all the credit he thought he had with Mademoiselle Cave to make her approve of him. He also told him that if he really were committed to having no other wife but Mademoiselle Angélique he shouldn't leave the troupe, adding that in the meantime his father might die or his passion abate or maybe be extinguished. Léandre protested that this would never happen. "Well then," said Destiny, "out of fear it may happen to your mistress, don't let her out of your sight. Join our troupe and become an actor. You won't be the first to do so who could have done something better. Write to your father. Make him think you're in the army and try to get some money from him. In the meantime I'll treat you like my brother and I'll try to make you forget the bad treatment you may have received from me when I was unaware of your merit." Léandre would have thrown himself at Destiny's feet if the pain he felt from the blows he had received over his entire body had allowed him to. At least he thanked Destiny in words so obliging and expressions of friendship so stirring that he was esteemed from that day on as much as one gentleman can be by another. Then they talked about looking for Mademoiselle Angélique; but the sounds of a loud commotion interrupted their conversation and made Destiny run down to the inn's kitchen, where what you will see in the next chapter was going on.

CHAPTER VI

Fisticuffs. Death of the Innkeeper and Other Memorable Things

TWO MEN, ONE DRESSED IN BLACK like a village school-teacher, the other in grey, who surely looked like an officer of the court, held each other by the hair and beard and from time to time punched each other ferociously. Each one of them was what his dress and mien purported. The one dressed in black, the village schoolteacher, was the parson's brother and the one dressed in grey, bailiff of the same village, was the innkeeper's brother. This innkeeper was in a room next to the kitchen, ready to expire from a high fever which made him so delirious he had smashed his head against a wall. His wound, combined with his fever, had weakened him to such an extent that when his delirium passed he was forced to abandon this life, which he may have regretted less than his ill-gotten gains. He'd been in the army for a long time, and had finally returned to his village, loaded with years and with so little honesty you might well say he had less of it than he did money, although he was very poor. But since women are often attracted by those things which they should least be attracted by, his unruly hair, which was longer than that of the other village peasants, his soldierly oaths, a plume he wore on holidays when it wasn't raining and a rusty sword that bounced against the old boots he wore even though he didn't have a horse, were all seen by an old widow who kept an inn. She had been wooed by the richest farmers of the region, not so much for her beauty as for the wealth she had amassed with her late husband by overcharging and by cheating the measure on wine and oats. She had always resisted all her suitors until finally an old soldier triumphed over an old innkeeper's widow. The face of this tavernish nymph was the smallest and her stomach the biggest in all of Maine, although this province abounds in potbellied people. I leave it to the naturalists to find the reason for this, as well as for the fat of the region's capons. To get back to this fat little woman, whom I see in my mind's eye whenever I think of her, she married her soldier without telling her relatives, and after growing old with him, and suffering too, she had the satisfaction of witnessing him die of a broken skull, which she attributed to a just judgement of God, since he had often tried to break hers. When Destiny entered the inn's kitchen, this innkeeper's wife and her maid were helping the village's old parson separate the combatants, who were bound together like two battling ships of the line; but Destiny's threats and the authority with which he spoke achieved what the good father's exhortations had not been able to, and the two mortal enemies separated, spitting out half of their bloody teeth, with nosebleeds and their chins and scalps skinned. The parson was a gentleman and a good judge of character. He very politely thanked Destiny, who, in order to please him, made the two hug like old friends when just moments earlier they would only embrace to strangle one another. During the reconciliation the innkeeper ended his obscure journey without alerting his friends, such that the only thing left to do when they entered the room after the peace had been made was to bury him. The priest said prayers over the body, and he said them well because he made them short. His vicar arrived to relieve him, and in the meantime the widow decided to howl with great ostentation and vanity. The brother of the deceased pretended to be sad, or really was, and the valets and maids did almost as good a job as he. The parson followed Destiny into his room, offering to be of service, an offer he repeated to Léandre as well, and they invited him to eat with them.

Destiny, who hadn't eaten all day and had exercised a lot, scarfed up his food. Léandre feasted on thoughts of love more than he did food, and the parson talked more than he ate. He told them many entertaining tales about the avarice of the deceased and the funny conflicts this dominant passion had caused with his wife as well as his neighbours. He told them the story, among others, of a trip the innkeeper had made with his wife to Laval. When they were on their way back the horse that carried them both lost two shoes. So he left his wife holding the horse by the bridle at the foot of a tree and returned to Laval, looking for the horseshoes everywhere he thought he had been, but he wasted his time, while his wife was losing patience waiting for him, because he had covered two leagues before he retraced his steps. She was getting very impatient when she saw him return barefoot, holding his boots and his stockings in his hand. She was surprised by this incongruity, but didn't dare ask him the reason for it because, by dint of obeying orders in the army, he had learnt to give them at home. She didn't even dare respond when he made her go barefoot, nor ask him why. She could only guess it was out of devotion. He made his wife take the horse by the bridle, and walked behind it to prod it. Thus did the man and the woman without shoes and the horse missing them on two of his hooves, after much suffering, reach home before nightfall, very weary. Their feet were so scraped and scratched they were barely able to walk for two weeks. He was never more satisfied with anything he'd done, and when he thought about it, he would tell his wife with a laugh that if they hadn't returned from Laval barefoot it would have cost them two pairs of shoes on top of the two horseshoes. Destiny and Léandre didn't react much to this tale the parson said would be a good one, either because they didn't find it as funny as the parson said or because they weren't in the mood to laugh. The parson, who was a big talker, didn't want to stop there and, addressing Destiny, told him that what he just heard didn't hold a candle to what he had yet to relate about the way the deceased had prepared himself for death. "About four or five days ago," he added, "he realized he wasn't going to survive. He didn't worry about his wife. He regretted all the fresh eggs he ate during his illness. He wanted to know how much his funeral would cost, and he even tried to bargain with me the day I confessed him. Finally, to finish the way he started, two hours before he died, he ordered his wife in front of me to bury him in a certain tattered old sheet he knew of that had over a hundred holes. His wife explained that he would be badly wrapped. He insisted he didn't want another one. His wife couldn't agree to this and, because she saw he was in no shape to beat her, she expressed her opinion more vigorously to him than she ever had before, without however forgetting the respect a decent wife owes her husband, however unpleasant he might be. She finally asked him how he could be seen in the Valley of Josaphat* with an ugly torn sheet over his shoulders, and in what kind of outfit he thought he would resurrect. The dying man got angry and swore the way he was used to when he was healthy. 'Hey, *Morbleu*!' he cried out. 'I don't want to be resurrected.' I found it as hard to keep from laughing as I did to make him understand he had offended God by getting angry, and even more by what he'd said to his wife, which was a kind of blasphemy. He performed a begrudging act of contrition, and on top of it we had to give our word that he wouldn't be buried in any other sheet than the one he chose. My brother, who had burst out laughing when he so loudly and clearly renounced his resurrection, couldn't stop laughing every time he thought about it. The brother of the deceased took offence at this and, one thing leading to another, my brother and he, each as much a brute as the other, grappled together after they finished trading countless punches, and they might still be fighting if they hadn't been separated." The parson finished his story, addressing himself to Destiny, since Léandre wasn't paying much attention to him. He took his leave of the actors, after again offering to be of service to them, and Destiny tried to console the distressed Léandre by doing his best to hold out hope. As damaged as the poor boy was, he looked out the window from time to time to see if his valet was coming, as if this would make him come any faster. But when you are waiting for someone impatiently, even the wisest are dumb enough to often look in the direction from which that person is supposed to come, and I'll finish the sixth chapter with that remark.

CHAPTER VII

*Ragotin's Panic, Followed by Misfortunes. The Dead
Body Adventure. A Rain of Punches and Other Surprising
Occurrences Worthy of Inclusion in this True Story*

LÉANDRE WAS LOOKING out the window of his room on the side where he expected to see his valet when, turning his head to the other side, he saw little Ragotin, his boots coming up to his belt, riding a little mule, escorted by Grudge on one side and Olive on the other, like a knight by his footmen. Going from village to village, they had got news of Destiny and, after following his trail, had finally found him. Destiny went downstairs to greet them and bring them to the room. At first they didn't recognize young Léandre who, in addition to changing his clothes, looked transformed. So that he would not be recognized for what he really was, Destiny ordered him to prepare dinner with the same authority as usual, and the actors, who recognized him thanks to this, no sooner remarked how elegant he was than Destiny answered for him and told them a rich uncle of his in the Bas-Maine had equipped him from head to foot and even given him money to force him to quit the theatre, which he didn't want to do, and so he left without saying goodbye. Destiny asked the others if they had learnt anything new pertaining to their quest and found out they hadn't. Ragotin assured Destiny that they left the actresses in good health, though very upset by Mademoiselle Angélique's abduction. Night fell; they dined and the newcomers drank as much as the others drank little. Ragotin drank himself into a good mood, challenged everyone to drink, like the tavern braggart he was, and joked and sang in spite of the others. Since no one joined him, and the innkeeper's widow's brother-in-law pointed out that it wasn't decent to make merry near the dead, he made less noise and drank more wine.

Everyone went to bed: Destiny and Léandre in the room they already occupied; Ragotin, Grudge and Olive in a small room near the kitchen and next to the body of the deceased, which hadn't yet been prepared for burial. The innkeeper's widow slept in an upstairs room that was next to Destiny and Léandre's. She went there in order not to witness the unpleasant sight of a dead husband and to receive the condolences of her friends, who came to visit in great numbers because she was one of the village's most important ladies and had always been as well liked by everyone there as her husband had always been hated. Silence reigned in the inn. The dogs were asleep, since they weren't barking. All the other animals were also asleep or should have been, and this calm lasted until between two and three in the morning, when suddenly Ragotin started screaming at the top of his lungs that Grudge was dead. All at once he woke Olive and alerted Destiny and Léandre to come downstairs to his room to mourn or at least to see Grudge, who had just suddenly died by his side, or so he said. Destiny and Léandre followed him, and the first thing they saw was Grudge walking around the room like a healthy man, although this is hard to pull off after a sudden death. Ragotin, who went in first, no sooner saw him than he recoiled, as if he had almost stepped on a snake or into a hole. He let out a loud cry, turned pale as a corpse and crashed into Destiny and Léandre with such force as he leapt out of the room that he almost knocked them to the ground. While his fear caused him to flee onto the grounds of the inn, where he risked catching his death of a cold, Destiny and Léandre asked Grudge for the details of his death. Grudge told them he didn't know as much about it as Ragotin, who was a little cracked. Olive, meanwhile, was laughing like a hyena. Grudge remained impassive and silent, as usual, and Olive and he revealed nothing more.

Léandre went to look for Ragotin and found him hiding behind a tree, trembling from fear more than from the cold, even though he was in his nightshirt. His mind was so filled with Grudge's death that at first he thought Léandre was the ghost and tried to run away when he approached. Then Destiny arrived, whom he took to be another ghost. They couldn't get the least word out of him, no matter what they said. Finally they grabbed him by the arms to bring him back to his room. But as they were about to go inside they came across Grudge, who was on his way out. Ragotin broke loose from his escort and, casting wild-eyed looks over his shoulder, threw himself into a thorn bush, where he got stuck from head to foot, and couldn't extricate himself fast enough to avoid Grudge, who called him completely mad and said he needed to be bound in chains. All three of them together pulled him out of the bramble. Grudge slapped him on his bare skin to show him he wasn't dead. Finally, the little frightened man was brought back to his room and returned to his bed; but he had barely got there when a clamour of female voices, which they heard coming from the next room, gave them an idea of what might be going on. They weren't the cries of a woman in distress. They were the horrifying screams of several women together – screams of fear. Destiny went over and found four or five women, along with the innkeeper's widow, who were looking under the beds and in the fireplace and who seemed very frightened. He asked them what was wrong, and the innkeeper's widow, half screaming and half speaking, told him she didn't know what happened to her poor husband's body. As she finished speaking she began to scream, and the other women, like a choir, answered in unison and all together made a noise that was so great and so pathetic that all the people at the inn entered the room and all the neighbours and passers-by entered the inn.

While this was going on, a master thief of a cat grabbed a pigeon that a maid had left half-larded on the kitchen table and, running away with his prey into Ragotin's room, hid under the bed where Ragotin had slept with Grudge. Wielding a stick, the maid followed him and, looking under the bed to see what happened to her pigeon, she began to shout as loudly as she could that she found her master and repeated this so often that the innkeeper's widow and the other women came over to her. The maid flew into her mistress's arms, telling her she found her master with such a transport of joy that the poor widow was afraid her husband had come back to life, and she turned noticeably pale, like a criminal being sentenced. Finally, the servant made them look under the bed, where they saw the dead body that was giving them so much grief. The difficulty wasn't so much getting him out from under the bed, although he was very heavy, as figuring out who had put him there. He was brought back into his room, where he began to be prepared for burial. The actors went into the room that belonged to Destiny, who couldn't make head nor tail of these bizarre events. As for Léandre, all he could think about was his dear Angélique, which rendered him as distracted as Ragotin was angry that Grudge wasn't dead: Grudge's mockery upset him so much that he was speechless, despite his tendency to talk incessantly and participate in all sorts of conversations, appropriately so or not. Grudge and Olive showed so little surprise at both Ragotin's panic and the transmigration of a dead body from one room to another, without any human involvement as far as anyone knew, that Destiny suspected they must have played an important part in this miracle. Meanwhile, the mystery was being cleared up in the inn's kitchen. A ploughman, back from the fields for lunch, hearing a frightened maid say her master's body had got up all by itself and walked, told her that, while passing by the kitchen at dawn, he'd seen two men in nightshirts carrying it on their shoulders into the room where it was found. The dead man's brother overheard what the ploughman said and found this behaviour reprehensible. The widow and her friends were informed in short order. They were all scandalized, and concluded in a single voice that those men could only be sorcerers who wanted to do something evil with the body.

While Grudge was being judged so harshly, he entered the kitchen to ask that breakfast be sent to their room. The brother of the deceased asked why he had carried his brother's body into his room. Grudge, far from answering him, didn't so much as look at him. The widow asked him the same question. He was just as indifferent with her, but she wasn't with him. She leapt at his eyes, as angry as a lioness defending her cubs (I'm afraid this comparison may be too majestic here). Her brother-in-law punched Grudge; the widow's friends didn't spare him either; the maids got involved and the valets too. But there wasn't room for a single man among so many hitters, and they got in each other's way. Grudge, alone against several others and, consequently, with several others against him, wasn't fazed by the number of his enemies and, making a virtue of necessity, began to move his arms with all of his God-given strength, leaving the rest to chance. Never has such an unequal fight been contested more closely. Grudge, who was calm under fire, used his skill as well as his strength, pacing his punches, and making them as efficient as possible. If he threw one punch that didn't land squarely on the first jaw it encountered but slipped, so to speak, it would contact a second jaw, and even a third, because he threw most of his punches with a half-pirouette, and one punch would produce three different sounds from three different jaws. At the sound of the combatants, Olive came down to the kitchen, and he barely had time to make out his companion among all those who were pummelling him when he was beaten himself, even more so than the one whose vigorous resistance was starting to wane. Two or three of those who were mistreated by Grudge fell upon Olive, maybe to get even. This only increased the noise. At the same time the innkeeper's widow was punched in the pupil, which made her see a hundred thousand candles (that's a precise number for something so uncertain) and put her out of action. She screamed louder and with more conviction than when her husband had died. Her screams attracted the neighbours who were in the house and brought Destiny and Léandre down to the kitchen. Although they arrived as peacemakers, undeclared war was waged on them. They weren't lacking in punches, and they made sure those who'd handed them out weren't lacking in them either. The innkeeper's widow, her friends and maids were yelling "Thieves!" and were only spectators to the fighting, some sidelined with a black eye, others with a bloody nose or a broken jaw, all of them with ruined hairdos. The neighbours had sided with their neighbour against those she called thieves. It would take a better quill than mine to depict adequately the beautiful punches that were thrown there. Finally, with animosity and fury gaining the upper hand everywhere, spits and pieces of furniture that could be thrown were being picked up, when the parson entered the kitchen and tried to stop the fight. In truth, as respected as he may have been, he would have found it very difficult to separate the combatants if their fatigue hadn't played a part. All acts of hostility ceased on both sides, but the noise didn't, because, with everyone trying to be the first to speak – the women with their high-pitched voices even more than the men – the poor fellow was forced to cover his ears and head for the door. This quieted the rowdiest. He entered the battlefield, and the innkeeper's brother, speaking up at his prompting, complained about the dead body being moved from one room to the other. He would have exaggerated this evil deed more than he did if he had less blood to spit out, not to mention the blood coming out of his nose, which he couldn't stop. Grudge and Olive admitted to what they were accused of, and protested they hadn't done it out of evil intent, but simply to scare one of their friends, which they had. The parson reprimanded them vigorously and made them understand the consequences of such an enterprise, which was no joking matter and, since he was a clever man and highly respected by his parishioners, he didn't find it difficult to patch things up between the parties. But Discord, with serpent's mane, hadn't yet accomplished everything she wanted to in this place. Howls that sounded like those of a hog having its throat cut came from an upstairs room; and the one who was responsible for them was none other than Ragotin. The parson, the actors and several others ran to his side and found his entire body, except his head, ensconced in a big wooden chest that held the inn's linens; and, what was unfortunate for the poor prisoner, the lid of the chest, which was massive and very heavy, had fallen on his legs and pressed down on them in a manner that was painful to witness. A powerful maid, who wasn't far from the chest when they came in, and who seemed to them quite distracted, was suspected of having put Ragotin where he was. And so she had, proudly, such that while she was busy making one of the beds in the room, she didn't deign to look at how Ragotin was being extricated from the chest, nor answer those who asked her where the noise they heard had come from. Meanwhile, the half-man was pulled out of his trap, and was no sooner on his feet than he ran to get a sword. He was prevented from reaching it, but no one could prevent him from reaching the big maid, whom he couldn't prevent from giving him such a big blow to the head that the vast seat of his narrow reason was shaken by it. It made him take three steps back, but this would have been backing up the better to jump forward, had Olive not held him by his trousers, just as he was about to strike his formidable enemy like a snake. Though in vain, his effort was violent. It broke his belt along with the silence of his audience, who began to laugh. The parson forgot his gravitas and the innkeeper's brother forgot to act sad. Only Ragotin didn't feel like laughing, and his anger was directed at Olive who, feeling aggrieved, carried him forthwith onto the bed the maid was making, and there, with Herculean strength, he finished off the process of pulling down Ragotin's trousers and, by raising and lowering his hands hard and fast upon his thighs and neighbouring areas, in no time turned them scarlet. The daring Ragotin bravely flung himself from the bed in his stockings, but such a bold move did not have the outcome it deserved. He stepped into a chamber pot that was left on the other side of the bed, unfortunately for him, and so deeply lodged his foot in it that, not being able to remove it with his other foot, he didn't dare leave the far side of the bed, for fear of further entertaining the others and bringing upon himself their teasing, which he tolerated less than anyone else. Everyone was surprised to see him so calm after he had been so agitated. Grudge suspected there had to be a reason. He made him come out from behind the other side of the bed, half coaxing and half forcing him. Then everyone saw where the impediment was, and no one could keep from laughing when they saw the metal foot the little man had fashioned. We'll leave him treading proudly upon pewter, in order to meet a group that entered the inn at the same time.

CHAPTER VIII

What Happened with Ragotin's Foot

I F RAGOTIN HAD BEEN ABLE to unpot his foot all by himself, without the help of his friends, I mean free it from the nasty chamber pot it had so unfortunately entered, his anger would have lasted at least for the remainder of the day. But he was forced to suppress part of his natural pride and toe the line, humbly asking Destiny and Grudge to contribute to the freedom of his right foot, or his left, I never learnt which. He didn't ask Olive because of what had happened between them, but Olive came to his aid without being asked, and he and his two comrades did what they could to bring him relief. The efforts the little man made to pull his foot out of the pot had swollen it, and those of Destiny and Olive made it swell even more. Grudge was the first to try, but so clumsily, or perhaps mischievously, that Ragotin thought he wanted to cripple him for life. He asked Grudge to stop helping him at once. Then he asked the others the same thing, and lay down on a bed while he waited for a locksmith to be summoned to hacksaw the chamber pot off his foot. The rest of the day went by peacefully at the inn, and somewhat sadly for Destiny and Léandre; the latter was unhappy that his valet hadn't returned with news of his mistress as he had promised; the former couldn't enjoy himself far away from his dear Mademoiselle Star, in addition to which he was affected by Mademoiselle Angélique's abduction and he pitied Léandre, whose face bore the marks of extreme distress. Grudge and Olive joined several locals who were playing boule, and Ragotin, after the work done on his foot, slept the rest of the day, either because he felt like it or because he preferred not to be seen in public, after all the bad things that had happened to him. The innkeeper's body was taken to its final resting place, and his widow, notwithstanding the thoughts of mortality her husband's death must have inspired in her, didn't forget to charge two Englishmen, who were travelling from Brittany to Paris, usurious rates.

The sun had just set when Destiny and Léandre, who couldn't leave the window of their room, watched the arrival at the inn of a coach pulled by four horses, followed by three horsemen and four or five lackeys. A maid came to ask them to give up their room to the party that had just arrived; and thus Ragotin had to show his face, even though he wanted to keep his room, and followed Destiny and Léandre into the one where he thought he'd seen Grudge die the day before. In the kitchen, one of the gentlemen from the coach recognized Destiny. It was the same counsellor from the parliament of Rennes he had met during the wedding that turned out to be so unfortunate for poor Cave. This senator from Brittany asked Destiny for news of Angélique, and expressed sadness when he learnt she hadn't been found. He was called La Garouffière, which makes me think he was more from Anjou than Brittany, because you don't see more Breton names starting with *Ker* than you do Angevin names ending in *ière*, Norman in *ville*, Picard in *cour* and those of people who live near the Garonne river in *ac*. To get back to Monsieur de la Garouffière, he was not without wit, as I have already told you, and didn't consider himself provincial in any way, it being his habit, during the six months that his parliament wasn't in session, to eat through some of his money in the inns of Paris and to wear black whenever the court was in mourning, which, all told, must have been a mark, if not quite of nobility, at least of non-bourgeoisie, if I dare use such an expression. Moreover, he was a wit by virtue of the fact that almost everyone claims to enjoy the entertainments of the mind, from those who know them to the presumptuous or brutal ignoramuses who boldly cast judgements on verse and prose, even though they believe it dishonourable to write well and, if it served their purposes, would hold it against a man if he wrote books, the way they would hold it against him if he were a counterfeiter. Actors profit by all this. They are lionized to a greater extent in the towns where they perform because, being the parrots or mockingbirds of the authors, and as even some of them are born with wit and are sometimes getting involved in writing plays – either of their own devise or based on borrowed material – there is a kind of ambition to knowing them or frequenting them. Nowadays justice has, in a fashion, been done to their profession and they are more valued than they used to be. It is also a fact that the theatre is a most innocent form of entertainment that can, at the same time, entertain and instruct the people. Today it has been purged, at least in Paris, of everything that was licentious about it. Would that it were too of the crooks, pages, lackeys and other human refuse that the ease of stealing coats attracts to the theatre even more than the base humour of the farces used to. But today the farce has been quasi-abolished and I dare say there are private gatherings where hearty laughter greets base and dirty witticisms which would scandalize the boxes of the Hôtel de Bourgogne.

Let's end this digression. Monsieur de la Garouffière was delighted to find Destiny at the inn and made him promise to dine with the company from the coach, which was made up of the groom from the wedding in Le Mans, of his bride, whom he was taking to his home in Laval, of Madame his mother, of a gentleman from the province, of a lawyer for the council and of Monsieur de la Garouffière, all related to each other and whom Destiny had seen at the wedding where Mademoiselle Angélique was abducted. Add to all those I just listed a servant or chambermaid, and you will find that the coach that carried them was very full. All the more since Madame Bouvillon (this was the name of the groom's mother) was one of the fattest women in France, though one of the shortest. I have been assured that she always carried, year in and year out, at least three thousand pounds of flesh, not including the other solid or liquid substances that make up the human body. After what I have just told you, you won't find it hard to believe she was very juicy, as are all short, fat women.

Dinner was served. Destiny showed up with his dashing good looks, which weren't dimmed by dirty linens, Léandre having lent him a clean shirt. He spoke little, as was his habit, and had he spoken as much as the others, who spoke a lot, he probably wouldn't have said as many useless things as they did. La Garouffière served him all the choice morsels on the table. Madame Bouvillon copied la Garouffière with so little discretion that all the platters on the table were emptied in an instant and Destiny's plate so full of chicken wings and thighs that I have often wondered since how it was possible to make, at random, such a high pyramid of meat on such a small base as a dinner plate. La Garouffière paid it no mind, so occupied was he talking about verse to Destiny and trying to make a good impression with his wit. Madame Bouvillon, who had her own designs, continued to serve the actor and, finding no more chickens to carve, was reduced to serving him slices of a leg of lamb. He didn't know where to put them, and held one in each of his hands until he could find a place for them somewhere, when the gentleman, who didn't want to remain silent in the face of his appetite, asked Destiny, with a smile, if he was going to eat everything on his plate. Destiny looked down at it, and was startled to see, almost reaching his chin, the pile of carved chicken that La Garouffière and Madame Bouvillon had erected as a trophy honouring him. He blushed and burst out laughing. Madame Bouvillon was disconcerted. La Garouffière laughed heartily and set the tone for the entire group, which burst into gales of laughter four or five times. The valets picked up where their masters left off and laughed in turn. The young bride found this so amusing that, bursting out laughing just as she was beginning to drink, she covered her mother-in-law's face and her husband's with most of what was in her glass, and sent the rest onto the table and the clothes of those who were sitting there. Everyone started to laugh, except Madame Bouvillon, who did blush a lot and stared at her poor daughter-in-law with an angry expression, which tempered her joy somewhat. Finally, everyone stopped laughing, because you can't laugh for ever. Some wiped their eyes. Madame Bouvillon and her son wiped the wine that was dripping off their eyes and faces, and the young bride apologized, while finding it difficult to suppress her laughter. Destiny put his plate in the middle of the table and everyone took back what belonged to them. They talked of nothing else during dinner, and the banter, good or bad, went very far, although the seriousness with which Madame Bouvillon quite inappropriately armed herself did put a crimp in the general cheer.

As soon as the table was cleared, the ladies retired to their rooms, the lawyer and the gentleman requested a deck of cards and played piquet. La Garouffière and Destiny, who weren't among those who are at a loss when they aren't gambling, held forth with great wit and had perhaps one of the best conversations ever heard at an inn of the Bas-Maine. La Garouffière intentionally spoke about all the things he thought would be most inaccessible to an actor, whose mind is usually more limited than his memory, and Destiny discussed them with real insight, demonstrating an intimate knowledge of society. Among other things, he made distinctions, with all the discernment imaginable, between women of great wit who only show it when they need to and those who only use it for show; also between those women who seem jealous of the buffoons known for vile humour, considered merry companions, women who not only laugh at their licentious allusions and double entendres, but also indulge in them themselves – who, in a word, are the neighbourhood lady jesters – and those who make up the most appealing and attractive part of the beau monde and are found in the best society. He also spoke about women who are able to write as well as the men who fancy themselves writers, and who, when they don't share the productions of their mind with the public, only do so out of modesty. La Garouffière, who was a real *honnête homme** himself, and who knew the type, couldn't understand how a country actor could have such perfect knowledge of *honnêteté*. While he admired him in silence and the lawyer and the gentleman, who had stopped playing because they had quar-relled over a card, yawned frequently from too great a desire to sleep, three beds were prepared for them in the room where they had dined, and Destiny retired to his companions' room, where he slept with Léandre.

CHAPTER IX

Ragotin's New Misfortune

GRUDGE AND RAGOTIN SLEPT TOGETHER. As for Olive, he spent part of the night mending his suit, which had come apart in several places when he had tussled with the angry Ragotin. Those who got to know this little Manceau noticed that every time he scuffled with someone, which happened often, he always unravelled or tore his enemy's clothing, in whole or in part. It was his trademark, and anyone who fought him hand to hand had to defend their clothing the way one defends one's face in a swordfight. When they went to bed, Grudge asked him how he felt, because he really looked sick. Ragotin replied that he'd never been in better health. They didn't take long to fall asleep, and Ragotin was fortunate in that Grudge respected the good company that had arrived at the inn and didn't want to disturb their sleep, otherwise the little man wouldn't have had a very restful night. Meanwhile, Olive worked on his suit and, after finishing everything he had to do, he took Ragotin's clothes and, as ably as a tailor, he shortened the doublet and the trousers and put them back in their place. Having spent the greater part of the night sewing and cutting stitches, he climbed into the bed where Ragotin and Grudge were sleeping.

They got up early, the way one always does at inns where the noise begins at dawn. Grudge again told Ragotin he looked sick. Olive told him the same thing. He began to believe it and, finding his suit more than four sizes too tight, he no longer doubted he'd swollen during the short time he'd slept and became very frightened by this sudden swelling. Grudge and Olive continued to exaggerate his sickly face and Destiny and Léandre, who were in on the joke, also told him he looked different. Poor Ragotin had tears in his eyes. Destiny couldn't help smiling, which made Ragotin very angry. He went into the inn's kitchen, where everyone told him what the actors had told him, even the people from the coach, who had got up early because they had a long stage to cover. They invited the actors to breakfast and everyone drank to the health of the sick Ragotin, who, instead of thanking them, left, grumbling at them and quite upset, to visit the town surgeon, to whom he described his swelling. The surgeon held forth on the causes and effects of his malady, about which he knew as much as he did algebra, and spoke to him for a whole fifteen minutes in the jargon of his art, which was as relevant to the subject as if he had spoken about Prester John.* Ragotin became impatient, and asked him, swearing to God admirably well for a little man, if he had anything more to tell him. The surgeon wanted to go on with his discourse; Ragotin wanted to beat him, and would have if he hadn't humbled himself before this angry patient, from whom he drew nearly a pint of blood and whose shoulders he suctioned, somehow. The treatment had just finished when Léandre arrived to tell Ragotin that, if he promised not to get mad, he would tell him about a trick that was played on him. He promised more than Léandre asked, and swore on his eternal damnation to keep all his promises. Léandre said he wanted witnesses to his oath, and brought him back to the inn, where, in the presence of all the masters and servants, he made him swear again, and informed him that his clothes had been shrunk. At first Ragotin blushed with shame, but then he turned pale with anger and was about to break his fearsome oath, when seven or eight people began to admonish him at once, so vehemently that, even though he was swearing at the top of his lungs, you couldn't hear anything. He stopped talking, but the others kept yelling in his ears and continued for so long the poor man thought he would lose his hearing. Finally, he got through it better than expected and began to sing as loudly as he could the first songs that came to his mind, which changed the loud noise of competing voices into great peals of laughter that travelled from masters to valets and from the scene of the action to all the parts of the inn, where different people tended to different business.

While the sound of so many people laughing together dies out somewhat like an echo, this faithful chronicler will now finish the current chapter under the eye of the benevolent reader, or malevolent, or however God made him.

CHAPTER X

How Madame Bouvillon Could Not Resist
Temptation and Got a Lump on Her Forehead

THE COACH, WHICH WAS ABOUT to undertake a long journey, was ready early. The seven people who filled it with no room to spare squeezed in. It left and, barely ten paces from the inn, the axle broke in half. The driver cursed his existence, and he was scolded, as though he were responsible for the life of an axle. Everyone had to get out of the coach and return to the inn. The passengers of the stranded coach were taken aback when they were told that in the entire area there wasn't a wheelwright closer than a big village three leagues away. They consulted one another and resolved to do nothing, since it was obvious their coach would be in no shape to go anywhere until the following day. Madame Bouvillon, who still had great authority over her son because all the family's wealth came from her, ordered him to get on one of the horses that carried the house valets and to put his wife on the other one and pay a visit to an old uncle of hers, parson of the same village where the wheelwright was to be found. The lord of this village was a relative of the counsellor and an acquaintance of the lawyer and the gentleman. They all decided to visit him together. The innkeeper's widow leased them pricey mounts, and thus Madame Bouvillon was the only one in her group who stayed behind at the inn, being a little tired or pretending to be. Besides, her round shape would not have allowed her to ride even a donkey, were it possible to find one strong enough to carry her. She sent her maid to Destiny to invite him to have lunch with her and, while she waited for lunchtime, she had her hair put up, curled and powdered, then put on a lace apron and gown, and made herself a wimple from a ruff belonging to her son. She pulled one of her daughter-in-law's wedding dresses out of a chest and adorned herself with it, transforming herself, in the end, into a fat little nymph. Destiny would have liked to have a relaxed lunch with his comrades, but how could he turn down his very humble servant, Madame Bouvillon, who sent for him as soon as lunch was being served? Destiny was surprised to see her so jauntily dressed. She greeted him with a jolly face, took his hands to have them washed and squeezed them in a way that seemed to suggest something. He thought less about eating than about why he was being summoned, and Madame Bouvillon reproached him so often for not eating that he couldn't answer. He didn't know what to say. Besides, he wasn't naturally talkative. La Bouvillon herself was only too ingenious when it came to finding a topic of conversation. When people who talk a lot find themselves in a tête-à-tête with another who doesn't talk much and who doesn't answer, the talkative ones do even more talking, because, judging the other person based on themselves, and seeing there was no reply to what they said, they tend to follow their own experience and believe that what they said didn't sufficiently appeal to their indifferent interlocutor; and they want to make up for their shortcoming by what they say next, which invariably is inferior to what they already said, and they won't stop talking as long as they have the other person's attention. You can always walk away, but because there are indefatigable talkers who continue to talk on their own, once they have been put in the mood by being with others, I think the best course to follow with them is to talk as much or more than they do, if possible, because everyone put together can't restrain a big talker as well as another big talker who interrupts him and forces him to become a listener. I base this observation on several experiences, and I may even be among those I condemn. As for the inimitable Bouvillon, she was the greatest sayer of nothings who ever lived. Not only did she speak by herself, she also answered herself. With Destiny's taciturn nature playing right into her hand, and aiming to please him, she covered a lot of ground. She told him everything that went on in Laval, the city where she lived, including all the scandals, and she didn't tear down individuals or entire families without rescuing them from the bad things she said about them by mentioning their good points. Every time she noticed a fault in her fellow man, she would protest that, although she herself had several faults, she didn't have that one. Destiny was mortified by this at first, and didn't answer her. Finally, he felt obliged to smile from time to time and to say sometimes, whether it was fitting or not, "How amusing" or "How strange".

The table was cleared as soon as Destiny finished eating. Madame Bouvillon made him sit next to her at the foot of a bed, and her maid, who let the inn's maids out the door first, closed it behind her as she left the room. Madame Bouvillon, who thought Destiny might have noticed this, said, "Do you believe that little scatterbrain who closed the door on us!"

"I'll open it, if you wish," replied Destiny.

"That's not what I'm saying," answered Madame Bouvillon, as she stopped him. "But you well know that two people alone together, since they can do as they please, can also be thought to do just about anything."

"It is not on the likes of persons such as yourself that bold judgements are passed," Destiny retorted. "That's not what I'm saying," said Madame Bouvillon. "But you can't take too many precautions against gossip."

"It has to have some basis in fact," replied Destiny. "And as far as you and I are concerned, the difference there is between a poor actor and a woman of your station is well known. Do you mind then," he continued, "if I go open the door?"

"That's not what I'm saying," said Madame Bouvillon as she went to lock the door, "because," she added, "maybe no one will notice that it's closed. And, if it's to be closed, it is better if it can only be opened with our consent." Having done as she said, she approached Destiny with her fat face inflamed and her beady eyes sparkling, and gave him food for thought concerning how he could honourably survive the battle it seemed he was about to wage. The fat sensualist removed her breast cloth and, without giving him much pleasure, spread out before Destiny's eyes at least ten pounds of flesh, which represented about a third of her bosom, the rest being distributed in two equal portions under her armpits. Her bad intentions making her blush (for the shameless blush too), her breasts were no less red than her face, and both combined could have been mistaken from a distance for a scarlet English bonnet. Destiny blushed too, out of modesty, while Madame Bouvillon, who had none left, blushed out of I'll-let-you-guess-what. She cried out that she had a bug on her back and, squirming under her clothes like someone with an itch, she asked Destiny to reach his hand down there. The poor boy did so, trembling, and meanwhile Madame Bouvillon, groping him under the hem of his doublet, asked him if he were ticklish. It was time to fight or give in, when Ragotin made himself heard on the other side of the door, banging on it with hands and feet as if he wanted to break it and yelling for Destiny to open it right away. Destiny freed his hand from

Madame Bouvillon's sweaty back to open the door for Ragotin, who was still making a hell of a racket and, wanting to pass between her and the table deftly enough to avoid touching her, his foot met something that made him stumble and strike his head against a bench hard enough to be momentarily dazed. La Bouvillon meanwhile, having hastily recovered her kerchief, went to open the door for the imperious Ragotin who, at the same time, pushed on the other side as hard as he could, making it slam into the poor lady's face with such force that her nose was bashed and she was left with a lump on her forehead as big as a fist. She cried out that she was dying. The little scatterbrain didn't offer the least apology and, jumping up and down and repeating, "They found Mademoiselle Angélique! Mademoiselle Angélique is here!" he nearly angered Destiny, who was calling as loudly as he could for Madame Bouvillon's maid to help her mistress, and couldn't be heard because of Ragotin's noise. The maid finally appeared with water and a white towel. She and Destiny repaired as best they could the damage the door too roughly opened had done to the poor lady. However impatient Destiny may have been to know whether Ragotin was telling the truth, he didn't yield to his impetuousness and didn't leave Madame Bouvillon's side until her face had been washed and dried and the lump on her forehead bandaged, but not without often calling Ragotin a scatterbrain, who, despite this, didn't stop tugging at him to make him come where he wanted to lead him.

CHAPTER XI

One of the Least Entertaining in this Book

IT WAS TRUE THAT MADEMOISELLE ANGÉLIQUE had just arrived, escorted by Léandre's valet. This valet was clever enough not to let anyone know Léandre was his master, and

Mademoiselle Angélique acted surprised to see him so well dressed, using her wits to say what Grudge and Olive had said naturally. Léandre was asking Mademoiselle Angélique and his valet, whom he passed off as one of his friends, where and how he had found her, when Ragotin entered, triumphantly leading Destiny, or rather dragging him, because he wasn't moving fast enough to suit his excitable temperament. Destiny and Angélique embraced with great expressions of friendship and with the tenderness people who really care about one another feel after a long absence, or when, after losing hope of ever seeing each other again, they are unexpectedly brought together. She and Léandre only caressed each other with their eyes, which communicated many things in the short time they met, putting off the rest until their first private encounter.

Meanwhile, Léandre's valet began his narration and told his master, as if he were speaking to a friend, that after he left him to follow Angélique's abductors, as Léandre had asked him, he had only lost sight of them at sunset, and the next day at the entrance of a wood, where he was surprised to find Mademoiselle Angélique alone, on foot and weeping. And he added that, having said he was a friend of Léandre and that he had followed her at his request, she had dried her tears and begged him to take her to Le Mans or lead her to Léandre, if he knew where to find him. "It is," he continued, "up to Mademoiselle to tell you why those who abducted her abandoned her like that, because I didn't dare talk to her about it, seeing her so distressed during our journey that I sometimes feared her sobs would suffocate her."

The least curious in the group were very impatient to learn from Mademoiselle Angélique the details of an adventure that seemed so strange, because what could one make of a girl so violently abducted and given up or abandoned so easily, and without the abductors being forced to do so? Mademoiselle Angélique asked if it would be possible for her to lie down but, as the inn was full, the good parson found her a room next door at his sister's, who was the widow of one of the richest farmers in the area. Angélique

didn't need to sleep as much as she needed to rest, which is why
Destiny and Léandre went to see her as soon as they knew she was
in her bed. As pleased as she was that Destiny was aware of her
love, she could not look at him without blushing. Destiny took
pity on her embarrassment and, to occupy her with something
besides losing her composure, asked her to recount what Léandre's
valet could not, which she did as follows:

"You can imagine how surprised my mother and I were when,
strolling on the grounds of the estate where we were, five or six
men entered through a little door in the wall that opened onto
the countryside, and grabbed me almost without looking at my
mother and carried me half-dead with fear to their horses. My
mother, whom you know to be one of the most resolute women
around, furiously pounced on the first one she saw and was
beating him so badly that, not being able to get away from her,
he had to call his companions for help. The one who came to his
aid, and was cowardly enough to beat my mother, as I heard him
boast during our journey, was the leader of the enterprise. He
didn't come near me that night, during which we travelled like
people on the run from someone. If we had gone through inhabited places my cries could have stopped them. But they avoided
as much as possible all the villages that were on their way, with
the exception of a hamlet, all of whose inhabitants I awoke with
my cries. At dawn my abductor came over to me and no sooner
looked at my face than, after letting out a shout, he assembled
his companions and met with them for about half an hour. My
abductor seemed as enraged as I was distressed. He swore enough
to frighten anyone who could hear him and yelled at almost all his
comrades. Finally their wild meeting ended and I don't know what
was decided. We started our march again, and I wasn't treated
as respectfully as I had been up to that point. They berated me
every time they heard me complain and swore at me, as if I had
caused them some harm. They had abducted me, as you know,
when I was in costume and, to hide this, they had covered me
with one of their capes. They came across a man on the way, to

whom they addressed some enquiry. I was surprised to see it was Léandre, and I think he certainly was very surprised to recognize me, which he did as soon as he saw my costume, which I intentionally uncovered and with which he was very familiar. Then he saw my face. I'm sure he's told you what he did. As for me, seeing so many swords drawn against Léandre, I fainted in the arms of the one who held me on his horse and, when I came to, I saw that we were travelling again and could no longer see Léandre. This made me cry even harder, and my abductors, one of whom was wounded, cut across the fields and stopped at a village yesterday where they camped like soldiers. This morning, at the entrance of a wood, they met a man who was escorting a young lady on horseback. They unmasked her, recognized her and, with all the joy shown by those who find what they are looking for, took her away with them, after striking her escort several times. This young lady cried out as much as I had, and I thought her voice sounded familiar. We hadn't gone fifty paces into the woods when the one I told you seemed to be the leader came up to the one who was holding me and said, referring to me: 'Make this loudmouth get down.' He was obeyed. They left me, vanished from sight and I found myself alone and on foot. The fear I felt when I realized I was alone might have killed me if Monsieur, who escorted me here and who had been following us, as he told you, hadn't found me. You know the rest. But," she continued, addressing Destiny, "I think I have to tell you that the young lady they preferred to me looks like your sister, my companion. She has the same voice. I don't know what to think, because the man who was with her looks like the valet you took since Léandre left you, and I can't get it out of my mind that it's him."

"What are you telling me?" Destiny said, quite worried.

"What I think," Angélique answered.

"It's possible," she continued, "to make a mistake about people's resemblance, but I'm afraid I'm not wrong."

"I'm afraid so too," replied Destiny, the expression on his face changed, "and I think I have an enemy in the province from whom

I have everything to fear. But who would have left my sister at the entrance to a wood, when Ragotin said goodbye to her just yesterday in Le Mans? I'm going to ask one of my comrades to go there as quickly as possible and I'll wait here to figure out what I have to do depending on the news he brings me."

As he finished speaking these words, he heard someone calling him from the street. He looked out the window and saw Monsieur de la Garouffière, who had returned from his visit and had something important to tell him. While he went to meet him, he left Léandre and Angélique alone, who were thus free to caress each other after such an unhappy separation and share each other's feelings. I think it would have been enjoyable to hear what they had to say, but it's better for them if their conversation remains private. Meanwhile, Destiny asked La Garouffière what he wanted. "Do you know a gentleman by the name of Verville, and is he one of your friends?" asked La Garouffière.

"He's the person in the whole world to whom I owe the most and whom I most respect, and I believe he is not indifferent to me."

"I think you're right," replied La Garouffière. "I saw him today at the home of the gentleman I went to visit. During lunch your name came up, and from that point on Verville could talk about nothing else. He asked me many questions about you I couldn't answer, and if I hadn't given my word that I would send you to see him (which he was sure you would do) he would have come here, even though he has business to attend to where he is."

Destiny thanked him for the good news he had brought and, having learnt Verville's location, he resolved to go there, hoping to hear from him news of his enemy Saldagne, who was sure to be behind Angélique's abduction and now appeared to have captured his dear Star, if she turned out to be the one Angélique thought she recognized. He asked his companions to return to Le Mans to cheer Cave with the news of her daughter's discovery, and made them promise to send him someone, or that one of them would return, to tell him what Mademoiselle Star's situation was. He learnt from La Garouffière what route to follow and the name of the town where he would find Verville. He made the parson promise that his sister would care for Angélique until she returned to Le Mans, took Léandre's horse and arrived that evening in the town he was looking for. He didn't think it wise to seek out Verville himself, lest he come across Saldagne, whom he suspected of being in the area. So he checked into a modest inn, from where he sent a little boy to tell Monsieur de Verville that the gentleman he wanted to see was asking for him. Verville came quickly, embraced him and held him for a long time without being able to speak, from too much emotion. Let's let them show their mutual affection like two people who care a lot about each other, and who meet again after having thought they would never see each other again, and let's go on to the next chapter.

CHAPTER XII

Which May Entertain as Little as the Previous One

VERVILLE AND DESTINY brought each other up to date. Verville amazed his friend with tales of Saint-Far's coarseness and of his brother's wife's virtue for enduring it. He sang the praises of the happiness he experienced with his own wife, and gave him news of the Baron d'Arques and of Monsieur de Saint-Sauveur. Destiny recounted all his adventures, without hiding anything, and Verville confirmed Saldagne's presence in the area, adding that he was as unprincipled as ever and very dangerous. Verville promised that if Mademoiselle Star had fallen into his hands, he would do everything in his power to find out and to serve Destiny, both personally and with the help of his friends, in whatever way he could to free her. "He has no place to stay in the area," Verville told him, "besides my father's house and the home of some kind of gentleman who isn't worthier than he is, and who isn't even the master of his house, being the youngest son. He has to pay us a visit, if he stays in the province. My father and the rest of us put up with him because he's our in-law; Saint-Far doesn't like him any more, whatever their relationship was like in the past. So I think you should come with me tomorrow. I know where you can stay. You will only be seen by people of your own choosing. Meanwhile, I'll have Saldagne watched. He'll be followed so closely he won't be able to do anything without our knowledge." Destiny found his friend's advice quite sound, and resolved to follow it. Verville returned to dine with the local lord, an old man, his relative, from whom he expected an inheritance. Destiny ate what was available at his inn and went to bed early in order to accommodate Verville, who wanted to leave at dawn to return to his father's.

They left very early as planned and, during the three leagues they travelled together, communicated a number of details they hadn't had time to tell each other before. Verville lodged Destiny with a valet whose marriage he'd arranged in town and who had a very convenient house one hundred and fifty yards from the Baron d'Arque's chateau. He gave orders that secrecy be maintained, and promised to come back soon to see him. Verville hadn't been gone two hours when he returned and told him he had lots of news. Destiny blanched and began to worry in anticipation, while Verville held out hope in advance for a remedy to the woeful news he had in store. "As I set foot on the ground," he said, "I came across Saldagne, who was being transported by four men into a room on the ground floor. His horse fell on him a league from here, and he is hurt. He told me he needed to speak to me, and asked me to come to his room as soon as a surgeon had examined his leg, which was badly twisted from his fall. Once we were alone, he said, 'It seems I must always reveal my wrongdoings to you, even though you are the least indulgent of my censors, and your wisdom always frightens my folly.' Following this, he confessed he'd abducted an actress with whom he'd been in love his entire life, and said he would tell me surprising things about this abduction. He said that the gentleman I told you was one of his friends hadn't been able to find him a dwelling in the whole province and was obliged to leave him; this man took with him the men he had furnished for Saldagne's enterprise, because one of his brothers, who was involved in smuggling contraband salt, was being watched by the archers of the Gabelles and needed his friends to protect him. 'Not daring to be seen in the slightest town,' he told me, 'because what I did had created quite a stir, I came here with my prey. I asked my sister, your wife, to keep her in her apartment, out of sight of the Baron d'Arques, whose strictness I fear, and, since I can't keep her here, and I only have two valets, who are as stupid as they come, I beg you to lend me your valet to lead her, along with mine, to my property in Brittany, where I will meet them as soon as I am able to ride again.' He asked me if I could spare several men, besides my valet, because, as dizzy as he might be, he could well imagine it would be difficult for three men to travel very far with a girl abducted against her will. For my part, I spoke about it as an easy thing, which he was quick to accept, the way madmen are quick to hope. His valets don't know you. Mine is very resourceful and faithful to me. I'll have him tell Saldagne he'll take along a dependable friend of his. That friend will be you. Your mistress will be forewarned. And the night they plan to cover a lot of ground, riding by moonlight, she will pretend to be sick as soon as they reach the first village. They will have to stop. My valet will try to get Saldagne's men drunk, which shouldn't prove too difficult; he'll facilitate your escape with the young lady and, making the two drunkards believe he knows where you went, he'll send them in the opposite direction."

Destiny found this proposal very feasible. Verville's valet, for whom he had sent, entered the room at that moment. Together they determined what needed to be done. Verville spent the rest of the day with Destiny, finding it hard to take leave of him after such a long absence, which, for all he knew, might be followed by a longer one still. It is true that Destiny hoped to see Verville in Bourbon, where the latter was supposed to go, and where Destiny promised to bring his troupe.

Night came. Destiny went to the place they had agreed to meet, accompanied by Verville's valet. Saldagne's two valets did not disappoint, and Verville himself delivered Mademoiselle Star into their hands. Imagine the joy of the two young lovers, who loved each other as much as could be, and the efforts they made not to show it. A few miles down the road, Star began to complain. She was urged to hang on until they reached a town two leagues distant, where she would be able to rest. She feigned increasing sickness. Verville's valet and Destiny voiced their concern in order to prepare Saldagne's valets, so they would not find it strange to stop a mere two leagues from where they had set out. Finally they reached the town and asked for lodging at the inn, which, fortunately, was full of guests and drinkers. Mademoiselle Star did an even better job of acting sick in candlelight than she had in the dark. She went to bed fully dressed and asked to rest for an hour, after which she thought she'd be able to get back in the saddle. Saldagne's valets, who were flat out drunks, let Verville's valet handle everything, as he carried out their master's orders. They attached themselves to four or five peasants who were as big drinkers as they were. The lot of them began drinking without paying attention to anyone else. From time to time, Verville's valet had a drink with them in order to egg them on and, under the pretext of going to check Star's condition, so she could leave as soon as possible, he went to tell her to get back on her horse, and Destiny too, to whom he gave directions. He returned to his drinkers and told them he had found their young lady asleep, which meant she would soon be able to get back in the saddle. He also told them Destiny had claimed a bed, and then he started to drink and toast the health of Saldagne's two valets, which by now was quite damaged. Their drinking was excessive and so was their drunkenness. They were unable to leave the table. They were carried to a barn, because they would have ruined any beds given them. Verville's valet pretended to be drunk and, having slept until dawn, abruptly awoke Saldagne's valets, telling them, with a distressed expression on his face, that their young lady had escaped, that he had sent his companion after her, and that they needed to get back on their horses and split up so as not to miss her. It took him over an hour to make himself understood, and I believe their drunkenness lasted over a week. Since the entire inn had got drunk that night, including the innkeeper's wife and the servant girls, it didn't occur to anyone to ask what had become of Destiny and his lady, and I don't even think anyone remembered them any more than if they had never been there in the first place.

While so many people sleep off their wine; while Verville's valet pretends to worry and urges Saldagne's valets to get going; and while the two drunks don't move any the faster for it, Destiny is covering a lot of ground with his dear Mademoiselle Star, filled with joy at having found her, and secure in the knowledge that Verville's valet pointed Saldagne's in the opposite direction. The moon was quite full that night, and they were on a highway that was easy to follow and that led to a village where we shall have them arrive in the next chapter.

CHAPTER XIII

The Sieur de La Rappinière's Bad Deed

DESTINY WAS VERY IMPATIENT to learn from his dear Star how she had ended up in the woods where Saldagne found her, but he was even more afraid of being followed. So he thought only of prodding his horse, which wasn't much of a specimen, and hurrying Star's mount, a powerful hackney, by shouting and using a switch he broke off a tree. Finally, the two young lovers felt reassured and, having exchanged a few words of love (for there was good reason to exchange them after what they had just experienced, and I'm sure they did, though I don't know any of the particulars) – after having, then, shared their love to their heart's content, Star told Destiny about all the help she had given Cave.

"And I fear," she told him, "that her distress will make her sick, for I've never seen its like. As for me, my dear brother, you can well imagine I needed as much consolation as she did, since your valet, having brought me the horse you sent for me, informed me that you had found Angélique's abductors and suffered serious injuries at their hands."

"Me! Wounded!" Destiny interrupted. "I was never in any danger of being wounded, and I didn't send you a horse. Something is going on here that I don't understand. I wondered why you kept asking me how I felt and if it didn't bother me that we were moving at such a fast pace."

"I'm delighted and worried at the same time," Star told him. "I was terribly worried about your wounds, but what you're telling me now makes me think your valet was bought by our enemies as part of some evil plot against us."

"It's more likely he was bought by someone who is too much of a friend," Destiny told her. "I don't have any enemies besides Saldagne, but he can't be the one behind my treacherous valet, because I know they beat him when he found you."

"And how do you know?" Star asked him. "Since I don't recall telling you anything about it."

"I'll tell you as soon as you tell me how you were taken from Le Mans."

"I can't tell you anything more than what I just told you," said Star. "The day after Cave and I returned to Le Mans, your valet brought me a horse sent by you and, pretending to be greatly distressed, told me you had been wounded by Angélique's captors, and that you wanted me to come to your side. I left within the hour, even though it was already quite late. I spent the night five leagues from Le Mans, in a place whose name I do not know. The next day, at the entrance to a wood, I was stopped by men unknown to me. I saw your valet beaten, which upset me no end. I saw them roughly throw a woman off a horse, and recognized Angélique. But the pitiful state I was in and my worries about your condition prevented me from thinking about her. I took her place and we travelled until evening, covering a lot of ground, most often through open country. We arrived well before nightfall at a country house where I noticed we were not welcome. That was where I recognized Saldagne, and the sight of him completed my despair. We continued on our way for some time, until we finally reached the house where they hid me, and from which you successfully delivered me."

Daylight began to appear just as Star finished relating her adventures. By then they were on the Le Mans highway and they hurried their horses in order to reach a town they saw in the distance. Destiny was eager to find his valet in order to discover what enemy they had to fear in these parts, besides the evil Saldagne. But after the nasty trick he had played on them, he wasn't likely to turn up where he could be found. Destiny was telling his dear Star everything he knew concerning Angélique, when a man, lying flat next to a hedge, so startled their horses that Destiny's almost fell under him while Mademoiselle Star's threw her to the ground. Alarmed by her fall, Destiny went to help her up as quickly as his horse would allow, which was still backing away, snorting and stumbling like the spooked horse he was. The lady wasn't hurt, the horses calmed down and Destiny went over to see whether the man by the hedge was dead or asleep. One could say he was both, since he was so drunk that, although he was snoring loudly (a sure sign he was alive), Destiny had a hard time waking him. Finally, after much pulling and shaking, he opened his eyes and Destiny realized he was none other than his own valet, the one he so wanted to find. The knave, drunk as he was, soon recognized his master, and seemed so upset upon seeing him that Destiny no longer doubted his guilt, whereas he had only suspected him of betrayal up to that point. Destiny asked the valet why he had told Mademoiselle Star he was wounded, why he had taken her from Le Mans, where Destiny had wanted him to lead her, and who had given him a horse; but he couldn't get a word out of him, either because he was too drunk, or because he pretended to be more so than he was. Destiny got angry, whacked him a few times with the flat of his sword, and after tying his hands with his horse's halter, used the one belonging to Mademoiselle Star's horse to leash the criminal. He cut a branch that he fashioned into a big stick, to be used should his valet refuse to walk willingly. He helped his Mademoiselle onto her horse, climbed onto his own and continued on his way, with his prisoner at his side like a dog on a leash.

The town Destiny had seen was the same one he'd left from two days earlier, leaving behind Monsieur de La Garouffière and his companions, who were still there because Madame Bouvillon was suffering from a vicious case of food poisoning. When Destiny arrived he didn't find Grudge, Olive and Ragotin, all of whom had returned to Le Mans. As for Léandre, he stayed with his dear Angélique. I don't need to tell you how she greeted Mademoiselle Star. One can easily imagine the expressions of affection that must have been exchanged by two girls who were very close, especially after the dangers they had experienced. Destiny told Monsieur de La Garouffière about the outcome of his trip and, after they met for a while in private, Destiny's valet was brought into one of the rooms of the inn. There he was questioned again and, as he again pretended to be mute, a gun was brought in with which to squeeze his thumbs. When he caught sight of it, he fell to his knees, burst out crying, begged his master's forgiveness and confessed that La Rappinière had made him do everything he had done, and promised to take him into his service as a reward. It was also learnt that La Rappinière was two leagues away, in a house, that he had usurped from a poor widow. Destiny again met privately with Monsieur de La Garouffière, who sent a lackey to tell La Rappinière he was needed for important business. This counsellor of the Rennes parliament exercised great power over the magistrate from Le Mans. He had saved him from the wheel in Brittany and protected him whenever he faced criminal charges. It wasn't that he didn't know he was a great scoundrel, just that La Rappinière's wife was something of a relative of his. The lackey sent to La Rappinière found him ready to get on his horse and ride to Le Mans. As soon as he learnt that Monsieur de La Garouffière was asking for him, he left to go meet him. Meanwhile, La Garouffière, who fancied himself quite the wit, sent for a portfolio, from which he produced all manner of verse, ranging from good to bad. He read them to Destiny, followed by a short story he translated from the Spanish, which you will read in the following chapter.

CHAPTER XIV

The Judge of Her Own Case

I T WAS IN AFRICA, ON THE ROCKY COAST, only an hour's distance from Fez, that Prince Muley, the King of Morocco's son, found himself alone at night, after getting lost while hunting. There wasn't the least cloud in the sky; the sea was calm and the moon and stars made it shine; it was one of those beautiful nights produced by hot climates that are nicer than the most beautiful days of our cold regions. The Moorish prince, galloping along the shore, entertained himself by looking at the moon and stars, which were reflected on the surface of the sea as in a mirror, when pitiful cries reached his ears. To satisfy his curiosity, he decided to investigate the area they were coming from. He spurred his horse, a barb if you will, in the direction of the cries, and found, among the rocks, a woman who was defending herself, as much as her strength would allow, against a man who was trying to tie her hands, while another woman attempted to gag her with a cloth. The arrival of the young prince interrupted the perpetrators of this violence and gave some relief to the one they were treating so badly. Muley asked her why she was screaming and the others what they were doing to her, but instead of answering, the man rushed towards him, brandishing a scimitar, and delivered a blow that would have severely wounded him, had he not avoided it thanks to the quickness of his horse. "Evildoer," Muley shouted at him, "how dare you attack the Prince of Fez?"

"I recognized you," the Moor replied, "but because you are my prince, and can have me punished, I have to take your life or lose my own."

As he finished speaking these words, he threw himself on Muley with so much fury that the Prince, valiant though he was, was reduced to thinking less about how to attack, and more about how to defend himself against such a dangerous enemy. Meanwhile, the two women were grappling and the one who, moments earlier, thought herself lost, prevented the other from fleeing, as if there were no doubt in her mind that her defender would prevail. Despair increases courage and sometimes gives it to those who lack it most. Although the Prince's valour was incomparably greater than his enemy's and seconded by uncommon vigour and skill, the punishment warranted by the Moor's crime made him risk everything and gave him so much courage and strength that the winner, between the Prince and him, remained uncertain for a long time. But Heaven, which usually protects those it raises above the rest, made the Prince's retinue fortuitously pass by the area, closely enough to hear the noise made by the combatants and the two women's cries. They hurried there and recognized their master just as, having struck down the one they saw bearing arms against him, he had him on the ground, where he did not want to kill him, saving him instead for an exemplary punishment. He forbade his people to do anything but attach him to a horse's tail, in order to prevent him from doing anything against either himself or others. The women rode with two horsemen and, in this equipage, Muley and his retinue arrived in Fez at daybreak.

This young prince ruled in Fez as absolutely as if he were already king. He called the Moor before him. His name was Ahmed and he was the son of one of Fez's wealthiest inhabitants. No one knew the two women, because the Moors (who are the most jealous of all men) take great care to hide their women and their slave girls from the eyes of the world. The woman the Prince rescued surprised him, and the entire court too, with her beauty, greater than had been seen in all Africa, and by a majestic demeanour, which a slave's miserable garment could not conceal from those who saw her. The other woman was dressed the way local women of some quality are, and could be considered pretty, although less so than the other one. But even if she could compete in beauty with her, the pallor fear had imparted to her face diminished her beauty as much as the former's was increased by the natural rouge an honest modesty applied to hers. The Moor appeared before Muley with the countenance of a criminal, and kept his eyes downcast. Muley ordered him to confess to his crime if he didn't want to die under torture. "I am well aware of what is being prepared for me, and which I have deserved," he answered proudly, "and, if there were some reason for me not to confess, no torture exists that could make me; but I cannot evade death since I tried to kill you, and I don't mind your knowing that the rage I feel at having failed torments me more than anything your torturers could invent for me. These Spanish women," he added, "were my slaves. One of them was able to adapt, even marrying my brother Zayed. The other one refused to change her religion and never acknowledged the love I had for her." He refused to add anything, no matter how much he was threatened. Muley had him shackled and thrown into a cell. Zayed's wife, the renegade, was put in a separate prison, and the beautiful slave was sent to live with a Moor named Zuleyma, a nobleman from Spain who had left that country because he could not bring himself to convert to Christianity. He was from the illustrious Zegris family, once upon a time of great renown in Granada, and his wife Zorayd, who was from the same family, had the reputation of being the most beautiful woman in Fez, and of possessing as much wit as beauty. She was immediately taken with the Christian slave's beauty, as well as her mind, after the very first conversations she had with her. If this beautiful Christian had been capable of finding consolation, she would have found it in Zorayd's affection, but, as though she wanted to avoid anything that could alleviate her pain, she sought only to be left alone in order to experience greater distress. When she was with Zorayd, she had to exercise great self-control to hold back her sighs and her tears. Prince Muley was very curious to hear her adventures. He had told Zuleyma this and, as he hid nothing from him, he had also admitted that he was inclined to love the beautiful Christian, and that he would already have let her know if the great distress that she exhibited hadn't made him fear the existence of an unknown Spanish rival who, as far away as he might be, would make it impossible for her to be happy, even in a place where he was absolute ruler. So Zuleyma ordered his wife to learn from the Christian woman the details of her life and through what circumstances she had become Ahmed's slave. Zorayd was as curious as the Prince, and did not find it difficult to learn the story of the Spanish slave, who felt she couldn't refuse someone who had been so friendly and affectionate towards her. She told Zorayd she would satisfy her curiosity as much as she wanted, but since she could only relate misfortunes, she was afraid her story would be very boring. "You'll see that it won't be," answered Zorayd, "because of my rapt attention and my empathy you will know that you won't be able to confide your secrets to anyone who loves you more than I do." She embraced her as she said these words, begging her not to delay any further the satisfaction she sought. They were alone and the beautiful slave girl, after wiping away the tears the memory of her misfortune caused her to shed, began to tell her story as follows:

"My name is Sofía. I am Spanish, born in Valencia. I was brought up with all the care that well-born, wealthy people like my parents bestow upon a girl who was the first fruit of their marriage and who from the earliest age seemed worthy of their warmest affection. I had a brother who was a year younger than me. He was as personable as it is possible to be. He loved me as much as I loved him, and our mutual friendship was such that when we weren't together there was a noticeable expression of sadness and worry on our faces that the most entertaining activities for children our age could not dissipate. So no one dared separate us. Together we learnt everything that is taught to children from the best families of both sexes, and everyone was amazed to see that I was no less skilled than he at rough cavalry exercises and that he was equally adept at doing everything that well-born girls do best. Such an extraordinary education made a gentleman who was a friend of my father wish to have his children brought up with us. He proposed it to my parents, who gave their consent. The proximity of our houses facilitated the plan. This gentleman was as wealthy as my father and no less noble. He also only had a son and a daughter who were more or less the same age as my brother and me. There was little doubt in Valencia that our two families would someday be united by a double marriage. Don Carlos and Lucía were equally likeable. My brother loved Lucía and was loved by her; Don Carlos loved me and I loved him too. Our parents were well aware of this and, far from objecting, would have arranged our marriages if we hadn't been so young. But the happy state of our innocent love was shattered by the death of my sweet brother. A high fever took him in a week, and that was the first of my misfortunes. Lucía was so distraught that no one was able to dissuade her from entering a convent. I fell gravely ill and Don Carlos was sick enough for his father to fear losing his children, so affected was he by the loss of my brother – whom he loved – the danger I faced and his sister's resolution. In the end, our youth cured us and time lessened our distress.

"Don Carlos's father died soon afterwards, leaving his son very wealthy and debt-free. His wealth allowed him to indulge his generous personality. The gifts he dreamt up flattered my vanity, made his love public and increased my own. Don Carlos was often at my parents' feet imploring them to defer his happiness no longer by giving him their daughter's hand. Meanwhile he continued with his lavish gifts. My father feared that he would eventually eat into his fortune, which convinced him to go ahead with the marriage. Thus was Don Carlos led to believe he would soon be his son-in-law, and Don Carlos reacted with such extraordinary joy it would have persuaded me he loved me more than life itself, if I didn't already believe it as firmly as I did. He organized an engagement ball in my honour, to which the whole city was invited. For his misfortune and mine, a Neapolitan count was in attendance, having come to Spain on important business. He found me pretty enough to fall in love with me and to ask my father for my hand in marriage, after learning the rank he held in the kingdom of Valencia. My father let himself be dazzled by the wealth and quality of this foreigner and promised him whatever he asked for. That very day he told Don Carlos he could no longer aspire to my hand, and he forbade me to receive his visits, at the same time ordering me to consider the Italian count the man I would wed upon his return from a trip he had to make to Madrid. I hid my displeasure from my father, but when I was alone Don Carlos appeared to my memory as the world's most attractive man. I reflected on everything that was disagreeable about the Italian count. I developed an intense aversion to him and felt I loved Don Carlos more than I thought possible, and that it would be equally impossible to live without him or be happy with his rival. I had recourse to tears, but this was a weak remedy for a sickness like mine. Don Carlos entered my room at that point, without asking permission, as was his custom. He found me in tears, and could not hold back his own, despite the plan he had to hide his true feelings until he could discover mine. He threw himself at my feet, and, taking my hands that he wet with his tears, he said, 'Sofía, I am to lose you and a foreigner you barely know will be happier than I because he is wealthier? He will possess you, Sofía, and you consent to it, you whom I have loved so much, who led me to believe you loved me too and who was promised to me by her father! But alas! By an unjust father, a greedy father who did not keep his word! If you were,' he continued, 'goods with a monetary value, my fidelity alone could afford you, and thanks to it you would be mine rather than anyone else's, if you remembered your promise to be faithful to me. But,' he cried out, 'do you think a man who was brave enough to raise his desires to your level isn't brave enough to take revenge on the one you prefer to him? And why would you find it strange if a poor unfortunate who has lost everything is ready to attempt just about anything? Ah! If you want me to die alone, my lucky rival will live, since he was able to win your heart and with it your protection. But Don Carlos, who is odious to you and whom you have abandoned to his despair, will die a death cruel enough to slake the hatred you have for him.'

"'Don Carlos,' I answered, 'are you teaming up with an unjust father and a man I cannot love in order to persecute me, and do you attribute to me as a private crime a misfortune we both share? Feel sorry for me instead of accusing me, and think up ways of keeping me for yourself instead of reproaching me. I have better reasons to reproach you myself. I could make you admit you never loved me enough, since you never knew me well enough. But we don't have time to lose in useless conversation. I will follow you anywhere. I allow you to undertake anything and I promise that I will dare to do anything in order to be with you always.'

"My words so consoled Don Carlos that he was as transported with joy as he had been racked with pain. He asked me to forgive him for having accused me of doing the injustice he thought was being done to him and, having explained to me that, short of allowing myself to be abducted, it was impossible for me not to obey my father, I consented to everything he planned and promised that the following night I would be ready to go anywhere he wanted to take me.

"Everything is easy for a lover. It took Don Carlos one day to put his affairs in order, withdraw money and arrange for a boat from Barcelona, which would set sail at whatever time he decided. Meanwhile, I wore all my jewellery, gathered all the money I could and, for someone so young, I did such a good job concealing my intentions that no one suspected anything. I wasn't watched, and so was able to slip away at night through a garden door where I found Claudio, a page who was dear to Carlos because he sang as well as his voice was beautiful and showed, in the way he expressed himself and his behaviour, more wit, more good sense and good manners than one would ordinarily expect from the age and condition of a page. He told me his master had sent him ahead to lead me to where a boat was waiting for us and where he wasn't able to take me himself for reasons he would explain later. One of Don Carlos's slaves whom I knew quite well joined us. We left the city easily and didn't have to walk very far before we saw a ship at anchor, and a sloop waiting for us by the shore. I was told that my dear Don Carlos would soon arrive, and that I should get into the sloop meanwhile. The slave helped me in, and several men I had seen on the shore that I took to be sailors made Claudio get in as well. He seemed to resist and make some efforts to stay on the shore. This added to the concern Don Carlos's absence already gave me. When I asked where he was, the slave told me proudly that there was no more Don Carlos for me. At the same time I heard Claudio's screams. He was crying, and saying to the slave, 'Ahmed, you traitor! You promised to get rid of a rival and leave me with my lover.'

"'Foolhardy Claudia,' the slave replied, 'should I keep my word to a traitor and should I have hoped that someone who isn't loyal to her master would be so enough to me to prevent her from sending the coast guard after me and deprive me of my Sofía, whom I love more than myself?'

"These words, addressed to a woman I thought was a man and that were incomprehensible to me, caused me such intense displeasure that I passed out in the arms of the perfidious Moor, who had not left my side. My fainting spell lasted a long time, and when I recovered I was in the cabin of a ship that was already far out to sea.

"You can imagine my despair, seeing that I was without Don Carlos and with the enemies of my religion instead, because I realized I was now in the Moors' hands, that the slave Ahmed had all kinds of authority over them and that his brother Zayed commanded the vessel. No sooner did this insolent Moor see that I had come to than he bluntly told me he had been in love with me for a long time and that his passion made him abduct me and take me to Fez, where it would be up to me to be as happy as I would in

Spain, while it wouldn't be up to him if I were to stop missing Don Carlos. I leapt at him, disregarding the weakness I still felt from fainting and with a skill and vigour he wasn't expecting, which I had acquired thanks to my education (as I told you). I pulled his scimitar from the scabbard, and was about to avenge myself if his brother Zayed hadn't grabbed my arm in time to save his life. I was easily disarmed, because, having missed my opportunity, I made no vain efforts against so many enemies. Ahmed, who had been frightened by my attempt, cleared my cabin, and left me in what state of despair you can imagine given the cruel change in fortune I had experienced. I spent the night grieving, and the following day brought no relief to my despair. Time, which often lifts similar burdens, had no effect on mine, and the second day on the ship I was in even greater misery than the sinister night when I lost my freedom, the hope of seeing Don Carlos again or of ever having a moment's respite for the rest of my life. Ahmed had found me so ferocious every time he dared appear before me that he no longer did. From time to time they brought me something to eat, which I rejected so stubbornly that Ahmed worried he'd abducted me to no purpose.

"Meanwhile, the ship had passed through the straits, and was nearing the coast of Fez, when Claudio entered my cabin. As soon as I saw him, I said, 'Bastard, who betrayed me, what did I do to you that you should make me the most miserable person in the world, and take my Don Carlos away from me?'

"'He loved you too much,' he answered, 'and since I loved him as much as you did, it wasn't a crime to try and eliminate a rival. But while I may have betrayed you, Ahmed betrayed me as well, and I would be as miserable as you if I didn't find some consolation in not being the only one who is miserable.'

"'Explain these mysteries to me,' I told him, 'and tell me who you are, so I know whether I am dealing with a male or a female enemy.'

"'Sofía,' he said then, 'I am of the same sex as you, and like you I have been in love with Don Carlos. But while we may have

burned with the same fire, our success was not equal. Don Carlos
has always loved you and always believed you loved him, while he
never loved me and must never have thought I loved him, since he
never knew who I really was. I am from Valencia, like you, and
wasn't born with so little nobility and wealth that Don Carlos,
having married me, would have been subject to the harsh criti-
cism meted out to those who marry below their station. But the
love he had for you consumed him completely and he only had
eyes for you. It wasn't that mine didn't do everything to exempt
my mouth from the shameful confession of my weakness. I went
everywhere I thought I would find him. I stood where he could
see me, and was attentive to him the way he would have been to
me if he loved me the way I loved him. I was master of myself
and my wealth, having lost my parents at an early age, and I
was often offered suitable matches. But the hope I had always
had of eventually inspiring Don Carlos to love me made me turn
a deaf ear to these offers. Instead of becoming discouraged by
my prospects, like any person would who, like me, had enough
attributes not to be scorned, my love for Don Carlos was fanned
by the very difficulty I encountered making him love me. Finally,
in order to have no second thoughts for not having tried everything, I got my hair cut and, having dressed as a man, I arranged
to be introduced to Don Carlos by a servant who had grown old
in the service of our family. He was a poor gentleman from the
mountains of Toledo, who pretended to be my father. My face
and mien, which your lover did not find unpleasant, led him to
engage me. He did not recognize me, even though he had seen
me many times, and he was soon as impressed by my wit as by
the beauty of my voice, my singing style and my ability to play
all the musical instruments with which persons of quality may
entertain themselves without shame. He thought he had found in
me qualities rarely seen in a page, and I gave him so many proofs
of discretion and loyalty that he treated me more like a confidant
than a servant. You know better than anyone that I am not exaggerating. You yourself praised me many times to Don Carlos in

my presence and did me favours that reflected well on me, but owing these to a rival only made me furious, so just as they made me more appealing to Don Carlos, they made you more detestable to the unhappy Claudia (for that is my name). Your marriage meanwhile was going forward, and my hopes were receding. The Italian count, whose wealth and pedigree dazzled your father as much as his ugliness and the flaws in his character repelled you, at least afforded me the pleasure of seeing yours dashed, and I was flattered by the insane hopes that any change inspires in the minds of the forlorn. Finally, your father preferred the foreigner you didn't love to Don Carlos whom you did. I saw the one who made me unhappy unhappy in his turn, and a rival I hated even unhappier than I, because I had not lost anything in a man who had never belonged to me, whereas you lost Don Carlos, who was all yours, and this loss, great as it might be, was perhaps a lesser misfortune than having as your eternal tyrant a man you could never love. But my prosperity, or more precisely my hopes, did not last. I learnt from Don Carlos that you had decided to follow him, and I was even employed to make the arrangements for the plan he had to take you to Barcelona and from there to France or Italy. All the strength I had up to that point with which to bear my ill fortune abandoned me after a hard blow that surprised me all the more, since it was completely unexpected. I was distraught to the point of sickness, and sick to the point of being bedridden. One day that I was complaining to myself about my sad fate and, believing I wasn't heard by anyone, I was speaking as loudly as I would have to some confidant, I saw the Moor Ahmed appear before me. He had listened to me and, after the embarrassment he caused me had passed, he said these words: "I know who you are, Claudia, since before the time you disguised your sex to serve as a page for Don Carlos, and if I never made it be known I knew, it was because I had a plan just like you did. I just heard you make desperate resolutions. You want to reveal yourself to your master as a girl who is dying of love for him and who has lost hope of ever being loved by him. Then you want to kill yourself in front of him to cause at least regret if you couldn't inspire love. Poor girl! What will you do by killing yourself other than further guarantee Sofía's possession of Don Carlos! I have much better advice to give you, if you're capable of following it. Take your lover away from your rival. The means are easy, if you'll believe me, and although it requires resolve, you won't need more than you had when you dressed as a man and risked your honour in order to satisfy your love. Listen to me carefully," the Moor continued. "I am going to share a secret with you that I never told anyone, and if the plan I am going to propose doesn't meet with your approval, you don't have to go along with it. I am from a noble family in Fez. My misfortune made me Don Carlos's slave and Sofía's beauty made me hers. I have told you many things in a few words. You think your misery is without remedy because your lover is abducting his mistress and taking her to Barcelona. It is actually your happiness and mine, if you are able to take advantage of the opportunity. I've dealt with my ransom and paid it. An African corvette is waiting for me in the harbour, near where Don Carlos is keeping another one ready to execute his plan. He's postponed it by one day. Let's act before he does. Go tell Sofía on behalf of her master to be ready to leave tonight when you come to pick her up. Bring her to my ship. I'll take her to Africa while you stay in Valencia, in sole possession of your lover, who maybe would have loved you as much as Sofía if he had only known you loved him."'

"Claudia's final words so exacerbated my suffering that, with a big sigh, I fainted again without showing the least sign of life. The cries let out by Claudia, who may have been repentant for ruining my happiness without furthering her own, brought Ahmed and his brother to my cabin. I was given every treatment imaginable. When I came to I heard Claudia attacking the Moor for betraying us: 'Infidel dog!' she yelled at him. 'Why did you convince me to reduce this beautiful girl to such a sorry state if you didn't intend to leave me with my lover? And why did you make me betray a man who is so dear to me, when that betrayal cost us both as much?

How can you claim to be of noble birth in your country when you are the most cowardly and treacherous of men?'

"'Shut your mouth, crazy girl!' Ahmed replied. 'Don't hold a crime against me that you were an accomplice to. I already told you that anyone who could betray a master, like you did, deserved to be betrayed, and, by taking you with me, that I was guaranteeing my life, and maybe Sofía's, because she might die of sadness if she knew you had stayed with Don Carlos.'

"The noise the sailors made, who were ready to enter the port of Sale, combined with the ship's guns and the shore's reply, interrupted Ahmed and Claudia's mutual reproaches and freed me for some time from the sight of these two odious people. We disembarked, Claudia and I had our faces veiled, and we were lodged with the perfidious Ahmed, in the house of a Moor who was one of his relatives. The next day we were brought by covered wagon to Fez, where, while Ahmed was joyously greeted by his father, I arrived the most dejected and despairing person in the whole world. As for Claudia, it didn't take her long to renounce Christianity and marry Zayed, the brother of the treacherous Ahmed. This nasty girl used every trick to get me to change religion as well and marry Ahmed as she had Zayed, and she became the cruellest of my tyrants when, having exhausted all kinds of promises, kindnesses and shows of affection, Ahmed and the rest of his family directed at me all the barbarity of which they were capable. Every day I had to exercise my fortitude against so many enemies, and I was better at enduring my hardships than I wished when I began to suspect that Claudia repented her meanness. In public she persecuted me with more apparent animosity than the others, while in private she sometimes did me favours that made me view her as someone who could have been virtuous if she had been raised to be. One day, while all the other women of the household had gone to the public baths, as is your Muslim custom, she came over to me, with a sad face, and said the following words:

"'Beautiful Sofía, whatever reason I once had to hate you, my hatred ended when I lost all hope of ever possessing the one who didn't love me enough because he loved you too much. I feel constant guilt for having made you unhappy and for having abandoned my God because I feared men. The least of my feelings would be enough to make me undertake the things my sex finds most difficult. I can no longer live far from Spain and any Christian land, with infidels among whom I know I can't find my salvation, neither in life nor after my death. You'll be able to judge whether my repentance is sincere by the secret I am about to confide, which will make you the master of my life, and give you the means to take revenge on me for all the pain I was forced to inflict on you. I have won over fifty mostly Spanish Christian slaves, all very enterprising men. With the money I secretly gave them, they have acquired a vessel capable of taking us to Spain, if God is favourable to my plan. It's up to you to follow my destiny, to save yourself if I succeed or, if you perish with me, to free yourself from the hands of your cruel enemies and end your unhappy life. Make up your mind, Sofía, and while we cannot be suspected of any plot, let's deliberate without wasting any time about the most important decision of my life and yours.'

"I threw myself at Claudia's feet and, judging her based on myself, I did not doubt her sincerity. I thanked her with as much expressiveness and depth of feeling as I could. I was thankful for the favour I thought she wanted to do me. We chose a day for our escape towards a place on the shore where she said rock formations would hide our small craft. That day, which I thought would be a happy one, arrived. We had no difficulty leaving the house and the city. I admired the benevolence of Heaven for the ease with which we were carrying out our plan, and I constantly thanked God for it, but the end of my trials was not as near as I thought. Claudia was only carrying out the orders of the perfidious Ahmed and, even more perfidious than he, she was only leading me to an out-of-the-way place at night in order to abandon me to the violence of the Moor, who wouldn't have dared undertake an assault on my modesty in the house of his father, who, though Muslim, was morally a good man. I innocently followed her – she, who was leading me to perdition – and I thought I would never be grateful enough for the freedom that I hoped to soon enjoy thanks to her. I kept thanking her and walking quickly over rough, rocky terrain to where she said her men would be waiting for her, when I heard sounds coming from behind me. I looked back and saw Ahmed grasping his scimitar. 'Loathsome slaves,' he yelled, 'so this is how you flee your master!' I didn't have time to answer. Claudia grabbed my arms from behind and Ahmed dropped his scimitar to join forces with the renegade. Together they did what they could to tie my hands with rope they'd brought for that purpose. Being more energetic and experienced than women usually are, I resisted the efforts of this evil pair for a long time, but eventually I felt myself weaken and, no longer able to depend on my strength, I resorted to screams which might attract some passer-by in this deserted place; I had just about given up, when Prince Muley appeared against all hope. You know how he saved my honour and probably my life, because I would surely have died of sorrow if the detestable Ahmed had satisfied his brutality."

Thus did Sofía conclude the story of her adventures, and the kind Zorayd encouraged her to trust in the Prince's generosity to procure her the means of returning to Spain. That very day she told her husband all that she had learnt from Sofía, which he communicated to Muley. Even though everything he learnt about the beautiful Christian's misfortune did not flatter his passion for her, virtuous as he was, he was pleased to know it, and to learn that she was emotionally attached to someone in her country, so as not to undertake, in the hope of a happy outcome, an enterprise he would later regret. He esteemed Sofía's virtue, and was motivated by his own to try and make her less unhappy than she was. He had Zorayd tell her that he would send her back to Spain whenever she wished, and after coming to this decision he stopped seeing her, trusting neither his own virtue nor her beauty. It was no simple task for her to put together a return trip. It was a long way to Spain, whose merchants did not trade with Fez. And even if she could find a Christian ship, young and beautiful as she was, she might find among the men of her own religion what she had feared finding among the Moors. Integrity is rarely encountered on a ship; honesty fares little better than it does in wartime, and wherever innocence and beauty are weak, the audacity of evil is emboldened by its advantage. Zorayd advised Sofía to dress as a man, because her height, more advantageous than most women's, would facilitate this disguise. She told her the idea came from Muley, who couldn't find anyone in Fez to whom he could confidently entrust her. Zorayd also told her he had been kind enough to provide for her sex's sense of decency by giving her a female companion who shared her religion and who would be disguised as well. He hoped this would alleviate the worry she might have to find herself alone on a ship among soldiers and sailors. The Moorish prince had bought from a Barbary pirate a catch he had made at sea. It came from a ship belonging to the governor of Oran that carried the entire family of a Spanish nobleman that, out of animosity, this governor sent to Spain as prisoners. Muley had learnt that this Christian was one of the best hunters in the world and, since hunting was the young prince's greatest love, he had wanted him as a slave and, the better to keep him, hadn't wanted to separate him from his wife, his son and his daughter. In the two years he lived in Fez in the Muley's service, he taught the Prince how to shoot with precision all kinds of game, both running and flying, as well as hunts unknown to the Moor. He had earned the Prince's good graces and become so necessary to his entertainment that the Prince never consented to a ransom and tried by various inducements and kind deeds to make him forget Spain. But his homesickness, combined with the idea that he would never be able to return, gave him a case of melancholy that ended with his death, and his wife's soon afterwards. Muley felt remorseful for not having granted them their freedom when they asked for it, people who had earned it through their service, and he wanted, as much as possible, via their children, to right the wrong he thought he had done them. The girl, named Dorotea, was Sofía's age. She was beautiful and intelligent. Her brother, who was no more than fifteen, was called Sancho. Muley chose both of them to keep Sofía company, and used this opportunity to send them to Spain together. Men's clothing in the Spanish style was made for the two young ladies and little Sancho. Muley showed his munificence with the quantity of jewels he gave Sofía. He also gave Dorotea beautiful gifts which, combined with those her father had already received from the Prince's generosity, made her wealthy for the rest of her life.

At that time, Emperor Charles V was waging war in Africa and had laid siege to the city of Tunis. He had sent an ambassador to Muley to negotiate a ransom for several noble Spaniards shipwrecked on the coast of Morocco. It was to this ambassador that Muley recommended Sofía using the name Don Fernando, a nobleman who did not wish to be known under his real name, while Dorotea and her brother were supposed to be in his party, one as a gentleman and the other as a page. Sofía and Zorayd could not part without regret, and many tears were shed by both. Zorayd gave the beautiful Christian a pearl necklace of such value that she would not have accepted it if the kind Moor and her husband Zuleyma, who loved Sofía no less than did his wife, hadn't made it known to her that she could not disappoint them any the more than if she refused this token of their friendship. Zorayd made Sophie promise to keep in touch by communicating from time to time by way of Tangiers or Oran or other places the Emperor controlled in Africa.

The Christian ambassador embarked at Salé, taking with him Sofía, who must be called Don Fernando from now on. He joined the Emperor's army, which was still outside Tunis. Our Spanish woman in disguise was presented to him as an Andalusian nobleman who had long been a slave of the Prince of Fez. She did not have reason enough to love her life to fear losing it in war and, wishing to pass as a caballero, she could not honourably fail to take part in combat often, as did many valiant men who filled the ranks of the Emperor's army. So she joined the volunteers, and distinguished herself at every turn, so gloriously that the

Emperor himself heard of the fake Don Fernando. She was fortunate enough to be near him when, in the heat of a battle in which
the Christians were at a marked disadvantage, he stumbled into
a Moorish ambush, was abandoned by his own troops and surrounded by infidels, and would likely have been killed, his horse
having already been under him, had our Amazon not helped him
onto hers and, assisting his valour by performing incredible feats,
bought the Christians enough time to regroup and rescue the
valiant Emperor. Such a brave deed did not go unrewarded. The
Emperor gave the unknown Don Fernando a lucrative commandership and the cavalry regiment of a Spanish lord who had been
killed in the most recent combat. He also gave her the equipage
of a nobleman, and from that moment no one in the entire army
was more esteemed and respected than this valiant girl. All the
actions of a man came so naturally to her, her face was so handsome, and made her appear so young, her valour was so admirable
in one so young, her wit so charming that there wasn't a single
person of quality in the Emperor's command who didn't seek
her friendship. One shouldn't therefore be surprised, what with
everyone praising her and even more so her heroic deeds, that the
Emperor made her one of his favourites.

During that time fresh troops arrived from Spain on the ships
that resupplied the army with money and ammunition. The
Emperor, accompanied by his top commanders, including Don
Fernando, wanted to review the new recruits. Among these newly
arrived soldiers she thought she saw Don Carlos, and she wasn't
mistaken. This preoccupied her for the rest of the day. She had
her men look for him where the new troops were quartered,
but they couldn't find him because he had changed his name.
She couldn't sleep that night and rose at dawn to go looking
herself for that dear lover, who had made her shed so many
tears. She found him, but he didn't recognize her because she
had grown taller and her face was tanned by the African sun.
She pretended to mistake him for someone of her acquaintance,
and asked him for news of Seville and another person whose

name was the first to pop into her head. Don Carlos told her she was mistaken, that he had never been to Seville and that he was from Valencia. "You look a lot like someone who was very dear to me," said Sofía, "and, because of this resemblance, I wouldn't mind becoming a friend of yours, if you don't mind being one of mine."

"The same reason," replied Don Carlos, "that makes you offer me your friendship would already have acquired mine if it were worth as much as yours. You resemble someone I loved for a long time, and you have her face and her voice, but you are not of the same sex, and obviously," he added with a long sigh, "you don't share her mood."

Sofía couldn't help blushing at Don Carlos's comment, which he didn't notice, maybe because his eyes, which were starting to well up with tears, couldn't see the changes in Sofía's face. She was moved and, no longer able to hide her emotions, she invited Don Carlos to visit her in her tent, where she would wait for him. She left him after telling him where she was quartered and that she was called Quartermaster General Don Fernando. When he heard that name, Don Carlos feared he hadn't paid him enough respect. He knew the Emperor had the utmost regard for him, and that, unknown though he might be, he shared his master's favour with the highest-ranking members of the court. He did not find it difficult to locate Don Fernando's quarters, which were known to everyone, and was received as well as a simple caballero could be by one of the top field commanders in the army. He again recognized Sofía's face in Don Fernando's, was even more surprised than he had been before and was most amazed by the sound of his voice, which penetrated his soul and renewed the memory of the person he had most loved in the whole world. Sofía, still unknown to her lover, invited him to eat with her, and after the meal, having dismissed the servants and given orders not to be disturbed, made the cavalry officer repeat that he was from Valencia and then tell what she knew as well as he did of their shared adventures up to the day of her planned abduction.

"Would you believe," Don Carlos told her, "that a girl of noble birth who had received so many proofs of my love and had given me so many of hers, was without fidelity or honour, had the ability to hide such major faults from me, and was so blind that she chose to follow a young page of mine who abducted her the day before I was supposed to?"

"But can you be sure?" Sofía said. "Chance is the master of all things and often enjoys confounding our logic with the most unexpected outcomes. Your mistress may have been forced to leave you and may be unhappier than she is guilty."

"I would thank God," Don Carlos replied, "if I could harbour any doubts about her guilt! All the losses and misfortunes she caused me would not have been difficult to bear and I wouldn't even consider myself unhappy if I could believe she were still faithful to me; but she is only faithful to the perfidious Claudio, and only feigned to love the unhappy Don Carlos in order to fool him."

"It seems, based on what you are saying," Sofía responded, "that you didn't love her very much, to accuse her without hearing her side and describe her as mean in addition to flighty."

"How could anyone be meaner," Don Carlos exclaimed, "than this impudent girl who, in order to shield my page from suspicion, the very night she disappeared from her father's house, left a letter in her room that was a masterpiece of deception and made me too miserable to forget it? I would like to recite it to you, so you can judge for yourself what deceit this young lady was capable of."

Letter

You should not have forbidden me to love Don Carlos after ordering me to do so. Merit as great as his could only inspire great love in me and, when the mind of a young person is taken, no room is left for material considerations. I am therefore leaving with the one you found good enough for me to love since my youth, and without whom it would be as impossible to live as it would be not to die a thousand times a day with a stranger I

couldn't love, were he even wealthier than he is. Our fault (if it
is one) deserves your forgiveness. If you grant it, we shall return
to receive it more swiftly than we fled your unjust treatment.
Sofía

"You can imagine," Don Carlos continued, "the extreme distress
Sofía's parents experienced when they read this letter. They hoped
I was still with their daughter, hiding in Valencia or not far away.
They kept their loss a secret from everyone, except the Viceroy,
who was their relative, and at the crack of dawn the law entered
my bedroom and found me sleeping. I was as surprised by this
visit as I could be, and after they asked me where Sofía was, I also
asked them where she was, which annoyed my interlocutors, who
roughed me up as they took me to prison. I was interrogated and,
faced with Sofía's letter, couldn't say anything in my defence. This
made it appear that I had planned to abduct her, but it was even
more apparent that my page had disappeared at the same time
as she. Sofía's parents organized a search, while my friends, for
their part, made all kinds of efforts to find out where the page
had taken her. It was the only way to show my innocence, but no
trace was ever found of the fugitive lovers, and my enemies then
accused me of killing them both. Finally, injustice aided by force
triumphed over oppressed innocence. I was told I would soon be
sentenced, and that the sentence would be death. I didn't expect
Heaven to deliver a miracle on my behalf, so out of desperation
I decided to risk a jailbreak. I joined forces with some bandits,
prisoners like me, and all of them men of action. We broke down
the doors of our prison and, with the help of our friends, we
reached the mountains closest to Valencia before the Viceroy could
be informed. We became the masters of the countryside. Sofía's
infidelity, her parents' persecution, everything the Viceroy had
done against me that I thought was unjust and, finally, the loss of
my property made me despair so that I risked my life whenever my
companions and I met resistance. This led to my acquiring such
a reputation among them that they wanted me to be their leader.

I had so much success as their leader that our troupe became a threat to the kingdoms of Valencia and Aragon, and we had the gall to exact tribute from these countries. I realize I am confiding very delicate matters," Don Carlos added, "but the honour you do me and my inclination make me willing to have you be the master of my life by revealing such dangerous secrets to you. Finally," he went on, "I got tired of being an outlaw. I stole away from my companions, who didn't suspect anything, and made my way to Barcelona, where I joined as a simple cavalryman the new recruits headed for Africa. I have no reason to care for life and, after making a mess of mine, I cannot make better use of it than against the enemies of my religion and in your service, as your kindness towards me has caused the only joy my soul has been capable of since the greatest ingrate among women made me the unhappiest man alive."

Unknown Sofía took unjustly accused Sofía's side, and left no stone unturned to persuade her lover not to pass judgement on his mistress before knowing more about her actions. She told the unhappy caballero that she felt for him in his misfortune, that it would make her happy to help him, and that to give him more concrete evidence of it than words alone, she asked him to be in her service. Then, when the opportunity presented itself, she would use her influence with the Emperor and that of all her friends to free him from the persecution of Sofía's parents and the Viceroy of Valencia. Don Carlos never agreed to everything the fake Don Fernando told him in Sofía's defence, but he agreed in the end to the offers she made him of her table and her roof. That very day the faithful mistress spoke to Don Carlos's colonel, and made him agree that this caballero, who she said was her relative, should serve under him – I mean her.

Now our unfortunate lover is in the service of his mistress, whom he believes dead or unfaithful. From the start of his service he feels perfectly at home with the one he takes to be his master, and finds it difficult to figure out just how he made himself so well liked by Don Fernando in such a short time. He is at the same time his chief of staff, his secretary, his gentleman and his confidant. The other servants have scarcely less respect for him than they do for Don Fernando, and he would surely be happy, knowing himself to be valued by a master who seems so likeable and that a secret instinct prompts him to like, if thoughts of Sofía lost – of Sofía unfaithful – did not constantly return to his mind, causing a sadness in him that the kindness of such a dear master and the improvement in his prospects could not overcome. Whatever tender feelings Sofía had for him, she was pleased to see him distressed, knowing that she was the cause of his distress. She spoke to him so often about Sofía and defended, sometimes with so much passion, if not anger and bitterness, the one whom Don Carlos nevertheless accused of failing to live up to her fidelity and honour, that he came to believe that this Don Fernando, who always brought up the same subject, had once been in love with Sofía and might still be.

The African war ended the way it is described in history books. The Emperor waged war later in Germany, Italy and Flanders, as well as other places. Our female warrior, under the name Don Fernando, added to her reputation as a valiant and experienced captain through several valorous and strategic actions, even though the latter quality is rarely seen in someone as young as the sex of this valiant girl made her appear to be.

The Emperor needed to go to Flanders, and asked the King of France permission to pass through his territory. The great monarch who ruled at that time wanted to surpass in generosity and openness a mortal enemy who had always had greater success than he and hadn't always been very gracious about it. Charles V was greeted in Paris as if he were the King of France. The handsome Don Fernando was among the small group of gentlemen who accompanied him and, if her master had spent more time in the world's most elegant court, the beautiful Spanish woman, mistaken for a man, would have inspired love in many a French lady and jealousy in the most accomplished courtiers.

Meanwhile, the Viceroy of Valencia died in Spain. Don Fernando trusted enough in his merit and his master's affection to dare ask for such an important position, and obtained it without incurring envy. As soon as he could, he informed Don Carlos of the success of his enterprise and gave him the hope that, as soon as he became Viceroy of Valencia, he would settle matters with Sofía's parents and obtain the Emperor's pardon for having been the chief of the bandits, and would even try to have his property returned in addition to helping him out in any other way possible. Don Carlos could have found consolation in all these wonderful promises if his tragic love had not left him inconsolable.

The Emperor arrived in Spain and went straight to Madrid, while Don Fernando went to take possession of his government. The day after the Emperor's arrival in Valencia, Sofía's parents filed a complaint against Don Carlos, who was the Viceroy's chief of staff and secretary. The Viceroy promised them justice and Don Carlos that his innocence would be protected. A new investigation was opened, witnesses were heard a second time and, finally, Sofía's parents, motivated by the sadness caused by the loss of their daughter and by a desire for revenge they thought legitimate, exerted so much pressure on the case that it was ready to be heard after only five or six days. They asked the Viceroy that the accused be sent to prison. He gave them his word that Don Carlos would not leave his residence and gave them a date when he would render his judgement. On the eve of that fateful day, which held the entire city of Valencia in suspense, Don Carlos asked for and received a private meeting with the Viceroy. He threw himself at his feet and said these words: "Tomorrow is the day you must make everyone know that I am innocent. Although the witnesses I produced completely exonerated me, I have come again before Your Highness as if I were before God, to swear that, not only did I not abduct Sofía, but the day before she was abducted I did not see her, I didn't hear from her, and haven't heard from her since. It is true that I was supposed to abduct her, but some unknown calamity made her disappear, causing her ruin or mine."

"That's enough," said the Viceroy, "you can sleep soundly. I am your master and your friend, and more aware of your innocence than you know, and, should I harbour any doubts about it, I would have to resist shedding light upon it, since you are in my house and of my house and you only came here with me because I promised to protect you."

Don Carlos thanked such an obliging master with all of his eloquence. He went to bed, but the impatience he had to see himself absolved didn't let him sleep. He got up at dawn and, clean and more elegantly attired than usual, attended his master's arising. No, I'm wrong. He only entered the room after his master was dressed, because, since Sofía disguised her sex, only Dorotea, disguised as well and privy to Sofía's disguise, slept in her room and gave her all the help which, given by someone else, could have revealed what she wanted to keep hidden. Don Carlos entered the Viceroy's room once Dorotea had opened it to everyone, and no sooner had the Viceroy seen him than he criticized him for waking up awfully early for an accused man who claims to be innocent, and told him that a person who doesn't sleep must have a guilty conscience. Somewhat confused, Don Carlos replied that the fear of being convicted hadn't kept him from sleeping so much as the hope of soon finding cover from his enemies thanks to the good justice rendered by His Highness. "But I find you too elegant and turned out," added the Viceroy, "and too relaxed for the day they will deliberate on your life. I no longer know what to think about the crime you're being accused of. Every time we discuss Sofía, you talk about her with less warmth and more indifference than I do. Yet I'm not being accused, like you, of having been loved by her and of having killed her, as well as, possibly, young Claudio, whom you accuse of abducting her. You say you loved her," the Viceroy continued, "and you are alive after having lost her, leaving no stone unturned to see yourself absolved and safe, you who should despise life and everything that could make you love it! Ah! Fickle Don Carlos, a new love must have made you forget the love you should have kept for the lost Sofía if you had truly loved her when she was all yours and dared to do anything for you."

Don Carlos, who was half dead from these words, wanted to reply, but the Viceroy didn't let him. "Be quiet," he said with a severe expression on his face, "and save your eloquence for your judges, because it won't work on me and I won't, for the sake of a servant, leave the Emperor with a bad impression of my impartiality. Meanwhile," added the Viceroy as he turned towards the captain of his guards, "secure him. Someone who escaped from prison is capable of breaking the word he gave me not to seek impunity by fleeing."

Don Carlos's sword was immediately taken from him, and he was an object of pity for those who witnessed him surrounded by guards, pale and disconcerted, and making an effort to hold back his tears.

While the poor gentleman repented for not having been wary enough of the mercurial mind of great lords, the judges who were supposed to try him entered the room and took their seats after the Viceroy had taken his. The Italian count, who was still in Valencia, and Sofía's parents appeared and presented their witnesses against the accused, who was so discouraged about his trial that he hardly had the strength to answer. He was asked to identify the letters he had sent to Sofía. He was confronted with Sofía's neighbours and servants, and finally the letter she left in her room the day of her abduction was produced against him. The accused had his servants testify that they had seen their master go to bed, but that he could have gotten up after pretending to fall asleep. He swore that he hadn't abducted Sofía and explained to the judges that he wouldn't have abducted her in order to leave her. But he was accused of no less than killing her and the page too, the confidant of his love. All that was left to do was judge him, and he was about to be condemned when the Viceroy had him approach, telling him, "Poor Don Carlos! You can well imagine that after all the marks of affection I showed you, that if I had suspected you were guilty of the crime you are accused of, I wouldn't have brought you to Valencia. It is impossible for me not to condemn you if I don't want to begin my duties by committing an injustice, and you can judge the displeasure your misfortune gives me by the tears it brings to my eyes. We could try for a settlement among the parties, if they were of lesser birth or less devoted to your ruin. Unless Sofía herself appears in order to exonerate you, you should prepare to die with dignity."

Carlos, despairing of his safety, threw himself at the Viceroy's feet, "You must remember, my lord, that in Africa, and from the time I had the honour of entering into Your Highness's service and every time Your Highness prompted me to relate the boring details of my misfortunes, I always told the same story. You must believe that in that country, and everywhere else, I would not have admitted to a master who did me the honour of caring for me what I would have to deny here in front of a judge. I always told Your Highness the truth, as to my God, and I am telling him again that I loved, that I adored Sofía."

"Say that you adore her, ingrate," interrupted the Viceroy, surprising everyone.

"I adore her," said Don Carlos, quite astonished by what the Viceroy had just said. "I promised to marry her," he continued "and we had agreed to go to Barcelona together, but if I abducted her, and if I know where she is hiding, I want to die the most cruel death. I can't avoid it, but I will die innocent, unless I deserve to die for having loved more than life itself a perfidious and unfaithful girl."

"But," cried out the Viceroy, a furious expression on his face, "what happened to this girl and your page? Did they rise to heaven? Did they hide under the earth?"

"The page was gallant," answered Don Carlos. "She was beautiful. He was a man. She was a woman."

"Ah! Traitor!" said the Viceroy. "How well you expose your vile suspicions and the low esteem in which you held your poor Sofía! Cursed be the woman who lets herself believe men's promises and then suffers their contempt because of her credulity! Sofía was no woman of common virtue and your page Claudio wasn't a man! Sofía was a faithful girl and your page a girl who had lost her way, who was in love with you and who stole Sofía from you so as to betray a rival. I am Sofía, and you are my unjust lover, an ingrate! I am Sofía, who has suffered unbelievable hardships for a man who didn't deserve to be loved and who thought me capable of the lowest infamy."

Sofía wasn't able to continue. Her father, who recognized her, took her in his arms. Her mother fainted, as did Don Carlos. Sofía left her father's arms to run over to the two people who had fainted and who came to just as she was wondering which one to care for first. Her mother wet her face with tears; she wet her mother's face with tears. With all the tenderness imaginable she embraced her dear Don Carlos, who thought he would faint again. He held fast however, and, not daring to give Sofía a full kiss, he made up for it by covering her hands with kisses. Sofía could hardly keep up with all the embraces and compliments she received. The Italian count, when it was his turn, wanted to talk about his claim to her, as she had been promised to him by her mother and father. Don Carlos, who heard him, let go of one of Sofía's hands, which he was avidly kissing, and, using his own to grasp the sword that had been returned to him, adopted a posture that scared everyone and, burying the city of Valencia in oaths, made it clear to everyone that no human power could ever deprive him of Sofía, unless she herself forbade him to think of her any more. But she declared that she wouldn't have any husband other than Don Carlos and begged them to approve of him or to resign themselves to seeing her shut up in a convent for the rest of her life. Her parents allowed her the freedom to choose whichever husband she wished and the Italian count left that very day for Italy or any other country he liked. Sofía recounted all her adventures, which everyone admired. A courier left to carry the news of this marvel to the Emperor, who kept for Don Carlos, after he married Sofía, the Viceroyalty of Valencia and all the benefits this valiant girl had earned under the name Don Fernando. He also gave the lucky suitor a principality his descendants enjoy to this day. The city of Valencia staged a magnificent wedding, and Dorotea, who changed back into women's clothing at the same time as Sofía, was married at the same time as she to a caballero who was a close relative of Don Carlos.

CHAPTER XV

The Sieur de La Rappinière's Insolence

THE RENNES COUNSELLOR finished reading his short story just as La Rappinière arrived at the inn. He distractedly entered the room where he was told he would find Monsieur de La Garouffière, but his beaming face visibly fell when he saw Destiny in a corner of the room, along with his valet, who was as disconcerted and frightened as a criminal being judged. La Garouffière closed the door to the room from the inside and then asked the brave La Rappinière if he could guess why they had summoned him. "Isn't it because of an actress that I wanted my share of?" answered the rascal, laughing.

"What do you mean, your share!" said La Garouffière, his face becoming serious.

"Are those the words of a judge such as you are and have you ever hanged a man as bad as you?" La Rappinière continued to try to make light of it and pass it off as a bawdy practical joke, but the senator's tone was so severe that that he finally admitted to his evil plan and offered weak excuses to Destiny, who needed all his wisdom not to dispatch a man who had tried to hurt him so cruelly after owing him his life, as we saw at the beginning of these comic adventures. But he still had to get to the bottom of another affair with the iniquitous magistrate that was of great importance to him and that he had communicated to Monsieur de La Garouffière, who promised to help him get the better of this evil man.

As hard as I've tried to study La Rappinière, I've never been able to discover whether he was less evil towards God than towards his fellow man and less unjust to his neighbour than inherently depraved. I only know with certainty that never has a man had as many vices together and to a greater degree. He admitted that he had tried to abduct Mademoiselle Star as boldly as if he were boasting of a good deed, and brazenly told the counsellor that he had never doubted the success of such an enterprise, "because," he continued, turning towards Destiny, "I had won over your valet. Your sister fell for it and, thinking she would find you where she was told you were immobilized with wounds, she wasn't two leagues from the house where I was waiting for her when God knows who took her from the big oaf who was bringing her to me, and who lost a good horse after receiving a beating." Destiny was turning pale with anger and also sometimes blushed with shame to see with what cheek this rascal dared speak to him about the offence he had tried to commit against him, as if he were talking of this and that. La Garouffière was scandalized as well and felt no less indignation against such a dangerous man. "I don't know," he said, "how you dare speak to us so frankly about the circumstances of an evil deed for which Monsieur Destiny would have given you a beating if I weren't there to stop him, but I warn you that he may still, if you don't give back a diamond locket you stole from him in Paris when you used to snatch coats. Doguin, your accomplice back then and later your valet, confessed on his deathbed that you still had it, and I declare that if you give us the slightest trouble in returning it, you will find me to be as dangerous an enemy as I have been a useful protector."

La Rappinière was stunned by this speech, which he had not been expecting. His ability boldly to deny an evil deed he had done failed him in his time of need. Stammering like a confused man, he admitted that he had this locket in Le Mans and swore endless oaths to give it back, which was more than anyone asked, because his word was of so little account. This was probably one of least murky deeds of his life, though it wasn't entirely pure, because although it is true that he did return the locket as promised, it wasn't true that it was in Le Mans, since he had it on him that very day, in order to be able to offer it to Mademoiselle Star, in case she hadn't been willing to give in to him for a trifle. This is what he confessed to in private to La Garouffière, hoping to regain his good graces, as he put the cameo locket into his hands to do with as he saw fit. The locket featured five diamonds of considerable value. Mademoiselle Star's father was painted in enamel and the face of this beautiful girl was so like the portrait that her father would recognize her from this alone. Destiny didn't know how to thank Monsieur de La Garouffière enough when he gave him the diamond locket. It exempted him from having to recover it by force from La Rappinière, who knew less about restitution than anything else and who could have used, against the poor actor, his position as a magistrate, which is a dangerous stick to put in the hands of an evil man. When the locket was stolen from Destiny, he had felt very bad; a feeling that grew even worse when he had to tell Star's mother, who treasured it as a token of her husband's affection. One can easily imagine that he felt great joy at having recovered it. He went to show it to Star, whom he found at the parson's sister's house in the company of Angélique and Léandre. They discussed their return to Le Mans, which they decided would be the next day. Monsieur de La Garouffière offered them a coach, which they declined. The actors and actresses dined with Monsieur de La Garouffière and his companions. They went to bed early at the inn and, at the break of dawn, Destiny and Léandre, each with his mistress sitting behind him, rode towards Le Mans, where Ragotin, Grudge and Olive were waiting. As for Madame Bouvillon, she pretended to be sicker than she was, so as not to receive a goodbye visit from the actor, with whom she was dissatisfied.

CHAPTER XVI

Ragotin's Misfortune

T HE TWO ACTORS WHO RETURNED to Le Mans with Ragotin were diverted from the direct route by the little man who wanted to treat them to a meal in a little country house whose proportions were in keeping with his diminutive stature. Although a faithful and exact historian is required to detail the important events of his history and the places where they occurred, I won't tell you very precisely where in our hemisphere the cottage was where Ragotin led his future brothers, whom I refer to thusly, because he hadn't yet been admitted to the vagabond brotherhood of country thespians. I'll therefore only tell you that the house was on this side of the Ganges, not far from Sillé-le-Guillaume. When he arrived, he found it occupied by a band of gypsies who, to his farmer's great displeasure, had stopped there under the pretext that their captain's wife was in labour, or rather because of the ease with which these thieves hoped to help themselves with impunity to the fowls of a remote farm far from the highway. At first Ragotin got mad in a little-angry-man way and threatened the gypsies with the sheriff of Le Mans, whom he claimed as a relative because he had married a Portail, and he gave a lengthy speech about this, to explain to his listeners in exactly what way the Portails were related to the Ragotins, not that his long speech tempered his excessive anger to any extent or prevented him from swearing scandalously. He threatened them furthermore with the sheriff's lieutenant La Rappinière, at the sound of whose name all knees buckled, but the Gypsy captain enraged him by addressing him politely, and had the impudence to compliment him on his bearing, which bespoke nobility and made him repent not a little for having mistakenly entered his chateau (that's what the rogue called his cottage, which was only protected by hedges). He added that the woman in labour would soon give birth and that the little band would move on after paying his farmer for what he had provided them and their animals. Ragotin was dying of pique at not being able to quarrel with a man who was laughing in his face while bowing and scraping, but the gypsy's composure was finally about to ignite Ragotin's bile when Grudge and the gypsy captain's brother recognized each other as long-lost old friends; this discovery was very helpful to Ragotin, who was surely courting trouble with his high-handed tone. Grudge asked him to calm down, which is what he wanted to do and what he would have done on his own if his ego had let him.

At the same time the gypsy lady gave birth to a boy. This caused great joy in the little band and the captain invited the actors to dinner along with Ragotin, who had already had chickens killed for a fricassee. Everyone sat down at the table. The Gypsies contributed hares and partridges they'd hunted along with two turkeys and two suckling pigs they'd stolen. They also brought a ham and tongues and a hare pâté that was consumed right down to the crust, which was eaten by four or five gypsy children who were serving the meal. Add this to Ragotin's fricassee of six chickens and you'll have to admit it wasn't a bad meal. The guests, besides the actors, numbered nine, all of them good dancers and even better merrymakers. They began by drinking to the health of the King and Messieurs the Princes, and then to the health of all the lords who welcomed small troupes in their villages. The captain asked the actors to drink to the memory of Charles Dodo, the new baby's great-uncle, who was hung during the siege of La Rochelle, through the treason of Captain La Grave. They inveighed against this double-crossing captain and against all sheriffs, and depleted Ragotin's supply of wine, the quality of which was such that the fun never turned into quarrelling and each of the guests, even the misanthrope Grudge, swore eternal friendship to his neighbour, kissed him with great affection and wet his face with tears. Ragotin was the perfect host and drank like a sponge. After drinking all night they should in all likelihood have gone to bed at sunrise. But the same wine that made them such docile drinkers inspired in them all simultaneously a parting spirit, for lack of a better term. The caravan packed up, not without including items of clothing belonging to Ragotin's farmer. The lord of the manor mounted his mule and headed for Le Mans without bothering to see whether Grudge and Olive were following him, paying attention only to sucking on a tobacco pipe that had been empty for over an hour. He hadn't gone a half-league, still sucking his empty pipe, which didn't produce any smoke, when the vapours from the wine suddenly knocked him out. He fell off his mule, which returned very patiently to the farm from where it had come. As for Ragotin, after several uprisings of his overloaded stomach, which did its duty to perfection afterwards, he fell asleep in the middle of the road. He hadn't been asleep for long, snoring like the lowest register of a church organ, when a man who was naked (the way Adam is described) but horribly bearded, filthy and grungy, approached him and started to undress him. This wild man struggled to remove Ragotin's new boots, that Grudge had taken from an inn thinking they were his, as I related somewhere in this true story. All his efforts, which would have awakened Ragotin if he hadn't been dead-drunk, as they say, and would have made him scream like a man being drawn and quartered, had no effect other than dragging him on the ground an arse-skinning five or six yards. A knife fell from the deep sleeper's pocket. The wild man grabbed it and, as though he wanted to flay Ragotin, right on Ragotin's skin split his shirt, his boots and everything he was having difficulty removing from his body. Having made a package of the stripped drunkard's clothing, he carried it away, fleeing like a wolf with his prey.

We'll let this man run off with his booty. He was the same madman who had previously frightened Destiny when he began his quest for Mademoiselle Angélique. But we won't abandon Ragotin, who isn't awake and really needs awakening. His naked body, exposed to the sun, was soon covered and stung by flies and gnats of various kinds that nevertheless failed to wake him. But he was awakened some time later on by a group of peasants who were driving a cart. No sooner did Ragotin's naked body come into view than they cried out, "There he is!" and, approaching him as quietly as possible, as though they were afraid to wake him, they secured his feet and legs, which they tied with thick ropes, and, having thus bound him, carried him to their cart, which they drove away with as much haste as a suitor abducting his mistress against her will and that of her parents. Ragotin was so drunk that none of the rough treatments he was subjected to could wake him, any more than the jolts of the cart that the peasants drove very fast and with so much haste that it tipped over in a bad rut full of water and mud, and as a consequence Ragotin tipped over as well. The cool temperature of the place he landed, at the bottom of which were several stones or something just as hard, and the shock of his fall woke him, and the bizarre state in which he found himself stunned him. He realized he was bound hands and feet and fallen in the mud. His head was spinning from his drunkenness and his fall, and he didn't know what to make of the three or four peasants who were helping him up from among the others who were righting the cart. He was so frightened by his adventure that he didn't even talk about what was such a great topic for a story, he who was by nature such a big talker. And right afterwards he couldn't have talked to anyone even if he had wanted to, because the peasants, after holding a secret meeting, untied the little man's feet only, and instead of explaining why or apologizing, in total silence turned the cart around in the direction it had come from and returned in as much of a hurry as they had come.

The discerning reader may be curious to know what the peasants had against Ragotin and why they didn't do anything to him. The circumstances are surely difficult to divine, and cannot be known unless they are revealed. As many efforts as I devoted to uncovering them, and after having talked to all my friends, I only learnt them recently, by chance, when I had given up hope, in the following manner. A priest from Bas-Maine, a bit mad from melancholy, and that a lawsuit had brought to Paris, wanted, while waiting for his suit to go to trial, to print some deep thoughts he had concerning the Apocalypse. His imagination was so prolific and he was so much in love with the latest productions of his mind that he hated the previous ones, and thus nearly drove the printer insane by making him print the same page twenty times over. This behaviour meant that he had to change printers several times, and eventually he came across the one who printed the book you are reading, where he read several pages of the story I have been telling you. This good priest knew more about it than I did, having learnt, from the very same peasants who had captured Ragotin in the manner I described, the motive for their enterprise. He knew the inaccuracies in my story and, having communicated them to my printer who was quite surprised (because he thought, like many others, that my novel was a made-up story) he didn't need much prompting from the printer to pay me a visit. It was then that I learnt from this true Manceau that the peasants who tied up the sleeping Ragotin were close relatives of the poor madman who was running around the countryside, whom Destiny met at night and who stripped Ragotin in broad daylight. They had planned to confine their relative, had often tried to do so, and had often been beaten by the madman, who was a large, powerful man. Some of the villagers, who saw Ragotin's body from afar gleaming in the sunlight, mistook him for the sleeping madman and, not daring to come closer for fear of being beaten, alerted the peasants, who took all the precautions you saw earlier, took Ragotin without recognizing him and, realizing he wasn't the one they were looking for, left his hands tied so he wouldn't try anything against them. The information I received from the priest made me very glad and I admit he did me a big favour; but I didn't do him a small one either when I advised him, as a friend, not to publish his bizarre ideas.

Someone may accuse me of having related a useless detail. Someone else may praise my honesty. Let's get back to Ragotin, his body soiled and bruised, his mouth dry and his hands tied behind his back. He stood up as best he could and, having looked in every direction as far as he could see without catching sight of houses or people, he took the first well-worn path he encountered, searching his mind for an explanation of what had happened to him. What with his hands tied the way they were, he was mercilessly tormented by a few stubborn bugs that attacked those parts of his body he couldn't reach. Sometimes he had to lie on the ground to crush them or force them to let go. Finally, he found a sunken path, lined with hedgerows and full of water, and this path led to the ford of a small river. He was happy to see it, intending to wash the mud off his body, but as he approached the ford, he saw a coach tipped over, from which the driver and a peasant, aided by the exhortations of a venerable man of the cloth, were pulling out five or six soaking-wet nuns. It was the old Abbess of Estival who was returning from Le Mans, where important business took her, and who was shipwrecked, thanks to her driver. The Abbess and the nuns pulled from the coach caught sight from a distance of the naked Ragotin, who was walking straight towards them. They were quite scandalized, even more so was Father Giflot, president of the abbey board. He quickly made the good sisters turn around, and shouted as loudly as he could to Ragotin to stop coming any closer. Ragotin kept on walking and stepped on a long board that was there to help pedestrians ford the river. Father Giflot walked ahead to meet him, followed by the driver and the peasant, and wondered at first if he needed to be exorcized, so diabolical was his appearance. Finally, he asked him who he was, where he was coming from, why he was naked, why his hands were tied, and asked all these questions with great eloquence while adjusting the tone of his voice and the movement of his hands to the meaning of his words. Ragotin answered him impolitely, "What do you care?" and, wanting to cross over on the board, pushed the Reverend Father Giflot so hard that he made him fall into the water. The good father took the driver and the peasant with him, and Ragotin found their way of falling so entertaining that he burst out laughing. He continued on his way towards the nuns who, their veils lowered, turned their backs to him in a line, their faces looking away at the countryside. Ragotin paid no attention to the nuns' faces, and walked past, thinking he was through with them, but Father Giflot didn't think he was through with him. He followed Ragotin, backed up by the peasant and the driver – the most quick-tempered of the lot and already in a bad mood because Madame the Abbess had scolded him – who broke away from the pack, caught up with Ragotin and, with his whip, got revenge on the skin of he who had wet his own. Ragotin didn't wait for a second lash. He fled like a whipped dog, and the driver, who wasn't satisfied with one lash, prompted him with several more that all drew blood from the skin of the thrashed miniature man. Giflot, although out of breath from running, didn't tire of shouting, "Whip him! Whip him!" at the top of his lungs; and the driver redoubled his efforts and was starting to enjoy himself when a mill offered poor Ragotin a refuge. He ran into it, with his tormentor still chasing him, and, finding the door to a courtyard open, entered and was greeted by a watchdog that bit him on the arse. He cried out in pain and ran from there into a yard with such abandon that he knocked over six beehives that stood at the entrance. This was the height of his misfortune. These tiny winged elephants, equipped with a proboscis and armed with a stinger, fiercely attacked the little naked body that didn't have any hands with which to defend itself, and wounded it horribly. His screams were so loud that the dog that was biting him was scared away by them – or rather by the bees. The merciless driver imitated the dog, and Father Giflot, whose anger had made him lose sight of charity for a time, repented for having been too vindictive and told the miller and his servants to hurry and not take so long coming to the aid of a man who was being mauled in their backyard. The miller extricated Ragotin from among the venomous and pointed daggers of these flying enemies, and although he was furious about his spilt hives, he wasn't without pity for the wretch. He asked him how in the devil he had managed to land under beehives, naked and with his hands tied. Had Ragotin wanted to answer him, he would not have been able, such was the extreme pain he felt throughout his body. A newborn bear cub that hasn't yet been licked by its mother is more recognizable as a bear than Ragotin was as a human, after the bee stings had swollen his body from head to toe. The miller's wife, as compassionate as a woman, had a bed made up for him and had him taken to it. Father Giflot, the driver and the peasant returned to the Abbess of Estival, and the nuns, who climbed back into the coach and, escorted by the reverend Father Giflot, mounted on a filly, continued on their way. It turned out that the mill belonged to the taxman Du Rignon or his son-in-law Bagottière (I never learnt which). This Du Rignon was a relative of Ragotin who, having made himself known to the miller and his wife, was treated with great care and successfully bandaged by the surgeon of a neighbouring burgh until his recovery was complete. As soon as he could walk, he returned to Le Mans, where the joy of discovering that Grudge and Olive had found his mule and brought it back with them made him forget the fall from the cart, the driver's lashes and the bee stings.

CHAPTER XVII

What Happened between Little Ragotin and Big Baguenodière

DESTINY AND STAR, Léandre and Angélique, two pairs of beautiful, perfect lovers, arrived in the capital of Maine without incident. Destiny put Angélique back in her mother's good graces by doing such a good job of highlighting Léandre's merit, breeding and love that Cave began to approve of the passion shared by this young man and her daughter as much as she had previously opposed it. The poor troupe hadn't yet done very good business in the city of Le Mans, but a nobleman who loved the theatre made up for the niggardly Manceaux. Having most of his property in Maine, he took a house in Le Mans and often entertained noble friends, courtiers as well as provincials, even certain Parisian wits, among whom were first-rate poets. In addition, he was a kind of modern Maecenas.* He passionately loved the theatre and all those involved in it, and that was what attracted every year to the capital of Maine the best theatre troupes in the kingdom. The lord I'm talking about arrived in Le Mans around the time our poor actors wanted to leave, dissatisfied as they were with the Manceau audience. He asked them to stay another two weeks as a token of their friendship and, to convince them, gave them a hundred pistoles, with the promise of another hundred when they left. He was anxious to put on a theatrical entertainment for several people of quality of both sexes, whom he had invited to Le Mans at the same time. This lord, whom I shall call the Marquis d'Orsé, was a big hunter, who brought to Le Mans his hunting equipage, which was one of the most beautiful in all of France. The fields and forests of Maine make up one of the most enjoyable hunting grounds in the entire country, be it for stag or hare, and at that time the city of Le Mans was filled with hunters attracted by news of this great entertainment, most with their wives, who were thrilled to see ladies of the court and be able to talk about it by the hearth for the rest of their lives. It's no small ambition for provincials to be able to sometimes say they saw in such and such a place at such and such a time courtiers, whose name they drop in brief phrases, as in, for example: "I lost my money against Roquelaure; Créqui won the pot; Coaquin is hunting stag in Touraine." But if you let them carry on about politics or war they won't stop talking until they've exhausted everything they have to say on the subject.

But I digress. Le Mans was full of nobility, great and small. The inns were full of guests, and most of the grand burghers who were hosting people of quality or friends among the local gentry quickly soiled all their damask and fine linens. The actors opened their theatre in the mood to do a good job, like the paid-in-advance actors they were. The bourgeoisie of Le Mans finally warmed to the show. The ladies of the town and the province were delighted to see ladies of the court every day, from whom they learnt to dress well, or at least better than they did, to the great benefit of their tailors, to whom they gave many old dresses to alter. There was a ball every night, where very bad dancers danced courantes very badly and where several of the town's young people danced in stockings of Dutch or Usseau cloth. Our actors were often hired to perform at private parties. Star and Angélique inspired love among the gentlemen and envy among the ladies. Inezilla, who danced the saraband at the actors' request, was admired. Roquebrune thought he would die of a love overdose, so much did his suddenly increase. And Ragotin admitted to Grudge that if he postponed much longer getting Star to be interested in him, France was going to be deprived of Ragotin. Grudge gave him hope and, to give him a demonstration of his esteem, asked to borrow twenty-five or thirty francs. Ragotin turned pale at this impolite request, repented for what he had just said and pretty much gave up on his love ambitions. But finally, boiling with rage, he put together the sum in all kinds of currencies from different purses and gave it with much sadness to Grudge, who promised that by the next day there would be progress.

That day they staged *Dom Japhet*,* a play as light-hearted as its author has reason not to be. There was a large audience, the play was well acted and everyone was satisfied, except for the unfortunate Ragotin. He arrived late, and as punishment for his sins he sat behind a provincial gentleman with a broad back, wearing a big cape that amplified his bulk. He was so much taller than the tallest that, even though he was sitting, Ragotin, who was only seated one row away, thought he was standing and constantly yelled at him to sit down like everybody else, not being able to believe that a sitting man's head wouldn't be on the same level as his neighbours'. This gentleman, named La Baguenodière, didn't realize for a long time that Ragotin was speaking to him. Finally Ragotin addressed him as "the gentleman with the green feather", and since he was wearing one that was quite bushy, quite dirty and not very delicate, he turned around and saw the little impatient man who rudely told him to sit down. La Baguenodière was so unmoved that he turned back towards the stage as if nothing had happened. Ragotin yelled at him again to sit down. He turned around again to look at him and once again turned back to face forward. Ragotin yelled again. La Baguenodière turned around for the third time, for the third time looked at the little man and for the third time looked back at the stage. During the entire play, Ragotin yelled just as loudly for him to sit down and La Baguenodière looked at him with enough composure to drive the entire human race crazy. You could compare La Baguenodière to a big mastiff and Ragotin to a pug that barks at him without the mastiff doing anything other than pissing against a wall. Finally, everyone paid attention to what was going on between the biggest man in the audience and the smallest one, and everyone began to laugh, while Ragotin started to swear with impatience and La Baguenodière did nothing other than stare at him coldly. This La Baguenodière was the biggest bully as well as the biggest man in the world. He asked with his customary frostiness two gentlemen who were sitting next to him why they were laughing. They answered frankly that it was because of him and Ragotin, intending to flatter rather than offend him. Offend him they did, however, and when a frowning La Baguenodière let go with "What idiots you are", they knew he had taken it badly, forcing each of them to respond with a big slap across the face. At first, La Baguenodière could only jostle them from left to right with his elbows, his hands being caught in his cape, and before he was able to free them, the gentlemen, who were brothers and very vigorous by nature, were able to slap him a half-dozen times, the intervals of which were by chance so well coordinated that those who heard them without seeing them thought that someone had clapped his hands six times at equal intervals. Finally, La Baguenodière pulled his arms out from under his heavy cape but, harassed the way he was by the two brothers who were punching at him like lions, his long arms were not free to move. He tried to step back and fell backwards onto a man who was behind him, knocking him over, along with his seat, onto the unfortunate Ragotin, who fell on another spectator, who fell on another, who fell on another and so on and so forth all the way to the end of an entire row of theatregoers, who were knocked over like bowling pins. The sounds of people falling, of trampled ladies, of those who were scared, of children crying, of people talking, laughing or complaining and of those who were clapping combined to make an infernal noise. Never did such a tiny cause produce such massive effects, and it was a miracle that not a single sword was drawn, even though the main conflict was between people who carried them and there were over a hundred in all among the audience. But what was even more miraculous was that La Baguenodière received punches and exchanged them with complete indifference and, moreover, that he hadn't opened his mouth after lunch to say anything besides the four unfortunate words that attracted a barrage of slaps, and didn't open it again until nightfall, such was the extent to which his taciturn and phlegmatic nature was in keeping with his size.

This ugly mess of people and seats all mixed together took a long time to untangle. While it was being done, and the most charitable in the crowd stepped in between La Baguenodière and his two enemies, horrible screams were heard coming from under the earth. Who else could it be but Ragotin? To tell the truth, once fate starts persecuting a wretch, it doesn't stop. The poor little chap's seat happened to be placed on the cover of the tennis court's drain. This drain is always in the middle of the court, right under the net. It is meant to receive rainwater and the board that covers it lifts up, like a box top. Since nothing lasts for ever, the drain cover of the tennis court where the play was staged was rotten and had given way under Ragotin, when a corpulent man along with his seat landed on top of him. This man's leg sank into the hole that now contained Ragotin. The leg was wearing a boot and its spur pricking Ragotin's throat was causing the terrible screams of mysterious origin. Someone gave the man a hand, and when his leg, which was caught in the hole, changed position, Ragotin bit his foot so hard the man thought he was being bitten by a snake and let out a scream that startled the person helping him, who let go from fear. Finally, he recovered, gave his hand back to the

man, who was no longer screaming because Ragotin was no longer
biting him, and the two of them together fished out the little man
who no sooner saw the light of day than he threatened everyone
with his head and eyes, especially those who were laughing at
him. He dived into the crowd of those who were leaving, cooking
up something glorious for himself and dire for La Baguenodière.
I never learnt how La Baguenodière and the two brothers were
reconciled, if they were. At least I've never heard of them harming one another since. And that was how the first play our actors
performed for the illustrious audience that gathered in the city
of Le Mans was disrupted.

CHAPTER XVIII

Which Doesn't Need a Title

THE NEXT DAY THEY PERFORMED *Nicomède* by the inimitable Monsieur de Corneille. In my opinion this play is
admirable and the one in which this excellent poet of the theatre
has been most original and has best displayed the fertility and
greatness of his genius, giving the actors proud characters who
are all different from one another. The performance was not
disrupted, which may have been because Ragotin wasn't there.
Hardly a day went by that he wasn't involved in some kind of
imbroglio, to which his excessive vanity and his thin-skinned and
presumptuous character contributed almost as much as his bad
luck, which up to that point had been relentless. The little man
had spent the afternoon in the room of Inezilla's husband, the
salesman of remedies Ferdinando Ferdinandi, a Norman who
claimed to be Venetian, as I already told you, a doctor of spagyrics
by profession and, to state frankly what he was, a great charlatan
and an even greater crook. Grudge, in order to get some relief
from Ragotin's constant pestering about his promise to make

Mademoiselle Star love him, made him believe the salesman was a great magician who could make the most chaste woman run after a man while in her underwear, but that he only performed such marvels for his close and most discreet friends, since he had got in trouble exercising his art for some of the greatest lords in Europe. Grudge advised Ragotin to do all he could to befriend him, which he assured him would not be difficult, the salesman being a sensitive man who easily liked those who showed a liking for him and who, once he had made a friend, was entirely devoted to him. You need only praise or respect a vain man and he will do as you please. The same doesn't apply to a patient man, who isn't so easy to influence, and experience shows that a humble person who has enough self-control to thank the one who rebuffs him will usually get what he wants; not so with the person whom the rebuff offends. Grudge made Ragotin believe what he wanted him to, and Ragotin right away went off to make the salesman believe he was a great magician. I won't repeat what he told him. It suffices to know that the salesman, who had been alerted by Grudge, played his role and denied being a magician in such a way as to lead one to believe he was. Ragotin spent the afternoon by his side while he heated an alembic for some chemical operation, and that day he wasn't able to get anything out of him, which caused the impatient Manceau to spend a sleepless night. The following day he entered the salesman's room while he was still in bed. Inezilla was not pleased because she was no longer of an age to get out of bed fresh as a daisy and she needed, every morning, to spend a long time in private before she was ready to appear in public. So she quickly slipped into a little dressing room with her moorish servant, who brought her her love munitions, while Ragotin brought Sieur Ferdinandi back to the subject of magic, and Sieur Ferdinandi was more open than before, but did not promise anything. Ragotin wanted to show him his largesse. He arranged for an excellent lunch to be served, and invited the actors and actresses. I won't tell you the details of the meal. You will only know that a great time was had by all and that huge quantities were eaten. After lunch, Destiny and the actors asked Inezilla to read a Spanish short story, one of those she wrote or translated daily, with the help of the divine Roquebrune, who had sworn by Apollo and the nine Muses that he would teach her all the nuances and beauties of our language in six months. Inezilla did not wait to be begged and, while Ragotin courted the magician Ferdinandi, she read in a charming voice the story you are going to read in the next chapter.

CHAPTER XIX

The Two Rival Brothers

D OROTEA AND FELICIA DE MONSALVE were the two most attractive girls in Seville, and even if they hadn't been, their property and pedigree would have made them popular with all the caballeros interested in a good marriage. Don Manuel, their father, hadn't settled on anyone, and Dorotea, his daughter who, as the eldest, was supposed to be married before her sister, had managed her responses and her behaviour so well that even the most presumptuous among her suitors had to wonder whether his declarations of love were well received or not. Meanwhile these beautiful girls never went to mass without a parade of well-dressed, would-be lovers. They couldn't take holy water without several hands, ugly or shapely, offering it to them at the same time. Their beautiful eyes could not peek from behind their prayer books without being at the centre of Lord knows how many intemperate gazes and they couldn't take a step in the church without having to acknowledge a bow with a curtsey. But, while their merit might have caused them great fatigue in public places and churches, it often attracted, under the windows of their father's house, entertainments that made bearable the strict confinement required by their sex and the customs of their nation. Hardly an evening went by when they weren't treated to music, and there was often running at the ring and tilting under their windows, which looked out onto a public square.

One day a stranger impressed all the other caballeros with his skill and was noticed by the two beautiful sisters, who thought he was a man shaped to perfection. Several caballeros from Seville, who knew him in Flanders, where he had commanded a cavalry regiment, invited him to run the ring with them, which he did, dressed in uniform. A few days later a ceremony took place in Seville to install a new bishop. The stranger, named Don Sancho de Silva, was in the church where the ceremony was being conducted, along with all the suitors of Seville. The beautiful de Monsalve sisters were there too, among other ladies veiled like them, in the fashion of Seville, and wearing a cape of thick cloth and a little hat covered with feathers. Don Sancho found himself by chance between the two sisters and a lady he accosted, but who asked him politely not to speak to her, and to make room for the person she was expecting. Don Sancho obeyed her and, turning to Dorotea de Monsalve, who was closer to him than her sister, and who had seen what happened between the lady and him: "I had hoped," he told her, "that being a stranger, the lady to whom I tried speak would not refuse me her conversation, but she punished me for having the temerity to think that my own was not unworthy of consideration. I beg you," he continued, "not to be as harsh as she was with a stranger you just saw mistreated and, for the sake of the reputation of ladies of Seville, to give him a reason to praise their kindness."

"You've given me a big one to treat you as badly as this lady did," Dorotea answered, "since you only came to me after she turned you down, but so that you may have no reason to complain about the women of my country, I am willing to speak to you for as long as the ceremony lasts, which should tell you that I hadn't arranged to meet anyone here."

"That surprises me, with your figure," said Don Sancho, "and it must be that you are quite fearsome or the suitors of this city quite shy, or rather that the one in whose spot I am standing is absent."

"And do you think," replied Dorotea, "that I know so little about how to love that in a suitor's absence I wouldn't avoid attending a gathering where he wouldn't be? Do not repeat the mistake you've made of passing judgement on someone you don't know."

"You would know," replied Don Sancho, "that I judge you more positively than you think, if you would allow me to serve you as much as I am inclined to."

"Our first impressions are not always reliable," said Dorotea. "Moreover, there is a great difficulty in what you are proposing."

"There is none that I wouldn't overcome in order to deserve belonging to you," replied Don Sancho.

"It isn't a matter of a few days," said Dorotea, "you may have forgotten that you are only passing through Seville, and you may also not know that it wouldn't please me to be loved only in passing."

"Grant me what I am asking," he told her, "and I promise I will stay in Seville for the rest of my life."

"What you are saying is very gallant," said Dorotea, "and it surprises me that a man who knows how to say such things hasn't yet chosen a lady hereabouts to whom he could address his gallant remarks. Might it not be the case that he doesn't think them worth the trouble?"

"It's rather that he doesn't trust the power of his words," said Don Sancho.

"Give me an exact answer to what I am going to ask," said Dorotea, "and tell me in confidence which of our ladies would have the power to keep you in Seville."

"I already told you that you could, if you wanted," Don Sancho answered.

"You haven't seen me," Dorotea told him, "so choose someone else."

"I will confess, since you've given me orders," Don Sancho said, "that if Dorotea de Monsalve had as much wit as you, happy would be the man whose merit she esteemed and whose attentions she tolerated."

"There are, in Seville several ladies who equal and even surpass her," Dorotea told him, "but," she added, "haven't you heard whether she favours one of her suitors over the others?"

"Since I consider myself far from being worthy of her," Don Sancho said, "I haven't really gone to the trouble of finding out anything about that."

"What makes you think you're not as deserving as the next man?" Dorotea asked. "Ladies' whims are sometimes strange, and often a newcomer's first approach makes more progress than several years of service on the part of suitors one sees every day."

"You're cleverly getting rid of me," said Don Sancho, "by giving me the courage to love someone other than you, which shows me that you have no desire to consider the services of a new suitor, who might do harm to the one with whom you have been engaged for a long time."

"Don't think that for a minute," Dorotea answered. "Believe rather that I am not so easy to persuade with gallant flattery to believe that yours is the effect of a growing attachment, even without seeing my face."

"If that is the only thing missing to my declaration of love in order to make it capable of being received," replied Don Sancho, "then, by all means, don't hide any more from a stranger who is already charmed by your mind."

"Yours wouldn't be by my face," answered Dorotea.

"Ah! You can only be quite beautiful," replied Don Sancho, "since you admit so frankly that you aren't. And I don't doubt that you want to be rid of me, either because I bore you or because all the room in your heart is already taken. So, it wouldn't be right," he added, "for the goodness you've shown in tolerating me to be further tested and I don't want to leave you with the impression that I intended simply to pass the time when I offered to spend all of it with you."

"In order to show you," said Dorotea, "that I don't want to have wasted the time I spent speaking with you, I would be so pleased not to end it without knowing who you are."

"I can do no wrong by obeying you. Please know, enticing stranger, that I go by the name Silva, which is my mother's, that my father is the governor of Quito, in Peru, that I am following his orders by being in Seville and that I have spent my life in Flanders, where I earned the army's best commands and a commandership of St James. That, in a few words, is who I am," he continued, "and it will be henceforth up to you to hear, in a less public place, what I want to be for the rest of my life."

"That will happen as soon as it can," Dorotea told him. "Meanwhile, without making any efforts to find out more about me, if you don't want to run the risk of never knowing me, be content with knowing that I am well born and that my face isn't scary."

Don Sancho left her side with a deep bow and joined a large group of rent-a-gallants involved in conversation. There exist a few sad ladies, of the kind who are always bothered by other people's behaviour but quite satisfied with their own, who are self-appointed arbiters of good and evil, although it is possible to wager on their virtue, the way it is on anything that isn't clear-cut, and who think that a little sanctimonious incivility and hypocritical posturing gives them a surplus of respectability, although the cheerfulness of their youth was more scandalous than the sadness of their wrinkles has been good at setting an example; such ladies, then, are likely to say, hardly knowing her, that Mademoiselle Dorotea is at the very least a scatterbrain, not only for having so suddenly made substantial advances towards a man she only knew by sight, but also for having let him speak to her of love, and that if a girl they had any power over carried on like that, she wouldn't be allowed in society for fifteen minutes. But let these ignoramuses know that each country has its own customs and that, while in France women and even girls who go everywhere freely, take offence, or should, at the slightest declaration of love, in Spain, where they are cloistered like nuns, one doesn't offend them by telling them one loves them, even when the one saying it isn't loved in return. They go even further: the ladies are almost always the ones who make the first move and who are the first taken, because they are the last to be seen by their suitors, whom they see every day in church, during walks, from their balconies and through their blinds.

Dorotea confided to her sister Felicia the conversation she had with Don Sancho, and admitted to her that this stranger was more appealing to her than all the caballeros in Seville, and her sister approved of her designs upon his liberty. The two sisters spent a long time philosophizing about the advantageous privileges men had over women, who were almost always married according to their parents' choice, which wasn't always to their liking, whereas men could choose appealing women. "As far as I am concerned," Dorotea said to her sister, "I am certain love will never make me do anything against my duty, but I am just as determined never to marry a man who doesn't possess all to himself what I might find in several others, and I would rather spend my life in a convent than with a man I couldn't love." Felicia told her sister that she had also made the same resolution and they strengthened each other's resolve with all the arguments their nimble minds could muster on the subject.

Dorotea found it difficult to keep her promise to Don Sancho to make herself known, and she told her sister how worried she was about it. But Felicia, who enjoyed solving problems, reminded her sister that a lady who was a relative of theirs, and a close friend to boot (which isn't always the case), would do everything she could to help her, since Dorotea's peace of mind was at stake. "You know very well," said her kind and most accommodating sister, "that Marina, who has been in our service for so long, is married to a barber who rents a cottage that is attached to our relative's house, and that the two buildings share an entrance. They are in a distant neighbourhood, and even if it were noticed that we were visiting our relative more than we ever had before, no one will pay attention to Don Sancho entering a barbershop, where he can moreover go at night and in disguise."

While Dorotea plans, with her sister's help, her amorous intrigue, while she gets her relative's help and gives Marina her instructions, Don Sancho thinks about his stranger and doesn't know if she promised to get in touch with him just to make fun of him and he sees her every day without realizing it, in church or on her balcony, receiving the worship of her suitors, all of whom Don Sancho knows and who are his best friends in Seville. He was getting dressed one morning, thinking about his stranger, when he was told that a veiled woman was looking for him. She was ushered in and gave him the note you are about to read.

Note

I would have been in touch sooner if I could have. If you still wish to see me, at nightfall be where the person who gave you my note tells you. She will meet you there and lead you to where I will be waiting.

You can imagine his joy. He enthusiastically kissed the heaven-sent ambassadress and gave her a gold chain she accepted without much of a fuss. She gave him a rendezvous at nightfall, in an out-of-the-way place she wrote down, where he should come alone. She then excused herself, leaving him the happiest man alive and the most impatient. Night finally arrived. He came dressed up and perfumed to the meeting place where the ambassadress from the morning was waiting. She took him into a little ramshackle house, which led to a very attractive apartment, where he found three ladies who were all wearing veils. He recognized his stranger by her figure and began by complaining that she wasn't lifting her veil. Without ceremony, she and her sister revealed to the lucky Don Sancho that they were the beautiful Monsalve ladies. "You see," said Dorotea as she removed her veil, "that I was telling the truth when I assured you that a stranger sometimes obtains in an instant what suitors one sees every day could not earn over several years, and you would be the greatest of ingrates if you didn't appreciate the favour I am doing you or if you judged me unfavourably because of it."

"I shall always value everything that comes from you as if it came from heaven," said the passionate Don Sancho. "And you'll see, by the care I take to keep what you've given me, that if I ever lose it, it will be through my misfortune rather than my fault."

> Then they spoke in present tenses
> Saying the things love makes us say
> When 'tis master of our senses.

The mistress of the house and Felicia, who both possessed *savoir-vivre*, moved away at an honest distance from our two lovers, giving them all the privacy they needed to share their love even more than they had, although they had already shared it a lot, and they made a date to share it even more, if that were possible. Dorotea promised Don Sancho to arrange it so they could see each other often. He thanked her as wittily as he could. The two other ladies participated in their conversation, and Marina reminded them to leave when the time came. Dorotea was sad; Don Sancho's face fell, but they had to say goodbye. The brave caballero wrote a letter the very next day to his beautiful lady, and received an answer that met his wishes. I won't show you their love notes because none of them ever became available to me. They often saw each other in the same way and in the same place as the first time, and came to love each other so much that without spilling their blood like Pyramus and Thisbe, they matched them in impetuous affection.

They say that love, fire and money can't be hidden for long. Dorotea, who couldn't get her gallant stranger out of her mind, was unable to refer to him casually and held him so far above all the other gentlemen of Seville that several other ladies with their own hidden love interests, who heard her constantly talk about Don Sancho and praise him to the detriment of the ones they loved, took notice and were offended. Felicia often warned her in private to speak with more restraint and, many times when they were with company, when she saw her give in to the pleasure of talking about her suitor, stepped on her feet hard enough to hurt her. A caballero in love with Dorotea was alerted by a lady who was one of his close friends, and had no trouble believing that Dorotea loved Don Sancho, because he realized that ever since this stranger had come to the city, the slaves of this beautiful girl, among whom he bore the heaviest chains, hadn't received the slightest favourable glance from her. This rival of Don Sancho was wealthy, well born and agreeable to Don Manuel, who nevertheless did not pressure his daughter to marry, because every time he talked about it she begged him not to marry her so young. This caballero (I just remembered his name was Don Diego) wanted to be certain of what he only suspected. He had a personal valet, one of those they call swell boys, whose clothes are as nice as their master's, or who indeed wear his, who set the fashion trends for the other valets and who are as envied by them as they are admired by the servant girls. This valet was named Guzmán and, having been born with a smidge of poetic talent, wrote most of the love songs of Seville, which correspond to the Pont-Neuf songs of Paris. He sang them accompanied by his guitar, and he didn't sing them without ornamentation, or embroidery of the lips or tongue. He danced the saraband, was never without his castanets, had wanted to be an actor, and introduced into the make-up of his character some bravery, though, truth be known, somewhat of the thieving kind. All these talents, combined with a certain learned eloquence, modelled on his master's, made him without question the target (if you will pardon the expression) of the amorous desires of every serving girl who considered herself attractive. Don Diego ordered him to charm Isabella, a girl who served the Monsalve ladies. He obeyed his master. Isabella noticed and thought herself lucky to be loved by Guzmán, whom she was quick to love herself and who, on his end, came to love her too, and to continue for real what he had only started to obey his master. While the most ambitious servant girls coveted Guzmán, Isabella was a good match for the greatest striver among the valets of Spain. She was beloved by her mistresses, who were generous, and could expect an inheritance from her father, an honest artisan. Guzmán therefore seriously considered becoming her husband; she agreed to it. They mutually swore marriage and lived together ever since as if they were married. Isabella was upset that Marina, the wife of the barber where Dorotea and Don Sancho met in secret, and who had served her mistress before her, was still her confidante in an affair of this kind where the generosity of a suitor is always involved. She had learnt about the gold chain Don Sancho gave Marina, about several other presents he had given her and she imagined she had received many more. She developed a deep-seated hatred of Marina, which is what led me to believe this good-looking girl was a bit self-seeking. So one shouldn't be surprised if, the first time Guzmán asked her to tell him whether it was true that Dorotea loved someone, she shared her mistress's secret with a man to whom she had given herself altogether. She told him everything she knew about our young lovers' intrigue and greatly exaggerated Marina's good fortune, who was being made wealthy by Don Sancho, and then she railed against her for garnering profits that should have belonged to one of the family's servants. Guzmán asked her to alert him when Dorotea would be with her suitor. She did, and he didn't fail to alert his master, to whom he told everything he had learnt from the not very loyal Isabella.

Don Diego, disguised as a pauper, waited at the door of Marina's dwelling the night his valet told him, saw his rival go in and, a little while later, saw a coach stop in front of Dorotea's relative's house, from which this beautiful girl and her sister stepped out, leaving Don Diego in a state of rage you can imagine. He resolved there and then to rid himself of such a formidable rival by removing him from this world. He hired assassins, waited for Don Sancho for several nights in a row and finally found him and attacked him, backed by two killers as well armed as he was. Don Sancho, on his end, was well equipped to defend himself and, beside a dagger and a sword, carried two pistols in his belt. At first he fought like a lion and realized that his enemies were out to kill him and that they were wearing protective armour. Don Diego was pressing him more than the others, who were only fighting as hard as they were paid to. He backed off from his enemies for a while to draw the noise of the fighting far from the house where his Dorotea was, but finally, fearing that he would get himself killed by trying to be too discreet and seeing that he was being hard pressed by Don Diego, he shot him with one of his pistols, laying him out on the ground half-dead, then called for a priest. At the sound of the gunshot the assassins for hire disappeared, Don Sancho ran home and the neighbours went into the street, found Don Diego, whom they recognized and who, as he lay dying, accused Don Sancho of killing him. Our caballero was alerted by his friends, who told him that, even if he wasn't sought by the law, Don Diego's relatives would not leave his death unpunished and would surely try to kill him no matter where he was. So he retreated to a monastery, from where he sent news to Dorotea and put his affairs in order, so that he could leave Seville when it became safe to do so.

The wheels of justice turned meanwhile, looked for Don Sancho and did not find him. After the first manhunts concluded unsuccessfully, and everyone thought he had got away, Dorotea and her sister, under pretext of devoutness, had their relative take them to the convent where Don Sancho was hiding, and there, with the help of a priest, the two lovers met in a chapel, vowed to be faithful to each other no matter what and parted with such regret and said such poignant things that her sister, her relative and the good father who witnessed it cried and still cry every time they think about it. He left Seville in disguise and, before leaving, sent letters to his father in the Indies. In these letters he informed him about the accident that forced him to leave Seville and retire to Naples. He arrived there without incident and was welcomed by the Viceroy, whom he had the honour of serving. Although he received all sorts of favours, he did not enjoy the year he spent there, because he had no news of Dorotea.

The Viceroy outfitted six galleys that he sent in an expedition against the Turks. Don Sancho's courage did not allow him to neglect such an opportunity to put it to the test, and the fleet's commander welcomed him onto his galley, giving him the best bedroom next to his own for his quarters, delighted to have along a man of his breeding and merit. The six Neapolitan galleys encountered eight Turkish ones almost in sight of Messina and didn't hesitate to attack them. After a long fight, the Christians took three enemy galleys and sank two. The Christian flagship was attached to the Turkish one which, being more heavily armed than the others, put up greater resistance. In the meantime the sea was getting rough and the storm increased so much in intensity that both Christians and Turks worried less about harming each other and more about protecting themselves from the weather. Both sides removed the grappling hooks that bound the galleys together and the Turkish flagship sailed away from the Christian one after the too daring Don Sancho had jumped into it, followed by no one. When he realized he was alone in the enemy's power, he preferred death to slavery, and at the risk of whatever might happen, dived into the sea, hoping that he might somehow be able to reach the Christian galleys, being a powerful swimmer, but the bad weather prevented his being seen, even though the Christian commander, who had witnessed his act, despaired of his loss, which he thought inevitable, and made his galley head for the area where he had jumped into the sea. Don Sancho meanwhile was splitting the waves with all his strength and swimming towards land, where the wind and the tide carried him. He was lucky to find a board from one of the Turkish galleys that had been smashed by cannon fire, and he put to good use this aid that he thought Heaven-sent. There wasn't more than a league and a half from where the combat took place to the coast of Sicily and Don Sancho reached it sooner than he hoped, aided as he was by wind and tide. He came ashore without accident and, after thanking God for having rescued him from such an extreme peril, he walked inland, pushing forward as much as his fatigue would allow, and, from the top of a rise, saw a hamlet inhabited by fishermen who turned out to be the most charitable to be found. The efforts he'd made during the combat, which had overheated him, and those he'd made in the sea and the cold he'd suffered both there and later, in his wet clothes, caused him to have a high fever that kept him in bed for a long time. Finally, he got better without doing anything other than resting. While he was sick, he decided to let everyone think he was dead, so he wouldn't have to protect himself so much from Don Diego's family, and in order to test Dorotea's fidelity.

He had made friends in Flanders with a Sicilian marquis, of the house of Montalto, named Fabio. He ordered a fisherman to find out if he was in Messina, where he knew he lived, and, learning that he was, he went there dressed as a fisherman and turned up at night at the Marquis's door. The Marquis Fabio had mourned him along with all those who had felt his loss. He was delighted to find his friend alive, after he had thought him dead. Don Sancho told him how he had survived and recounted his adventure in Seville without hiding his great passion for Dorotea. The Sicilian Marquis offered to go to Spain and even to abduct Dorotea, with her consent, and bring her to Sicily. Don Sancho didn't want to take advantage of such extreme expressions of friendship from his friend. But he was delighted that Fabio would accompany him to Spain. Don Sancho's valet, Sanchez, was so distraught by the loss of his master that, when the Neapolitan galleys went to Messina to refresh themselves, he entered a monastery, where he planned to spend the rest of his days. The Marquis Fabio sent word to him through the superior, who had received Sanchez on the basis of the Sicilian nobleman's recommendation and who had yet to give him his habit. Sanchez thought he would die of happiness when he saw his dear master again and had no intention of returning to his monastery. Don Sancho sent him to Spain to prepare his arrival and to report news of Dorotea, who meanwhile thought, along with everyone else, that Don Sancho was dead. News of his death travelled all the way to the Indies. Don Sancho's father died of grief when he heard the news, leaving to another son he had seven hundred thousand pounds, on condition that he give half to his brother if news of his death turned out to be false. Don Sancho's brother was called Don Juan de Peralto, after their father. He set off for Spain with all his money and arrived in Seville a year after Don Sancho's departure. With a different name, it was easy for him to hide that he was Don Sancho's brother, which was important to keep secret because of the long stay his business required him to make in a city where his brother had enemies. He saw Dorotea and fell in love with her, as his brother had, but she didn't love him in return. This beautiful distraught girl could love no one after her dear Don Sancho. Everything Don Juan de Peralto did to appeal to her only bothered her, and every day she refused the best matches in Seville that her father proposed to her.

During that time, Sanchez arrived in Seville and, following his master's orders, he tried to learn about Dorotea's conduct. He learnt from the city's rumour mill that a wealthy caballero, recently arrived from the Indies, was in love with her, and was courting her with all the gallant attentions of a refined suitor. He wrote to inform his master, representing the situation as more dire than it was, and his master imagined it to be even worse. At Messina, the Marquis Fabio and Don Sancho boarded Spanish galleys bound for home, and sailed without incident to Sanlúcar, where they took a coach to Seville. They arrived at night, and stayed in the lodgings Sanchez had found them. They kept the room the next day, and at night Don Sancho and the Marquis Fabio went to take a walk in Don Manuel's neighbourhood. They heard instruments being tuned up under Dorotea's windows, followed by excellent music, after which a lone voice accompanied by a theorbo sang the lengthy complaint of a tigress turned into an angel. Don Sancho was tempted to charge the serenaders, but the Marquis Fabio stopped him, explaining that this was about all he could do if Dorotea obliged his rival by appearing on the balcony or if the words of the song gave thanks for favours received rather than the complaint of an unhappy suitor. The serenaders left, perhaps dissatisfied, and Don Sancho and the Marquis Fabio left as well.

Meanwhile, Dorotea began to find the Indian caballero's love most irksome. Her father, Don Manuel, was extremely anxious to see her married, and was certain that if this Indian, Don Juan de Peralta, rich and from a noble family as he was, offered to be his son-in-law, he would be preferred over all the others, and she was under greater pressure from her father than she had ever been. The day after the serenade that Don Sancho and the Marquis Fabio had sampled as well, Dorotea discussed it with her sister and told her she could no longer tolerate the Indian's attentions and that she found it strange he made them so public before speaking to her father. "It's behaviour I've never condoned," Felicia told her, "and if I were in your place, I would treat him so badly at the first opportunity that he would soon become disillusioned about his chances of appealing to you. As far as I'm concerned, I never liked him," she added. "He doesn't have that good air about him which can only be acquired at court and there is nothing polite about his great expenditures around Seville, nothing that doesn't smell like a foreigner." She went on to paint an unflattering portrait of Don Juan de Peralta, forgetting that when he first appeared in Seville, she had admitted to her sister that she didn't find him unappealing and that, every time she mentioned him, it was to praise him enthusiastically. Noticing her sister so changed, or pretending to be, in the feelings she once had for this caballero, Dorotea suspected her of being as fond of him as she wanted to make her believe she wasn't. To find out, she told her she hadn't been offended by Don Juan's attentions through any kind of aversion she had for him. On the contrary, finding something of Don Sancho's air in his face, he would have been more capable of appealing to her than any other caballero in Seville; besides, she knew that being wealthy and from a prominent house, he would easily obtain their father's consent. "But," she added, "I can no longer love anyone after Don Sancho, and since I can't be his wife, I'll never be another's and I'll spend the rest of my days in a convent."

"Even if you hadn't really made up your mind about carrying out such a strange plan," Felicia told her, "you couldn't have upset me any more than you have by telling me."

"Don't doubt it," answered Dorotea. "You will soon be the best match in Seville, and it's what made me want to see Don Juan in order to persuade him to have the feelings of love for you that he has for me, after having disabused him of the notion that I would ever consent to marry him. But I will only see him to ask him to stop bothering me with his attentions, since I see you have such an aversion to him. Truth be told," she continued, "that makes me sad because I don't see anyone else in Seville to whom you could be as well married as him."

"He is more indifferent to me than hated," Felicia told her, "and if I told you he didn't appeal to me, it was more to accommodate your feelings than from any aversion to him."

"Admit, my dear sister," Dorotea replied, "that you aren't being forthcoming, and that when you told me your low opinion of Don Juan, you didn't remember you had sometimes given him very high praise, and that you feared more that he would appeal to me too much than discover that he didn't appeal much to you."

Dorotea's words made Felicia blush and become disconcerted. Her mind confused, she said a quantity of disconnected things that defended her less than they convicted her of what her sister was accusing her, until she finally confessed she loved Don Juan. Dorotea did not disapprove of her love and promised to help her as much as she could. That very day, Isabella, who had broken off with her Guzmán after what happened to Don Sancho, got an order from Dorotea to go find Don Juan, bring him the key to the door of Don Manuel's yard and tell him that Dorotea and her sister would wait for him there at midnight when their father had gone to bed. Isabelle, who had been bought off by Don Juan and who had done what she could to burnish his image in her mistress's mind, without success, was very surprised to see this change and pleased to bring good news to someone who had only got bad news from her and from whom she had already received many presents. She ran to this caballero, who would not have dared believe his good fortune had she not put the key to the yard in his hand. He put in hers a small potpourri purse filled with fifty pistoles, which made her at least as happy as she had just made him.

As luck would have it, the very night Don Juan was supposed to enter Dorotea's father's garden, Don Sancho, accompanied by his friend the Marquis, was spying on this beautiful girl's home in order to get a better idea of his rival's situation. Don Sancho and the Marquis were on Dorotea's street at eleven o'clock when four well-armed men stopped near them. The jealous suitor thought it was his rival. He went over to the men and told them he planned to use the space they occupied and asked them to move. "We would out of civility," they told him, "if the space you are requesting weren't absolutely necessary to a plan that shall be executed in plenty of time for you to execute yours." Don Sancho's anger was at the boiling point; putting his hand to his sword and charging these men that he found impolite was one and the same. Don Sancho's surprise attack caught them off guard and made them retreat, and with the Marquis charging them as vigorously as his friend had, they fought badly and were pushed back to the end of the street at a fast pace. There, Don Sancho received a light wound on the arm and pierced the man who had wounded him with such a thrust it took him a long time to remove the blade from his body and he thought he'd killed him. The Marquis, meanwhile, chased the others, who ran away as fast as they could when they saw their companion fall. At one end of the street Don Sancho saw people with lights coming, who had been alerted by the noise of the fighting. He feared it might be the law; it was. He hurriedly fled into the street where the fight had started, and from that street to another, in the middle of which he found himself face to face with an old caballero carrying a lantern and who had put his hand to his sword when he heard the noise Don Sancho was making as he ran in his direction. This old caballero was Don Manuel, who was on his way home after playing cards at a neighbour's, as he did every night, and was about to enter his home through the garden door, which was next to where Don Sancho encountered him. "Who goes there?" "A man," Don Sancho answered, "who urgently has to pass by, if you don't stop him." "Perhaps," said Don Manuel, "you have run into some trouble and you need shelter; my house is nearby and could be useful to you."

"It is true," answered Don Sancho, "that I need to hide from the law, which may be looking for me, and since you are generous enough to offer your house to a stranger, he puts himself entirely into your hands and promises never to forget the favour you have done him and to take advantage of it only for as long as needed for those who are looking for him to have gone away."

Thereupon, Don Manuel opened the door to the yard with his key and, having ushered Don Sancho inside, had him wait in a stand of laurels while he went to give orders to hide him in the house without being seen by anyone.

Don Sancho didn't wait long among the laurel trees before he saw a woman coming towards him who said, "Come, my caballero, my mistress Dorotea is waiting for you." At the mention of that name, Don Sancho realized he might well be in his mistress's house and that the old caballero was her father. He suspected Dorotea of having made a rendezvous with his rival at the same place and followed Isabella, more tormented by jealousy than by fear of the law. Meanwhile, Don Juan arrived at the appointed hour, opened the door of Don Manuel's yard with the key Isabella gave him and hid in the same laurels Don Sancho had just left. A moment later he saw a man coming towards him; he prepared to defend himself in case of attack and was surprised when he recognized Don Manuel, who told him to follow him and that he was going to take him to a place where he wouldn't have to be afraid of being caught. From Don Manuel's words, Don Juan conjectured that Don Manuel might have been sheltering someone in his yard who was hiding from the law. He could do nothing else but follow him and thank him for his kindness, and it is easy to believe he was no less upset by the danger he was running from than angry at the obstacle now foiling his amorous plan. Don Manuel led him to his room and left him there to go have a bed made up in another one.

Let's leave him in the distress he must be in, and turn to his brother Don Sancho de Silva. Isabella led him to a room on the ground floor that looked out on the yard where Dorotea and Felicia awaited Don Juan de Peralta, one as a mistress yearning to appeal, the other to tell him she could not love him, and that he would be better off trying to appeal to her sister. Don Sancho entered the room where the two sisters were waiting. Their surprise was so great that Dorotea fainted dead away and, if her sister hadn't held her and helped her to a chair, she would have fallen to the floor. Don Sancho didn't move. Isabella was frightened to death and thought that the dead Don Sancho was appearing to them in order to avenge the wrong her mistress was doing to him. Felicia, though frightened to see a resuscitated Don Sancho, was even more distressed by her sister's state. When she finally recovered her senses, Don Sancho addressed her: "While the rumours of my death, ungrateful Dorotea, excuse to some extent your lack of loyalty, the despair it causes in me wouldn't leave me enough alive to reproach you. I wanted to make everyone believe I was dead so that my enemies would forget me, not you who promised to love only me, and who so quickly broke her promise. I could seek revenge and make so much noise with my cries that your father would wake up and find the suitor you are hiding in his house. But I must be mad! I'm still afraid of your displeasure and it distresses me more that I must not love you any more than it does that you love another. Enjoy your new lover, unfaithful beauty. Don't worry about any obstacles to your new love. I'll soon deliver you from a man who could reproach you your whole life long that you betrayed him when he risked his life to see you again."

Don Sancho wanted to leave after these words, but Dorotea stopped him and tried to explain herself when Isabella, quite frightened, told her that Don Manuel was coming. Don Sancho only had time to hide behind the door. The old man reprimanded the girls for not having gone to bed, and while his back was turned to the door, Don Sancho left and, entering the yard, went to the same stand of laurel where he hid before and where, summoning the courage to contend with whatever might happen, he waited for an opportunity to leave. Don Manuel had entered his girls' room in order to get some light and from there to open the door of his yard to the officers of the law who were knocking on the door, because they were told Don Manuel had taken into his house a man who might have been one of those who were fighting in the street. Don Manuel didn't try to stop them from looking in the house, thinking that they surely wouldn't make him open the door to his room and that the caballero they were looking for was safely shut inside. Seeing that he couldn't avoid being discovered by the many officers who had spread out in the yard, Don Sancho left the laurel wood and, coming up to Don Manuel, who was very surprised to see him, whispered in his ear that a man of honour kept his word and never abandoned someone to whom he had extended his protection. Don Manuel asked the sheriff, his friend, to leave Don Sancho under his guard, something he easily obtained, both because of his quality and because the wound was not serious. The law withdrew and Don Manuel, having recognized, by the same words he said to Don Sancho when he first saw him, and that this caballero repeated, that he really was the caballero he invited into his yard, had no doubt that the other one was some suitor brought into his house by his daughters or Isabella. To get to the bottom of it, he had Don Sancho de Silva led to a room and asked him to stay there until someone came to fetch him. He went into the one where he had left Don Juan de Peralta, to whom he pretended that his valet had come in with the officers and was asking to speak to him. Don Juan knew that his personal valet was quite sick and in no shape to come looking for him, and that he wouldn't have done so without permission, even if he knew where Don Juan was, which he didn't. He was therefore very disturbed by what he heard from Don Manuel, whom he answered by saying that the valet could wait for him at home. Don Manuel then recognized him as the young gentleman from the Indies who was attracting so much attention in Seville and, being well aware of his pedigree and his wealth, resolved not to let him out of his house until he married the one of his daughters with whom he'd had the least contact. He spoke to him a while longer to further clear up the lingering doubts that were still troubling him. Isabella, from the stairs, saw them conversing and went to tell her mistress. Don Manuel glimpsed Isabella and thought she had just delivered some message to Don Juan from his daughter. He left him to run after her while the torch that was lighting the room finished burning and went out on its own.

While the old man was searching in vain for Isabella, she informed Dorotea and Felicia that Don Sancho was in their father's room and that she had seen them talking. The two sisters ran over at once. Dorotea wasn't afraid to find her dear Don Sancho with her father, as she had decided to confess that she loved him, that she had always loved him, and the reason for the rendezvous with Don Juan. So she went into the room just as Don Juan was leaving. In the dark she mistook him for Don Sancho, stopped him by grabbing his arm and said, "Why do you run away from me, cruel Don Sancho and why didn't you listen to how I could have answered your harsh accusations? I admit that they couldn't be harsh enough if I were guilty of what you have in some way reason to believe, but you know very well that there are false things that sometimes appear to be truer than the truth itself, which does come out in time. So give me the time to show you this truth by straightening out the confusion your bad luck and mine and perhaps several others' has created. Let me explain myself and don't risk being unjust by being too quick to condemn me before I'm even convicted. You may have heard a caballero loves me, but have you heard that I love him too? You may have seen him here, because it is true I sent for him, but when you discover to what end, I am sure you will be remorseful for having hurt me when I gave you the greatest proof of fidelity that can be given. Why can't he be here, this caballero whose love bothers me! You would know by what I would tell him, if he ever had the opportunity to tell me he loved me and if I ever read the letters he wrote to me. But my misfortune, which always put him in my sight when his presence was unwelcome, prevents me from seeing him when he could help enlighten you."

Don Juan had the patience to let Dorotea speak without interruption in order to learn even more than she had just revealed to him. Finally, he may have been about to quarrel with her when Don Sancho, who was going from room to room looking for the way out to the yard that he had lost, and who heard Dorotea's voice speaking to Don Juan, moved towards her as quietly as possible, but was nevertheless heard by Don Juan and the two sisters. At the same time, Don Manuel entered the room with the light that several of his servants carried ahead of him. The two rival brothers saw each other and were seen looking proudly at each other, their hands on the hilt of their swords. Don Manuel stepped between them and ordered his daughter to choose one of them for a husband, so he could fight the other one. Don Juan spoke up and said he was ceding any and all claims, if he ever had any, to the caballero who was standing in front of him. Don Sancho said the same thing, and added that, since Don Juan was invited into Don Manuel's house by his daughter, it would appear that she loved him and was loved by him and, as far as he was concerned, he would rather die a thousand deaths rather than get married with the least reservation. Dorotea fell to her knees in front of her father and begged him to listen to her. She told him everything that had happened between her and Don Sancho de Silva before he killed Don Diego out of love for her. She then explained how Don Juan de Peralta had later fallen in love with her, the plan she had to disabuse him of any notions he might have and to propose that he ask her sister's hand. She finished by saying that, if she was unable to prove her innocence to Don Sancho, she wanted to enter a convent the next day, and spend the rest of her life there. Thanks to her narrative the two brothers recognized each other.

Don Sancho was reconciled with Dorotea, whose hand in marriage he asked Don Manuel for. Don Juan also asked him for Felicia's, and Don Manuel received both as sons-in-law with a satisfaction for which there are no words.

At dawn, Don Sancho sent for the Marquis Fabio, who came to share in his friend's happiness. The whole thing was kept secret until Don Manuel and the Marquis had persuaded a cousin, heir of Don Diego, to forget his relative's death and come to an understanding with Don Sancho. During the negotiations the Marquis Fabio fell in love with this caballero's sister and asked for her hand in marriage. He happily received a proposal that was so advantageous to his sister, and from that point agreed to anything that was proposed to him in Don Sancho's favour. The three marriages happened the same day. Everything worked out well for everyone concerned and for a long time, which is food for thought.

CHAPTER XX

In what Way Ragotin's Sleep Was Interrupted

THE PLEASANT INEZILLA finished reading her story, which made her listeners regret it wasn't any longer. While she was reading it, Ragotin, who, instead of listening, had started to converse with her husband about magic, fell asleep on his chair, as did the salesman. Ragotin's sleep was mostly involuntary, and if he had been able to resist the vapours of the food he'd consumed in such great quantities, he would have been attentive out of politeness to the reading of Inezilla's story. He wasn't completely asleep, often letting his head fall to his knees and bringing it back up, sometimes half asleep and sometimes waking up with a start, as one does more often than elsewhere at a sermon when it is boring.

There was a ram at the inn, to which the rabble that is always coming and going in such places was accustomed to lowering their heads with their hands in front, which the ram would charge and strike with his head, as rams do by nature. Now this animal had the run of the inn, even entering the rooms where he was often given food to eat. He was in the salesman's while Inezilla read her story. He saw Ragotin, whose hat had fallen off, and who (as I already told you) often lifted and lowered his head. He thought it was a champion challenging him to put his valour to the test. He took five or six steps back the way one does before jumping and, taking off like a horse at the start of a race, with his head armed with horns he smashed into Ragotin's, which was bald on top. He would have broken it like a clay pot given the force of the collision, but luckily for Ragotin, he struck it while it was being lifted and thus only superficially scraped his face. The ram's charge so surprised those who saw it that they were riveted by it, without nevertheless forgetting to laugh. Such that the ram, who was accustomed to charging more than once, could without impediment use as much room as he needed for a second charge and rashly crashed into Ragotin's knees, just as, in a daze from the shock of the ram, his face scratched and bloodied in several places, he lifted his hands to his eyes, which were causing him considerable pain, having been equally smashed, each one by its own horn – because the ram's horns were at the same distance from one another as the eyes of the unfortunate Ragotin. The ram's second charge made him open them. And he no sooner recognized the author of this damage than he hit the ram out of anger on the head with his fist, badly hurting his hand in the process by striking a horn. He was enraged by this, and even more so by the laughter of the audience, whom he blamed in general, and he was furious when he left the room. He also tried to leave the inn, but the innkeeper stopped him to settle the bill, which he may have found as unfortunate as the ram's blows.

END OF THE SECOND PART

Notes

p. 3, *The Coadjutor*: Jean-François Paul de Gondi (1613–79), Cardinal de Retz, author of the famous *Mémoires* (1717).

p. 6, *tennis*: The ancestor to modern tennis, it was played indoors, in establishments called *tripots*. It is still played today, as real tennis.

p. 8, *Mondory… Dangerous ghost who troubles my sleep*: Mondory was the stage name of Guillaume Desgilberts (1594– 1653), regarded as one of the finest stage actors of his time. The line quoted is the first line of the play *La Mariane* (1636) by Tristan L'Hermite (1601–55).

p. 14, *Bellerose was too affected… Floridor too stiff*: Bellerose and Floridor were the stage names of Pierre Le Messier (1592–1670) and Josias de Soulas (1608–71), two famous actors of the time.

p. 14, *Hardy*: Alexandre Hardy (*c.*1570–1632) was a prolific playwright, mainly known for his tragedies.

p. 21, *the Litters*: A litter was a carriage hung on poles, and borne by and between two horses.

p. 24, *Corneille… when Rotrou died*: The playwright Pierre Corneille (1606–84) was the foremost tragedian of his time. Marc-Antoine Girard de Saint-Amant (1594–1661) was a contemporary poet, while Charles Beys (1610–59) and Jean de Rotrou (1609–50) were playwrights.

p. 25, *Roland*: Roland (736–78) was a famous knight who fought for Charlemagne and whose heroic death during the Battle of Roncevaux inspired epics such as the anonymous eleventh-century *The Song of Roland*.

p. 25, *a story taken from a Spanish book*: The third story from *Los alivios de Casandra* (1640) by Alonso de Castillo Solórzano (*c.*1584–*c.*1647).

p. 25, *Donkey Skin*: A popular French folk tale, later made famous in 1694 by Charles Perrault (1628–1703), in which a princess flees from her father disguised in the hide of a magical donkey.

p. 33, *Polexandre… Illustre Bassa… Cyrus*: *Polexandre* (1632–37) is a heroic novel by Marin Le Roy de Gomberville (1600–74). *Ibrahim, ou l'illustre Bassa* (1641) and *Artamène, ou le Grand Cyrus* (1649–53) were long *romans-à-clef* by Madeleine de Scudéry (1607–1701).

p. 33, *Esplandián or Amadís*: Amadís is the protagonist knight of the fourteenth-century epic (first published in 1508) *Amadís of Gaul*. Esplandián is his illegitimate son, who follows in his footsteps in further chivalric romance novels.

p. 34, *unknown Urganda*: Urganda the Unknown is a magical priestess in *Amadís of Gaul* (see second note to p. 33).

p. 37, *not the first Rinaldo of this dangerous Armida*: In the epic poem *Jerusalem Delivered* (1580) by Torquato Tasso (1544–95), the witch Armida ensnares the knight Rinaldo.

p. 43, *Garnier's*: Robert Garnier (1545–1601) was a poet who hailed from the Maine province in which *The Comic Romance* is set.

p. 43, *La Flèche School... the rout of Ponts-de-Cé*: The school at La Flèche, the Collège Royal Henry-le-Grand, was an important Jesuit school founded in 1603 by King Henry IV of France, now a prestigious *lycée* and military school under the name of Le Prytanée. Ponts-de-Cé was the site of a battle in 1620 in which the army of King Louis XIII easily defeated the forces of his mother Maria de' Medici, who wanted to regain power, having been regent until her son had come of age.

p. 44, *Pyramus and Thisbe... the lion*: *Pyramus and Thisbe* was a 1617 play by the poet and dramatist Théophile de Viau (1590–1626), recounting the tragic tale, popularized in Ovid's *Metamorphoses*, of the ancient mythological lovers Pyramus and Thisbe. Pyramus commits suicide after mistakenly believing that Thisbe has been killed by a lion, who appears in Act IV of the play.

p. 49, *Mairet's Soliman*: A play, first performed in 1630 and published in 1639, by Jean de Mairet (1604–86), a famous dramatist in his time.

p. 57, *The antipathy... between Jacob and Esau*: This rivalry between the sons of Isaac, recounted in Genesis, started in the womb over who would be the first-born and continued after Esau sold his birthright to Jacob, the conflict continuing between their respective descendants after their deaths.

p. 58, *Latin Land*: In other words, the Latin Quarter, domain of the University and the clerics.

p. 58, *Plutarch*: Plutarch (46–*c*.120 AD) was a Greek-born Roman historian and essay writer. The debate over whether modern or ancient texts were a better source of knowledge and education was a very topical one at the time.

p. 58, *Amadís of Gaul... L'Astrée*: For *Amadís of Gaul* see second note to p. 33. *L'Astrée* (1607–27) is a major pastoral novel, extremely successful in its time, by Honoré d'Urfé (1567–1625). The lengthy multi-volume narrative centres on the love story between the shepherdess Astrée and her lover Céladon.

p. 74, *Théophile*: See note to p. 44.

p. 95, *Exaudiat*: A musical setting of Psalm 20, which contains the phrase "*Exaudiat te Dominus*" ("May the Lord hear you").

p. 99, *Augustus's over Antony*: A reference to Augustus (63 BC –14 AD), the first Roman Emperor (r.27 BC–14 AD) and his ally Marcus Antonius, the general and statesman, with whom he had previously formed the Second Triumvirate which briefly ruled Rome before the Empire.

p. 100, *Manceaux*: Residents of Le Mans.

p. 110, *wool-snatchers*: Thieves who snatch coats and capes.

p. 112, *Chimène*: Don Rodrigue's love interest in the tragedy *Le Cid* (1637) by Corneille.

p. 113, *Laurel-muncher*: Word coined by Pierre de Ronsard (1524–85) to designate bad poets.

p. 114, *mithridate*: Poison antidote, cure-all sold by charlatans.

p. 116, *the late Phaeton*: In Greek mythology, the son of Helios, who was fatally struck down by Zeus after he endangered the earth while driving his father's sun chariot.

p. 118, *honnête homme*: "A cultured person, combining nobility of feeling with that of birth; socially appealing thanks to their integrity, discretion and taste"(*Dictionnaire du Français classique*, Larousse, 1992).

p. 119, *Aristotle's rules*: The three classical unities prescribed for drama by Aristotle in his *Poetics*: unity of action, time and place.

p. 119, *Cassandre, Cléopâtre… son of Pippin's*: *Cassandre* (1642–45) and *Cléopâtre* (1647–58) were novels by Gautier de Costes de La Calprenède (1609–63). For *Polexandre* and *Cyrus* see first note to p. 33. Scarron is mocking all of these novels for their excessive length. Pippin the Short (714–68, r.752–68) was the first King of the Franks, and his son and successor was Charlemagne (742–814, r. 768–814), or "Charles the Great".

p. 135, *an alguacil… a commissaire*: A constable, a police officer.

p. 144, *the Lapiths ran after the Centaurs*: In Greek myth, the human Lapiths fought against the half-horse Centaurs at the wedding feast of Pirithous, after a Centaur attempted to rape the bride.

p. 146, *the love of self*: *L'amour propre* corresponds most often to *ego* in modern English usage. It was an important word/concept in seventeenth-century French discourse.

p. 152, *Roger et Bradamante by Garnier*: *Bradamante* was a 1580 play by Robert Garnier (see first note to p. 43), focusing on the love story between Roger and Bradamante, characters from *Orlando Furioso* (1516–32) by Ludovico Ariosto (1474–1533).

p. 167, *Valley of Josaphat*: A valley mentioned in Joel 3:2, named after the fourth King of Judah (ninth century BC).

p. 180, *honnête homme*: See note to p. 118.

p. 181, *Prester John*: In the medieval imagination, a legendary benevolent Christian king, believed to be descended from the Magi and to have ruled somewhere in the East.

p. 237, *Maecenas*: The Roman Gaius Maecenas (*c.*70–8 BC) was an advisor to Emperor Augustus, and a wealthy patron to poets such as Horace and Virgil.

p. 239, *Dom Japhet*: *Dom Japhet d'Arménie* (1653), a play by Scarron himself.

Extra Material

on

Paul Scarron's

The Comic Romance

Paul Scarron's Life and Works

Paul Scarron was born in 1610 in Paris. His father was an important counsellor in the Parliament of Paris. Unlike the English Parliament, the French assembly had no political power: it existed to ratify royal edicts and act as the supreme court of France. The magistrate members of these assemblies (for they existed in the provinces as well) were called Robins, after the robes they wore. They made up the *noblesse de robe* (the nobility of the robe), an important thread in the social fabric of *Ancien Régime* France, a highly literate class neither entirely noble nor entirely bourgeois. Scarron's mother died when he was only three, and when he was seven his father remarried by all accounts an extremely avaricious and controlling woman, who is likely to have influenced her step-son in several ways. Scarron called her "the world's most litigious lady", as she filed multiple lawsuits, seeking to favour her own children over those of her husband's first wife. Scarron's sense of humour and taste for mockery and satire may have developed early on, as a way of defending himself against the brutal and unfair treatment meted out by his stepmother. Such was the quarrelling in the Scarron household that thirteen-year-old Paul was sent to live with relatives for two years in Charleville, a town in the Ardennes, later famous as the home of Arthur Rimbaud. Scarron is thought to have completed his education in Paris afterwards, but he did not follow in his father's footsteps. It is unlikely that his stepmother would have tolerated the expense of fifty thousand livres required to purchase a post in the Parliament. Nor did his father think that he was well suited for the law. With limited options, he chose the church instead, despite a lack of aptitude for religion, and at age nineteen he became an *abbé*.

Birth, Background and Youth

Although *abbé* means abbot in English, a concordat passed between Pope Leo X and Francis I of France (between 1515 and 1521) gave the kings of France the right to nominate, for almost all French abbeys, 255 *abbés commendataires* who received income from a monastery without needing to render a service. Since those *abbés* only rarely commanded an abbey, they often worked in

Career as an Abbé

wealthy families as tutors or spiritual directors. Although wearing the small collar and robe could procure social advantages (which Scarron already possessed), an *abbé* could wear civilian garb whenever he wished. For the next three years, while receiving an allowance from his family, Abbé Scarron led a happy-go-lucky life in Paris, frequenting salons, making his literary debut, befriending other writers, courting young ladies.

Move to Le Mans   In 1633 he moved to Le Mans, the most important city (population 10,000 at the time) of the province of Maine (today the *départements* of Sarthe and Mayenne) where much of *The Comic Romance* takes place. He held the position of "domestic" in the house of the "affable and tolerant" Bishop of Le Mans, although his functions are not known. After the Bishop's death, Scarron remained in Le Mans until 1640, enjoying the excellent local cuisine, experiencing provincial life and frequenting the local aristocracy, the Comte de Belin in particular, a theatre enthusiast, through whom Scarron met important dramatists, including Rotrou, and for whom he wrote two arguments against *Le Cid*. Here he became acquainted with the kind of travelling theatre troupe depicted in *The Comic Romance*.

Ailment   It was during the end of his stay in Le Mans, from late 1638 through early 1640, that he began to be afflicted by the fast-moving disease that would eventually leave him a paraplegic. It appears to have been some form of rheumatoid arthritis. There are several stories, probably apocryphal, that attribute the origin of his illness to hours spent in freezing water under a bridge, or in a swamp, to escape either arrest after a "carnival" prank, or an irate husband, etc. Whatever the cause, Scarron's physical state, which involved a degenerative disease, eventual near-total paralysis, chronic pain and a severe twisting of the body exacerbated by a carriage accident, was accompanied by twenty years of prolific artistic production. After his death, a medal struck in Scarron's honour carried the motto "I conquered pain through laughter and playfulness".

Writing Career   Scarron moved back to Paris in 1640. In 1643 he published
Flourishes   his first book, a collection of burlesque verse. He also received a grant of 500 écus from the Queen, along with the title of "Queen's Invalid". Between 1644 and 1652, influenced by the burlesque of recent Italian authors, such as Bracciolini, Tassoni and Lalli, Scarron became famous as the leading proponent of the burlesque genre in France. In 1644, he published *Typhon*, the first of the French burlesque epics. From 1648 to 1652 he

turned out *Virgile travesti* in instalments, an epic parody of Virgil's *Aeneid* that was the most popular of his writings during his lifetime. Our notions of parody and satire, combined with the earthy and farcical elements of *The Comic Romance*, might lead us to think that burlesque poetry was, if not vulgar, at least very down to earth. This was not the case. As Scarron conceived of it, burlesque poetry was meant to charm and entertain literate society, with the kind of stylistic pyrotechnics developed by Clément Marot (1496–1544) applied to the parody and satire of the Greek and Latin classics so familiar to seventeenth-century readers. After a long period of dormancy, the Marot tradition was in vogue again by 1630. It reigned at the Hôtel de Rambouillet (the first and most famous of the salons), where ballades, rondeaux and *blasons* were the order of the day. As early as 1640, the baroque poet Saint-Amant said of this poetry that it had nothing in common with "dull and ridiculous clowning", but was seasoned with "kindness and sharp wit". Ultimately, the burlesque, as practised by Scarron to satirical ends, embraced many of the literary trends of his time, trends that are often contrasted for the sake of analysis and categorization, but that in fact often coexisted and overlapped: preciosity, the baroque and neo-classicism.

Beginning perhaps as early as 1643, and until his death in 1660, Scarron wrote nine plays, several of which were hits, adding to his renown. These were adventure comedies in the Spanish fashion, not unlike those written by Thomas Corneille, Quinault and others. Scarron's originality derived not only from the burlesque elements he added, mixing farce with melodrama, but also from the strength of his style. His plays were an important part of Molière's troupe's repertoire, and his influence on a number of Molière's comedies is clear. *La Précaution inutile* (*The Useless Precaution*) in particular influenced *School for Wives*, as well as works by Sedaine, Diderot, Beaumarchais and Stendhal. It is the story of a constantly cuckolded man who marries a woman he thinks too dumb to cheat on him. This substantial experience in the theatre contributed not only to the content but also to the form of *The Comic Romance*.

It is likely that the impetus for *The Comic Romance* came from his house guest Esprit Cabart de Villermont, a young world traveller and polymath, who introduced Scarron (already well-versed in Spanish) to Spanish fiction, to *Don Quixote*, and the *novelas* of Cervantes, María de Zayas y Sotomayor and Alonso de Castillo Solórzano, among others. Villermont suggested that Scarron produce a new translation of *Don Quixote* instead of translating *libertin* philosopher Gassendi from the Latin, as Scarron had planned. Pre-Enlightenment philosophy, though connected to Scarron's world view (and Molière's) in intriguing ways, did not seem well suited as a genre to Scarron's comic and artistic temperament. Scarron rejected the *Don Quixote* translation on the grounds that it had already been done. Instead, he undertook to write his own novel, inserting his translations (adaptations really) of four Spanish *novelas* into what would become *The Comic Romance*.

Marriage to Françoise d'Aubigné

Villermont was also responsible for initiating what became perhaps the most salient feature of Scarron's biography. It was Villermont who introduced Scarron to sixteen-year-old Françoise d'Aubigné, the granddaughter of Protestant general and poet Agrippa d'Aubigné, author of *Les Tragiques*, a classic of French literature, considered the only successful epic poem written in the French language. Françoise was beautiful and intelligent, though a poor orphan. She impressed Scarron, who married her, though the union resembled an adoption more than a marriage: he was forty and had lost the ability to do anything but speak and move his hands. The fact that he had lost his mother at a very young age may have meant that he identified with his young bride; it was not the only time he "rescued" a young woman. Ultimately, they both benefited greatly from the relationship, which seems to have been based on mutual affection and respect. Scarron appears to have thoroughly educated his wife, whose early correspondence reveals that she had only been semi-literate when they met. For her part, Françoise grew up to become a formidable woman: after Scarron's death she became the illustrious Madame de Maintenon, the mistress and later the wife of Louis XIV. She founded Saint-Cyr, one of the first schools anywhere to offer girls a rigorous formal education. Napoleon preferred her writing style to Madame de Sévigné's. She was devoted to her paralysed, misshapen husband, and together they hosted, in the Marais neighbourhood of Paris, one of the great salons of the seventeenth century, the golden age of salons. Guests ranging from fellow writers to the most powerful men in the court enjoyed Françoise's quiet dignity, grace and sparkling conversation, in combination with Paul's extraordinary narrative imagination and irrepressible high spirits. A sense of their respective personalities (and their relationship) can be gleaned from two documents. The first is from Scarron's testament (written in burlesque verse!). In it he bequeaths permission to his wife to marry again – likely to be the most successfully executed of his orders – "because it is true, in spite of myself, I have forced her to fast, which should give her a good appetite; let her enjoy it then a little, and may her prudent wisdom not have recourse to a paralytic, but may she enjoy the benefits which the sacred ties permit". Six years after his death, still not remarried, in a letter to her friend Ninon de l'Enclos (the most celebrated courtesan of the time, who had her own salon and does not seem to have suffered any kind of social exclusion) the widow Scarron complained about a suitor:

> *What do you think of the comparison someone has dared make me of this man to M. Scarron? My God! What a differ-ence! Without fortune, without pleasures, [Scarron] attracted good company to his home. He would have hated this man and banished him. M. Scarron had that charm which the whole world knows and that kindness of heart which almost everybody discovered in him. The other one is neither bril-liant, nor funny, nor reliable. When he speaks he is ridiculous. My husband's background was excellent. I corrected his licences. He was neither foolish nor vicious at heart, of a recognized integrity, of a disinterestedness without example.*

The two parts of his widely acknowledged masterpiece, *The Comic Romance*, were published in 1651 and 1657 respectively. They were probably written in 1650 and 1656. The third part was unfinished upon Scarron's death in 1660, and none of it survives. Two "continuations" were written by others, but they are devoid of the qualities found in the first two parts. *The Comic Romance* tells the story of a travelling theatre troupe mostly in and around the province of Maine.

It was very popular with the public in both France and England (where there were eight editions of the English trans-lation of 1700 during the eighteenth century), and is generally acknowledged to be a classic of French literature that occupies an important place in literary history, not least because of its influence on Henry Fielding and the eighteenth-century English novel in general. In Fielding's case, while the introduc-tion to *Joseph Andrews* does not mention Scarron by name, as it does Cervantes, Fielding's espousal of what he terms

The Comic Romance

"Comical Romance", his description of it, and the text of *Joseph Andrews* itself, all point to the obvious influence of *The Comical Romance*, as it was known in English. As a burlesque production, *The Comic Romance* is a synthesis of imported genres, and appears almost post-modern in its mixtures or juxtapositions – of primarily farce, adventure narrative and preciosity.

Beyond any models however, much of the work's originality derives from Scarron's extraordinary narrative verve. His contemporaries considered him the best pure storyteller of his time, and one of the most coveted invitations in Paris was to Scarron's bedside to hear the paralysed author "try out" his story by reading it aloud to a select audience. Storytelling is so important to this work that the author regularly signals his presence, or the presence of his proxies – characters who tell their own stories or who engage in actual storytelling by relating the two María de Zayas y Sotomayor and two Alonso de Castillo Solórzano *novelas* Scarron adapted from the Spanish, and included in his text. Far too numerous to list, the author's consistent interruptions and disruptions of the narrative include many such instances as the last sentence of the first chapter: "He accepted her offer, and while the animals ate, the author rested awhile and began to think about what he would say in the second chapter." At one point a character is able to fill in missing elements of a story he tells when he discovers it in print, at Scarron's publisher, told in its entirety, to the amazement of Scarron's friend de Luynes, "who had thought, like many others, that my book was invented". Scarron produces every kind of narrator, from omniscient, to unreliable, to ignorant. While these and the many other related devices Scarron uses shatter conventional fourth-wall narrative illusion (anticipating and probably influencing the early "avant-garde" works of Diderot and Sterne), in his hands they contribute to another kind of aesthetic illusion. Tapping into the oral origins of narrative, the multitudinous devices that signal the author's presence combine with writing that possesses a breathless immediacy to give the reader the illusion of being a listener. This quality has much to do with tempo, and Scarron rarely departs from presto.

Scarron is not making fun of what he parodies (the way, say, Voltaire does) so much as he is riffing: using adventure or romance as familiar themes performed almost extemporaneously in new and unexpected ways. Ultimately *Le Roman comique* is as much about storytelling itself as it is about the stories it tells. Thus it seems strangely appropriate that it was unfinished, that it lacks closure.

Like Don Quixote, *The Comic Romance* is an anti-romance, and like its illustrious predecessor, part of the modern novel's foundation in parody. Scarron's antagonists were not the same as Cervantes's though. But they were equally or even more unreal, too exalted and idealistic to have much to do with human reality. By the mid-seventeenth century, the romance in France had become bloated (eight, ten or more volumes were common) and possibly even more phantasmagorical than the tales of knights sent up by Cervantes. Scarron pokes fun in particular at La Calprenède and Scudéry for their interminable narratives and endless poetic descriptions of, say, a forlorn lover languishing on a terrace overlooking the sea. In *The Comic Romance* the narrator calls *Le Grand Cyrus* "the world's most well-furnished book". Like Cervantes, Scarron was interested in what he calls speaking in "more human terms", right after the parody of the heroic style with which he opens his novel. In Part I, Chapter 21, where the characters debate the merits of different kinds of novels, one of them lauds *novelas* for being written "within human reach" while the troupe's pompous and silly "author", Roquebrune, "said with absolute conviction that there was no pleasure to be derived from reading novels if they weren't made up of the adventures of lords, and of powerful lords at that". When he goes on to call *Don Quixote* "the silliest book I've ever seen", Roquebrune is told to take care "that it doesn't displease you through your fault rather than his". The title *Le Roman comique* explicitly refers to theatre. It means something like "the theatrical novel", a title that in English would lose the rich connotations of the secondary meanings of the French *comique*, which are adequately conveyed by calling it *The Comic Romance*, since what we now call romance novels are not that far removed from the romances Scarron had in mind when he appended the oxymoronic adjective "*comique*" (comic or comical in addition to "of the theatre") to the noble noun "*roman*" (meaning romance then, and novel in more contemporary French).

But *The Comic Romance* is more than a straightforward comical puncturing of idealism. It never strays far from a dialectical give-and-take between high and low. Besides the bitter and cynical actor, Grudge, the core of the troupe is composed of the noble leading man Destiny and the virtuous actresses Star, Cave and Angélique. The farce is provided by would-be-author hangers-on, the "finger puppet" Ragotin and the "poet" Roquebrune, as well as a number of characters encountered along the way. As the troupe moves through lower Maine they are shadowed by fallout from the lives Destiny and Star led before joining the theatre. Recounted by Destiny to Cave and Angélique, their story, which suffers many comic interruptions, forms the bulk of the adventure narrative until the past catches up to the present. Twice in each part of the book there is a pause in the action as a character narrates a *novela*, each time a moral tale concerning the psychology of love, in which virtue is achieved through great effort. Although the style of each of these dimensions of the text differs from the others, they all seem related to some form of what we would now call realism: comic realism, of course, but also plausible adventure in a "real world", which seems to foreshadow the eighteenth-century novels of Prévost and Marivaux, and psychological realism in the adapted *novelas*, anticipating Madame de Lafayette's *La Princesse de Clèves*. It is significant that the changes Scarron makes in his adaptation of the four *novelas* are in the direction of greater realism, editing out fairy-tale elements and overwrought descriptions and adding such details as having a hero "wash his teeth" after a meal, while maintaining a more formal, florid style than in the rest of the novel. Idealism within on a more "human reach" coexists with the most down-to-earth farce. Scarron's parody of adventure narrative yields a new model – a more human adventure narrative.

Among its themes, identity, abandonment and adoption loom large. What could be more "real" or important to many or perhaps most of us, not just to Scarron? It is difficult not to view the diminutive Ragotin as Scarron's alter ego; the butt of so many jokes, he resembles a human pin cushion. Perhaps this is the author's way of lashing out at his own physical condition. But the book also contains a number of ideal alter egos, Destiny and the heroines, who struggle against external obstacles to live ethical lives, leading us to think of Scarron's entertaining comic fiction as having a surprisingly important ethical dimension. Perhaps not so surprising when one considers that ethics and entertainment were the twin pillars of seventeenth-century French literature, from outright

"French moralists" such as Pascal and La Rochefoucauld to all those like Molière for whom pleasing the public was the stated goal of their art. Scholarly readers of *The Comic Romance* tend to marvel at the work's "remarkable blending of patterns and flavours". Among these, the blending of ethics and entertainment might be the most significant; for it may hold the key to the "human reach" Scarron sought. Is this not the "moral" of the following passage from Part One, Chapter XIII, which concludes with the author's wink to himself?

The Baron d'Arques had a very large collection of novels in his library. Our tutor, who in Latin Land had never read any, who at first forbade reading them and who repeatedly condemned them in front of the Baron d'Arques, to render them as odious to him as the Baron had found them entertaining, became so taken with them himself that, after devouring the old ones and the modern ones, he admitted that reading good novels educated while entertaining, and that he thought they were no less able to instil noble sentiments in young people than Plutarch. Thus he encouraged us to read them as much as he had previously steered us away from them. He advised us to start with the moderns, but they were not yet to our taste and, until the age of fifteen, we enjoyed reading the likes of *Amadis of Gaul* far more than the likes of *L'Astrée* and the other beautiful novels written since, through which the French have shown, in this as well as a thousand other things, that while they do not invent as much as other nations, they perfect more.

We should also not overlook another kind of realism in *The Comic Romance*, probably the most commonly noted. This is the depiction of provincial everyday life in seventeenth-century France. Among important writers, Scarron's was one of a very few. And of course the depiction of the travelling players gives us some idea of what Molière's years touring the provinces might have been like. At one time it was thought that Scarron's troupe really was Molière's Illustre Théâtre and *The Comic Romance* primarily a *roman-à-clef*. In the final analysis though, what most sets apart *The Comic Romance*, besides what Jean Giono called "an art the colour of magic", is the riotous life poor paralysed and suffering Scarron breathed into it.

Translator's Note

Until the present translation there was no published modern English translation of *The Comic Romance*. The earliest translation is from 1665, convincingly attributed to John Bulteel. This translation influenced what became the "standard available" translation of 1700, judged "most readable", published in *The Whole Comical Works of Scarron*. The latter is known as the Brown-Savage translation, although a committee of translators was involved. There were seven editions of it in the 18th century. A later translation by Goldsmith (1775) has been shown to be little more than a recasting of Brown-Savage. Brown-Savage was reissued in 1892, and a facsimile of the 1892 edition was published in 1968. For a scholarly analysis of these translations see *Scarron's* Roman Comique *and Its English Translators* in *Robert Drury's Journal and Other Studies* by Arthur Secord, (University of Illinois Press, 1961). Although the previous translations contain inaccuracies, apparently unmotivated infidelities and infelicities, their overarching egregious flaw seems primarily a function of their age. The English translation from 1700 feels stylistically distant from Scarron's original. Scarron's French resembles modern literary French far more than the Brown-Savage translation does any kind of modern English. The reason for this has to do with the work many French writers had done since the sixteenth century to create a relatively minimalist and transparent literary style that came to be known as classic or neo-classical. The effect makes reading a seventeenth-century French text akin to reading a nineteenth-century English one. Thus it may be that Scarron's novel is more translatable into English now than it was at the time of its publication, when "literary" English was, for lack of a better term, busy. For example, in the opening chapter there is a tussle at the front of the cart. According to Brown-Savage: "The squabble had been occasioned by the servant of the tennis court falling foul upon the carter, without saying why or wherefore; yet the reason was because his oxen and mare had been a little too free with a truss of hay that lay before the door." My translation reads: "It was the tennis court's servant who had attacked the driver, because his oxen and mare were helping themselves to a pile of hay in front of the door." Here and elsewhere, my translation is closer to the original than Brown-Savage. In the passage cited, only the decision to use "driver" for "carter" is a departure, and "were helping themselves to" is less literal than "had been a little too free with", only in order to use a con— —nglish idiom that corresponds to the original French. As is often the case here, and unlike most translations, more faithful is more readable. Simply put, the Brown-Savage is busy, clunky and archaic, whereas the original remains lithe and, in its directness and transparency, seems modern. This is not to minimize the difficulties of any translation where a difference in eras is added to the difference in languages. At the very least it seems safe to say that Scarron's unique voice, however it may have been heard by eighteenth-century readers of the Brown-Savage translation, is no longer audible to readers of that translation today.

Select Bibliography

Standard Edition:
The Classiques Garnier edition (2010) of *Le Roman Comique*, edited by Claudine Nédelec, is the most authoritative edition to date.

Biographies:
Forsythe Phelps, Naomi, *The Queen's Invalid: A Biography of Paul Scarron* (Baltimore, MD: Johns Hopkins University Press, 1951)
Leca, Ange Pierre, *Scarron, le malade de la reine* (Paris: Éditions Kimé, 1999)
Magne, Émile, *Scarron et son milieu*, 7th edn.(Paris: Émile Paul Frères, 1924)

Additional Recommended Background Material:
Buckley, Veronica, *Madame de Maintenon the Secret Wife of Louis XIV* (London: Bloomsbury, 2008)
Koritz, L.S., *Scarron satirique* (Paris: Klincksieck, 2000)
Parish, Richard, *Scarron: Le Roman comique* (London: Grant & Cutler, 1999)
Secord, Arthur, *Scarron's* Roman Comique *and Its English Translators* in *Robert Drury's Journal and Other Studies* (Champaign, IL: University of Illinois Press, 1961)